TRINITY

Feathers and Fire Book 9

SHAYNE SILVERS

ARGENTO
PUBLISHING

CONTENTS

Shayne Silvers

Trinity

Feathers and Fire Book 9

A TempleVerse Series

ISBN 13: 978-1-947709-40-9

© 2020, Shayne Silvers / Argento Publishing, LLC

info@shaynesilvers.com

HARK! THE HERALD ANGELS SCREAMED...

War is coming to the City of Fountains.

The Four Legendary Creatures are free, the Seven Sins are running wild, the vampires are getting thirsty, and the Vatican is ready to enter the front lines.

And Callie Penrose is at the heart of it all. The Horsewoman of Despair flicked the first domino, and the consequences are echoing throughout the various halls of power in all corners of the world. As the streets of Kansas City threaten to become raging rivers of blood, one of those closest to Callie is kidnapped, and she is forced to choose between her heart and the people who depend on her to keep them safe.

To value ***duty*** over ***love***.

As the pillars of Heaven begin to crumble, it becomes increasingly obvious that all these events are coordinated rather than coincidental. Callie may have flicked that first domino, but how much can her heart handle when she learns that some of her closest friends set all the dominos up in the first place.

Now is the time when success truly depends on how Lucky Callie can be, and whether she can determine which friends have been paid thirty pieces of silver to stab her in the back. Angels shall weep, and demons shall laugh.

Humanity will burn and gods shall die in the wake of a Horsewoman betrayed.

DON'T FORGET!

VIP's get early access to all sorts of book goodies, including signed copies, private giveaways, and advance notice of future projects. AND A FREE NOVELLA! Click the image or join here:
www.shaynesilvers.com/l/219800

FOLLOW AND LIKE:
Shayne's FACEBOOK PAGE:
www.shaynesilvers.com/l/38602

I try my best to respond to all messages, so don't hesitate to drop me a line. Not interacting with readers is the biggest travesty that most authors can make. Let me fix that.

I squinted at the lethal warrior across from me, carefully sidestepping as I focused on his hips. He mirrored my every move, like a dark phantasm reflecting up from a puddle of blood. The dance of death was at hand.

Beams of early morning sunlight pierced the shadows of the park, desperately, mercilessly, attacking the last vestiges of night in their never-ending battle of dark versus light. My foe had used the sun against me before, striking the very moment I squinted at the unanticipated brightness. I tried luring him into a similar trap, but he smiled devilishly and stepped in the opposite direction.

"I'm growing bored," my foe drawled. "Attack when your enemy least expects it, from a place she least—"

He interrupted his own lecture as he abruptly blurred forward and swung his katana low in an attempt to take out my thigh. I dove towards him to disrupt his timing, thrusting my blade at his gut. I felt a whisper of fabric against the edge of my sword, but I knew he had only moved enough to avoid my strike. I hadn't almost gotten him.

He'd merely wanted to expend as little energy as possible to avoid my attack.

Which was why I simultaneously rocked forward with a swinging elbow to hammer his jaw while he gloated about dodging my blade.

Well, that had been my intent.

But this was Ryuu, not some half-assed swordsman looking to bolster his self-confidence. Ryuu embodied self-confidence. To him, admitting self-confidence was like bragging about being able to breathe. Pointless.

He pivoted and rolled with my elbow—impossible as it seemed—and rapped the knuckles of my sword hand with the flat of his blade. My hand spasmed and I dropped my katana even as he bumped his hip against mine and used it as a fulcrum to flip me over his body and slam me down into the dew-laden grass carpeting our make-shift arena. He rode me down to the grass, straddling me in a half mount as his arms shifted to pin my elbow and extended wrist to the ground near my ear. I rabbit-punched him in the ribs with my free hand—once, twice, three times—earning only soft grunts as consolation prizes.

His weight atop me shifted, and I wrapped my legs around his hips to prevent him from decoupling or riding higher into a full mount that might wind up giving him a more advantageous position where he could trap me into an arm bar. He'd done that twice this morning already. I snatched one of his forearms, jerking it low between us and trapping it against my belly as I squeezed his body against me with my legs, which brought his shoulder into contact with my cheek.

"Nice," he growled, panting heavily as he struggled to free his arm without giving up his position. The heat of our bodies momentarily distracted me, and then I began noticing other positives about our entanglement—and not in an aspect limited to wrestling. The ebb and flow of our hips, arms, hands, and chests flexing, twisting, pressing, grinding together in a passionate embrace that could either signify love or hate, war or peace.

We were not just wrestling on four dimensions, because layered on top of the grunts and squeezes of the visually documentable physical realm and the ephemeral white-water rapids that was the passage of time were the quantum entanglements of our minds and our motivations. Our sin and our virtue. Our past and our present.

The space between us was life and death, and it was a heady, spiritual, incalculable plethora of immeasurable dimensions. It existed and didn't exist at the same time, always shifting, never shifting, depending on if it was being observed and when.

The contact points between us—although ever shifting and writhing— was the intersection of the two loops of infinity or the ouroboros that visually depicted a snake eating its own tail but symbolically implied an eternal struggle of eat or be eaten, kill or be killed. Together, we were infinity.

Alone, we were two circles bumping and grinding.

Which was also fun, and entirely distracting.

"Your mind wanders, Penrose," Ryuu breathed into my ear, sounding amused as he continued to struggle in an effort to slip free of my leg lock trapping our hips together. "I wonder on the topic…" Thankfully, he couldn't see my face or I would have head-butted him. His breath smelled of spicy cinnamon and green tea, and I felt my mouth water instinctively as I spotted a drop of sweat on his neck, barely an inch away from my lips.

For a single moment, I wanted nothing more than to lean forward and lick it up.

Yum.

I felt my tongue tingle in the back of my mouth, and then I realized that Ryuu was no longer struggling or teasing me about my focus. I shifted my head to the side, keeping my chin tucked in case it was a ruse to conquer an opening in my defenses. I caught a glimpse of his face and realized that it was calm but perfectly still. Frozen. I frowned, unsure about this strange new tactic. I could still feel him breathing and pinning me to the ground but he looked as if he'd had a sudden thought that required his full attention. Was he admitting defeat? *Or maybe you gave him an unprofessional bodily reaction to contend with*, I thought to myself with a wicked grin. This close, I probably would have noticed such a tactic. No, scratch that. I *definitely* would have noticed.

"You two should just fuck and get it over with," a familiar voice purred in an encouraging tone.

Since I was upside down, I pressed the back of my skull to the grass and shifted my eyes up to try and look behind me. Aphrodite, the goddess of sex, was sprawled out on the quilted blanket Ryuu had laid out earlier. She wore a shiny, satin toga that stretched from one shoulder to mid-thigh and scandalously flaunted side-boob as it barely managed to cover both of her breasts. A gold belt was cinched around her waist, looking as if it was made of golden medallions, the ends hanging lower than the actual toga. She wore golden sandals with straps that crisscrossed up to her knees before tying into pretty bows. Her thick, shiny brown hair was perfectly styled and hung down her back and over her covered shoulder, emphasizing the opposite bare shoulder and the hollow curves of her collarbone. Her somewhat large,

5

almond-shaped green eyes glittered like dew on fresh-cut grass. I took a silent moment to honor my hatred of her raw beauty and the primal sense of physicality her very aura inspired.

Maybe, just maybe, she'd been pouring gasoline on my libido while I'd been wrestling Ryuu.

Then again, maybe not. Ryuu hadn't noticed her presence, and he probably would have if she'd been toying with my emotions. It had also been years since I'd made any decisions after midnight, so to speak. *Abstinence makes the suck grow suckier*, I thought to myself. It was in First Corinthians. Somewhere.

She was unashamedly nibbling on the cheese and crackers, grinning at us. I couldn't actually glare at her from my current position, so I growled my displeasure. "Hey, goddess of sex. Good morning. I've been better, thanks for asking."

"I did not ask. It is painfully apparent to me that you have not had a good morning...yet. You haven't even had a mediocre morning. An orgasm a day keeps the carnage at bay," she said in a sing-song voice. She gestured encouragingly with a shooing flutter of her long, tan fingers. I scowled...as scowly as I could manage from my disadvantaged position. She let out an impatient sigh at my reaction and shifted her position to lean back on both elbows and gaze at the sky. "Oh, don't be a prude. I'll look away, my dears. Just get it out of your system. You're obviously not learning much about real wrestling. Any one of my boy toys could have pinned the both of you before they hit puberty."

Ryuu growled, shocking the hell out of me and causing me to reflexively squeeze his hips tighter. Which...introduced me to an interesting new development. Ryuu had *definitely* heard the conversation, ladies. "Is...that...so?" Ryuu rasped, slowly lifting his chin and shifting his attention to Aphrodite. I pretended I had died, even though I was stuck staring at his Adam's apple and pinned beneath his obviously operational secret shinobi tool.

Aphrodite glanced over sharply, giving Ryuu an impressed smile. She nodded her approval at his ability to snap out of whatever magic she had used to freeze his body but not his awareness or hearing. She then ruined it by taking a full three seconds to eye him up and down with a smokier, hungrier grin before settling on his eyes. Ryuu didn't react or comment. He just stared back, and I wished I could have seen his eyes, because her face paled and her smile faded a hair—which was the equivalent of a terrified scream from anyone else. "I retract my statement," she said in a soft, respectful tone. Her appraising green eyes flicked to me for a moment before returning to his. "Are we still wearing masks, Ryuu?" she asked, emphasizing his name in such a way that told me she was obviously referring to him, specifically.

He gave her a slow, stiff nod. "I would have presumed that wearing a mask would earn me your blessing, Aphrodite. Kink-shaming seems hypocritical for the goddess of sex."

2

Aphrodite blinked. Then she burst out laughing, dissipating the budding tension between the pair. "So be it. Well, if you're not going to have a go at each other, come join me. We have much to discuss."

Ryuu peeled off of me with such agility that it almost felt like he'd used magic. No groans, grunts, or awkward gropes. One minute we were pressed together like peanut butter and jelly, and the next he was looming over me, extending his hand to help me up. I swatted it away with a narrow-eyed glare, and didn't bother to hide my groan as I rose up to a sitting position. My knee popped and I belted out a curse as Old Death taunted my apparently arthritic body of less than thirty years.

I managed to regain my feet without further incident and then I brushed off my hands, studying Ryuu thoughtfully. "Masks, huh?" I asked him under my breath. I wasn't disappointed or angry with him. I knew he had secrets. I was more curious than anything else, especially now that I realized Aphrodite knew at least one of those private details.

He gave me a subtle, unashamed nod.

"Okay," I whispered back with a small smile to let him know it wasn't a big deal. "Let's go see what she has to—"

"You know I can hear you," Aphrodite interrupted in a dry tone. "You're less than six feet away."

We left our wooden practice swords in the grass and joined her on the blanket, scooping up our water bottles in unison like we always did after a sparring match. Usually, we took the break to reflect on the bout, not to be scrutinized by a love doctor. *The* love doctor. Aphrodite watched us drink with an amused smirk, reminding me of an adult watching her preteen child interact with their first crush—when neither child had been brave enough to openly admit their feelings but to everyone else it was painfully obvious. That awkward surprise encounter at the mall that innocent daughters feared and villainous mothers coveted. I couldn't figure out which one of us was Aphrodite's child in my imagined scenario.

"So," I asked, growing agitated, "just stopping by to tease us? I already told you that I needed to have a talk with—"

She snapped her fingers, cutting me off. "Nate Temple is going to be executed before the next sun rises. Problem solved."

My eyes practically bulged out of my head and Ryuu choked on his water even as his eyes flicked to his black katana propped up against a nearby stump. "*What?*" I demanded.

Aphrodite nodded, solemnly, using Ryuu's cheese knife to pare off a few slices from the wedge. "That's what happens when there is an unspoken war with double-crossing schemers on both sides. Everyone is a double agent, so who knows who is really working for whom? Cheese?" she asked, extending me a slice.

I shook my head, firmly, but Ryuu reached out to grab it and pop it in his mouth. His calculating gaze never shifted even a millimeter from the goddess' eyes as he chewed.

Aphrodite continued slicing away at the cheese, humming softly as she worked. "It's all about the children. Always was. Always will be. Well, that and power, of course. Nate is much the same, even though he sees himself as so much different. It is rather a...divine comedy, one might say." And her eyes flicked to me so swiftly that it felt like a slap.

Was she referring to the Divines I had just saved from Purgatory last night? Dante Alighieri had authored the book *The Divine Comedy*, a first-hand account about *Inferno*, *Purgatorio*, and *Paradiso*—Hell, Purgatory, and Heaven. I kept my face calm, meeting her gaze directly. "I don't see much comedy in the death of a close friend. Even less so in the death of a fellow Horseman. Or the Catalyst." I had spoken to Aphrodite a few days ago, and she'd informed me that Nate was imprisoned but relatively safe.

"Death," Aphrodite mused. "I wish we had less death, don't you, Ryuu? Immortality makes men rather paranoid, especially when they learn there is always a catch."

He stared at her so blankly that he may as well have been a statue. "Balance. Yin and Yang," he said, calmly.

Aphrodite smiled her agreement, and then sliced her palm with the knife. Deeply. Golden ichor—the blood of the gods—welled up in her palm and she studied it with morbid curiosity. "Godkillers walk the world again, those pesky little cockroaches," she said with an amused smirk. "Halo Breakers, Beasts, new Horsemen...what is this world coming to?" She lifted her fist and squeezed it, letting a drop fall into her other palm. It splashed, resembling liquid gold. "Ah, yes. That was why I interrupted you. Because the world is coming to an end. No need to worry about the Omega War. That was yesterday's news." She gauged our reaction for a few moments, enjoying the stunned looks on our faces. "So, if you ever wanted to remake that old classic film, Saving Ryuu's Privates," she said, "now is your chance. Before the fireworks start." My cheeks blushed beet red and I couldn't make myself look in Ryuu's direction. "War is often started as a consequence of sex, so it might as well end a war, for once. Go out with a big O and a standing ovation, naturally," she said, leaning back on one elbow with a devilish grin, obviously intending to supervise and critique our debut acting careers.

I opened my mouth, not entirely sure what I intended to say, when Ryuu dove forward in a roll and drew his black katana, the Angel Killer. He remained in a defensive crouch, positioned between us and whatever had spooked him.

I spun to see he was protecting us from a tall young woman, almost skeletal, standing before us with a dazed look on her face. We were in a somewhat secluded clearing of a mostly quiet park outside of the city limits, so we should have heard or seen her approach. Yet here she was, out of the blue. Aphrodite hadn't even noticed her approach before Ryuu reacted.

The goddess of sex gave her a condescending sneer. "The five-dollar-a-pop Johns are on the other side of the park, devil tramp," she said in a haughty tone. "No one has time for your sob story."

I arched an eyebrow at her crass tone, instinctively wanting to defend the poor, helpless woman, but something about the dazed look in the woman's eyes gave me pause. It was the vacant, glossy-eyed look of death, not drugs. And then the woman smiled, moving only her lips. Her face, eyes, cheeks, and body language did not reflect a smile. The contrast told me she was a hollow, husk of a soul trapped inside her own body. "I just want to watch, Aphrodite," the woman said in a strange, detached voice, looking as if someone was speaking through her. "Let the children play, why don't you? Where's that gung-ho attitude you used to have when your husband still visited your bed? That *carpe diem*? That *joie de vivre*?"

Aphrodite rose to her feet and her eyes began to flicker with a golden glow. "I warned you once, Lady Lust. Begone or be goned. The old rules are no longer so strictly enforced," she warned in a chilling tone. And I noticed that Aphrodite now clutched a pair of ribbons around her fists, looking like boxing tape made of silk. Except they were not tightly wound, allowing the loops to hang loose like she was an unraveling mummy. Stranger still, the ends twitched in a breeze that did not exist. I sensed no magic from her.

Long, black claws suddenly extended from the tips of Lust's fingers, ripping through her flesh with such force that the woman's eyes bulged and watered in protest of the Archdemon riding her body. I sucked in a breath at this undeniable proof. It really was Lust, one of the Seven Deadly Sins.

"I'm going to peel away your skin and lick you on the inside," the possessed woman said in Lust's hungry rasp. It made my skin crawl to see the woman's obvious terror at her own words. Lust hadn't partnered with this woman; she had raped her body and her mind.

"I haven't even had my goddamned coffee yet," I muttered, reaching for my katana and drawing the blade. I didn't want to hurt the woman, but Lust would leave me no choice.

Which was the whole point, of course.

3

The possessed woman shrieked like a banshee and tackled Aphrodite.

Or she tried to, anyway.

Aphrodite backhanded her so hard that I felt the crack of bone on bone in my own fingers. The poor woman crashed to the ground, rolled, and then head butted our wooden stump. She twitched for a few moments and I slowly looked up at Aphrodite. "Good lord, woman. She's possessed. Maybe pull your punches and don't kill her."

Aphrodite was inspecting her nails, pursing her lips in displeasure. "I did. Watch," she said, turning back to her foe.

The woman groaned, rising up on her elbows to support her weight. Her jaw hung loose and to the left, completely detached. I winced to see tears streaming down her cheeks and blood dribbling from her lips, because Lust was still inside those eyes, using the poor girl like a punching bag. I took a step forward, preparing to exorcise the Archdemon from the girl—if such a thing was even possible with an Archdemon.

The girl held up a pale hand, her fingernails split and bleeding from the horrible black claws that looked like mutated thorns. "Step closer and I'll kill her. I will cast her soul down to the pits of despair where she may burn for eternity. This one lusted after fame and fortune, allowing drugs and sex to consume her from the inside out. She. Is. Mine."

I paused, narrowing my eyes. "What do you want, Lust? Too cowardly to confront me yourself?"

She snorted. "I have a healthy appreciation of your lust for violence. It gets me off. Just think, I can sit back and hurl dozens of young men and women at you, relishing and delighting as your denied thirst for blood consumes you from the inside out. The longer you persevere against this internal war inside you, the longer I can sit back and pleasure myself. Every fight you win will only break you further, bringing my climaxes to greater heights. Your pain and denial will be my ecstasy," she said in a dreamy hum. "Denying your own desperate desire to murder because you deceive yourself with the lie that they are helpless victims, even when you know they are their own worst enemies. That the only way to get to me is through them. In pursuing me, I will make you a monster of your own conscience."

I glared back at her, stepping forward and holding out my hand to tell Ryuu to stand down, because he looked ready, willing, and able to stack up the bodies for me if it would save me from pain. He gave me the briefest of nods, acknowledging my request. For now. I focused on Lust, wondering if she'd been manipulating my wrestling match with Ryuu, rather than Aphrodite's now seemingly wholesome attempts. If Lust knew me well, she would know that I did not, in fact, want to cross that line with Ryuu until I'd cleared my conscience by speaking with Nate—a man who was apparently scheduled for execution tomorrow night. I took a calming breath, focusing on the matter at hand.

"I do not have a lust for violence, and I definitely do not have a thirst for blood," I said with more confidence than I felt. "But I do enjoy eviscerating evil nihilists."

"No thirst for blood, Count Dracula? Please!" the girl scoffed as the demon forced her to keep talking despite the agony of a fractured jaw. Then she lifted a claw to her throat and, without warning, pierced the thin flesh and began to drag it across. Blood spilled down her neck, and one of Aphrodite's ribbons snapped out, wrapping around the woman's wrist to pull it away from causing further harm. The girl moved to use her other hand and another ribbon lashed out from Aphrodite's hand. The girl strained and snarled, unable to battle the restraints. It made me cringe to see someone so bony and hollowed out struggling with such ferocity, like a caged animal railing at the bars. She looked like she hadn't eaten in days. Ryuu's face was set in a grim frown, knowing he was impotent here. He could fight, but the only person to battle was an innocent, malnourished shell of a woman being manipulated like a puppet.

"What do you want, Lust? Leave this woman out of it," I demanded.

"Where are my brothers?" she hissed. "All this chaos a few days ago, Nephilim slaughtered, Lord Pride and Lord Wrath in the thick of it with the pious Archangels making an appearance, and now the city is as quiet as a tomb. No one knows anything, and no one can find them. You are the common denominator. You were to be my sister-in-law, yet now my brothers are missing. What did you do to them?"

I stared at her, shaking my head at the reminder that Wrath had presumed to be my husband. "Lady, I have no fucking idea what happened to Pride or Wrath." And...that was actually true. I didn't know what had happened to Pride or Michael in Purgatory, and I did not know where Wrath or Gabriel had fled. I didn't know why they had been working together without telling their fellow Sins or Archangels. "I might have a few more pieces to the puzzle because all the fighting happened around me, but I sure as hell don't have any answers."

She sneered, obviously not believing me. Her gaze ignored Aphrodite entirely and settled on Ryuu. "Yet here you have the Halo Breaker on a leash, humping your leg on command. The only man capable of killing the highest echelon of angels and demons."

Aphrodite snorted. "There has been zero humping, of that I can assure you. I'm likely more upset about it than you are. If you want us to treat you with any modicum of respect, stop being a coward. You came to the orgy wearing a meat suit for protection, all while telling us how provocative and promiscuous you are. Take off your clothes and let's see what you're working with," Aphrodite purred. Something about her tone drew my attention away from Lust, and I blinked to see Aphrodite now sauntering closer in a sashaying sway. I missed the part where her silk toga had slipped off and fallen to the ground a few paces back, but she was nailing the rest of her catwalk.

Even Ryuu stared, bug-eyed, and his free hand absently tore at his collar, popping one of the buttons so fast that it shot into the woods like a bullet. I grinned at him, feeling a sense of liberation overcome my anger and fear as I nodded my support. He was appreciating beauty and raw talent, and I found nothing wrong with window shopping. I wouldn't have even minded the suggestion that we try on a few of the samplings rather just imagining—

I froze, noticing that I was tugging at my own top. I lowered my hand to see a broken button in my palm and that my bra was almost entirely exposed. I hastily re-clasped one of the buttons, having to skip the torn button so that my top was crookedly closed. Better than the alternative. Ryuu had noticed my reaction and it must have snapped him out of Aphrodite's fog of hornytopia as well. He gave me a flat look, obviously embarrassed that he'd failed as a bodyguard.

I shook my head reassuringly, hiking a thumb behind me at Aphrodite. Then I touched my thumb and forefinger to form a circle that left my remaining fingers standing up in a gesture that meant *perfection*. He grunted, glanced past my shoulder at Aphrodite, and then gave me a very slight, guilty shrug of agreement. I grinned, turning back to Aphrodite.

A light pink fog surrounded her, glittering at her feet with a hazy glow. Around Lust, a similar bright red fog collided against the Olympian's, the two forces crashing over each other like silent waves, creating riptides of competing passions. I realized that some of the pink fog had reached out tendrils to me and Ryuu, as if we were a part of Aphrodite's power, or she was using us in some way, which explained our sudden desire to rip our tops off.

One of Lust's tendrils of red fog reached out to me like a curious octopus. It touched my shin before I could react, and I gasped when it immediately dissipated as if repelled by me. I stared at the two women, who were glaring at each other from a few paces away, acting as if they couldn't see their war of fog.

"Callie Penrose might take issue with killing this poor child, but I do not," Aphrodite said in a soft, gentle, soothing tone that made Lust visibly cringe and pull back. "I know what your victim has done to herself, and despite all your manipulations and attempts at tainting her, I sense a flicker of love in her heart. She has a *daughter*, Lust. And I can see that no matter what you do to her, or encourage her to do to herself..." Aphrodite said, almost in a whisper, as she advanced another step, "that you will never, *ever* smother that love a mother has for a child. You will beat your head against a wall in your efforts, but I can assure you her last thoughts before death will not be guilt. They will be memories of her watching, from a distance, a beautiful little girl being raised by two loving godparents. That the mother loved her daughter enough to give the child away in a last-ditch, desperate attempt to shield the young girl from her own mother's demons. You already lost, Lust. You simply do not know it yet."

Lust snarled, straining against the ribbons. Dozens of ephemeral red tentacles suddenly erupted out of the fog blanketing the ground and hammered into the poor woman. I gasped in horror.

Then I stared, dumbfounded, as the tendrils faded away, pushed back by a tiny orb of pink light over the mother's heart. The red fog hissed and steamed and I swore I heard distant screams as the pink light grew brighter and stronger, pushing against Lust's vices with Aphrodite's love. Even the red fog on the ground faded and retreated, being devoured by the pink light and fog of genuine love. Within moments, no red fog remained and I heard a distant, almost imagined scream of outrage.

Our demons are coming for you, Callie Penrose. They will rip you and your people to shreds, turn them against each other, filling the streets with hate until you deliver us Pride and Wrath's whereabouts. The rest of the Seven will tear you apart from the inside out, saving the physical pain until after your soul has been thoroughly tortured and shredded to ribbons...

Then she was simply gone. "Bye, Felicia," I muttered. "You're a real peach."

The girl smiled crookedly, and my own heart broke to see that her whole face brightened up like the sky when the sun comes out from behind a cloud. A real smile, not one planted there by Lust. The mother let out a shuddering wheeze and then her head dropped to her chest as she collapsed to the ground.

Aphrodite let out a weary breath and the ribbons restraining the girl came unbound of their own accord, whipping about wildly. I stared at the woman, concerned. "Did you kill her?" I asked, softly.

Aphrodite shook her head. "No. She is stronger than she looked," she said, smiling down at the woman. "A mother's love is one of the strongest powers in creation. It is why Lust had to work so hard to turn her, which is part of the fun, in her opinion." She crouched down and cupped the girl's cheek. The woman suddenly convulsed, let out a whimper, and then her body totally slackened as she began to breathe deeper with a sleepy smile on her gaunt cheeks.

"Did you just heal her?" Ryuu asked, sheathing his blade.

Aphrodite snorted, glancing at me from over her shoulder. "Bad news, Callie. Ryuu doesn't recognize a female orgasm. This does not bode well."

My cheeks burned bright red and Ryuu began stammering an incoherent rebuttal that made Aphrodite smile even wider. Ryuu finally gave up, muttering unhappily under his breath, something about being outnumbered and facing a rigged jury. Aphrodite leaned close to the mother and brushed her hair back. The mother still wore a smile and her skin seemed to grow even brighter, giving her hollow cheeks an almost rosy glow. Healthier. The goddess of sex kissed her on the forehead. Ryuu and I both gasped as the woman simply disappeared.

Aphrodite rose to her feet and turned to face us, her every movement visibly captivating and entrancing. "I know some excellent healers who can give her the care she deserves. Maybe she will even be able to see her daughter one day. The one she dreams about every single night," she added, with an empathetic and incredibly raw smile on her face that made my heart break.

I remembered my last conversation with the Olympian. She wanted nothing more than to free her husband's daughter—the girl he loved more than anything in the world. And Aphrodite's sole goal in life was to grant him that wish. To save his daughter.

Pandora.

The curious part was that Pandora wasn't necessarily a prisoner. She worked for Nate Temple, willingly and happily. But Hephaestus, Pandora's father, was a prisoner of Zeus, apparently. Zeus' repeated threat to harm Pandora if Hephaestus ever disobeyed the Father of the Olympians was stronger than any chains, so Hephaestus remained a prisoner to keep his daughter safe.

I stared at Aphrodite, thinking very deep thoughts on the topic of preconceived perceptions and actions. Aphrodite...had impressed me.

She frowned at our shirts, suddenly looking annoyed. Then she planted her fists on her hips, flaunting her nudity. "That's all you could manage? I thought for sure my fog would get you two topless, at least. Here I am at a birthday party, and I'm the only person dressed in the appropriate attire. It is considerably rude of you, I'll have you know," she said. Before I could respond, Aphrodite snapped her fingers and her silk toga whipped through the air and hit her shoulder, where it immediately slithered over her oiled flesh like a snake, draping the goddess' hatefully perfect curves until she was once again moderately covered. She Mary Poppins'ed her own skimpy nightgown. The goddess of love was apparently stronger than the Archdemon of lust—which was actually a relief, all things considered.

Knowing what I did now, I wondered if Lust was also based on an actual demon's name, like when I had discovered that Pride was actually Lucifer. Was he a one-off or the norm? Was Satan lurking around somewhere or was he kind of like God, keeping as far away from the sandbox as possible, preferring to watch his kids play from afar.

Aphrodite walked up to our blanket and returned to her earlier position. "Now, where were we?" she asked, patting the blanket. "I won't bite." Then she grinned wickedly. "Unless you ask very nicely."

4

I stared at her, struggling to process her words. I knew she had a flair for the dramatic, but I also knew there was a calm, collected, mostly sane and empathetic individual beneath her facade. Her every waking moment was devoted to saving the daughter of the man she loved.

Pandora was the closest way to get her back into Hephaestus' good graces.

"Tell us what the hell you meant about Nate and the Omega War," I said, joining her on the blanket. "Were you talking about the Seven Sins?"

She let out a tired sigh and leaned back against the stump. "No. I was not. That complicates the situation even further, I'm afraid. Are you quite certain that you don't wish to let out some aggression with a wholesome, old-fashioned *ménage à trois?*" she asked, sounding hopeful. I shook my head firmly and Ryuu averted his eyes as he began furiously polishing his sword.

Not *that* sword.

Aphrodite pouted, picked up the whole wedge of cheese, and then began gnawing on it, which made the hair on the back of my arms jump right up. She was...eating her feelings. Aphrodite was having a nervous breakdown and trying to hide it behind stuffing her face. She was concealing her panic attack by taunting us with a panty attack.

"What did you mean when you said the Omega War is over?" I repeated.

"It was kind of a big deal," I said, sarcastically. "It's in the name and everything. What could possibly be worse than the *end*?"

Aphrodite was quiet for a few moments, her gaze distant. "One of the Masters winning before all the players for the Omega War were even on the board," she said between chews. She finally let out a sigh, leaning her head back against the log. And in that simple pose...

Okay. I had to hand it to her. Aphrodite was *banging*, as the kids called it. Her throat and slender neck looked as if it had been preserved in olive oil, giving her skin a natural, permanent, silky glow. Each vein and tendon and muscle were clearly visible and begging to be kissed, caressed, tickled, or bitten.

Her silk toga did little to hide her perfect cleavage, and her long, delicate fingers actually made me want to nibble them and play kissing games. Her long legs were crossed, and her calves drew the eye like iron to a lodestone.

And this was the reaction she was having on *me*, a heterosexual woman. Despite how reserved Ryuu typically was, I could sense that his pulse was about twice as fast as normal. Just being in her presence was affecting his heart rate, despite what his mind told him. My own heart skipped a beat at the realization and I barely stopped myself from frowning. How did I know Ryuu's pulse? What the hell was that all about? But as I looked at his neck, I could tell he was at a steady seventy beats per minute, much faster than his usual resting heart rate.

"Who are we talking about, Aphrodite?" I asked, focusing back on the matter at hand. Maybe Aphrodite's presence was sending us into some sort of collective mind space of fornication—a power of hers that encouraged groups to fully experience the joys of sex from every possible angle and perspective. I had to admit, it was probably something I could accomplish with my own magic, if I really set my mind to it. A temporary shared mental scape that would allow me to not only feel the sensations of my own body from a lover, but to layer in his sensations of what my body was doing to him. I realized I felt a little dizzy at the concept, and that I was smiling absently. I shook my head, firmly, and took a calming breath as I admitted a universal truth.

Callie's beaver needed to start a war with the EPA by building the goddamned mother of all dams. Or the world would burn if I didn't get laid. Soon.

"Zeus," Ryuu said in a grim tone. "You are saying he is a Master?"

Aphrodite hesitated, looking frustrated. "I honestly do not know. Whatever he is might be just as bad. Or worse." She took another bite of the cheese, looking troubled. "Perhaps it is more accurate to say that the first shots of the Omega War are coming sooner than we anticipated. If those shots work as intended, there may not be an Omega war. Or, better put, the Omega War will be hopeless."

"What do you mean?" I asked, closely watching her eyes for any sign of bluffing or deceit. Aphrodite had helped me in the past, but she had also explicitly said not to trust any Olympians. She herself was an Olympian.

"You must start gathering your forces. Take off the masks. Find out who is whom."

"The Masters," I breathed. "You really are talking about the Masters. It wasn't hyperbole."

"Yes," she said, meeting my eyes. "You, *Master* Dracula," she said, enunciating the title that I had acquired with my new job, "need to entrench yourself and find out who they really are. Any of them. Hell, simply find out who are *not* Masters. And then you need to start crafting weapons as fast as your forges can make them. Darling and Dear are already waiting at Castle Dracula to assist you. It is time to fire up the furnaces of Eternal Metal."

I eyed her up and down, trying not to panic. "What if you are one of the Masters?" I asked, not wanting to talk about the Eternal Metal at Castle Dracula. Supposedly, I needed a very specific type of blacksmith to do as she suggested. Mine had been killed during my takeover of Dracula's stronghold. The Eternal Metal was somehow fused into my very body, giving me the ability to call up the Silver claws. I'd hypothesized that it also had something to do with my bloodline as an descendent of King Solomon and our ability to trap demons. I glanced down at the Seal of Solomon on my thumb, frowning, pensively. Had my mother known all along that I would take Castle Dracula for myself? That I needed to in order to have a chance at surviving the Omega War?

Aphrodite opened her mouth to argue and then let it click shut. "To be completely transparent, I can't honestly say whether I am one or not. What deals and agreements have I made and to whom? What if I sold my soul to them long ago and don't even know it? I am talking to one right now, after all. For all I know, you received a welcome kit and a letterman's jacket. Maybe the Masters are the good guys in the story and our perception is entirely wrong. I simply don't know anymore," she hissed, sounding on the verge of tears. "That is what is so insidious about all of this. Old lines, alliances, blood feuds...they are all being rewritten. Some are working for these Masters and don't even know it."

I nodded, knowingly. I didn't take offense at her hypothetical of me being part of the club. I had similar doubts and concerns. "Well, you're a goddess. Do something goddess-like."

She scoffed. "I think...gods are *part* of the problem. We might be the *entire* problem. I believe we need the new Horsemen—and you guys really need to come up with a better name, for what it's worth. New and Old Horsemen is going to get very confusing in the days ahead. Especially if you're pitted against each other." My brief smirk of agreement shattered at the thought of warring with the Biblical Four Horsemen. "I think this is part of what makes Nate so special. He is the Catalyst. He has already killed an Olympian and an Asgardian. What if...all gods are part of the Masters? What if we, by trying to be the good guys, are being played? Who the hell even came up with the term, Masters?"

I bit my tongue, deciding that I really didn't want to let her know that Nate Temple's ancestor had founded the alleged Masters club centuries ago. "Well, I literally have beef with both Heaven and Hell right now," I reminded her. "Olympus and Asgard sounds like a Nate problem."

Aphrodite shook her head solemnly. "Don't underestimate yourself, and don't overestimate Nate Temple. He will need allies of his own. He is only one man..." she sighed. "For him, it might already be too late," she added in a soft whisper. "Carnage begets Carnage..." she breathed so quietly that I almost didn't hear it.

I narrowed my eyes. "What do you know, Aphrodite? What is going on? Where is Nate? I knew he was in trouble last time we spoke, but you made it sound like he was relatively safe for the time being. What has changed?"

Her lips clamped shut and her eyes grew misty. "I...cannot say," she croaked, sounding miserable. "Literally. I don't know how I managed to say as much as I already have."

Ryuu cleared his throat. "I've been warding us, but it's fading rapidly, as if it's being shredded apart by acid." I turned to him with a frown, only now noticing the sweat beaded on his forehead and the fact that his jaw was clenched so hard it looked like he might crack a tooth. His hands were balled up in fists and they were shaking. No wonder he hadn't been participating in our discussion.

Aphrodite dipped her head in gratitude. "Thank you for that, D—" she cut off abruptly, and her eyes widened nervously, as if afraid Ryuu might kill her for the slip up. "Thank you, *Ryuu*," she said, instead.

He dipped his chin in a jerking motion, obviously preoccupied with his ward. What name had she been about to use? Did I know any Asian myths that featured a murderous ninja with a name starting with the letter D?

My mind wandered with hastily made-up options. *Dave the Unbearable. Daryl the Stoic. Donald the Great. Dennis the Menace.*

"Heed the call, Horseman," Aphrodite said, interrupting my mental rolodex. "No matter what, *heed the call*. Even if you are in the middle of executing your foe, saving your father's life, rescuing a child..." She leaned closer to me, staring straight into my eyes and pinning me in place. "Heed. The. Call."

I swallowed under the intensity of her gaze.

Aphrodite cocked her head as Ryuu let out an exhausted sigh. She pursed her lips, glancing left and right, and then she let out a Greek curse that I couldn't translate. Her tone told me the gist of it. Before I could even open my mouth, she winked out of existence.

I spun to Ryuu to see that he looked pale and exhausted. Which, for Ryuu, was saying a hell of a lot. I had never once seen him tired. It almost made him look like he was on the verge of death in comparison to his usual endless endurance and stamina. He licked his lips and I realized they were parched. I scooted closer and lifted my water bottle to his mouth, forcing him to drink or drown. He guzzled the water and I couldn't help but stare at his lips and tongue, realizing that I held the back of his head with one hand and that my chest was pressed against his shoulder. His arms shook weakly, struggling to even hold himself upright.

"What the hell were you up to, Ryuu?" I whispered, wondering why Aphrodite had fled so abruptly even though there was obviously no threat in the park. Ryuu would have been on his feet—no matter how tired—if there was any immediate danger. Even if it killed him. Or he would demand that I Shadow Walk us away if he couldn't stand.

He met my eyes, swallowing the last of the water. I lowered the bottle and cupped the side of his cheek, brushing my thumb against his stubble. His dark eyes were deep and dreamy to me, even though they frightened most everyone else.

"I was protecting us from her family," he said, eyeing the sky. "We probably shouldn't talk openly about who we shared breakfast with, and who she might be related to. In fact, we should probably pretend none of that ever happened until we are absolutely certain of our privacy. None of those topics are open for discussion any longer. The only St. Louis friend I want to hear about is Alucard, because he is your vampire."

I nodded nervously. "Okay...Daryl," I said, taking a stab at his secret name.

He blinked, looking momentarily confused. Then it dawned on him and he grunted, shaking his head. His eyes drifted from mine, hesitated on my jawline—arresting my breath for a moment—and then shifted to the blankets. I composed myself by lowering my hand and followed his gaze to the dusty bottle he'd brought along with the blanket, cheese and crackers. "Sake?" he asked in a hoarse tone.

"It's nine in the morning."

Silence stretched between us. "Sake?" he repeated.

I nodded, staring at the bottle. "Sake."

24

I sat on the blanket, leaning my back against the tree stump, considering my eventful morning. Our earlier training had been exhausting, but the surprise cameos from Aphrodite and Lust had left me feeling wrung out and hung to dry. And not in the fun way. My muscles were sore, my once white training garb was now missing a button and was also scuffed and stained from grass or dirt where Ryuu had flipped me down to the ground or pinned me after grappling. I had sweated so much that my hair was damp at the temples and plastered to my neck.

Yet all I could think about was the equally sweaty warrior sitting in front of me. Ryuu was fumbling inside his duffel bag, giving me a rare moment to study his muscular, handsome frame unobserved—a rare delight, because the man seemed to have eyes in the back of his head, always catching me at the most damnable moments. Like when I was trying to get my gawking on. I recalled the more pleasant moments from our morning's adventures—his body pressing me to the ground as we vied for control and dominance.

When training with him, he pulled exactly no punches, hitting me as hard as he would have hit any man. He didn't treat me like a dainty little flower. He treated me like I needed to be treated—as a student. None of the bowing and scraping and apologizing I got from almost everyone else, and none of the little jokes and teasing I got from those closest to me—like Cain or Claire.

When the practice swords came out, we were master and student. Period. And his only goal was to whittle away at me until I became the most dangerous and beautiful possible form of myself. One who could protect herself in absolutely any situation. He didn't care that I had magic and that I might not need to be a master swordsman. His belief system was to pretend that every individual weapon at one's disposal was the *only* weapon at one's disposal. So, he treated me like my only source of protection was the sword.

Then, when the sword failed, he trained me how to use my body as a deadly weapon.

His devotion to that simple philosophy was strangely endearing. He treated his cherished black katana—the Angel Killer, as I'd heard it called—as if it were his lover. Murmuring to it when he checked it each night for nicks or burrs—of which there were never any, since it was a supremely powerful magical artifact. I didn't quite know what his sword was or what it represented, but it was obviously powerful enough to make an Archangel and Archdemon hesitate. Still, every night before going to bed, he spent a few moments speaking to, or perhaps praying over, his dark blade. Wiping it with a soft cloth before silently slipping it back into its sheath.

With the same affection one might use to tuck a child into their covers at night after reading them a bedtime story.

As much as I wanted to know the story behind his blade, and the story behind him, it wasn't the right time. It almost felt like such a scenario was akin to meeting his mother and father, and that was not something a girl took lightly when...

I blushed slightly. We weren't officially dating. As much as we both wanted to, there were a few things I knew I had to do before I made a move or encouraged him to make one.

That whole Nate Temple chestnut. We'd been dancing around a relationship for about a bajillion figurative years, sharing nothing more than a lone kiss and a few exhausted naps. Every time we'd attempted to try more, some big nasty monster had interrupted our plans, keeping us apart and delaying our chances at a relationship.

In that spell of romantic tension, I'd finally come to terms with the fact that I had moved on past Nate. He was an amazing man, but I was no longer sure he was the right man for *me*. But I needed to break that news to him, directly, before I entertained any romance with Ryuu. And now Aphrodite was warning us that Nate was to be executed tomorrow, putting me in a position where I had to choose between St. Louis and Kansas City—between helping my friend, Nate, and protecting the innocents of my home. Without any specific details, of course. Where was the fun in that? This newsflash from Aphrodite combined with Gunnar's gravelly call waking me up from a dead sleep this morning to tell me that Hermes was helping in the search for Nate and that he wanted me to come to St. Louis to help. Grouchy from being woken up, I'd told him I was busy with problems of my own so I couldn't make any promises. Now, knowing that Nate was scheduled for execution...I felt like a cold-hearted bitch. Things had obviously deteriorated since Gunnar's call.

Especially when considering Aphrodite's other comments to me. Her warning to fire up the forges at Castle Dracula and work with Darling and Dear to make enchanted weapons and armor was just the cherry on top. Especially since I had no capable blacksmith to handle the mysterious metal.

And the remaining Sins were a very serious problem, as confirmed by Lust's interruption this morning. They had not heard from Wrath and didn't know what had happened to Pride. Wrath, for whatever reason, had not informed his fellow Sins about me rescuing the two missing Divines—the White Tiger and the Vermillion Bird—from Purgatory. Or that my trip to the cursed, soul-sucking place had allowed me to accidentally combine Archangel Michael and Archdemon Lucifer—Pride—into one sentient being named Lucky. An Anghellian, whatever that was. It seemed no one had been informed that angels, demons, and their graces had been trisected at some point and the three parts banished to each of the three Christian realms: Heaven, Hell, and Purgatory.

But what did that mean? Lucky was no longer an angel or a demon. In fact, he seemed entirely human but with two spectral sidekicks he could summon up that absolutely knew how to open cans of whoop-ass on Archangels and Archdemons alike.

So, was Lucky more powerful than the Sins and the Archangels? Or was he as frail as a human?

Wrath had also not told anyone about him working with Archangel Gabriel, which was very concerning. Was Wrath turning a new leaf or was Gabriel breaking bad? In summation, I had a lot on my plate without having to worry about Nate or the Olympians and the precursor to the Omega War.

I wasn't going to be the one to tell anyone, or anything, about Lucky until I had some solid answers.

Which meant I couldn't hand over Pride. Because he no longer existed.

The rescued Divines, Zoe and Bai were recovering from their centuries-long banishment in Purgatory, and it was more than likely that their mental fortitude, possibly even their sanity, was about as reliable as carrying water with cheese cloth. Or Swiss cheese.

Yet both Heaven and Hell equally feared the dangers of the Four Divines uniting together. No one would tell me why.

My godparents, Samael and Lilith, were now betrothed and itching to get hitched. In the past, my mother had worked with them, encouraging them to form a Trinity with two of the Divines each.

Samael with the Black Tortoise and Azure dragon, Xuanwu and Qinglong.

Lilith with the White Tiger and Vermillion Bird, Zoe and Bai. In an effort to protect them, Lilith had seen fit to hide them in Purgatory where no Archangel or Archdemon could hunt them down. Risking their very souls and sanity had been a better alternative than handing them over, which gave me a good estimation of exactly how dangerous they just might be, even though I knew no specifics. I was really getting sick and tired of the consistent shoulder shrug responses to the ridiculous number of vitally important developments.

Now that they were saved, I was hoping someone would start shedding some light on the topic, but I wasn't holding my breath. I would find my own answers. King Solomon, my ancestor, had libraries and libraries and libraries of books. He had to know something. That was my next stop today —to get answers on the Four Divines, the Seven Sins, the Seven Archangels, and the one Anghellian cocktail I'd made with Lucifer, Michael, and their shared grace I'd inadvertently saved from Purgatory.

Now, it seemed Lust intended to make my life difficult. Maybe Lucky would have some helpful information on his dysfunctional Brady Bunch of a family.

Ryuu poured the sake into the two cups he'd scrounged up from his duffel bag and held one out to me. I accepted it with a forced sigh, commanding myself to relax rather than continue stressing myself out. I lifted the cup between us in a nonverbal cheers, but neither of us took a drink. The cup was warm, and I found myself smiling at the preparation it must have required. He had smuggled it here in a thermal blanket of some kind to keep it warm.

He let out a sigh and stretched his legs out, leaning his back against the stump almost directly beside mine. Ryuu unfastened the top buttons of his jacket and fanned his neck in a cooling gesture. I frowned, remembering I had broken one of my own and that my jacket was now crookedly closed in addition to being dirty and grass stained. Thanks to Aphrodite's persuasive fog. The jacket felt like it was trying to choke me, and a small breeze of amazingly refreshing air caressed my exposed flesh in such a way that I almost groaned in ecstasy.

Ryuu looked at me and chuckled. "It's not that hot, you big baby—" He cut off abruptly, noticing my wardrobe malfunction and the likely possibility that undoing a button might be a decision I could not later correct. "Oh. Well, it's just a bra. I promise not to complain."

I rolled my eyes and smiled, bumping my shoulder against his. "Pig." Rather than pulling away, I remained pressed against him and I felt his pulse begin beating steadily faster. As did mine. I still wasn't sure what to make of that newfound awareness, but I could no longer shrug it off. I could absolutely sense his pulse.

I felt Ryuu's eyes on me, so I slowly turned to face him. My heart skipped a beat as our gazes locked, and I realized, for the first time, that our noses were only a hands-width apart. His dark eyes blazed hungrily as he studied me without blinking. A slight breeze blew between us, kissing our feverish lips and sending a few strands of my hair to dance, tickling our noses as we continued our silent staring contest.

Ryuu leaned ever so slightly closer, his eyes drifting to my lips, and I felt his pulse slow, growing deeper and more pronounced. My own heart thundered in my chest, speeding up as if diametrically opposed to his. I bit my lower lip, my eyes betraying me and shifting to his mouth.

He leaned closer by maybe a millimeter and I suddenly regained control of my body, snapping out of the almost euphoric daze that had overcome me. I jerked my chin away and stared down at my boots like they were an anchor. My breath came short and shallow and the tips of my fingers tingled as I struggled, internally, with anger, excitement, and resentment at ruining our moment. Why had I turned away? One kiss couldn't hurt, could it?

But it could, and it would.

So long as I hadn't spoken with Nate, it would tarnish any potential relationship I had with Ryuu—no matter how fucking goddamned bad I wanted to grab him by the ears and inhale his breath until I made his eyes roll back into his head. Damn Aphrodite for messing with my head. It had been hard enough without her meddling, but now I felt like a hormonal wreck. I clenched my fist and punched the ground, imagining Nate's stupid face. Aphrodite's stupid face.

Part of me seriously considered bundling Ryuu up in a web of air, pinning him to the ground, and then Shadow Walking to St. Louis, to Nate, where I would efficiently proceed to slap him in the face to get his attention, tell him how I felt, and then Shadow Walk my horny ass back to Kansas City to my captive ninja so I could give Callie Dracula what she damned well craved and deserved.

I wanted nothing more than for this Shinobi Knight to slay my va-dragon. Now. I was a damsel ready to undress, or the village was in danger. Or something. Unfortunately, I knew I was the only one preventing my happy ending. Not Ryuu. He'd...just tried to kiss me. I was sure of it.

A cold chill rolled down my spine as I remembered that Nate was in trouble and that my emotions were overriding my rational thinking. Another shudder ran through me at a more concerning thought. Had Lust returned to mess with my head? I risked a glance at our surroundings, checking for outside influence. I didn't feel any magic or see any fog, though, so I let out a breath of relief. And guilt. This was becoming a real concern, reminding me of a few of Aphrodite's offhanded comments.

An orgasm a day keeps the carnage at bay. Carnage begets carnage. What had she meant by that? She had warned me about Carnage before, but I wasn't quite sure what she had meant. It was some kind of mental malady, which might explain the apparent splash of jet fuel now coursing through the engine of my sex drive.

"My apologies," Ryuu said in a rasping, clipped growl as he rose to his feet. "I should take a quick walk and leave you to your thoughts." He bowed and spun on a heel, already walking as I lifted out my hand in a feeble, pathetic attempt to stop him. I bit my lip, for a different reason entirely this time. Shame, anger, and guilt at hurting his feelings when we both damned well wanted what he'd made a move to do. None of this would have happened if I hadn't continued encouraging him. Call me stupid and old-fashioned, but I knew myself well enough to know that until I spoke my piece directly to Nate, I would feel guilty about any direct action with Ryuu.

My hand fell and my shoulders slumped as I tucked my knees to my chest and wrapped my arms around them. I brushed a loose strand of hair behind my ear, suddenly feeling very, very cold as my eyes grew blurry.

6

I don't know how long I sat there, wallowing in frustration and anger, but it felt like a year.

I felt Ryuu's presence behind me, but I couldn't force myself to turn and meet his eyes. I wanted to apologize, but I also wanted to hit him. This wasn't my fault. Why had he tried to kiss me? Why hadn't he just fucking manned up and kissed me regardless of me turning away?

Even as the thought crossed my mind, I knew it wasn't fair. I would have been pissed off if he had. Thrilled, but upset all the same. I fidgeted with my glass, wondering if I should pour myself another sake. Or maybe pour two glasses of sake as an olive branch between us—a gesture of goodwill. He shared my reservations about acting on our feelings before speaking with Nate, so he shouldn't have tried kissing me. Then again, I shouldn't have stared at him all doe-eyed and twitterpated.

I poured myself another glass of sake. Then I set the bottle on the stump in clear view of Ryuu in a vaguely conciliatory gesture—like sheathing a sword. He stepped into view and I forced myself to look up. I sucked in a breath to see the frosty anger crackling in his eyes.

"Too much to drink," I said in a knee-jerk response, hoping to shrug off the failed kiss and my reaction. "I'm a lightweight," I said, unable to maintain eye contact with the now furious ninja. I wanted to just forget any of it had ever happened. Right now, I felt like saving Nate from execution for the primary benefit of coming clean with him so that I could resolve the constant tension between me and Ryuu. Also to save Nate from death, of course...

But mostly to save Callie's happy spot from eternal lonely hermit status.

Ryuu's silence was a looming, terrifying, physical presence. I honestly couldn't decide what he was about to do.

He made no move to approach or argue. Apologize or forgive. I half expected him to tackle me to the blanket and force his damned lips where he knew I damned well wanted them—ethical and moral quagmires dismissed in one desperate act of violent passion. Frustrated at my own twitchiness, I finally flicked my gaze his way, unable to handle the suspense any longer. He did the one thing I had not anticipated. At all.

His face had changed. It was now blank, devoid of any personal feelings —as if the moment had never happened. Was that how he wanted to play it? I found myself growing angry at the thought, even though I had tried to do much the same thing with my bullshit excuse about being a lightweight.

Realizing that his act of denial hurt my feelings, I understood that my act of denial had probably hurt his feelings.

Relationships were fucking *difficult*. It sure had increased my reliance on mentally cursing. I swore almost every other sentence in my mind, so full of emotion that I was fairly sure the cursing was the only thing preventing me from having a nervous breakdown.

Ryuu stood there, silently, like...he was merely my platonic and stoic bodyguard. A man doing a job. Not dismissive but indifferent and without empathy. He was still furious—I could see that much in his eyes. In fact, he looked angrier than I had ever seen him. Even when fighting Archangels and Archdemons to keep me safe. He looked as if his eyes could cut metal.

I fidgeted, needing to avert my eyes from his razor-sharp glare. "What almost happened a few minutes ago," I said in a shaky tone, "never happened." He was loudly silent. I felt myself growing angry at his contin- ued, surprisingly effective tactic, and I lifted my eyes to his, bolstering my courage to stand firm. I abruptly sucked in a breath and jerked back to see that he had somehow managed to look even angrier than before! "I...I have feelings for Nate," I lied, lamely as hell, even though he knew very well that I no longer did. He'd also heard me clarify that lack of feeling for Aphrodite's benefit less than fifteen minutes ago. Why had I said such a stupid thing?

Ryuu closed his eyes and I could have sworn I heard his jaw crack and his teeth grind together. "Then I guess I will echo your lie." I frowned, cocking my head in confusion. "I apologize for my actions," he said—in a tone so dry and deadpan that he may as well have drawn a picture of Nate and stabbed it in the forehead with his katana while stating they were the bestest of best friends.

My lips thinned and I decided it was time to be a little cruel rather than letting him talk down to me. "I was not lying, Ryuu," I muttered. Because although the romance had faded, I did still love him. I just wasn't *in love* with him. The two of us were not compatible for what we both truly wanted. On the other hand, many of Nate's characteristics and traits...yeah, I loved them. Ryuu had all the good ones and few of the bad ones.

And many more that Nate didn't have.

Ryuu didn't even bat an eye. "This isn't the Riverboat Casino. Doubling down on a lie will not save you."

I stared at him a moment, unable to speak. He...had just called me out. Correctly. And a very significant part of me—about 206 bones voting unanimously—wanted to rip off my clothes, scream FTW, and then take advantage of the cruel ninja with overwhelming aggression. Damn. What was the half-life of Aphrodite's fog? Was I full of free radicals or was this what happened when a cup runneth over?

Instead of acting on my fantasy, I took a calming breath and brushed my hair behind my ear. I patted the stump he'd occupied when setting up our picnic hours before.

Ryuu disobeyed me, kneeling down on the blanket in front of me instead. "We have more training to do, so we should make this brief," he said.

I scowled. He was even more stubborn than me! "I'm sorry for hurting you, Ryuu."

He studied me in silence for a few moments, and his eyes were void of any compassion or peace, as if he were acknowledging words spoken by a stranger. "Are you ready to continue training, then?"

I clenched my jaw. What the hell was this ice-cold demeanor? He knew the tension between me and Nate was still present. He was the one who first made an issue out of it. "Stop being an asshole. I'm trying to apologize."

He leaned forward, and his eyes were downright *merciless*. "Then stop being a fool. I don't care for your apology. I want your *heart*." He chose words that countered my own, and they hit me like a fist to the gut.

He...wanted my *heart*. Not *hey, I really wanted to kiss you*, or *sorry for crossing a line but I couldn't help myself*. Not even a *I think I really like you*.

No. His words had been an invading army wielding a battering ram against my castle gates, demanding my surrender, and telling me in no uncertain terms that he would take my castle one way or another.

And I'm not ashamed to admit that his words, tone, and body language flat *did it* for me.

His dominant defiance was so fucking sexy that my anger was almost feeding into my lust, fueling it like gasoline on a fire. I decided that I really, *really* liked him furious. Not right now, but kind of. It was maddeningly confusing, bringing thoughts of Lust and Aphrodite back to mind. Was I being manipulated? Was he? I knew I couldn't make a move, even without the Nate topic, until I knew for certain that our thoughts and passions were our own.

To add to my own confusion, I felt a tear spill out from my right eye and roll down my cheek.

Ryuu's stern glare cracked and he winced compassionately—proving that all men are suckers—before he reached out a hand to brush away the tear. I repaid him in kind.

I slapped the shinobi spirit out of him with a meaty THWACK that resounded through the park like a crack of thunder, even sending a pair of birds fluttering and squawking from a nearby tree.

7

Ryuu hadn't even attempted to block it, and my palm stung as a result of his firm jaw not giving an inch from my full-forced blow —which caused the force of my slap to redouble back onto my hand. If he had recoiled with the blow, the excess force would not have rebounded into my hand. Which was the secret to breaking boards in martial arts—you punched *through* the board. Because if you pulled your punch and didn't break it, all the force you used bounced right back into your knuckles, making them hurt like hell.

The wooded clearing was silent for a few moments. And then...

Ryuu began to laugh. He had a perfect red handprint on his cheek, and he was fucking *laughing*. I opened my mouth, not sure if I wanted to yell at him, apologize, slap him again, or laugh with him.

Ryuu held up a hand, forestalling me. "That was the most honest thing you've said in ten minutes. Your honesty echoed throughout the park." He smirked. "And my skull."

I couldn't bite back the small smile at the corner of my mouth, but I managed to let out a sigh of defeat. "Fine. You win, fucking ninja Jedi," I snapped, folding my arms. "I'm not sure *what* Nate and I have! Happy now?"

Ryuu stared at me with a patient look on his face. He did not nod or smile at my submission. He didn't gloat either. He wasn't even ignoring it. It felt like...he was waiting for more. As if I'd only dipped my toes in the pool of honesty rather than jumping all the way in. I wanted to cower under that intense look because he was right. He wasn't going to let me get away with a bullshit apology. He wasn't accepting it.

Damn him and his fucking jawline and that smug confidence. He was doing exactly what he did in training—refusing to let me avoid confronting my failures. He was holding up a mirror and waiting for me to be honest with myself.

And him.

I let out a nervous breath, gathering my courage and wondering what I could say to come clean about the whole Nate and Callie situation. "I think we are perfect for each other, but I also fear that we are not," I mumbled, not entirely sure how to come clean while being honest about my feelings for Nate and my interest in Ryuu. I didn't love Nate any less than before, but I had to admit that my love for Ryuu might go way beyond anything I had ever felt for Nate.

Ryuu watched me, giving me a slight nod of encouragement. "Thank you for admitting what I have known for some time now," he said gently. "That is all I ask for—honesty." He paused, a smile tugging at his lips. "Well, that is not *all* I ask for," he admitted, openly grinning.

I blushed, glancing down at my boots, but I failed to hide my smile. I was going to punch him again if he kept antagonizing me. The necessity of me speaking with Nate wasn't solely about my own guilt or clearing my conscience. It was also about responsibility. After all was said and done, Nate and I would have to work together as Horsemen for the approaching Omega War. Or Aphrodite's pre-war tailgate party. Romantic complications or bitter resentments could be potentially world-ending if he lost trust in me for sneaking a kiss on the side. I knew how Nate felt about betrayal—I felt much the same. No matter what, daggers needed to be buried or they would be seen as daggers to the back.

Like the first time Ryuu had met Nate. That had gone to shit quickly, and it had been my fault for letting my emotions get between the three of us. Pettiness had almost caused bloodshed between two men I most admired and loved.

So...a little bit of honesty for Ryuu's troubles. "I can no longer sense Nate," I whispered, admitting a secret I hadn't shared with anyone. It had been that way for a week. Ryuu's smile evaporated in an instant. "Gunnar and Alucard are anxious, but I shrugged it off as their typical neurosis related to every half-cracked idea Nate decides to act upon," I said with a hollow smile. "He's apparently been missing for over a week."

"You spoke with the other Horsemen?" Ryuu asked.

I nodded with an apologetic shrug. When I received the call from Gunnar this morning, I hadn't shared the details with Ryuu, knowing Nate was a sore point between us. Gunnar also hadn't given me any actionable information worth sharing. I knew Alucard would contact me if things grew dire. I was his boss, in a way. I was also his fellow Horseman.

I cleared my throat, knowing it was time to come clean now that Aphrodite had muddied the waters in front of Ryuu. "And Hermes," I admitted, trying to act nonchalant about namedropping. At the time, waking up to a highly irregular call from Gunnar, I'd been groggy and irritable. Then, to have him pass the phone to a man claiming to be Hermes had almost been enough to make me hang up, declaring the whole thing a stupid prank. That they had found Nate, but he was on a job helping the Olympians and would be incommunicado for a while. But after Aphrodite's warning...I was no longer as suspicious of Hermes' identity. I was suspicious of Hermes' intentions. "He said the Olympians were helping search for Nate. To call on them if we needed anything." I swallowed grimly. "They found him, but he is doing something for them as a gesture of thanks. He hasn't visited Chateau Falco to talk with Gunnar and Alucard. Why not?" I mused, knowing Ryuu wouldn't have an answer.

Ryuu frowned, struggling to process my story. I didn't blame him. Had he been missing, or hadn't he? How long had he been out of the prison Aphrodite had mentioned because Gunnar hadn't mentioned anything about a prison, which was why I'd been hesitant to agree to meeting with Gunnar and his new pal, Hermes. "That...is good, right?" he asked, obviously confused thanks to Aphrodite's visit and grim warning.

I shook my head. "They *say* he's back, but I do not *sense* him," I repeated. They had to have been lying, because as a fellow Horseman, I had grown accustomed to the small part of me that could sense Nate's general location. The same way I could sense Gunnar and Alucard right this very moment. Gunnar and Alucard had to know something was wrong, because they should be able to sense that Nate wasn't back either, despite what Hermes claimed. We were all Horsemen.

Ryuu grimaced. "What about our own...problems? Kansas City is ready to blow."

I let out a weary sigh and a faint nod. "I know. But something is wrong. I can feel it," I said, tapping my chest. "I think it's a Horseman thing."

"Where might he be?" Ryuu asked, forgetting all about the shattered kiss now that danger had once again lifted her ugly head.

I stared down at the ground. "I do not know. He's just *gone*. Maybe he's in Fae. Or Asgard. Or Niflheim." It was possible that the fact he was in another realm was preventing me from sensing him. Or it could be a justification I was using to lie to myself. My instincts screamed something was off. "He hops realms all the time, but this feels different," I finally said, unable to lie to him with throwaway answers. Because...I was scared to discover the truth. What if something had happened to him? I'd been so concerned about my love life, angels, and demons that I hadn't paused to think about the very real dangers he faced back in St. Louis—ones that had the potential to spill over into Kansas City or affect all of us in the Omega War that we would all supposedly protect humanity from.

Which had probably been Aphrodite's freaking point.

"What can I do?" Ryuu asked in a foreboding tone.

I shrugged, frustrated. "Nate never tells me anything. Never lets me in. How am I supposed to help my friend if he keeps me in the dark?" I whispered angrily, punching my fist into my thigh.

Ryuu stared at me intently, catching onto the term I had used. Friend. I'd called Nate *friend*. He didn't gloat, but...

Ninjas were masters at concealing their true movements, so I knew there was a small but powerful flicker of excitement at my words. But danger was on the table, so that would have to wait. Goddamned chivalry. Goddamned responsibility. Goddamned Olympians.

Goddamned ninjas and Anghellians and Carnage.

"Well, I can't do anything about Nate right now, but I intend to visit my ancestor, Solomon. He and Last Breath have billions of books in the temple libraries. If anyone has answers about Anghellians, Divines, the Sins or even the Omega War, it would be them."

He nodded. "Then let's go—" He cut off abruptly, glaring past my shoulder at something behind me. "Legion is a dozen feet behind you."

⚝ 8 ⚝

I spun with a growl, ready to throw down some serious magic. Legion worked for Wrath, and I needed the Sin to deal with his crazy sister, Lust, before she sent a dozen more possessed, violent victims after me in an effort to discern Wrath's location.

A familiar older gentleman with a mustache and a bowler hat stood waiting for me, holding a briefcase with both hands in front of him, revealing that he held no weapons and obviously intended no harm. I lurched to my feet, hearing Ryuu do the same.

"Callie Penrose," Legion said with forced cheer. "May we speak with you about a matter of some urgency?"

I narrowed my eyes, suspicious of his tone. I wasn't going to confirm my identity, not with his penchant for legal contracts and that notoriously dangerous briefcase of his. "Who I am," I said, choosing my words carefully, "depends on if you have a hella-legal summons in that briefcase. You're not trying to serve Callie Penrose papers, are you, Legion? She and Wrath never even made it to the public courthouse, so a divorce settlement would not be necessary."

He licked his lips with an uneasy smirk. "We fear Kansas City will be immolated in the next forty-eight hours unless we find Wrath as soon as possible. Pride as well. Some of the other Sins grow restless."

I stared at him. "That was not a yes or no." I had almost forgotten about his casual use of the plural when referring to himself. It kept me on my toes, paranoid of an ambush. Then again, Legion could multiply into countless clones of himself, so it wasn't necessarily paranoia. It was common sense.

He let out a frustrated breath, puffing out his cheeks and making his mustache jiggle. "We are not serving you papers! Show some respect for the Apocalypse and listen to us, you vapid little child!" An insignia of a burning, shattered crucifix blazed to life on the front of his leather briefcase. That symbol and his downright frantic response stopped my breath, reminding me of the time I had spent in the Doors—the test of King Solomon to confirm my birthright.

The last step of my journey had been to jump through a stained-glass window of a white-haired girl and an older father figure. The pair had been holding hands, standing before a shattered, smoldering crucifix just like the one on Legion's briefcase. The new Four Horsemen had occupied the corners of the stunning window—before I'd been offered the job of Horseman of Despair. I had referred to the white-haired girl as a vapid little child, but only Solomon and Last Breath had been present to hear me say it. To my understanding, the window had been a depiction of the end of the world, making me and Roland the central two figures holding hands. Yet I was also one of the Horsemen at the corners, which was oddly unsettling.

A depiction of the past—me as a child.

A depiction of the present—me staring at the massive window.

A depiction of the future—me as the Horseman of Despair to ride beside Nate Temple, the Horseman of Hope, in the upcoming Omega War. A war I had not yet known about.

Aphrodite's earlier visit, and the warning she'd given me, hit me even harder after seeing Legion's briefcase and hearing his declaration about my city possibly being destroyed in the next two days.

But Ryuu had rightly reminded me that we were not to talk about the Masters or the Omega War, especially not with potential enemies like Legion, a greater demon who worked as Wrath's on-call lawyer and gopher. I needed to find out what he knew, but I needed to play this very carefully. I motioned for Legion to approach. "Swear that you do not wish me harm and you may come closer."

He had lifted his foot to take a step but abruptly halted. He looked up, chewing over my words. "*We* would appreciate you using the proper pronouns. *You all*, will suffice."

I stared at him for about three seconds, and then I burst out laughing at the insanity of it all. Even Hell was politically correct. Who knew? "Sure," I said, smiling warmly because I could tell my laughter only emphasized my unintended slight. "Could y'all swear that y'all do not wish either of us harm, and then come on down yonder to this here Hillbilly feast," I said, mocking my own Missouri roots in an effort to appease him. I gestured at the blanket and food. "Yeehaw."

Legion cocked his head and took off his hat with a confused frown. "We represent many clients, so we may not speak on their behalf. Many of them, as you well know, wish you gratuitous eons of suffering and hopeless anguish," he said, in a tone about as polite as I had ever heard. "Yeehaw," he said, tasting the word for himself. "Do y'all swear the same? Not to harm us?"

"Amen to that, Legion!" I waved a hand, grinning at his honesty. "Swear for y'all selves and then mosey on down. A truce for the duration of y'alls visit plus one hour."

For a morning so young, it was shaping up to be a real scorcher—in more ways than one.

Legion made the appropriate promise and then clicked the heels of his fancy dress shoes together before shuffling closer. He stopped a few feet away, eyed the blanket with haughty distaste, and chose to remain standing. Ryuu coughed into his fist, reminding me he was present.

Wow.

An agent of Hell had just picnic-shamed me. Silently informing me that my blanket wasn't refined enough for his social circles—a man whose most notable circle was which level of Hell he called home. They must have a gated community with personal security, sulfur-picket fences around every decadent and meticulously hellscaped lawn, and private misery pools in every backyard.

Talk about a low blow. Straight from the seventh circle.

I let out a weary sigh, realizing that he truly did look terrified beneath his calm facade. It was in the subtleties: his eyes darted left and right at the slightest breeze or tumbling leaf in his peripheral vision; he was breathing shallow and fast; and his lips were pursed and pale. If he had been playing poker, I would have called his bluff. The question was what, exactly, he was bluffing about. Was he scared for Wrath's fate or was he attempting to set me up? The Archdemons didn't care about the fate of Kansas City. Hell, they'd fully hoped for it to burn, so his threat about immolation wasn't as shocking as the first time I'd heard it. That's why the Seven Sins had stopped by this urban stretch of Route 666 on their Summer of Love road trip in the first place. Well, that, and for Wrath to surprise marry me, apparently.

"Okay. What's got Legion looking constipated?" I asked, keeping my features blank.

He shifted from foot to foot, ever so slightly, before beginning. "We cannot find Lord Wrath or Lord Pride. Both were last seen in your presence. Pride outside his hideout where you killed a dozen Nephilim, and Wrath at Castle Dracula for a dinner with your...godparents," he said, looking as if he wanted to vomit at the term, "Samael and Lilith—"

"Which Legion knows because Envy was spying on me," I said, not wanting to keep saying *y'all* in case it got stuck in my verbal repertoire for the next week or so. Southern drawl was as sticky to the tongue as molasses.

Legion flinched, almost dropping his bowler hat. He managed to keep hold of it, grimacing nervously as his eyes flicked left and right again, looking fearful of the very real danger of Envy popping up behind him to impale him in the digestive off-ramp with a red pitchfork. If demons did have sphincters, his was all sphunct'd up. He gave me the faintest of nods in response to my accusation, licking his lips nervously. "We must find Lord Wrath. We fear for his safety," he rasped. "We are his and we don't know what to do without him. Our ability to replicate is weakening. We cannot multiply as fruitfully as yesterday."

His eyes bore into mine with an almost accusatory gleam. I blinked. Legion couldn't duplicate himself? "Wait. Do you think I *killed* him?" I asked, incredulously. "Is that why Lust paid me a visit and all but threatened to disembowel me if I didn't hand over her brothers?" Legion's eyes bulged at the mention of Lust visiting me and I saw beads of sweat pop out on his temples. "I didn't but not for a lack of trying. I'd be carrying his head around on a pike for all to see if I'd managed to pull that one off. Hell, I'd be on a beach, soaking up the sun, lugging his corpse around like Weekend at Bernie's."

Legion didn't blink, seeming to assess me for deceit. Finally, he took stock of Ryuu, only to find the ninja shrugging and nodding. "I would advise against vacationing with a corpse, but he was alive the last we saw him," the ninja said, and I knew he was choosing his words very carefully. Because Legion was incorrect on one fact. We had seen both Pride and Wrath at

Xuanwu's estate when we had opened a portal to the Neverwas—or Purgatory, as his breed called it.

If Legion didn't know about that, Wrath hadn't told anyone about me turning Pride and Michael into an Anghellian. Or the fact that Wrath had been working with Archangel Gabriel, his sworn nemesis. Wrath was keeping secrets from his own demon servant. I could guess at why he hadn't shared his rekindled friendship with his brother, Gabriel, but why not throw some shade at Pride instead? It would have been the perfect cover for his own crimes.

Awful pun, but where the hell was Wrath?

"Where are the other Sins? Have you guys checked with them?" I asked, my mind working at about a million miles an hour, considering a dozen different factors. Legion was not a good liar and he was ignorant and needy —the perfect mark for a con artist. I could use that.

Legion shrugged, dejectedly. "We have not. We fear them without the protections of our Master."

An idea began to formulate in my mind, and I began talking before I'd reached a solid conclusion. "Wrath fled when I turned him down at our dinner. We argued, obviously, but he walked out on his own two feet, not happy with my reaction to his proposal. He said he was going to rally the other Sins for an emergency meeting now that our wedding was off the table." I chose my words very carefully, speaking them off-handedly as I made sure my body language was equally disinterested and dismissive. Not my demon, not my problem. I needed to come across as genuine and uncaring, giving him a sliver of a hope that he might be able to intercept his boss at this fictional meeting.

He needed to believe that I had way more important things to worry about than Wrath's current location.

Legion frowned, giving me a doubtful look. "Lord Wrath despises his brothers and sisters. He would never call such a bizarre formal meeting."

I shrugged, leaning back on my elbows. "I said as much myself, mocking him for his idea."

Ryuu cleared his throat. "You said, and I quote, *if you want to pout and cry to your dysfunctional family about a woman rejecting you, it only reaffirms my decision. Go to hell, Wrath.*" His words hit Legion like a kick to the nuts, and I realized I was chuckling in surprise at Ryuu's improv skills. I hadn't intended him to back up my lie, let alone expected him to pour extra salt on Legion's pride in the process.

Legion opened his mouth, wordlessly, obviously wanting to smite Ryuu for the ninja's Hellish equivalent of blaspheming. Sinspheming? Demonizing? Whatever.

9

I waved a hand absently. "After the Pride situation with the Nephilim, Wrath kind of went crazy. Maybe he was even jealous that I visited Pride. If you guys recall, that was part of my agreement—to meet each and every Sin before considering his betrothal. Maybe he thought he could convince them to play nice with me when I came calling. He didn't have a reason to be jealous, though, because I haven't seen Pride since the multiple homicide of the Nephilim. Even Michael, who takes particular pleasure in pointing out my flaws, hasn't popped up to remind me how sinful I am." I shrugged. "Maybe he forgot to tell you guys about the meeting?"

Legion shook his head firmly, looking lost deep in his own thoughts. "I will continue searching. My main concern is what the rest of the Seven Sins will do in his absence. You said Lust visited you?"

I nodded. "Via a possessed woman less than an hour ago. Here, actually."

I knew I would garner no friends from Heaven by being too loose-lipped or helpful to Legion, so this was the best I could do. Because Legion had seemed to entirely forget that I had a clan of ninjas at my disposal, and they were known for being particularly sneaky.

Legion stared at me, looking miserable. "We don't know what to do," he said with sad, puppy-demon eyes.

I let out a breath, muttering unhappily. "How about this. I promise to let you guys know if I run into him, but only if you guys promise to give me a heads up if he's heading my way. Deal?"

He nodded adamantly, fumbling with the buckles on his briefcase in his abundance of excitement. "Let us just draw up a contract—"

"No. This is a personal pact between you guys and me. More binding than any contract. Ryuu is my witness."

Legion cocked his head, lowering his briefcase with a thoughtful look. "How archaic..." he mused. He glanced about the park, frowning. "We must sacrifice an innocent woodland creature and paint the Bindings of Damnation on each other's faces. Which creature would you prefer? The younger the better. Innocent blood is the equivalent of your upcoming improved mobile network when it comes to sacrificial communications. Superior service even in the most abysmal of locations."

Ryuu stared at him flatly and I had to forcefully click my jaw closed. "How about a simple handshake, psychopath? We can spit on our palms first, if you guys want to make a big ceremony out of it."

Legion frowned, looking disappointed. "That's not very dignified," he complained with a pompous air. He lifted a finger to reveal a shining black claw. "Maybe just a little prick to seal the deal?"

"Legion?" I asked in a calm, serious tone. He looked up at me, eyes hopeful. "A little prick never seals the deal, no matter what you guys were told."

Ryuu coughed violently into his elbow, trying not to stare directly at Legion.

Legion narrowed his eyes at the ninja, realizing he was the brunt of another joke. He stomped his way up to me and spit in his palm. "Fine. We swear to give you fair warning if Lord Wrath intends to visit you...in exchange for you alerting us to his whereabouts the moment you locate him."

I spit in my palm and shook hands, staring him in the eyes as we connected. I felt a faint pulse of heat and a whiff of sulfur in the air, which was less than appealing. I noticed something hovering above his head and reflexively swiped my other hand at it, believing it to be a mosquito.

Legion hissed and leapt away from me, putting at least six feet and his briefcase between us. "How dare you?!" he snarled, indignantly. I stared back at him, baffled.

Ryuu had leapt to his feet and drawn his black blade, keeping the both of us in his peripheral as he occupied the space between us. "Easy now," he urged in a calming tone. "Easy. Just a misunderstanding."

"*Misunderstanding?*" Legion sputtered, practically quivering with outrage. "She tried to touch our private parts!"

I scratched at my ear, fighting a smile. "I swatted at a fly. Unless you guys are admitting that you guys really are a collective of dickheads, I didn't go near any private parts."

Legion scowled at me before shifting his glare to Ryuu. "She mocks me. You saw!"

Ryuu nodded in commiseration. "I can assure you, it was an honest mistake. She did not intend to touch your halo."

"OUR HALO!" he shrieked, infuriated at the whole pronoun thing on top of my unintentional molesting.

The hair on the back of my neck practically jumped out of my skin. "Wait. WHAT?!" I demanded, competing with Legion for loudest crazy person.

Ryuu apologized and continued speaking with Legion, who now refused to acknowledge my existence. "May I have a piece of...Legion's essence so that we can reach out to you guys when the time is right?" Ryuu asked the affronted demon, struggling to address him properly.

Legion nodded, tugging at a few strands of hair with more force than necessary. He handed it over to Ryuu and then held out his palm, expecting Ryuu to return the favor. Ryuu reached onto his shoulder and lifted a long strand of pale hair. I narrowed my eyes. Of course. From our wrestling. I must have shed a few hairs on him. Legion took it with a derisive sneer, mumbled something privately to Ryuu in the tone of a displeased butler, and then disappeared in a puff of smoke.

"He didn't say goodbye to me," I grumbled, placing my hands on my hips and squaring my shoulders as I glared at Ryuu. "Maybe ask my permission before you give my hair to Wrath's manservant."

Ryuu rolled his eyes. "It was not your hair," he said, looking entirely too proud of himself. I frowned. "Claire," he explained, reaching into his pocket to pull out another strand. "I took a few from the brush on her nightstand when you grew concerned about her loyalties. I wanted my ninjas to keep an eye on her for you." He saw the anger flicker away from my face, and the concern rapidly replace it. "I have not sent anyone after her. I was going to discuss it with you before making such a decision, but I wanted to have the means to do it promptly if you agreed to it."

I stared at him, not sure if I was proud, relieved, or troubled by his well thought out plan. I had almost forgotten about Claire and the concerns I had about her proximity to Envy while he'd been snooping around Castle Dracula. "Why was her hair on your shoulder?" I asked.

He smirked, sheathing his katana. "When you shook hands, I pulled it from the vial in my pocket while you were both distracted." He lifted a small glass vial from his pocket, slipped Legion's hair inside it, corked it, and then tucked it back into his pants. "I knew we would need a way to track him. That is why you purposely antagonized him, correct? Subconsciously encouraging him to check on the rest of the Sins so we could locate them?"

I nodded, deciding that I really wanted to slap and kiss Ryuu at the exact same time. Competence was the sexiest quality a man could have, but add in the brains to scheme, a graceful lethality, and a body designed to inspire Classical Greek statues...

And my panties practically felt combustible.

But I was a professional, so I didn't actually leapfrog his face and ride him down to the ground while gripping his hair for handlebars. Yes, I envisioned it, but I was a lady, first. "I really need to call Nate," I muttered to myself under my breath.

Judging by the way Ryuu's pupils dilated, he definitely heard me and wholeheartedly agreed. I shrugged off the thought, still concerned about Lust and Aphrodite's potential manipulation of my sex drive.

"So, you can track his movements with that hair?" I asked, gesturing at the vial.

"My men can do it without being seen. They will work in rotation so that they are not recognized." He pulled out his phone and made a call, speaking in low tones as he paced back and forth. I watched him, absently; my eyes appreciated his not overly muscled frame, but my mind was a tornado of anxiety.

Halo. Ryuu had said I'd almost struck Legion's halo. What the hell? Had I actually seen a flicker of his halo, not the fly or mosquito I had assumed? Or had I seen a fly and simply made a serious social faux pas while trying to shoo away the pest?

Ryuu finished his call and turned back to me. "Legion just privately told me he anticipates at least two murders every day until Pride and Wrath are found. Could be more, of course, possibly two from each of the remaining Sins. I told my men to ratchet up the patrols on the streets."

I blinked at him. "Wait. They're going to attack my people until I give them something I don't have?"

Ryuu nodded with a grim resignation in his eyes. "Falls in line with Lust's parting threat. We need to find Wrath and come up with an answer about Pride."

I gritted my teeth and clenched my fists. "Or we could save ourselves the trouble and kill all the Sins," I growled.

He grinned wolfishly, nodding. He opened his mouth to speak, but then his eyes shifted beyond my shoulder right as I felt a familiar wave of power flare up behind me. "Sense a disturbance in the Force, I do," I said, turning to face our newest uninvited guest.

Eae, the angel known as the Demon Thwarter loomed before me, his wings flared out for dramatic effect.

I groaned. "Did you put up a damned internet ad about our location?" I asked, glancing at Ryuu.

Both men ignored me. "Callie Penrose!" Eae's voice boomed through the clearing like a megaphone. "Eden calls, and you have been summoned for judgment—"

"Remember that time we ran you over with a car?" I interrupted him. I leaned forward, cupping one hand around the side of my mouth. "*Twice!*" I whisper-shouted. Then I leaned back, assessing his wings. "I can hardly tell. Promise."

10

The angel pursed his lips and his wings sunk a few feet lower at my cruel reminder. He had been disgraced in recent years after failing to manage a problem with Nate Temple in St. Louis. He had since chosen to hitch his wings up in Kansas City, relegated to being the guardian angel of one of the most awful, spiteful old women I had ever had the displeasure of meeting: Greta, former assistant to the CEO at Temple Industries.

She was worse than any demon I'd ever met. She was the embodiment of holier-than-thou.

I think Eae would have preferred falling from grace. At least demons could have dignity. The side benefit to working for her was that she was now employed at Abundant Angel Catholic Church—A2C2, for short—so he moonlighted with First Shepherd Fabrizio.

If he had expected a more welcoming reunion between us, he had been sorely mistaken, and had now been corrected with extreme prejudice.

I didn't hate him or anything. He was actually the best angel I'd met, but I had learned that angels were better remembered than experienced. A rearview mirror look was recommended when it came to angels. They were the vacuum cleaner salesmen of yesteryear, popping up unannounced to convince you to invest in something you couldn't responsibly afford and didn't even know you needed three minutes ago. If they managed to slip past your defenses and set up shop in your living room, it was in your best interest to grant whatever vague, non-binding assurances were necessary to get them walking, tumbling, or flying out your front door, depending on your state's definition of self-defense.

Missouri had the Castle Doctrine.

And very few vacuum cleaner salesmen, coincidentally.

Yippee-ki-yay, Carpet-sucker!

Unfortunately, the Castle Doctrine offered no protection from angels.

"I was sent here to put you on notice," Eae said in a calmer tone, even though his words were actually a direct threat. He pulled out a rolled parchment and extended it to show me one side that was decorated with elaborate runes. "This is the arrest warrant for Archangel Michael. Heaven has questions about his involvement in the mass execution of a dozen innocent Nephilim. There are...conflicting stories, so we must detain and interrogate him."

I managed to keep my cool, knowing that the claim was utter bullshit. The Nephilim had not been even remotely peaceful. Eae swallowed uneasily after he finished speaking, and I could tell that he did not want to be here. At all. He was working under orders. From one of the other Archangels, most likely. Like the Sins, there seemed to be seven who received the most notoriety in the Bible. I really needed to brush up on that topic, because it seemed they were part of the legal team investigating me. "What does that have to do with me?" I finally asked in a calm, crisp tone.

"You were a witness to the event in question. This writ demands you turn over Michael or share any information you have on his whereabouts." He swallowed again. "Upon threat of execution. The Nephilim will have justice."

Ryuu took a step forward and I held out my arm, halting him. Eae immediately shielded himself with one of his wings and pulled the parchment away to keep it safe. Ryuu smirked. "Made you flinch."

Eae's lips thinned. "I have no quarrel with you, Halo Breaker, but I am aware of your reputation. I am merely the messenger of this decree, since it was determined that I have experience negotiating with Miss Penrose." And to his credit, I realized that his tense attitude and somewhat prickly demeanor did not seem to be directed at me, per se. He came across as frustrated about his current assignment, knowing that our history would offer him no protection and that it was essentially a suicide mission or a declaration of war against the White Rose, the Horseman of Despair, Count Dracula, and the wielder of the Holy Spear.

He wasn't wrong.

His boss had thrown him into the gladiatorial arena as a sacrifice and it pissed him right the heaven off.

I studied him, thoughtfully. "Who sent you, specifically? If this is about Michael, does that mean Gabriel sent you?"

Eae shook his head, but I noticed a flicker of unease in his eyes upon hearing Gabriel's name. "We have not seen Lord Gabriel in some time. Do you know where he is?"

I was silent for a few moments, trying to get a firm understanding of the shifting sands beneath each possible answer I could give. Gabriel had been working with Wrath, but it sure didn't seem like Eae knew that—neither had Lust or Legion. Did Eae's boss know—whichever Archangel had sent him to me—what Gabriel was up to? Had Wrath been working undercover for Gabriel or the other way around? Who was *good* and who was *bad*? Because I was getting pretty damned confused about who I could trust these days: some Olympians, but not all Olympians; some angels, but not all angels; some demons, but not all demons.

Since no one seemed to have knowledge about Gabriel and Wrath's rekindled brotherhood, I could not in good conscience give either Heaven or Hell a firm answer. I was the rope between both sides of the family tug-of-war.

"I saw Gabriel a few days ago, and it was not a cordial meeting," I finally said.

Eae cocked his head, reading my wary tone underlying the words. "Why would a meeting with the leader of the Archangels not be cordial? Did he disapprove of your actions?"

I could tell that Eae was also speaking between the lines, as if he believed he was being watched. Hell, maybe he wasn't sure if I was trustworthy, fearing that I was attempting to entrap him. Talk about trust issues. Neither one of us knew if we were on the same side, but both of us believed that, as individuals, we were on the right side. We just didn't know if our supposed teams were on the right side.

"Gabriel was working undercover at Castle Dracula as a servant, spying on my people. And me, of course," I explained, gauging his response.

Eae's eyes widened slightly at my accusation, but then narrowed with suspicion and doubt. "Impossible. Gabriel would not hide his awesomeness."

I grunted at his dated application of the word. "Awfulness, perhaps. There was nothing honorable about his undercover work. It was straight up spying, and I don't know why he thought it necessary."

"Did Michael know about this?"

I shared a long look with Ryuu, hoping for guidance. He gave me a discreet shake of his head. Finally, I turned back to Eae. "Listen, don't take this the wrong way, but I'm not sure you are at the right pay grade to hear the answers to your questions. Neither of us has enough verifiable information to continue this conversation without frightening the crap out of each other. There are things happening in this city that make no sense, and I'm not talking about the Freaks. I'm talking about *your* family squabbles. The Sins and the Archangels."

Eae took a dangerous step forward. "You are not *listening* to me," he hissed, with an almost manic look in his eyes, more like he was pleading with me—almost like a hostage trying to send a coded message in a ransom demand or proof-of-life video. "The Nephilim demand justice, and they *will* have it."

Ryuu drew his blade a few inches to reveal cold black steel. "Careful, Demon Thwarter. Callie Penrose is listening, and I am watching," he warned, pointedly glancing at Eae's feet. "The White Rose is being as honest as she possibly can. We have observed agents of Heaven working at odds with each other, and it leaves us in the moral conundrum of having to judge their motivations and pick one over another—which seems a contradiction. We do not desire this duty, but we will fulfill it with all the honor it requires, which means we need to ask difficult questions and stand firm on our convictions." Eae nodded after a few moments, looking as if he wanted to commiserate with us and speak freely. Problem was, I knew he couldn't do such a thing. Eae was a stickler for red tape and following the rules. "Having said that," Ryuu continued in a dispassionate tone, "your brothers have provided adequate provocation for an...attitude adjustment."

I slowly turned to look at Ryuu and his lazily calm demeanor. Eae opened his mouth to argue, thought better of it, and finally closed his mouth with the sound of clicking teeth. I burst out laughing. "Attitude adjustment?" I asked, dryly. "Subtle."

Ryuu frowned pensively and then nodded. He sheathed his blade all the way and cracked his knuckles, and then shook his wrists as if to loosen them up before a workout. "You are correct," he said, smiling at me. He shifted his attention to Eae. "I should take a more hands-on approach. Any attempt to lay a finger on Callie Penrose, and I will choke you to death with your own halo. I will not need Angel Killer to make you weep. Your brothers will hear you cry and they will quiver in fear. The Pearly Gates will weep blood and as the Pillars of Heaven crumble and fall, I will stand tall beside the White Rose." Eae's face paled and he stared into Ryuu's eyes with palpable, silent fear. "Tell me my threat is an empty one, Eae. Please. The White Rose hasn't outright said so, but I think she believes my reputation is...overinflated or dramatized." He did not look over at me, but rather stared into Eae's eyes. "Tell her that my threats are empty and that I will not do this thing. Please."

Eae's shoulders shook and he stared back at my ninja, actually quivering. "You...do not exaggerate," he croaked, sounding like he hated himself for admitting it where anyone else could overhear. His eyes flicked up towards the sky and he shuddered, looking torn.

I stared at Ryuu, wondering if I really wanted to know about his past or not. "Did you just accuse me of nagging?"

He smirked. "I *defended* your right to nag, technically."

"We will talk about this later," I grouched, turning back to Eae. "Ryuu will stop threatening you. Right, Ryuu?"

He shrugged. "I've already finished threatening. All that is left is the doing. As long as I'm here, Callie is behind my aegis, and everything in front of my aegis will be destroyed, utterly. Archangel, Archdemon, Nephilim." He shrugged. "These titles are meaningless to me. They are all lightning bugs at dusk, proclaiming that their ass makes them worthy."

Eae nodded stiffly, obviously not appreciating the metaphor. "Understood," he said, very wisely slipping my execution order out of view.

"I feel like we got off on the wrong foot, Eae." He turned to me with a wary look. "How have you been? Having fun with the Shepherds?"

He considered my words. "They are under new management, and there have been some...growing pains."

I arched an eyebrow. "Did they fire Fabrizio as First Shepherd?"

Eae shook his head firmly. "No. They cleaned out the Conclave and hired a new leader. Father Ignatius. My time is mostly spent at Abundant Angel Catholic Church, so I often hear First Shepherd Fabrizio's vociferous displeasure."

I smiled. "He used naughty words, didn't he?"

Eae just smiled, the first genuine smile of the morning. But his eyes remained haunted and paranoid.

"Okay. What do you think you know about the Michael situation?" I asked, not wanting to be the first one to share my side of the story with the Nephilim. Because...Michael *had* killed a dozen of them, but only to protect me and Pride from their overzealous hunger to see me dead. They'd been deceived with false accusations about me. We'd had to hide Michael and Pride from a full-scale manhunt from both Heaven and Hell as both sent out arrest warrants blaming the other side of the family. The biblical Hatfield and McCoy's feud. But there was an entirely good chance that I might let slip one tiny sliver of information that would reveal I knew much more than they thought and that I had been complicit in aiding the fugitives escape from the law. Which would then mean angels, not Nephilim, would be hunting me down for execution, and Ryuu would be forced to kill large swaths of heavenly hosts because he was very adamant about keeping his word, and he'd just made a declaration to Eae that he now had to stand behind. If I was in danger, angels would die by his hand.

"The dead Nephilim," Eae said. "You were there, as was Pride and your godfather, Samael."

"For the record, they shot a rocket-propelled grenade at me before even announcing why they were there. They intended to interrogate my smoldering ruins, but Michael, Pride, and Samael had strong opinions against that—each for different reasons." I took a calming breath, knowing that it was best if I didn't say more. Gabriel and Wrath had both seen me after that altercation, but if they were now both missing...

I wasn't required to volunteer incriminating information. I felt a strange sensation that made my shoulder blades twitch, as if we were being watched. I glanced up at the sky, frowning, but I saw nothing alarming.

Finally, I shrugged, turning back to Eae. "Why do you think they haven't returned to Heaven or reached out to you? Any theories? What's the running gossip around the blessed wine cooler? Maybe they don't believe they will get a fair trial. The terms *martyr* and *black flag* comes to mind."

Eae shook his head. "I am not at liberty to say. What are your theories? What's the running gossip around the cursed blood cooler?" he asked, trying to sound cool by flipping my words.

"Cold blood is gross, from what I hear. Maybe a blood fondue fountain would work, but I'd have to take a closer look at Castle Dracula's operating budget for office equipment."

"What can you tell me about Michael? Give me *something*," he pleaded.

I folded my arms. "I'm not sure I can do that. Even if I could, I don't know if I *should*. Something smells off about this whole thing. Why did they send you when they know I have Ryuu as a nuclear deterrent? And what did you mean about the Nephilim demanding justice? Speak plainly."

Eae closed his eyes, murmuring under his breath as he debated my request. After a few moments, he opened them and his features took on a grim resignation—a man walking to the gallows with his head held high.

I instantly grew uneasy, as did Ryuu.

Eae surprised the hell out of me by revealing a long ivory claw where his finger had been. The only reason I didn't instantly murder him was because he turned the claw towards himself and sliced into his own palm. He smeared the blood down his face and then drew an intricate rune on his throat in a practiced gesture. The structural cartilage of his wings suddenly flared with light as dozens of glowing runes sprang to life from shoulder to tip. Enochian script. The one on the tip of his wing looked familiar, but it rapidly began to fade and then fizzled out as I stared at it. The next one started to do the same, and I realized that it was a countdown.

Ryuu was glaring past Eae, staring at the ground, and I noticed a ring of golden light in the grass that trapped us all within its circumference. I clenched my jaws. "A trap," I snarled, rounding on Eae.

"No!" Eae hissed, holding out his palms in a *don't shoot* gesture. "A ward that lets us speak privately, but it won't last long," Eae said, eyeing the fading runes extending down his wings. He was right. The second to last one had also winked out, leaving about a dozen on each wing.

Ryuu pursed his lips, keeping his hand rested on the hilt of his sword. "Speak."

Eae nodded. "I was told that if Callie Penrose does not immediately cooperate in the capture of Michael, Nephilim hit teams will strike. Repeatedly. Until she complies. I am entirely sure I am being watched, so if you want to prevent any innocent lives being taken by these independent teams, you need to help me help you."

I took an aggressive step forward, checking the runes on his wings and the ring surrounding us. "What do you mean, *hit teams will strike*? Where? Who? Are you saying they are coming after me? Or are the Nephilim staking out my people?" I demanded, realizing that both Heaven and Hell were putting me firmly in their scopes—and they didn't even know the full story of what I had actually done in making an Anghellian. I quite literally could not give them what they demanded.

"They told me no more than that," Eae assured me in a desperate tone. "I would guess that your allies are already under surveillance or they would not have told me about the strike teams. It sounded to me like they wanted to hit you before you had a chance to gather your forces. They did not want me to serve as a warning without teeth. They know and respect your ability to wreak havoc, and that if we warn you with mere words, you will form an allied army of monsters and demons to knock down any Nephilim assassins.

This leads me to believe that your actions, right here and now, will determine someone's fate. In less than five minutes."

"A five-minute warning?" I snarled incredulously, clenching my knuckles. "This was never intended to be a friendly negotiation. They sent you to buy them time! How long is this ward? Are we trapped inside?"

"No. You may pass through without issue. It guards only against eavesdropping."

Ryuu was utterly silent, so it took me a moment to notice that he had actually closed half the distance between him and Eae. His face was utterly blank, and his hands were empty, but he looked like he wanted to get them dirty.

"Ryuu. Stop," I said, sternly. "He didn't have to tell us any of that. He could have said his piece and then left when we told him we didn't have answers about Michael. Or after mentioning retaliations from Nephilim for noncompliance."

Eae was nodding fervently.

Ryuu kept walking, not speeding up or slowing down. Just a steady march of death closing in on the angel.

"In fact, he probably put himself in danger by being so open, didn't you, Eae?" I said, louder.

Eae nodded rapidly, realizing the situation was spiraling downhill fast.

Ryuu continued his slow, graceful pace, not making a sound. He was almost within striking distance.

Eae closed his eyes and fell to his knees, spreading his arms and wings out wide as he silently muttered a prayer, tilting his head back so that his face looked to the heavens. The runes were about halfway gone.

Ryuu came to a stop before him and silently assessed the praying angel. Then he reached out with one hand for the top of the angel's head, and I had no doubt that I was actually going to see him grab the halo and proceed to choke Eae to death with it, just like he'd vowed earlier. I didn't see any indication of a halo like I'd apparently seen with Legion. I also knew that there was absolutely nothing I could do to stop Ryuu. Nothing I wanted to do, to be completely transparent. It was unfortunate for Eae that he'd been forced into such a terrible position, sent out like a dog with a message, but that wasn't what his brothers had done. They had inadvertently sent me a hostage, and I was pretty sure Ryuu knew it. If we could kill or capture Eae for a message we didn't like, they might think twice about aggravating us further by killing any of my allies.

Ryuu's fingers touched Eae's hair and the angel flinched. I stared at the empty space above Eae's head, trying to see any sign of the halo before Ryuu came into contact with it, but I noticed nothing out of the norm.

The Halo Breaker pinched a few strands of Eae's hair and shifted them to the other side of the angel's head, correcting the part down the center of the angel's skull. I hadn't even noticed Eae's hair had a part until Ryuu fixed it.

Ryuu stepped back with a satisfied grunt and brushed his hands together. "That was bothering me this whole time. Now you're looking like a million bucks."

Eae peeled his eyes open and stared up at Ryuu in disbelief. "You...fixed my hair?" he croaked, trembling as if he'd soiled himself for no reason and couldn't decide whether he was okay with it or not.

Ryuu nodded, extending his hand to pull Eae to his feet. The angel hesitantly held out his hand and let himself be pulled up. Face to face, Eae was much taller than Ryuu, but it didn't look that way. "For being honest with Callie."

Eae lifted both hands to check his hair, looking as if he couldn't quite believe his luck and needed to verify that his halo hadn't been snatched up by ninja sleight of hand.

Ryuu moved so swiftly that it was a blur, and I heard a meaty *thump* followed by Eae's lung crushing groan. The angel doubled over, wheezing around Ryuu's fist, which was firmly folded into Eae's ribs where he'd delivered the mother of all uppercuts. "That was for not being honest *sooner*." He pulled his hand away and Eae's knees buckled, sending him crashing back down to the ground with a pathetic whimper.

Ryuu turned away without a sliver of compassion on his face, gave me a nod, and then slowly returned to his original position closer to me. I watched him the whole way, my jaw hanging open. It wasn't an arrogant strut, but his oozing confidence gave me vague stirrings that made me think of the words *covet* and *lust*.

"Well," I said, letting out a breath as I glanced at the recovering angel. "I'm not really sure where we go from here. Are you returning to the angels who sent you here as a hostage victim? You do see that, now, right? That you were sent out as a sacrificial lamb to buy them time?"

Eae nodded. "Y-yes," he rasped, slowly rising to his feet and clutching his ribs. "But the only way to stop this is to find out who is behind it all, if not Gabriel. I am beginning to see duplicity in more than one angel, situations where I know their words contradict their actions. I can be of more use on the inside, and very little use by *your* side."

I nodded. "But that doesn't help me *now*. Who have they been watching?" I asked, checking his runes. I estimated that we had a minute or two, tops, before he would be unable to speak freely. "Anything, Eae. Who should I protect?"

Eae shot me a desperate, impotent look. "Someone close to you but not someone who will push you so hard you will no longer cooperate. An underling of lesser importance. Likely more than one so you know it was intentional."

"They are all important, Eae," I snarled, grinding my teeth.

"I know! I'm just explaining their intentions. Killing Claire or Cain would put you on the warpath and make you uncooperative, which they don't want. So, it will be a follower you might not even know. One of your many vampires, for example. You are Count Dracula and are responsible for all of them, but you hardly know them all and you certainly don't love all of them as family."

I ran a hand through my hair, realizing that keeping my people safe was an impossible task. He was right. It would be a nameless soldier. That's what I would have done. "Damn them all!" I shouted, panting furiously.

Ryuu watched me with surprisingly compassionate eyes, and I realized that he was entirely aware that it might end up being one of his own men—a nameless ninja. My anger turned to guilt and I tried to mirror his compassionate look. I probably failed, but I hoped the sentiment came across clearly.

My people were not *unimportant* to me...even if I didn't personally know them.

But I was suddenly very aware that I had done a pretty shitty job at uniting them and letting them know I appreciated them and their support. I could have at least brought them all to Castle Dracula. The place wasn't perfect since Archangels and Archdemons could enter with abandon, but at least there were enough armed monsters to keep an eye out and police the figurative streets.

Which was the only answer I could think of. I turned back to Ryuu. "We need to get everyone to Castle Dracula."

Ryuu stared at me, not agreeing or rejecting. If his ninjas were at Xuan-wu's warded estate, they would be safe. But most of them spent time patrolling the streets of Kansas City, which meant any one of them might be experiencing their final moments, destined to die in five minutes. "I can have my men do a roll call to see who doesn't reply from the street patrols. The others can retrieve their body and bring them to..." I trailed off, eyeing Eae, realizing that I needed to choose my words carefully, "the spa."

Because Xuanwu had a rebirth pool in his pocket dimension, the training field. Aala, Ryuu's sister, could see about bringing back a murdered or injured ninja, if they were one of the targets. And if Eae's warning turned out to be true.

Ryuu nodded. "You realize that your plan will empty the streets of Kansas City and leave it defenseless and up for grabs?" I nodded. "And that it will herd everyone you care about all into the same place. Much easier for your enemies to attack in full force and do the most damage without fear of being flanked."

I nodded again. "I know, Ryuu, but I'm running out of better options."

Eae glanced down at his wings, grunting to see only one glowing rune left. He looked back up at me with a forlorn look. "When this fades, I will need to play my part so as not to arouse suspicion. We cannot be seen as allies."

I nodded, clenching my sword. "We've done that before. When we ran you over with a car."

He smirked, nodding his head. Then his face went utterly calm and the last rune winked out. The ring of light around us also disappeared, and the blood on Eae's face and chest crumbled away like dry ash in the breeze. "Be warned, Callie Penrose. I will pass on your response, but know that the next encounter between us will not be with words. Michael has been declared a criminal, and all those who associate with him are deemed guilty."

I nodded. "So. Be. It."

Eae studied us for a few more moments, glaring furiously for the sake of his handlers.

A blur of tanned skin and feathers abruptly swept down from the sky and tackled Eae, driving his face into the dirt and using it as a brake pad for a skid that lasted at least thirty feet. I stared in disbelief.

"Riddle me this," Ryuu said, entirely too pleased with himself.

❧ 12 ❧

It took me a few moments to see through the tufts of sod and grass and feathers to verify that it was indeed Phix, the sphinx, the queen of riddles. Now that I saw her with my own eyes, I felt her presence in my mind, realizing that it was her who I had sensed watching us minutes before Eae flung up his ward. I'd shrugged it off, too concerned about my allies in danger to give it any further scrutiny.

"Don't you ever put my White Rose inside a ward without my permission!" Phix screamed, throttling the poor angel as she gnashed her teeth at him.

Ryuu's amusement had shifted to mild concern as he shot me a look. "Should we—"

"Nah," I said. "Nate's put him through worse. Phix is just giving him a friendly *hello*—"

"I will rip out your grace and floss my teeth with it!" Phix snarled, palming the angel's forehead with her massive paw and banging the back of his head into the ground with each syllable.

I continued speaking. "Peaceful greeting between allies—"

"I will pluck every single feather from your overcompensating wings and burn them with Greek fire!" she roared, batting his face from left to right with alternating swats of her paw. The talons slicing across his face emitted a scraping, metallic sound rather than tearing his flesh to ribbons with fountains of blood. This made me curious, since Ryuu had readjusted his internal organs with one punch. She finally hurled herself up into the air, circled him with powerful sweeps of her wings, and then glided back to me, landing by my side. Ryuu studied her thoughtfully and then gave her an approving nod. She nuzzled up even closer, ducking under my arm as she let out an affectionate purring sound.

Which wasn't weird at all since, from the feline's chest up, she was a perfectly curved bombshell of a naked human woman, from navel to million-watt smile to salon commercial hair. Her breasts were on full display and would best be described as *insurable*—perfectly shaped, large enough to draw every eye without resembling a teenaged boy's favorite anime, and resilient to gravity in every way. So, a naked chick was pressed up against my side, physically forcing me to wrap my arms around her shoulder as she purred at me loud enough to tickle my armpits. Apparently, I'd been adopted as a founding member of the Furry Scouts of America.

"Hey, um, Phix," I said under my breath, knowing it sounded lame and not wanting Eae to see my discomfort. "I thought you were training with Grimm to be..." I trailed off, not wanting to officially announce her new role as my Horseman's ride so that she wasn't targeted by Eae's handlers. "Training for your new job."

"That's what you get for thinking," she said, haughtily. Ryuu's eyes widened slightly and he very wisely chose to keep his focus on Eae. "I've been assessing the city from the air, getting a better read on the layout. Can we go to war soon, because I am hungry, and this place is a boiling kettle. It wasn't even this bad with Roland's red dome. Well, close," she admitted.

The angel had scrambled to his feet, gasping in horror at the grass stains on his white wings. He slowly turned, aiming his glare at Phix like a drawn arrow. "You will suffer for your insolence, creature—"

"Horse," Phix snarled, aggressively. To further muddy the water, she abruptly shifted into an entirely human form and I almost tripped over my own full-body muscle spasm. I had been entirely sure she couldn't do that, and it gave me instant reservations about choosing her as the official ride to the Horsewoman of Despair. A vision of me piggybacking on her shoulders, entering the Omega War like it was a game of chicken in a fraternity house pool.

"What the hell, Phix?!" I hissed, unable to stop myself from inspecting her now human lower half. Her newly revealed ability invited very important questions. Did she still have paws or could we now go shoe shopping together? Her thighs were a sun-kissed bronze that glistened like suntan oil and there wasn't a single blemish or hair to be seen—even as my attention drifted to her pelvis. I abruptly shifted my gaze to her hands. Her nails were bright purple. What the hell?

"Horse?" Eae sputtered, staring at her lower confessional booth with a dumbfounded expression on his face.

She nodded adamantly. "I identify as a horse, given my recent promotion to Despair's most trusted confidante." And there it was. So much for secrets. She somehow managed to cast challenging glares at both Ryuu and Eae, giving them equal levels of disdain. Looks like she was aiming for *Callie's BFF* status, competing against my tutor and potential boy toy.

"You cannot *identify* as a horse!" Eae sputtered, infuriated. "That is ridiculous."

"You identify as a good angel, so I thought it was make-believe day," Phix said, smugly. "Now, begone, creature." She made a shooing gesture with one hand, volleying his own term for her existence right back at him. Eae's face darkened and I shot him a discreet, apologetic look.

Eae winked out of view, much like Legion had. I absently wondered if it was a form of Shadow Walking for the elites.

Ryuu pulled out his phone and made a call, probably to his ninjas. I disentangled myself from Phix, gave her a flat glare, and then sat down on a log. I snatched up the bottle of sake, and took a long, healthy swig, staring off into the park.

Phix rolled her eyes and shifted back into her sphinx form with a relieved sigh. "So itchy being human," she muttered before curling up into a ball and closing her eyes.

I shook my head, feeling mentally exhausted for so early in the morning. "How did training go, Phix?" I asked, absently. She didn't respond. She didn't even open her eyes. "Right. Great talk," I muttered.

I took a sip of sake and stared off into the clouds while Ryuu continued on the phone.

"Demons and Nephilim on my ass, threatening to kill my friends, and I don't know how to tell them that their own bosses are behind it all. Gabriel and Wrath. Oh, and Aphrodite shows up to tell me Nate's scheduled for execution by an Olympian, but he's helping the Olympians, and I shouldn't trust the Olympians because they are starting a pre-war that could determine the fate of the Omega War. And now demons and Nephilim are both targeting my people." I took another swig, feeling Ryuu sit down beside me. He reached for the bottle and took a drink of his own. "Who do I trust, Ryuu?" I asked, leaning my head against his shoulder and wanting to do nothing more than cry. Just a little.

"The White Rose should always trust herself," he said, softly. "She has good instincts."

I grunted. "Doesn't feel that way sometimes. And you just missed the slow pitch chance to say I could trust *you*. If this was a Hallmark Christmas movie, you would have just ruined the plot."

He took another drink of the bottle, pondering my words. "This is not a Hallmark Christmas movie," he finally said with a rather disgusted look on his face.

I frowned, shaking my head. Apparently, Ryuu and I would never be watching cheesy romance movies together. However, digging deeper...it was actually an incredibly sweet thing to say to me. I often did judge myself too harshly and second guess my actions, but I couldn't let him know that. "That was actually a worse thing to say," I told him. "The only thing you forgot to do was buy me a bouquet of flowers and then stomp on them rather than giving them to me."

He chuckled. "I would rather empower you than give you a crutch to lean on—even if that crutch is me. You don't need to look to someone else to fight your battles. You need to fight your own, trust your instincts, and know that you have what it takes to save yourself. These qualities are priceless."

I sighed, snatching the bottle from him. I lifted the bottle to my lips and began to drink.

"For everything else, there's Ryuu," he added in a low, foreboding growl, drawing his black blade a few inches. I choked on the sake, spewing it out in a mist of alcohol. I glanced over at him, wiping my lips with my sleeve. "The screams of your foes dying will almost be as loud as your followers cheering," he assured me with a cool smile. "And you can always trust me, Callie Penrose."

Phix chuckled wickedly, lazily digging her claws into the grass and tearing up furrows in the hard ground.

Ryuu's phone chirped and he glanced down with a frown. He stared at the screen for a few moments and let out a soft breath. When he looked up, his eyes were hard and brittle like a frozen pond. "One of my men was found dead. Jin. He had an angelic rune carved into his forehead."

I clenched my fist and let out a growl. "Eae was right. They're sending a message. How quickly can your men get him to Aala's rebirth pool?"

Ryuu shook his head. "Jin's severed head was sitting atop a wooden chest of ashes. His own ashes."

I let out a furious hiss, rising to my feet as my vision tunneled with rage. "So much for them being the good guys."

Ryuu shook his head. "They think we are the bad guys. All is fair in love and war. Men often commit violence in direct proportion to their level of fear. I would say they are very, very frightened of you and my men," he said with an almost feral smirk. "I will show them the true depths of fear. We are safe at Xuanwu's but not when out in the streets. My men will have to be more vigilant—they've grown sloppy in their duties. Jin was not vigilant. Now, the Nephilim will have to be vigilant of *me* because it is considered rude not to reply to a message that they spent so much time crafting. My response will be...poetic," he vowed.

I wrapped my arms around him in a tight hug, resting my forehead against his. "We will avenge him, Ryuu." I hadn't meant for it to be a romantic gesture; more of a camaraderie for the fallen. But the tension between us suddenly ratcheted up at warp speed, our pulses doubling within seconds as I noticed I could taste his breath. Phix's purring grew significantly louder and I quickly pulled away, embarrassed. I scowled at her for good measure, but she wasn't looking at us. Maybe she'd felt our pulses speed up, too. What was causing my newfound awareness of heartbeats?

There was one obvious answer, but I knew I wasn't a vampire, so I forcefully dismissed that fear.

I frowned, noticing a symbol on Phix's rump. "Hey! Is that a fucking *tattoo?*"

Phix lifted her head to look back at me, blinked lazily, and then nodded. "I am now a creature of darkness, fighting the light."

I arched an eyebrow, sputtering incoherently. "Pardon?" I finally managed.

"Grimm was adamant that there is a conspiracy afoot. A group working behind the scenes that no one even knows exists. He calls it Rainbowgate, and he thinks they are the real power behind the Masters."

I blinked, trying not to laugh. Then I leaned forward, inspecting the symbol. It appeared to be a rainbow with a lightning bolt bisecting it and shattering the peak like it was a bridge of glass. It also looked crude, more of a brand than a tattoo. "Did, um, anyone else get these...badges of honor, or just you?" I asked, fearing that she was the victim of one of Nate's unicorn's frequent pranks.

She narrowed her eyes. "Do not patronize me, woman." There were so many things wrong with that comment that I decided to let it go. "Grimm also had one. As did Ratatouille."

I grunted. "Who the fuck is Ratatouille?"

She gave me a slow grin. "Oh, you will see."

"Why do you need a tattoo? Doesn't that let everyone know you know?" I asked. "What is this group called?"

Phix glanced left and right, looking suspicious. "Promise not to repeat what I am about to tell you?" I nodded. Rather than speaking out loud, she spoke directly into my mind, hijacking my thoughts. *The Rainbownatti. We are Legion.*

I was silent for about five whole seconds. Had Grimm really roped her into one of his crazy conspiracies, turning his hatred for rainbows into a form of the Illuminati? "You can't say *we are Legion* anymore. It's hyperbolic. The real Legion is here in Kansas City. It's identity theft." She frowned, pensively. Then she shrugged. I folded my arms. "And it's ridiculous. I think Grimm is pranking you."

"That's what one of *them* would say," Phix said, with a suspicious glare.

I rolled my eyes, turning back to Ryuu. "Let's get out of here. I need to talk to Lucky about his two families. We need a solution to this madness."

"Who is Lucky?" Phix asked, standing up behind me.

I sighed and quickly caught her up on the high points of my recent adventures. She stared at me, looking stunned. Then she glanced past me at Ryuu. "I'm holding you responsible for this. I thought I was leaving her in capable hands when I left for work. All you had to do was babysit her."

"Hey!" I snapped. "You joined a cult and got a tattoo! You want to lecture Ryuu on responsibility?"

"I was training for my job and I discovered the true evil plot behind the Omega War. You broke into Purgatory and essentially murdered Archangel Michael and Archdemon Pride by making this...Anghellian—which is an incredibly ridiculous name. It's not a real thing. Wake up, Neo."

I flung my hands up in the air at her trying to out-pop-culture me with a Matrix quote. "Of course it's a real thing! I was there—HEY! Don't you *dare* walk away from me, young lady!" I hissed, glaring as she did exactly what I told her not to do. Did Nate have these kinds of problems with Grimm? Weren't they supposed to work *for* the Horsemen, not boss them around?

"I'm suddenly very interested in the naked man over by the angel fountain," Phix said from over her shoulder. "You should be, too."

"What?!" I demanded. "Why is there a naked man in a public park? And stop walking away from me while I'm talking to you!" Ryuu calmly began gathering up our gear, realizing that we were leaving one way or another, whether by Phix's command or mine. I snapped my fingers. "Put that down. We're not going anywhere. You don't take orders from a pissy cat."

He froze, his eyes widening. I heard Phix's purr change to something decidedly less friendly. "Pussy cat?" she asked in a warning tone.

"Pissy, as in, being a real bitch to her *boss*, the Horsewoman of Despair, when she's stressed out of her mind, crabby, angsty, worried sick about more of her friends getting killed when she can't tell her friends from her foes—"

I was suddenly tackled to the ground and smothered by a weighted blanket of sleek, hot fur. A gentle, massive paw clamped over my mouth and I looked up to see Phix looming over me. She gave me an affectionate smile, her purring threatening to recalibrate my pulse as she shifted her paw to cup my cheek. "You need to cut loose. Let off some steam." Her purple eyes shifted to Ryuu and she smirked wolfishly. "Might I suggest you take the ninja and—"

I screamed, letting out a full-bodied shriek that emptied my lungs and echoed throughout the park. Phix smiled even wider, purred louder, and waited for me to finish.

"You mentioned saving two Divines from the Neverwas—a white tiger and a red phoenix," she said in a soft voice.

"Get off me. Now. Or I will personally remove your stupid tattoo with a rusty scalpel," I warned.

She ignored my threat, pinning me down with her massive weight. "The naked man at the nearby angel fountain had a white tiger and a fiery bird on leashes."

I froze, gawking up at her. "Lucky," I breathed.

She nodded. "My thought as well." Then she calmly extracted herself and turned away, waiting patiently.

I climbed to my feet, dusted off my pants, and then rounded on Ryuu, pointing at our training gear. "Pick that up. We're going to the angel fountain to beat the holy hell out of an Anghellian." He sighed, not bothering to point out that this conflicted with my order from ten seconds ago.

My phone rang so I answered it without looking. "White Rose. What do you want?"

Roland grunted on the other end of the line. "Not a good time?" he asked in a grim tone.

"I wouldn't have answered like that if it was, Roland," I said, thinking about Lucky and wondering why the hell he was here at all, let alone naked and walking the Divines on leashes. They were all supposed to be resting at Xuanwu's, not wandering around in public. They'd all three been sleeping when Ryuu and I left to train this morning. What if Eae's handlers had spotted him?

"Well," Roland muttered, "sorry for inconveniencing you. If you're too busy, perhaps I can schedule a meeting with your secretary to discuss the murdered remains of one of your vampires near my church," he said in a frigid tone. "Oh, wait. You do not have a secretary."

I clenched my jaw at his news and his tone, feeling like my temples were throbbing so hard they might explode. "Watch it, Roland. I'm in a mood today."

"A category five bitch-icane," Phix called out in a loud shout, ever so helpful.

I flipped her off and then turned away, focusing on Roland. "Let me guess. Severed head propped up on a wooden chest of ashes."

The line was silent and I could practically see the shock on his face through the phone. "How did you—"

"Like I said, rough morning. I need you to round up every single vampire you can and get them to Castle Dracula. Now."

"Of course," he said, sounding troubled. "Who hit us?"

I hesitated. "Drive-by Catholicism," I muttered, thinking of Lust and Eae's eerily similar threats.

"*What?* The Vatican Shepherds?" he growled.

I shook my head. "No. Definitely not. Bad metaphor. This was an indirect consequence of..." I let out a frustrated breath, not trusting the privacy of our call, and I didn't have time to turn it into a twenty-minute conversation. "Listen, Roland, just do as I ask. I don't have time to chat right now. Ryuu and I are about to get Lucky and I'm fed up with interruptions."

The other end of the line was completely silent and I almost glanced down to see if we'd been disconnected. "Well..." Roland said, sounding as if he was struggling to find the right words. I understood. One of ours had just been murdered and I was telling him to retreat. "I...will get everyone to the castle. Protect yourself, Callie," he said, his words sounding awkward and stiff.

"I don't need protection, Roland. He does. I'm going to make him scream. He's already running around naked, so it's high time I show him who's boss." Roland attempted to deter me, but I hung up the phone and slipped it into my pocket. "Let's go get Lucky."

Ryuu was frowning, thoughtfully, scratching at his jaw at some private thought. Phix began trotting away, leading us towards the fountain.

🦁 14 🦁

I strolled through the park, taking deep breaths of the scintillating scent of fresh growth riding the gentle breeze of early morning air. This time of day, the birds were singing delightedly, the park was relatively quiet, and the world could almost be seen as a calm, peaceful, tranquil place.

The world was not a calm, peaceful, tranquil place.

The homicidal, psycho, riddle-cat stalked through the park at a steady clip, doing her best to remain out of sight. Phix kept to the ground rather than flying where anyone and everyone could see her. I watched her slip through the woods like a jaguar, keeping her wings tucked close as she guided us towards where she had last seen Lucky and the two Divines—who should have still been recovering from their banishment in Purgatory.

The Neverwas. The Night Currents. I'd heard numerous names for the place, and each revelation had only caused me more consternation. Why was it called Purgatory—a Christian reference—if other entities were imprisoned there? And how had no one known that angels and demons stored their graces there for a rainy day? Correction—why had the angels and demons been ripped into thirds in the first place, and then had their memories of such trauma wiped? In my analysis, the only one high enough up on the food chain for such a decision was the Notorious G.O.D.

We hadn't seen many park-goers, but I'd seen a few joggers weaving in and out of sight on winding, distant trails. Hopefully, Lucky's nudity hadn't attracted a crowd or a local news channel reporter. More importantly, I hoped Eae and his cohorts hadn't spotted him. As I thought about the numerous threats against me and my allies, I realized I had one more call to make.

I pulled out my phone and dialed as we followed Phix.

Fabrizio answered on the third ring. "Callie!" the First Shepherd of the Vatican death squad answered, sounding out of breath and suspicious. "Were your ears burning?"

I frowned, still scanning the park for Lucky or any sign of my hunters. "No. I wanted to warn you—"

Ryuu grunted, drawing my attention with a subtle shake of his head. "Careful. He works for *his* superiors, first. Not you," he reminded me. "And his *ultimate* superiors are no longer your fans."

I nodded, knowing full well that I was taking a big risk in calling him. I was no longer just Callie Penrose. Angels and Nephilim saw me as a threat because of the murdered Nephilim and Michael's disappearance. I was also the Horseman of Despair with the Spear of Destiny in my possession. Last, but certainly not least, I was Count Dracula, and the Shepherds were in an eternal war with vampires.

But Fabrizio and those working at A2C2 were my friends. They might or might not be safe from Nephilim, but they certainly needed to know that demons were on the hunt in Kansas City. I wasn't even sure if Fabrizio knew that the Seven Sins were in town. Would Eae have been permitted to tell him?

"Callie?" Fabrizio asked, sounding more concerned. "You still there? Warn me about what?"

"Yes. I'm here," I assured him, reconsidering how much to say over the phone. "I wanted to get your take on a hypothetical. Can we meet up later today?" I asked, choosing to follow Ryuu's advice.

The phone was silent for a few moments. "Um. Sure. I was going to call you to request a meeting as well," he said in a guarded tone that instantly made the hair on the back of my neck rise up. I just couldn't get a damned break today.

"Oh?" I asked. "Business or pleasure?" Eae had mentioned a change in management at the Vatican, so maybe Fabrizio was wading into the political swamp. That was a dangerous game for him to play because I was his friend and ex-colleague as a Shepherd, but I was also his enemy as the new Count Dracula.

Again, there was a long pause and I could have sworn I heard an audible gulp. "Both, actually," he said in a tone that I couldn't quite place. "If you are no longer...busy, I could meet you now."

Ryuu had sensed my tension and was staring into my eyes with a dangerous look—silently asking me if I needed a blade in the dark for the First Shepherd. I shook my head at him in answer, trying to decipher Fabrizio's strange behavior. "I'm actually still in the middle of—" I froze, suddenly suspicious. "Wait. How did you know I was busy right now?"

I heard a kerfuffle on the other end, and it sounded suspiciously like two grown men slapping and wrestling over the phone. "Oh. I was just chatting with Roland, and he might have told me—vaguely, of course—that you were...preoccupied. He wanted to make sure you had protection."

I stopped walking, wary of his overly careful, clipped words. I mentally picked apart his statement, and began to wonder if he was speaking in code. Had Roland told him about Lucky? I almost had a panic attack at the thought. What if Fabrizio blabbed to Eae or his superiors in the Vatican? I took a calming breath. Or maybe Roland had warned him about the vampire killer. Of course, I couldn't outright ask Fabrizio what he knew, because I didn't know how secure the line was. My new life purpose was to get my ass out of this cursed park before someone else decided to drop in and pay me a visit. I decided to play it safe. Silence or hesitation would only make him suspicious and more concerned.

"Oh. He's nothing I can't handle," I said, smiling at the fact that the two older men were being incredibly overprotective of me—as if I didn't know how to handle myself in dangerous situations. He made a strangled sound on the other end and I hastily clarified in an effort to assuage his fear. "And for the record, I never leave home without protection these days," I said, laughing as I saw Ryuu scowling at the phone. I waved a hand to let the ninja know he didn't need to murder the two grumpy old priests. "You two need to stop acting like I'm a child and get over it. I'm a big girl now and, believe it or not, I am allowed, even encouraged, to make bad decisions all on my own. And stop gossiping."

He sounded like he had the phone halfway in his mouth, breathing directly into it. "I'm just...you never..." he trailed off, sounding frustrated as he struggled for the right words. "I care about you, Callie, and Roland was very—"

There was another scuffle and I heard the phone fall to the ground, accompanied by a growl that definitely belonged to Roland. "I didn't tell you a thing! You opened this nightmare box all on your own."

"Roland!" I snapped, pursing my lips. "You're supposed to be collecting vampires, not gossiping. What did you tell him?" Of course, he couldn't hear me.

"Then why did you tell me anything in the first place?" Fabrizio snapped at Roland, followed by more wrestling and a few slaps and punches, grunts and curses.

"I am leaving!" Roland shouted in the background. "Remember, you did this to yourself!"

"This is *your* church!" Fabrizio argued. "You can't leave! I will leave!" I heard a heavy slam, a long silence, and then muttered cursing. Someone picked up the phone, grumbling unhappily. "Okay, I'm back. Sorry," Fabrizio said.

"What the *hell* is going on over there? Roland is supposed to be on a job! What did he tell you?"

Fabrizio hesitated. "We were heading to his church for a coffee when we found...the ashes he told you about. After he called you, he mentioned being...concerned about you. That you might be making ill-advised decisions and that he couldn't help you since you sent him off to collect vampires."

I let out a sigh of relief to hear no mention of Lucky. I unclenched my fist, waving off Ryuu's concern. "Oh. Don't worry about me. I'm in great hands with Ryuu. He works me hard, leaving me feeling like I've been wrung out to dry, but I wouldn't have it any other way." Ryuu nodded with smug pride at my accolades of his training abilities.

"Ryuu," Fabrizio said in a fatherly tone that made me grin. He really was treating me like his daughter!

"Ryuu is even better than Roland, but I'll kill you if you tell him that."

The phone dropped again and I heard something shatter. "Roland?" Fabrizio wheezed. "We need to talk. Soon."

I shrugged. "Sure. Like I said, Ryuu and I are just wrapping up a few things and then we can meet. I'll call you when I'm finished?"

"Y-yes. We should meet in private. Sensitive topics being what they are."

I frowned, masking my phone from Ryuu, knowing he wouldn't like that aspect one bit. "What are you working on?" I asked, hoping it didn't have anything to do with the Seven Sins, which might lead him to questions about Lucky.

"Just...staying busy. You know me," he said, cagily.

"I heard about new management. Father Ignatius. Is that what has you acting so strangely, old man? Paranoia?"

He laughed, a forced sound, but at least it was closer to his usual self. "Yes. We definitely need to talk about that. Hence the privacy."

I considered his request and then shook my head. "I won't go anywhere without Ryuu. I trust him and he needs to know what's going on."

My ninja beamed proudly, dipping his chin. I shrugged back. With so many people wanting to kill me, and him being the only Halo Breaker I knew, it was a simple equation. I noticed that Phix was trying to get our attention from thirty yards away, pointing through the trees where I assumed the angel fountain was. I hadn't realized we'd walked so far.

"Ah. Well. About that..." Fabrizio said, sounding anxious again. "It's probably best if it's just you and me."

"Why?" I frowned. "Wait. Is this because he can..." I trailed off, not wanting to say it out loud. "His nickname. The rumors about him being able to do something that no other man can do?"

Fabrizio choked and coughed on the other end of the line. "*What?*"

I hesitated. How the hell did I say it without saying it? He could kill Archangels and Archdemons. They called him the Halo Breaker. "Um. I'm trying to beat around the bush, Fabrizio, because I don't know how secure this line is. I'm talking about his very unique...sword. He has a reputation that makes some men very...uncomfortable." I waited, listening to Fabrizio continue to choke and sputter. In that moment, I wondered if the rumor of Ryuu being known as the Halo Breaker was *not* common knowledge. Perhaps I shouldn't have said anything at all. "You know what? Never mind. Who listens to rumors, right? As long as it's brief, I'm sure Ryuu wouldn't mind giving us some privacy. He has a few errands to run for me this morning."

Fabrizio let out a gasp of relief. "Okay. Perfect. Call me as soon as you can. We have so much to discuss."

I nodded absently. "Yeah. Sure," I murmured, speaking low as we neared Phix. She was motioning for us to be silent as she pointed her paw through the thick foliage to reveal a fountain and what looked like fire. "Hey. I need to go. Things are really...heating up here, and I need to get my head in the game. Ryuu is glaring at me because I'm being a bad student right now."

Ryuu rolled his eyes. "Get off the phone," he whispered, harshly. "It's time for you to show me what you can do."

I nodded, eyeing the fountain as I ignored Fabrizio's muttered cursing. Ryuu was giving me a test. On top of dealing with Lucky and the unpredictable Divines, there was a high likelihood that an angel or Nephilim had seen the trio and was keeping a curious eye on them. Entering the open might spring a reaction. The Divines were playing in the pool on the other side of the statue, so all I could clearly see was a lot of fire and splashing from two large creatures. Lucky was sitting on the statue's shoulder, singing raucously as if he'd been sidetracked stumbling home from the bar after last call.

I gripped the phone, staring at Lucky as I made my goodbyes to Fabrizio. "Head back to Abundant Angel and make sure you have towels and a blow dryer."

"What?" Fabrizio demanded.

"Because I'm going to be filthy and wet. Oh, and warm up the confessional booth. I'm about to start sinning all over this man," I said, glaring at Lucky. I knew he was going to make things difficult. I just knew it. From what I'd seen, he had retained more of Pride's incorrigible traits than those of the responsible Michael.

The only way to control Lucky was overwhelming force. I hung up and pocketed the phone.

The statue looked at least ten-feet-high; a beautiful angel statue with outstretched wings standing over a wide pool of shallow water, looking like she was singing a hymn. The pool stood in the center of a clearing with only two jogging trails coming near it—one on the far side of the pool and one between me and my targets.

The scene reminded me of the fountain and pool where I had first encountered Last Breath, the protector of Solomon's Temple. He had a reputation as a legendary, supernatural assassin, able to shift at will but most often resembling an overly muscled Asian man or a bipedal white tiger with glowing blue eyes. He could summon up a fog to conceal his movements, and I had never seen anyone move as fast as he could.

Then again, I hadn't known Ryuu back then. I found myself smiling, imagining the two competing in an obstacle course for baddest, fastest badass. I scanned the tree line, searching for Heavenly or Hellish threats.

Phix rolled her eyes. "You think I didn't already do that? Twice?"

I ignored her, pointedly. Lucky was still naked, still singing, but was now standing on the angel's shoulders, balancing on one foot in a precarious wobble. He held an impossibly long, gaudy, bedazzled leash in each hand, wielding them like reins for the two unruly Divines splashing around in the pool.

Zoe, the giant Vermillion Bird, was currently on fire, even though she was standing in the pool of water. The water was boiling and steaming all around her, transformed into a hot spring by her flames. The splashing water only momentarily doused her fiery form; it crackled back to life immediately after the water landed.

Bai, the White Tiger, was pouncing about in the water, swiping at imaginary prey. Her sleek white fur seemed to glow as if under a black light, emphasizing the pitch-black stripes that served to break up her form and distort the eye.

"Xuanwu and Qinglong will be livid," Ryuu growled.

"Goddamn it, Lucky," I whispered. Ryuu looked like he'd been kicked in the nuts while hearing factual evidence that Buddha was actually a genocidal maniac.

"I told you," Phix said, matter-of-factly. "They look like they are having fun, at least. Those must be retractable leashes, or he would have already fallen." She was staring at Lucky, appraising this supposedly dangerous being with a look of mild disappointment.

I grunted, stepping out of the trees, and making my way towards the fountain with a forced smile. "Technically, you're partially right," I told Phix from over my shoulder. Because Lucky was one third Lucifer, a fallen angel.

Lucky finally noticed our approach and grinned toothily as he gave Bai's leash a playful tug. "I'm the Tiger King, bitches!"

Ryuu growled at Lucky's disrespectful joke. I groaned, snatching at Ryuu's wrist right as he prepared to draw his dark blade. He closed his eyes and visibly relaxed under my grip. I gave him an uneasy smile and released him.

"Cold up there?" Phix asked, grinning.

Lucky cocked his head and placed his hands on his hips before granting us a proud thrust and wiggle that made Ryuu curse and me groan. "How unoriginal. A cat being catty." Then he grinned at her.

The two Divines seemed unconcerned about our arrival, but they were eyeing Phix curiously, sniffing at the air and keeping her in their peripheral vision. The sphinx casually prowled closer, not making eye contact, allowing them to feed their curiosity without making them defensive.

"You're not wearing any *pants*, Lucky," I finally said, checking that no one was nearby to see his current state of undress.

He smiled. "She isn't wearing a shirt," he said, pointing at Phix.

I folded my arms and began tapping my foot. I saw a pile of clothes lying in the grass. "Get down and get dressed. You're supposed to be behind Xuanwu's ward. Everyone is looking for you, and everyone wants those two dead." I frowned, shaking my head. "No, everyone thinks those two are *already* dead. They need to heal from their ordeal before you put them in serious danger, and I would feel better if Xuanwu made that final decision. Or Qinglong."

Lucky frowned. "No one can sense what or who I am, and everyone will think these two are just your everyday magical creatures," he complained. "We are anonymous."

I stared at him in disbelief. "Except you're naked, and Regulars don't know magical creatures exist!" I hissed.

He blinked and then gave me a slow nod. "I forgot about that part. That could complicate things." He scratched at his jaw. "Couldn't we just kill any Regular witnesses?" he mused, thinking out loud. Then he snapped his fingers. "No. Wait. Don't tell me. That's...wrong?" he finally said, emphasizing the last word in a higher-pitched, questioning tone as if he was guessing on a pop quiz in school.

I closed my eyes and counted to three. "Yes, Lucky. Killing innocent people is wrong."

"Ah!" he shouted, snapping his fingers and then pointing at me excitedly. "But do we *know* they are innocent? Better to be safe than sorry, right?"

Ryuu slowly shook his head in stunned disbelief. "Is he serious right now?" he murmured to me.

I nodded. "Pride drives the bus as far as I can tell. Maybe Michael is inside somewhere, rattling the cage like an imprisoned conscience." I scanned the park, silently praying no joggers rounded the curving trails on a morning run. I gave Lucky a warm smile. "You're standing a dozen feet in the air, naked, and you want to talk about safety?" I asked in a syrupy sweet tone. "Come on down and get dressed. I've already had unexpected visitors this morning, and two of my men have been murdered because I wouldn't turn you in. Both sides of your family," I said, meaningfully.

Lucky narrowed his eyes. "Well. We should probably do something about that," he said, and I caught faint flickers of ephemeral silhouettes looming over each of his shoulders. One was red and one was yellow, and the easiest way to describe them was to say they looked like Incredible Hulks in full suits of armor. Thankfully, they flickered away again as Lucky took a calming breath.

I let out my own sigh of relief, echoed by Ryuu. Phix was speaking softly with the two Divines, spinning in slow circles to show off her form—and her tattoo. Great. One day out of Purgatory and Phix was trying to indoctrinate them into Grimm's Rainbownatti secret society. Lucky cleared his throat, sounding strained. He gave me a guilty shrug. "Okay. I'm better. Anxiety is not good for me." He shifted his attention to Ryuu. "Does your sister have any Xanax? That has to be the best multivitamin I've tried since I rose up from Hell."

"That would be a drug, not a vitamin," Ryuu said. Then he turned to me, speaking in a softer tone so as not to be overheard. "How does he not know these things? I've heard him make a dozen pop culture references."

Lucky frowned, and there was something sinister about it. Violent and deadly. I felt a shiver of fear run down my spine. "Tell me something, Halo Breaker," Lucky said in a decidedly darker tone. I set my hand on the hilt of my katana as Lucky's specters crackled to life over his shoulders, all three glaring directly at Ryuu. Their eyes began to glow with golden light, mirroring Lucky's own eyes. The Anghellian spread his arms and the two specters did the same.

I gasped as power immediately crackled through the air, causing my nose and fingers to tingle with sharp pain as loose strands of my hair rose up off my head. The clouds above began to thicken and darken like iron filings drawn to a magnet, shutting out the sunlight within moments. This was exactly the kind of thing I'd wanted to avoid. A fucking spectacle.

"Lucky. Dial it back!" I shouted, trying to be heard over the whipping wind that was now creating slapping waves in the pool below. Oblivious to the stormy water, Zoe's tail fanned out in an arc of fire. Phix and Bai hunkered lower as if preparing to pounce, their tails twitching and their eyes dilating like Lucky had just cracked open a kilo of catnip.

The Anghellian did not hear me, or chose to ignore me, and chaos reigned supreme.

❧ 16 ❧

A golden hologram of a full-sized man suddenly sprang to life, hovering over the water. Lucky's voice was cold and ancient, sounding like a harmony of three voices rather than one—a dying whisper, a bestial roar, and a raging shout. "Have you ever had your entire existence ripped into thirds so fiercely that you felt it on the full spectrum of time itself, Halo Breaker? The nightmarish, panic-inducing anticipation of what the pain might feel like *before* it happens, the excruciating savagery of being skinned alive in the moment it *actually* happens, and the bone-deep, eternal, full-body ache of pain that you know will never fade from that old, unhealed wound long *after* it happened?" The golden silhouette tore into three separate men with a screech that made my teeth ache and my skin crawl. They were all hunched over and had changed colors. One was still gold, sporting a halo and feathered wings. One was a sickly figure of pale, purple mist. The last was red with horns, sharper bat-like wings, and a tail.

Ryuu stared back, spending a moment to focus on each apparition as he gritted his teeth. The wind whipped his hair back and forth across his face. He did not blink, and he did not show fear. He looked respectful. "I have not."

Lucky nodded. "Each piece of me had its mind raped and wiped of all memory, and then each of us was sent to different foster homes to be raised with a false confidence and origin story," he continued in his hauntingly powerful trinity harmony of a voice. "Those pieces have now been slammed back together—all the physical pain, all the mental horrors, and all the lies that represented the bedrock of our separate existences. Three worlds have collided in a spiritual force the equivalent of the Big Bang. Right. Here." He tapped his chest and then clapped his hands together with a deafening crack, like lightning. The three silhouettes slammed together in an explosion of light that momentarily blinded me. "Let there be light!" Lucky laughed—a harsh, cynical sound.

"Lucky!" I begged. "Stop. Please."

"Cut me a little slack, Halo Breaker," Lucky continued, ignoring me entirely. "And when I ask for a Xanax, maybe skip the judgment and show a little empathy."

My vision was slowly returning, and the winds were dying down. Ryuu's Shadow Skin whipped around him, crackling and snapping like a cape, and the Halo Breaker met Lucky's gaze with steadfast resolve. His pulse was slower than I'd felt at any point so far today. "Diva."

His single word response went off like a stick of dynamite.

Bai let out a spitting roar that I felt in my chest. Her tail began twitching back and forth as she hunkered low. Metal spines rose up from the depths of her almost glowing white fur, resembling an angry, albino porcupine. And then she lunged for the lip of the pool, closer to Ryuu...

Which sent a wave of water directly at Zoe, soaking her and dousing her flames in a hissing explosion of steam.

Zoe screamed and spread her dripping wings with a crisp snapping sound, like a wet towel whipping an unprotected ass in a high school gym class shower. The wings erupted with flaming light as her peacock-like tail snapped out like a metallic fan—the weapon—except coated in hungry fire fed by napalm.

My eyes bulged at the sudden escalation Ryuu had ignited. "Let's all calm down," I urged, jerking my attention between Ryuu, Lucky, and the Divines. "Help me out, Phix!"

Phix was already pacing back and forth, keeping her violet eyes locked onto the two Divines, but not doing anything to prevent an attack.

Lucky stared back at Ryuu, and I let out a breath of relief when I saw that he was no longer flanked by his specters or looking like he was one hiccup away from destroying the Omegaverse.

He finally burst out laughing, doubling over and slapping his knees. "Diva!" he crowed, unable to catch his breath.

Then his foot slipped, and he squealed like a child as he fell from his lofty height.

"Mommy!" he cried, lashing out for a handhold to catch his fall. He managed to grab onto one of the wings, hugged it like a spider monkey, and let out a triumphant shout. The statue wobbled violently, and I realized that his display of power had beaten the hell out of it, knocking it loose from its pedestal. The Divines tugged at their leashes in an attempt to get clear of the unstable statue. The force of their effort caused the wing to crack and fall, finally casting Lucky down to the pool with the rest of the statue toppling the opposite direction.

The stone crashed into the fountain, sending a wall of water directly into the Divines, soaking them anew. Thankfully, it served to cool their tempers enough that they no longer looked ready to attack Ryuu. Lucky choked and coughed his way out of the water, gasping and wheezing like he'd survived a shipwreck rather than a middling fall into a pool. "I'm alive!" he rasped, swiping his soaked, long blonde hair out of his eyes.

Ryuu was there, hoisting him out of the pool and onto the grass, laughing so hard that he could barely remain upright himself. "Diva," he repeated, shaking his head and patting Lucky on the back.

Lucky looked up with a proud smirk. "Diva," he agreed.

The Divines shook off their fur and feathers, spraying water in every direction. In the deluge, the magical leashes had winked out of existence. Zoe's feathers sizzled and crackled back to life with puffs of steam, and Bai promptly began licking her leg, primping. As cats do.

I let out a breath, shaking my head as I stared at Lucky, unable to fight the smile creeping onto my face at his grin. "Mommy?" I asked, trying not to laugh.

He grinned as he wiped the damp hair back from his eyes. "Seemed fitting." He climbed to his feet with the two Divines, ruffling Bai's fur playfully—seemingly unharmed by her razor-sharp metal spines. Then he leaned down to peck Zoe on the beak with a loud smooching sound. The fire trickling back to life over her feathers didn't appear to harm him; they even seemed to diminish under his touch, as if calmed by his gesture.

"Does Xuanwu know you took them out in public?" I asked.

He shook his head, not meeting my eyes. "I wanted to take them for a walk," he said in a soft, compassionate tone. "Do something fun for them. They have been prisoners long enough. Changing their prison cell from Purgatory to their brother's house and having everyone treat them like they're made of glass isn't healthy. They're the strongest gals I've ever met," he said, proudly. "Ain't ya?" he asked, ruffling Bai's forehead with his knuckles. She yawned, revealing massive steel fangs that I'd almost forgotten about.

I pulled my hair back over my shoulder, using the motion to mask the tears that abruptly blurred my vision. That...was actually incredibly kind. Bai again shook her body and emitted a playful yowl, spraying Lucky, and then plopped down on the grass to lick her still glowing fur. She looked bigger and stronger than when we had first rescued her from Purgatory. I tried not to think about the metal spines and silvery tint to the Divine White Tiger's fur.

I decided to think of Zoe as a red phoenix rather than her official title, the Vermillion Bird. It sounded like a haughty, made up word for the color red, useful only in impressing colleagues who no one liked at art exhibits no one wanted to attend. And I was from Kansas City—we didn't ever speak of the alleged St. Louis baseball team that shall not be named, so calling her Red Bird was off the table.

They both looked much healthier than when I'd saved them last night, but they definitely still seemed thin and weak—malnourished and with severely atrophied muscles.

One major concern was that their brothers, Xuanwu and Qinglong, could speak. It hadn't even been twenty-four hours yet, but I knew they were concerned that their sisters had not spoken yet. Was that a problem? Was something wrong with them, or was it simply because they had spent such a long time in Purgatory and weren't in the practice of speaking?

Part of me was concerned about the surprisingly strong bond they shared with Lucky. Maybe they recognized his Grace from Purgatory. It was entirely possible that they had formed their bond centuries ago, looking out for each other in the Neverwas. A gang.

A Trinity, even. I still wasn't entirely sure what that entailed, and I fully intended on grilling my godparents on the specifics.

Originally, the girls had been bonded to Lilith in a Trinity. Much like Samael's Trinity with Xuanwu and Qinglong. But Lilith's bond had been a long time ago, and the last time they had seen her had been when she sent them to Purgatory. Had that broken their Trinity? Had Lucky's Grace replaced Lilith?

Granted, Lilith had only done so to keep them safe, but after a few hundred years, perhaps they had been driven to a state of madness where they now saw her act as a betrayal. I wouldn't blame them. Purgatory was a world where souls eternally fed upon one another. One day you were the predator, the next day you were the prey. They definitely hadn't shown any eagerness to leave Lucky's side, let alone seek out Lilith. Xuanwu, Qinglong, and Lucky were pretty much their favorites—treating me like I hadn't been there at all.

Well, not really. But compared to the adoration they showed their brothers and Lucky, I felt a little jilted. Seeing an animal love on someone else over me—when I had been the key to saving them—felt like a kick to the teeth.

But I had plenty of other things to focus on.

The most important thing to me was the affectionate looks they gave Lucky. They loved him, dearly, and he obviously felt the same way about them. Their bond was definitely healing them.

I hadn't realized how much pain Lucky was in until he'd scared the living hell out of me with his display of raw power. Xanax could prevent the end of the world, apparently.

I glanced up at the sky. The clouds were now drifting away, allowing the sun to shine through in places, but the freak storm and the now destroyed statue were going to draw attention. "We really need to get the hell out of here—"

A winged man slammed into the ground with an earth-shaking thud, barely three paces away from me. Two Gateways screamed to life, one on either side of the angel as he rose to his feet. Two hardened warriors—Nephilim—stepped through.

"Fuck this park," I muttered, drawing my katana. "It's literally the worst."

The Divines and Phix snarled in a spitting, coughing warning, agreeing with me as I glared at the new arrivals.

Lucky cleared his throat, pointedly. "Do I need to put my pants on for this?" he whispered to Ryuu.

Ryuu laughed. "Oh, I don't know. This should be over fairly quickly."

Eae scowled angrily, and the Nephilim fingered the hilts of the two long daggers they each wore sheathed at their hips.

"I'll go ahead and put my pants on," Lucky muttered. "It's all fun and games until someone loses a testicle."

Ryuu laughed even harder.

❧ 17 ❧

E ae stared me down, his face blank and cold. But I saw a flicker of
warning and apology in his eyes.

"Not good odds, guys," I said, slowly sheathing my katana. I
patted the hilt with my palm and then lowered my hands to my sides. I
focused my powers and felt my Silver claws slowly extend from between my
knuckles—for when a sword wasn't a personal enough touch. Also, it made
angels and Nephilim nervous to see a reminder of my ties to Solomon.

"I came to see if you had reconsidered my generous offer," Eae said,
curling his lip at my claws.

My mind raced, knowing I needed to get Lucky and the Divines as far
away as possible, before Eae or his Nephilim started asking difficult questions. "I'm a little busy," I said, pointing a thumb at Lucky—who was struggling to put his pants on—and the two Divines, who were watching the new
arrivals with barely restrained violence. "A witch tricked these three morons
into drinking her potions and now I have to figure out how to return them
to normal and wipe their memories." I shrugged. "Seriously, though. Fuck
this park. I am *never* coming back."

The Nephilim eyed the two Divines and Lucky, apparently recognizing
Phix and Ryuu by their looks or reputations. Probably both. I made sure not
to stare, but in my peripheral vision it seemed like they bought my lie. As
long as I could get my allies out of here before one of them overreacted and

obliterated my witch potion story. I heard Phix calmly speaking to Zoe and Bai and I sent up a silent prayer that she was here. A fellow...creature was someone they could relate to, and it seemed she was keeping them calm. For now. But Phix was also a homicidal monster with an incredibly short fuse, as Eae had personally experienced just this morning.

If the Nephilim showed any disrespect, the situation was going to get messy fast.

I cringed to see Lucky stink-eyeing Eae as he zipped up his jeans. He had a mischievous smirk on his stupid face that I didn't like at all. He was on the verge of doing something stupid to his little brother. I hoped Ryuu could keep him in line, but I knew he would be more focused on countering Eae if the angel decided to act his part too authentically for the Nephilims' benefit. Ryuu was the only one who could kill an angel, after all.

"I have not reconsidered your offer. I've barely even had time to think about it," I said. "Give me until tomorrow to see what I can find out about your request."

"How many more of your followers must die before you do the right thing, Dracula?" one of the Nephilim asked.

I slowly turned to look at him as Phix let out a long, slow whistle. He was about my height and had shaggy, light brown hair with pale blue eyes. His fellow Nephilim had sandy blonde hair with bright green eyes and was an extremely tall, broad-shouldered, Nebraska farmer type. His unassuming strength would be easy for most to overlook, but I could tell it had been earned by tossing hay bales at dawn while his pale-eyed buddy likely mastered the shake weight with a battalion of bros chugging Muscle Milk at his side, cheering him on. He just had that pompous little shit vibe to him.

The two Nephilim did not wear a uniform or robes or anything that would make them stand out in a crowd. They both wore jeans, sneakers, and a plain white t-shirt and they would have fit in on any college campus in America. They each wore a thin metal band around their right wrist, reminding me of those copper bracelets some athletes wore. I tried to think back on the other Nephilim I had met, but I didn't remember any of them wearing matching jewelry. And those Nephilim had worked for Nameless, a corrupt angel who had ultimately fallen from grace. Literally. I'd encased him in the Silver magic of the Solomon bloodline at the moment he fell. His statue now resided inside Roland's church.

Maybe the golden cuffs signified rank?

I turned my nose up at the pale-eyed prick. "You look like you should be in a boy band. How about you remain silent while the adults are talking."

The muscles of his jaw clenched and his cheeks darkened. The farm boy's eyebrows almost climbed right off his head as he coughed a laugh into his fist.

The prick Nephilim took an aggressive step forward but the farm boy grabbed him by the shoulder and squeezed, halting the prick in his tracks. "She makes a good point, and your comment was cruel. Stand down, Quentin."

Lucky burst out laughing. "Quentin?" he hooted.

Damn it.

Quentin winced in pain but still managed to glare at Lucky. "Let go of me, Adrian," he growled.

Adrian waited a few more moments to make sure Quentin wasn't going to do anything stupid, and then released his grip. He gave me a discreet nod and mildly apologetic frown.

I dipped my chin back, respectfully. "Thank you, Adrian."

Quentin rested his hands on the hilts of his daggers, cocking his hips to stand in an arrogant pose as he chose to openly leer at Phix's breasts with a wicked grin. Seriously? Where was Heaven recruiting the Nephilim from these days? A career fair booth in Hell?

Preventing myself from committing murder had never been so hard.

Eae didn't visibly sigh in relief at Adrian's effective diffusing of the situation, but his slow blink was proof that he was toeing a fine line in being my double agent. He had control, but not as much as he should have. Adrian the farm boy *Nephilim* had quelled the drama, not the *angel*. And none of them seemed disturbed about the upside-down authority structure. Who was pulling the strings upstairs? I really needed to talk to Solomon after this and get a refresher on the Archangel hierarchy.

But I had to get us out of this confrontation without bloodshed, first. Thinking of the murdered ninja and vampire, I felt my own quiet, unquenchable rage flickering dangerously within my breast. Heaven had already spilled blood. Perhaps we were way beyond a peaceful compromise. A very strong part of me wanted to play tit for tat and kill the two Nephilim —even though I kind of liked Adrian—but that would put Eae in an impossible situation and ruin my chances at getting inside information.

Adrian wore a pensive frown, shifting his gaze between the Divines, the ruined statue, and the retreating clouds overhead. "A potion did all of this?"

Eae was studying the Divines now, and I watched as his face slowly changed to horror. "Daemons," he breathed. Phix stepped in front of them, protectively. He'd recognized them for what they were. He turned to look directly into my eyes with a skeptical, suspicious stare.

I kept my face devoid of all reaction. "That's ridiculous."

Quentin frowned. "I thought the surviving Daemons were a turtle and a dragon?" he said, suddenly wary.

Eae's face had gone as pale as a sheet and I knew, beyond a shadow of a doubt, that there was no more room for peace. Angels feared the possibility of all four Divines existing, especially in the same place at the same time. I didn't know why, but I knew Eae could no longer feign ignorance. He'd just caught me in a lie—one that had dire consequences for his kind. He couldn't reveal our alliance in front of his Nephilim without being branded a traitor.

In fact, this little revelation that all four Divines were alive and well would very likely change Eae's opinion about working with me. I might have actually just become his enemy for my proven lie of omission. He'd seen how unsurprised I was to see Zoe and Bai, which meant I had known of their presence during our earlier encounter and hadn't told him.

Eae shifted his glare to Lucky and he was suddenly holding a gleaming, golden spear as thick as my forearm. "Who are you?"

Lucky stared him down with his fearless smirk. "I'm not sure I like your tone, Eae."

The angel clenched his spear tighter, pursing his lips. Then he abruptly stiffened, his eyes widening slightly. "How...did you know my name?" he rasped.

"I cursed your name under my breath the moment you arrived," I growled. "Your problem is with me. My associates are not under your jurisdiction and do not have to answer your questions," I said, gesturing for my allies to back up. "Right, Ryuu? We wouldn't want them to feel threatened," I said, meaningfully. "More than one diva can ruin a party."

Ryuu caught my meaning—*don't let the Divines or Lucky lose their shit*. "Correct, White Rose. They are under the protection of the shinobi and the Black Tortoise." In my peripheral vision, I saw him shoving Lucky back towards the Divines. Lucky was the only one who could calm them down and he was also too flippant for a tense situation like the one we now faced.

And if Eae pressed him too hard, he was likely to hulk out into Anghellian mode and destroy anyone who looked at him sideways.

Phix stepped up beside me, eyeing the two Nephilim up and down and licking her lips with a provocative smile. A wave of dizziness swept over me and I gripped her shoulder for support, blinking dazedly. I knew it wasn't an attack because Eae and his Nephilim shot me suspicious glares like I was trying to deceive them. As I fought it off, I started feeling dull thuds all around me like someone was thumping a bass drum in a collection of steady, double cadences.

Heartbeats. I was sensing heartbeats again.

Ryuu's was slightly faster than normal, likely since he was too far away from me and torn between keeping the Divines safe, Lucky in check, and protecting me from the angel. Phix's heartbeat was light and quick, eager for action. She spoke, helping distract the Nephilim from my strange reaction. "The man who created it doesn't need it, the man who bought it doesn't want it, and the man who needs it doesn't know he needs it. What is it?"

Adrian and Quentin stared at her warily. "I don't have time for childish riddles," Quentin grumbled, shifting his attention towards Lucky and the others as if devising a way to reach them. Eae looked torn between hating me and wanting to flee, but not knowing how best to accomplish either. My dizziness had faded but I still felt...muted, as if everything was slower and more dramatic than it actually was.

Adrian finally shrugged. "A riddle."

Phix grinned broadly. "No. But that was a *very* clever answer."

Eae leaned towards me, gritting his teeth. "Explain yourself. Now."

I shrugged, woodenly. "Dizzy spell," I murmured, shaking my head.

"What is the answer to the stupid riddle?" Quentin asked, absently, risking a quick glance at Phix's chest when he thought she was focused on Adrian.

"A coffin," Phix mused, slowly turning to face him. "And if you stare at my chest again without my express permission, there won't be enough pieces of you left to require one. A commercial trash bag will suffice."

Quentin snarled and lunged for Phix, pivoting on his feet and drawing both of his forearm-length daggers, surprisingly fast, in an attempt to murder the sphinx.

18

My strange perception vanished like a popped bubble and everyone froze, just like when I used my Horseman's Mask or focused on speeding up my senses.

Except...I hadn't intentionally done anything. My gaze locked onto Quentin's outstretched daggers. He'd actually thrown one at Phix and it was currently floating between them, frozen still. Once time resumed it would almost immediately sink into her chest, and he was already swinging his other dagger at her for a follow-up attack.

Eae's eyes had begun to widen and his mouth was open in a silent shout. Phix had a similar look on her face and she had already begun leaning to the side to try and avoid the dagger. I knew that she wouldn't be fast enough.

My eyes settled on Quentin's vulnerable throat and I smiled. I felt a sharp flash of pain in my gums and tongue, and then I tasted my own blood, making me shudder with pleasure. I explored with my tongue to feel my canine teeth had grown significantly longer and sharper. I sucked in a surprised breath, feeling my flesh tingle and a newfound set of instincts completely take over my mind and body.

Save Phix. The Nephilim already killed two of yours. Eye for an eye. Blood for blood. Take them.

The next thing I knew, I had blurred forward and swatted the airborne dagger out of harm's way with my claws. Then I palmed Quentin's face and sank my new fangs into his neck. Nephilim blood filled my mouth and my knees buckled as I let out a rapturous groan. I didn't just take his blood; I felt something being drawn out of me at the same time.

And with it came a sense of completion. A powerful rush of energy that made me feel like I was physically buzzing.

I heard a tinny ringing in my ears that grew louder and louder until I felt a faint popping sensation in my chest. A shockwave of power whipped out of me in a perfect circle, sending everyone in my proximity flying and tumbling.

Quentin fell to the ground at my feet, his neck ravaged and my claws sliding out of his abdomen in a soft, bloody whisper. I didn't remember stabbing him but his hot blood flowed over my knuckles like warm oil. I heard a sharp metallic *click* before time returned to normal and sound came blasting back at full volume.

Eae scrambled to his feet, staring at my mouth with a horrified look on his face. "What have you done?" he hissed, staring at the blood dripping down my chin and claws. Phix had regained her feet and was crouched low, ready to pounce as she glared at the angel. Adrian was slowly rising to all fours, moaning painfully.

I stumbled back a few steps, feeling panicked yet hauntingly energetic. My skin was vibrating and pulsing. I licked my lips and shuddered. "It... tastes like honey," I rasped.

Rather than reply, Eae lifted his massive spear and hurled it at me. There was a blur of motion and a chiming *clang* that sent the spear flying off to the side where it tore through a tree wider than my waist. The tree fell, groaning and creaking before it crashed down to the ground with a resounding *thud*. I realized I was smiling and that my eyes were locked onto the man now standing between me and Eae.

Adrian, the last Nephilim.

Except he now had long silver claws extending from his fists, identical to mine. He stared at Eae, licking his lips with a feral twinkle in his eyes. "You do not touch the White Rose," Adrian said in a low, basso growl. I felt like raising my hand or tapping him on the shoulder to ask what the fuck was going on.

Eae curled his lip in outrage, eyeing both of us with a livid glare. "You were not supposed to know about that, Callie Penrose," he growled. "No one was supposed to know." He took a step closer—

Adrian leapt forward, slicing his claws through Eae's stomach and then pummeling the angel with his fists and claws. Eae grunted with each blow, too shocked to react to the Nephilim's rage.

I wiped the blood from my mouth, realizing that no one but Eae seemed to have noticed how I'd killed the first Nephilim, Quentin. Phix's eyes had gone straight for my claws, spotting the blood and then dismissing the murder from further scrutiny.

Rather than waiting for an explanation, or for Adrian to possibly shift his bloodthirsty rage and claws on someone else, Phix tackled him from the side. They skidded into the fountain and Phix slammed his head into the stone with a hiss. "Enough of this insanity," she snarled. Adrian twitched, blood dripping from the wound on the back of his head. She glanced over at me with a merciless shrug. "He had crazy eyes."

Eae finally crashed to his knees, clutching at his throat. I hadn't even seen Adrian slice his neck but there was now a fan of blood down his chest. I stared in disbelief as his eyes fluttered closed. Then his wings fell limp and boneless as he finally toppled to his side next to Adrian. Blood instantly began to pool on the ground from his messy wounds. I sucked in a sharp breath as the blood touched Adrian's claws and was instantly absorbed like it had been sucked up from a straw. Phix had already loped back to the Divines to calm them down, so she hadn't noticed Adrian's claws drinking the blood. Adrian's wounds immediately healed, the blood no longer dripping from his head, and he began to breathe easier.

My eyes bulged in disbelief.

Ryuu and Lucky stepped up beside me, ignoring Adrian and staring at Eae with blank faces. They obviously hadn't noticed Adrian's swift recovery. Their presence was probably the reason behind Phix's abandoning me rather than staying to protect me from Eae when he woke back up. I heard Phix speaking in soft, comforting tones to Zoe and Bai, reassuring them that they were safe. I glanced back, frowning to see they looked surprisingly skittish. I wasn't sure if it was the swift speed and violence of the confrontation—of my hyper speed, subconscious, primal instinct to attack Quentin—or the fact that an Angel had just gotten his ass kicked by a friendly.

To protect *me*. The now-healed Adrian—thankfully unconscious—had protected me from his boss.

Ryuu pursed his lips, shifting his gaze from Eae to Adrian. "The Nephilim killed the angel," he said, sounding troubled.

My eyes widened in horror. Ryuu...was right. Eae was not breathing. "What have we done?" I whispered, staring at the dead angel. "I thought only you could do that?"

Ryuu considered my question, studying the angel. "It depends on how strong they are. Anyone can kill an angel. Even you, Callie. But only if your heart is fully invested in the act. It's all about passion of purpose. When it comes to the First Sphere of angels like the Seraphim, the Cherubim, the Thrones, and the *real* Archangels..." he said, cracking his knuckles. "I'm your man."

Lucky gripped my shoulder with a nervous look in his eyes. "We need to leave. Now," he whispered. "The rest of the Archangels will sense this and come to lay vengeance. We must be nowhere near this...unveiled secret. I must be nowhere near this, specifically."

I pointed at the body. "Adrian killed his angel boss, not me. That's fairly obvious by looking at the wounds," I said, pointing. "And why do you not look surprised to learn that Nephilim are bloodsucking holy vampires?" I hissed, pointing at Adrian's claw, which was noticeably drinking up Eae's pool of blood. Ryuu grunted, his eyes widening a hair. So, he hadn't noticed it either.

Lucky shook his head, firmly. "No one speaks about it. I'm surprised Eae even knew about it, to be honest. Good talk, now let's go," he pressed, attempting to pull me away.

"Wait!" I snapped, feeling like my mind had snapped in two. "They're actually freaking *vampires?*"

Lucky pondered my question, glancing at the skies anxiously. "Kind of? Why do you think Heaven and Hell lost their collective shit the moment you became Dracula? They knew you were already a Horseman, but to then see you take over the entire Sanguine Council? How long until you took over their elite, secret, Nephilim vampire army, leaving them defenseless here on Earth? Yeah, they were fucking terrified of this exact thing."

I felt a migraine coming on. "Is that why Hell really rose up? The Sins escaping and coming to Kansas City? Why Wrath was so adamant about marrying me?"

Lucky nodded. "This conversation would be so much more fun not standing over a crime scene." I narrowed my eyes and began tapping my foot. Ryuu looked just as incredulous, which meant it truly was a giant secret. Lucky let out a frustrated breath. "Fine. The Sins came as a direct retaliation to Heaven scoping out your city. We weren't going to let them have all the fun. The moment you became Dracula, it sent a shockwave throughout the cosmos. A crack in the foundation of their eons of power. Our eons of power," he corrected. "That is why the angels have all been so scared of you, trying to tame you and manipulate you. You also hold their spear, of course. It's almost comical how many times you've unintentionally punched them in the nose."

I stared down at Eae, seeing him in a new light.

Ryuu suddenly cursed. "I took some of his hair. And Eae thought he was being watched at our earlier meeting."

"Get rid of the hair!" I hissed, glad that he had remembered. The angels who found his body might have used it to track us down. I studied the two Nephilim with a nervous frown, realizing that it wasn't the only evidence of my presence here. I'd bitten Quentin in the neck and slurped his blood. Had Ryuu and Lucky not noticed me doing it? I remembered how time had slowed down, only resuming after the shockwave of power erupted out of me. Quentin was very dead, but Adrian was merely unconscious after his claws had consumed Eae's blood.

I frowned, noticing Adrian's bracelet had broken off. I flicked my gaze to Quentin's body to see that his had also broken off. A chill ran down my spine. Had my shockwave ripped off their bracelets, breaking their servitude with Heaven and the angels? Was that how I'd unknowingly drawn Adrian into defending me from Eae? Lucky hadn't mentioned anything about the bracelets, but it made sense. The Nephilim hadn't seemed aware of their vampiric abilities, and the angels would have needed a way to keep them in line rather than have them revolt at their enslavement.

"We can't just leave him here," I said, indicating the unconscious Adrian. "He's now a murderer and no longer bound to their will. They will kill him."

Lucky gave me a wry look. "You want to adopt this vampire Nephilim? Who knows how much restraint he has now that he's tasted angel blood. What if he turns into a monster? We don't know how to control him while he adapts to his new...appetite." Lucky said, warily. He pointed at the bracelet. "That is how they keep the vampire Nephilim in line and unaware of their latent natures. And that is also the extent of my knowledge."

Although glad to hear confirmation about the bracelets, I shook my head, pensively. "Not vampire. He used claws. He's something different."

Ryuu shrugged. "You saw how he looked at you, Callie. That was a worshipful and adoring look." I tried not to flinch, recalling my own sudden thirst for blood. What the hell was going on with me? Sensing heartbeats and now growing fangs? I didn't have any new thirst or hunger on my mind, and I actually felt decidedly sick to my stomach at the thought of drinking from Quentin's neck. However...I also felt a thrill of anticipation at the rush of power I'd felt. I tried to keep all this from my face, not wanting my friends to suddenly look at me as a monster. "The moment you broke his bracelet, he would have been flooded with new, overwhelming hunger like typical, freshly turned vampires," Ryuu continued. "Instead of avenging his partner, he immediately rose to defend you."

Was that why I now felt a responsibility to him? I'd woken him up, freed him, and...I was supposed to just let him take the fall for killing Eae?

Ryuu stepped forward. "I could stab Eae in the heart to make it look like I murdered him with Angel Killer. That way they won't know we discovered their Nephilim secret."

Lucky snapped his fingers. "Brilliant idea. Do that. Then we can go get some barbecue, because I am famished."

19

I shot Lucky a disgusted look and then turned to Ryuu. "That will put you on Heaven's Most Wanted list."

He shrugged. "It is the only logical explanation they might buy. Who else could kill an angel if not the Halo Breaker?" he asked, glancing over both of his shoulders as if searching for a nonexistent patsy. "And he will not be the first angel I've killed. How do you think I earned the moniker?" he asked in a dry tone. "I'm already on their Most Wanted list. I will just have to lay low for a while. I'm good at living in the shadows, and we also have the demon assassins to deal with. I won't be bored."

With a sick feeling in my stomach, I nodded. "Thank you, Ryuu. We can take Adrian back with us to try and figure out what this is all about. I'm sure Castle Dracula has a safe place to stow him where he can't go on a rampage."

Lucky chuckled, "As long as you don't have any angels hiding at Castle Dracula, you should be fine. If this Nephilim wakes up to see another angel, his instincts might take over."

I nodded, assessing Lucky. "He didn't attack *you*, Lucky. You really aren't an angel any longer, are you?"

He shook his head. "Maybe he would have reacted if I'd called up my bodyguards," he said with a thoughtful frown.

I nodded, approaching the two open cuffs on the ground and scooping them up. I discreetly touched the puddle of Eae's blood with my own claws and cringed as they drank up the angel's blood just like Adrian's had done. Damn it. The Nephilim really were tied to me. Why was I only now growing fangs and sensing heartbeats? I buried the fear deep, not wanting to add to the drama we were already facing. No one else seemed to have noticed my thirsty claws as I saw Ryuu rest the tip of his sword over Eae's heart.

"I feel like we should say something," Lucky said, frowning.

I nodded, rising to my feet. "That's very thoughtful. You probably knew him best." Ryuu stepped back, dipping his chin respectfully and holding his katana at his side.

Lucky cleared his throat, studying his fallen brother. "Eae, Demon Thwarter, Angel of Heaven..." he said, rattling off the titles by rote and with surprising respect, "was the biggest asshole I ever met."

Silence stretched over the park and Ryuu and I gawked at the Anghellian with horrified looks.

He noticed our attention and shrugged. "What? I'm not going to lie over his grave. People don't magically become better people once they die. Guy was a total prick."

Ryuu rested his sword back on Eae's chest. After a moment, he grunted, looking startled. "The prick is apparently still alive," he said in a calm tone.

My heart dropped into my stomach. "What?" I hissed, leaning forward. I tried to force my new senses to obey. After a few unsuccessful moments, my temples began to throb and I was about to give up. That's when I finally heard it. A very faint, weak pulse coming from Eae's chest.

"Want me to kill him anyway?" Ryuu asked, glancing over at me. "He made it abundantly clear that he is no longer on our side. He is your direct enemy. Do you know why he had the sudden change of heart? Was that blast of magic something you meant to do?" he asked, still pressing the katana against Eae's heart.

I blinked at the onslaught of questions, knowing I had no good answers. I didn't want to talk about my fangs or the shockwave of power. I wanted to talk to Adrian when he woke up and see if I could get any information from him. Maybe Solomon knew something about this—another reason to go visit him. He also might know something about the cuffs I had pocketed. "Don't execute him," I finally said. Not wanting them to know I could now sense heart beats, I feigned ignorance. "Are you sure he's actually alive? Or is he going to bleed out in the next five minutes anyway? Because I'd rather not take him with us and get caught transporting a dead angel."

Ryuu studied Eae pensively. "I think he's actually going to make it. His wounds are slowly healing." He looked over at me with a meaningful look. "My other comment still stands. He wants to kill you now. For this," he said, gesturing at the Nephilim. "He might have answers, but he won't give them up easily, and you also want to take Adrian with us. The Nephilim who tried to murder Eae in your name. You are asking for trouble a dozen different ways, and we already have Legion to deal with. Possibly other angels and Nephilim. And Olympians," he reminded me.

I nodded. "I know, but we can't execute him when he's helpless and sleeping. Maybe we can convince him to talk to us. We already know he's suspicious of his superiors. We have to take the chance. Maybe seeing that Adrian is alive will prove to him that I'm not the monster he fears."

"Prick," Lucky reminded us, shaking his head.

Ryuu pulled his sword away. "As you wish. I can take both of them to Aala, along with Lucky and the girls. Perhaps my sister can tweak their chakras and give all of us some much-needed answers, him included," he said, in a surprisingly compassionate tone as he glanced at Adrian. "I'm sure he will have many, many questions about his...enslavement. And it's difficult to remain angry after a dip in the Rebirth Pond," he said with a smile. My responding smile was bitter and hollow. Ryuu and I had been planning on taking a private swim there after our training. "Xuanwu and Qinglong can keep them in line when they wake up."

Phix approached with the Divines, handing them off to Lucky. "They're good. Just trying to get a grip on their new world. They seem to have a kill first, question later mentality, which I totally appreciate," she said with a playful smile, bumping her shoulder against Bai. "But I am mature and responsible, so I talked them down."

Lucky knelt down in front of Zoe and Bai. "Looks like no skinny dipping for us, girls."

I rolled my eyes at both of them. "I need to talk to Fabrizio and then Roland about the vampire mass exodus. We can meet up at Castle Dracula after." I dreaded the private talk Fabrizio had requested, confident that the topic would only add to my growing list of problems, but I owed it to him to at least hear him out. Especially now that I'd just hospitalized his resident angel, eaten a Nephilim, and exposed another as a new flavor of clawed vampire.

Ryuu considered my words, looking like he was calculating risks. Rather than argue that I shouldn't be left unattended, he nodded. "I will track Legion after I get these two sorted and check on my ninjas."

I smiled, strangely happy about his agreement. He hadn't tried to coddle me and get overprotective, although I knew part of him wanted to. He trusted me, and that made me inordinately proud. It wasn't that I wanted his approval, but knowing how dangerous he was, it was the fact that he gave it freely that made me cherish it so much more.

I also wanted some time to clear my head about a few things—the brooding ninja, my apparent vampire fangs and enhanced senses, my war against Heaven and Hell, the Olympians, Nate Temple's whereabouts, and to clarify what I needed to ask Solomon. I had questions about the Archangels and the overall hierarchy of Heaven, the Nephilim vampires and their cuffs, and any information he might have on Anghellians or the Seven Sins. Privacy would do me some good.

"Take Xylo with you so I can find you if I finish up, first," I told him. He nodded, looking like I'd just asked him to babysit my kid brother. As dangerous as Xylo was, he was impressively gullible and aloof to the current world.

"I'll go with you," Phix said. "A Horseman needs a horse, after all."

I thought about it and shrugged, turning my back on the others to give her a warm smile. "It will be nice to catch up with you, Phix."

She casually wiped at her chin with her paw while staring me straight in the eyes. "Yes. We have so much to discuss," she said in a meaningful tone. My eyes widened and I wiped at my own chin, finding a speck of Nephilim blood I had missed. Phix assessed my face and gave a faint nod. So, she *had* seen me bite Quentin.

"I am hungry," Lucky reminded us. "And I'm not picking up my prick of a brother. I'll get the cute little nephilpire holy badger." He scooped up the Nephilim without further ado and ripped open a Gateway of golden light. I blinked in surprise, not realizing he could do such a thing. The Divines hopped through, forcing Ryuu to hurry up or be left behind. Ryuu picked up Eae in a fireman's carry and then shuffled through the Gateway. Not a moment too soon, because it winked shut behind him, catching a few angel feather tips that fluttered to the ground of the park.

"He really doesn't like the angel," Phix observed. I slowly turned to face her, uneasy about the topic at hand. "Hop on, Callie," she said in a gentle tone. "Fangs do not make you a monster."

I hung my head as I complied, feeling the buzzing high begin to fade as I hopped onto her back. "But drinking Nephilim blood might seal the deal," I argued.

"Did it make you feel good?" she asked as she swept her wings and took us to the sky.

I wrapped my arms around her waist so that I wouldn't fall off. "People will see you!" I hissed.

She laughed, shaking her stupidly beautiful hair in my face. "Grimm taught me how to hide. We could fly through downtown and not be seen."

"Well, you're going to need to braid your hair or something," I said, spitting out a tuft of her curly locks.

She laughed even harder. "You never answered my question."

I was silent for a few moments, pretending that the wind was washing away the taint I felt in my soul. Because...it had felt good. Way too good. "Yes. Like an alcohol buzz," I said.

"Well, you are a vampire," she reminded me. "You might not need human blood, but that doesn't mean you can't have treats every now and again. Do you feel any kind of craving? Hunger? Thirst?"

I thought about it, analyzing myself. "No," I admitted with a frown. "Thinking about it makes me feel sick. The rush was nice, but I don't have a hankering for more or anything."

Phix nodded. "Then you should be fine." We sailed through the air, preferring silence. "Should be..." I heard Phix say in a softer tone, as if speaking to herself.

"Just keep an eye out for avenging angels. Or demons." I thought about Aphrodite. "And Olympians, I guess."

I didn't necessarily want to meet with Fabrizio, but I'd promised, and I had also learned that ignoring problems from the Vatican Shepherds only served to exponentially increase them. So, I'd find out what had Fabrizio concerned and then get back to saving my vampires and ninjas, interrogating a Nephilim, and saving Eae's life. Only then could I focus on what to do about Lucky and the Divines.

I hefted the Nephilim cuffs in my hand, thinking. My father had been a Nephilim. Maybe my mother had studied these cuffs in her laboratory. Solomon's Temple might have more answers than I had originally thought. I could also ask Last Breath to do some digging for me while I finished my other errands.

❧ 20 ❧

Phix had dropped me off outside the church, promising to scout out the city in an attempt to locate any of the Sins.

Not knowing what else to do, I knocked on the massive doors to A2C2. My clothes were a mess, and I needed a shower. I glanced down at my demon sensing boots, frowning. They were of no use in detecting arch-class beings, but they might give me a warning if any of the assassins Legion had warned about decided to try anything inadvisable. So far, the demons hadn't attacked my people. Just the Nephilim.

I would focus on the arrest warrants from Heaven and Hell once I knew my people were safe and secure at Castle Dracula. In a way, I might have inadvertently discovered a solution to the Nephilim assassins. Use the Dracula shtick of waving my hand in front of their faces and calling them to my side of the battle lines. I would still have to worry about the angels, but my people would be safer.

I realized I wasn't staring at my boots, but the actual steps beneath me. This spot, exactly, was where I had been abandoned by my parents as a child. This spot was where I, as an adult, had raged at the doors through some crazy time distortion in Solomon's Doors, wanting nothing more than to hug my baby self and give her a word of loving encouragement. Instead, I had become the monster who infamously terrorized the church that night—the source of my own childhood nightmare.

I shuddered, shaking off the thought as the door opened. A wizened old woman peered out at me from the gloomy, candle-lit interior, like it was some medieval castle. "You," she rasped in a pious tone.

"Me, Greta. It's so nice to see you," I lied, cursing my luck. "Is that a new rosary?"

She narrowed her eyes suspiciously. "This is the Lord's house. You are not welcome here."

I blinked, hearing a group of children walking with their nanny down the sidewalk behind me. "I see your wrinkles and your fond feelings for me have only increased in your old age—"

"Tithe and repent your sins," she snapped, waving a golden cup in front of my face.

I blinked, leaning away from the gaudy cup. "Are you really trying to shake me down? In the Lord's name?"

She rattled the cup more aggressively, letting me know there were actually some coins and bills within. "Tithe and support Abundant Angel's good work!" The nanny and her children had stopped to stare at me and I felt my cheeks heating up. Greta eyed the broken button on my coat. "Make it good. The Lord sees our hearts, but you're doing your best to distract him," she said, glaring at my chest and the minimal cleavage displayed by the crooked button.

I narrowed my eyes, dangerously. "You've got to be kidding me," I growled, reaching into my pocket. It was easier than arguing with her. I could always Shadow Walk into the church, pop up behind her, and pinch her ass, but then she'd really think I was the devil. I didn't have any spare change, but I found a crumpled wad of paper. I pulled it out to discover that it was my emergency hundred-dollar bill. Greta's eyes glittered like Smaug for a moment, zeroing in on her take—I mean, the Lord's blessing, of course. "Here," I snapped. "Now let me through already."

"Is that all? You are supposed to give ten-percent." She eyed me up and down in a very judgmental manner. "Corners must not pay as well as they say."

My ears caught fire and I seriously considered smacking the dentures out of her mouth. Instead, I reached for the door and decided I was going to invite myself in. The old woman lunged in an attempt to freaking *bite* me, of all tactics, but I managed to shift my hand to a section of the door above her head. I abruptly felt a burning sensation on my fingertips and noticed a rune come to life on the interior wall behind Greta. My eyes widened in alarm and I grabbed Greta by the shoulder as my hair began to rise up at a sudden wave of electric energy in the air. I opened my mouth to warn her but God was simply not on my side this morning.

An invisible fist struck me in the gut, sending me tumbling down the stone stairs to bang the back of my head on the hard ground. Fortunately for her, I had managed to pull Greta away from the attack, but unfortunately for me, she fared better since I'd lost my grip after the metaphysical blow. She hadn't even lost her balance. I propped myself on my elbows, staring up the stairs at the door, blinking languidly as my vision tunneled and spun. My fingers tingled but they weren't injured, and the electric energy in the air seemed to have condensed into that single strike and then dissipated.

What the hell had just happened? Had I triggered a defense ward on the church?

"Are you okay, ma'am?" the walking nanny asked, looming over me. "You took quite the fall." She held out a five-dollar-bill, waving it back and forth like bacon to a dog. "Here. Take this and go get something warm to eat. There is no shame in living on the streets, but that is no excuse to attack an old woman."

I clenched my jaw, grinding my teeth. I sat up, swatted the nanny's hand away, and glared up at Greta, who was now shaking an admonishing finger at me. "Harlot! Jezebel!" she shrieked, loud enough to cause the nanny and kids to grow silent, stop, and stare. I felt them back away from me like I was a contagious leper.

"Oh, hell no!" I growled, climbing to my feet and ignoring the wave of dizziness that overcame me as I stormed up the stairs in a weaving march of violence incarnate.

Greta's face paled and she clutched her golden cup to her chest, backing towards the open doorway and screaming at the top of her lungs. "Father David! I'm being attacked!"

I heard shouting from within the church as I reached the top of the steps. I paused, waiting for my vision to steady, and scanned the doorway more carefully, looking for other runes I might trigger. "What is wrong with you, Greta?" I demanded. "Why would you shout such horrible things?"

Fabrizio came skidding to a halt beside her. He saw me, blinked, and then glanced back at the rune I had triggered. It was no longer visible, but it confirmed my thoughts. Fabrizio had put it there. Why? And why had it affected *me*? The church welcomed dozens of strangers each week, so it couldn't be an all-encompassing ward designed to block out all non-approved members. Even Freaks were welcomed with open arms here. Then again, it wasn't a day of service, so maybe Fabrizio had amplified it. Or the news he wanted to share with me was so dire that it had made him paranoid.

Father David peered his head out for a second, saw me, and then flashed me an awkward, goofy smile. "Good morning, Callie. It's so good to see you."

I grunted. "Likewise," I said, dryly, rubbing the goose egg on the back of my head. My dizziness had faded and I didn't feel nauseated, so the prognosis was probably just a funcussion.

Greta made a moaning sound, clutched her chest, and then dramatically cowered against the wall in theatrical fear. "Oh, praise the Lord," she moaned, really hamming it up. "I thought she was going to *kill* me!"

"What is *wrong* with you?" I demanded, taking an aggressive step forward.

Fabrizio was suddenly blocking the entrance with his arms outstretched. "How about we take a walk, Callie. Let cooler heads prevail."

"Fine!" I growled, glaring at Greta. "Tell the spiteful, racketeering, mafia hag to give me back my money."

Fabrizio arched an eyebrow. "What?"

I nodded, pointing an accusing finger at her. "She made me pay a cover charge for Club Salvation, here, demanding that I tithe to get in. Pretty sure that, although tithing is *encouraged*, it is never used as a *bludgeon* or a *threat*. Or maybe I'm just old fashioned."

Father David shot Greta a stern look. "Is this true, Greta?"

Greta turned to shoot me a hateful scowl that only I could see, and then turned to give Father David the warmest, most grandmotherly, charitable smile I had ever seen outside of politics and infomercials. "I asked the woman—"

"Callie!" I growled. "You know my damned name!" Fabrizio gave me a subtle shake of his head and his eyes flicked past my shoulder in a meaningful way. I heard the children murmuring amongst themselves, still standing behind us with the nanny, watching the free show. I folded my arms and imagined eating Greta's heart. Raw.

"I asked the woman," Greta repeated in a more forceful tone, pretending she was the only one who hadn't heard me shout my name, "if she would be willing to chip in for the youth choir's trip to St. Louis next month. I may have been a bit forceful, but you know how protective I am of the little children."

Fabrizio gave me a wary look. "Well, good job, Callie. Thank you for supporting the choir. Now, let's go—"

"I want my money back. And an apology," I said, firmly.

Father David sucked in a breath and Fabrizio closed his eyes for a moment, begging the Lord for patience. "The choir really could use your help, Callie."

I settled Father David with a warm smile of my own. "This is the first time I've heard anything about a choir. Greta just lied to your face, Father David."

"I would *never!*" she shrieked. "Horrid, horrid woman!"

I held out my palm. "Money. Now. I worked very hard for it. On the streets, as you so eloquently put it, Greta."

Father David blanched at that bit of information and gave Greta a stern glare. "Return her money, Greta."

Her face darkened for a moment, but no one else seemed to notice. She plucked a five-dollar-bill from the cup and handed it to Fabrizio. "I hope you're pleased with yourself," she muttered, turning away to leave.

"I'll be happy when I get the other ninety-five, woman. I gave you a hundred."

Greta froze and I thought she might actually make a run for it. Then she glanced down into the cup, feigning surprise. "My mistake." She pulled out the hundred and handed it to Father David.

He studied her with a disappointed look. Then he held it out to me. "My apologies for her...mistake," he said.

I waved a hand, dismissively. "No worries, Father David. Keep it. I just wanted to make sure it was in safe hands." Greta actually shrieked before storming back into the church. I winked at Father David. "I'd think twice about sending the choir to St. Louis. Dangerous place these days."

He frowned. "I haven't heard anything on the news..."

I leaned closer, speaking in a low tone. "The kind of danger that is too...*Freaky* to show up in the news," I said.

His face paled and he looked sharply at Fabrizio. The First Shepherd nodded. "I second Callie's advice."

"I...see," Father David murmured. "I apologize for Greta's poor attitude. It is her grandson's birthday and she has been unable to reach him. He is not answering his phone and it is troubling her greatly."

I shrugged. "Not my problem. I'm sure Yahn will call her when he's got time. He's probably busy with his girlfriends." In my anger at the old hag, I'd almost forgotten that Yahn, a shifter dragon from St. Louis, was her grandson. In fact, Greta had lived in St. Louis before deciding to move her crotchety ass to my city. She was also close with Eae, which I had definitely forgotten about until this exact moment. I suddenly felt very, very guilty.

Had...she felt him get injured? Was that what had her all bitter and cruel? Eae had been her guardian angel for some time now. I wasn't sure how permanent that was, because I never saw him with her. But he had been working closely with Abundant Angel, so maybe his job requirements had broadened to serve the church while watching over Greta.

Nevertheless, I'd almost killed her angel this morning. Maybe her poor attitude was actually justified, whether she knew it or not. I really hoped she couldn't see some angelic stain to my aura or she was liable to begin telling stories about how I'd been an accomplice in the beating of her guardian angel.

Fabrizio was staring at me with a grim frown. The door to the church had closed and we were standing on the steps. "Hi..." I said, awkwardly. "Did you ask me something? I hit my head when I fell, so I'm kind of spacey right now."

"Did you say girlfriends? Plural?"

I shrugged, realizing Yahn's relationship status had startled him. "No one really knows, to be honest. Dragons look at romantic relationships a lot differently than we do. Yahn seems to be in a throuple with the Reds, twin sisters and shifter dragons, from St. Louis who work with Nate Temple. Or maybe they're just teens having some fun. Never seemed relevant to ask. Until I find them naked in my bed, I couldn't care less. In Yahn's case, dreams do come true—and I do mean that in all its clever interpretations."

He blushed at my phrasing. "Dragons," he said, deadpan. "Greta's grandson is a dragon."

I smiled. "Keep up, old man. He's a rainbow dragon. He can change colors like a chameleon, camouflaging at will. He can even be transparent if he wants to. The perfect spy. Incredibly rare, apparently."

Fabrizio nodded, thoughtfully, looking more familiar with Yahn's military capabilities than his love life. "I think I need an espresso. Or whatever offensive re-creation they have of it here in America. I'm a glutton for punishment, but caffeine is caffeine."

I wrapped my arm around his shoulder. "I love you unconditionally, Meatball. But I am on a time crunch."

21

We had made small talk about dragons, my ninjas, and vague allusions to an increased number of demon sightings in the city while walking to a nearby coffee shop. The Brewbacca wasn't my usual haunt, but the sign had a Wookie in Ray Bans sipping a coffee, so it earned my vote. Everyone inside smelled like fresh soil and marijuana, and wore enigmatic emblems of the Hippie Trinity, a powerful trifecta of beanies, beards, and Birkenstocks, so I knew the beans had been officially blessed by the Vegan, the Burning Man, and the Hipster Spirit.

Fabrizio was a Star Trek fan, so I had to bully him through the door with a Gibbs swat to the back of the head.

After much grumbling and complaining, we were sipping and doctoring our drinks with sugar and milk when I noticed an older man at the table next to me. He was reading the newspaper carefully, murmuring sagely to what looked like could be his grandson across the table. The boy was fascinated, staring at the older man with curiosity as he sipped on a juice box and nibbled a muffin. Whenever his grandfather looked up, the boy would quickly look away, pretending he hadn't been staring, and the grandfather would chuckle good-naturedly.

"I caught you that time, boy," the grandfather said in a playful growl.

"When can I learn to read, Pop-Pop?" the boy complained. "Can you teach me?"

For the faintest of moments, I saw a flicker of fear in the grandfather's eyes. Then it was gone, replaced by a huge grin. "Pop-Pop isn't a very good teacher, and you deserve the best. Reading is the only way to rise in this world," he said. "If you can read, you can do *anything*."

The boy's eyes flashed with excitement. "Anything?" he breathed, wistfully. "I can learn to fly?"

His pop-pop chuckled. "Well, if you learn to read, you could become a pilot or an astronaut. That's more exciting than flapping your arms around like a turkey!" he teased, dropping the paper and flapping his elbows with a dramatic squawk.

I smiled warmly, stirring my drink as I wondered what my biological grandfather had been like. I hadn't even seen my adoptive father, Terry Penrose, in what felt like years. There was a vacuum in my heart that could only be filled by a father's love, a cup of cocoa, and a night spent watching a raging Missouri thunderstorm.

"What's it say, Pop-Pop?" the boy asked, practically bouncing in his seat.

The older man nodded wisely, staring down at the paper. The headline showed a picture of children playing on a playground, laughing happily. "It looks like a new playground is opening soon. We'll have to go check it out to make sure the slide works properly," he said, somberly.

The kid grinned toothily, nodding his agreement. Just then, the door to the shop opened and a married couple walked in. The boy spun to look and then let out a squeal. "Mommy! Daddy! Pop-Pop found a new park!"

I frowned, reading the headline under the picture of the playground. *Mayor vows to close dangerous playground.*

I discreetly leaned over. "Excuse me."

The old man glanced over at me with a surprised but heartfelt smile. "You trying to give an old man a heart attack?" he chuckled. "I haven't seen a woman as beautiful as you since I met my wife seventy years ago, God rest her soul."

I blushed, unable to bite back my own smile. "Thank you, but I don't know if I'm witty enough to keep up with a rascal like you." He guffawed, slapping his callused palm on the table. I glanced up to make sure the boy and his parents weren't within earshot. They still stood at the door, looking over a collection of mugs for sale. I jerked my chin towards the man's paper. "It says they're closing that park, sir."

His smile fractured and he clutched at his chest. "Oh, dear. That's terrible. I saw the picture and thought..." he trailed off, obviously horrified that he would need to break his grandson's heart. "Now where am I going to take him? He was so excited," he rasped, crestfallen.

"Did you not read the headline?" I asked with a compassionate frown.

He slowly turned to look up at me, and gazed directly into my eyes. "I... never learned how to read," he admitted in a sad voice. "I always start our play dates here with me pretending to read the paper so that he learns how important reading is. I'm a farmer," he admitted, tugging on the straps of his overalls. "His parents don't have a lot of money, and they live in a part of town where it's easier to join a gang than get a proper education. So I do what I can to feed his curiosity."

My heart broke at the shame in his eyes but hearing how hard he worked to make sure his grandson didn't follow a dark path made me want to wrap my arms around his shoulders and weep. The parents walked over, tugging along by the boy. I leaned away so as not to intrude. The mother smiled at the old man. "Hey, dad. We saw your truck out front while we were running errands, so we wanted to say hello before we run to work."

"Give me your wallet, Fabrizio. Now," I breathed.

He nodded, slipping it into my palm with a curious frown. I opened it and pulled out all the cash he had. I counted it and smiled, spotting four hundred-dollar-bills. I folded them in half two times and palmed them. Then I leaned down to the old farmer and extended my hand. "My name is Callie. It was a pleasure meeting you, old rascal."

The farmer, looking flustered by his current park dilemma, nodded politely and traded grips with me. I pressed the money into his palm with my fingers and smiled when his confused eyes flashed up to mine. "C-Callie," he repeated, sounding even more flustered than a moment ago.

I smiled and pulled my hand away. I eyed the playground picture on the newspaper and curled my lip. "Stop teasing the boy and tell him where you're really taking him," I said, folding my arms.

The farmer looked panicked, opening and closing his mouth wordlessly. "I-I..."

I waggled a finger at him. "Your tricks won't work on me." I turned to the parents and the boy, smiling knowingly. "My dad is just like him. Always pulling pranks on me when I was a little girl, stealing my nose and—"

"Digging coins out of your ears because you didn't clean them well enough," Fabrizio said in a loud voice as he leaned into our conversation, holding his fingers wide to show they were empty. The boy stared, transfixed as Fabrizio reached behind my ear and I felt a faint tendril of magic in the air. The boy gasped as Fabrizio pulled his hand away, now pinching a large silver coin between his fingers. He flicked it to the boy with a chuckle.

I rolled my eyes, elbowing Fabrizio playfully. "See?" Then I scooped up my drink and waved goodbye as the boy stared down at the coin in his hand, amazed. I leaned down to the old farmer. "You're doing it exactly right, Pop-Pop. Go show him the best day ever or I'll have words with you the next time I see you," I warned.

His lips trembled and a tear rolled out from his eye as he nodded. "Thank you, Callie," he whispered. Then he turned to his grandson. "How about we ditch this lame-o joint and go to...*Worlds of Fun.*"

The parents gasped, stunned, stammering about money. The boy bolted upright like a rocket, whistling like a teakettle.

The old man flashed the parents the cash I'd slipped him, making their jaws drop even further. "A guardian angel gave me a lucky lottery ticket," he said with an easy shrug. "I was going to surprise the boy, but I wanted to read my newspaper in peace for a few moments before he started acting like a crazy turkey!" He grinned down at the boy and mimicked the elbow flapping and squawking again. The boy did the same, and soon the entire store was staring at us, looking just as baffled as the parents.

In the chaos, I tugged Fabrizio's sleeve, pulling him towards the door. The old man caught sight of me and dipped his chin while mouthing a silent *thank you*. I smiled back. The parting twinkle in his eyes warmed my heart, and stayed with me for a very long time as Fabrizio and I slipped out the door.

22

We walked the streets in companionable silence, sipping our drinks under a cloudy sky. For the first time today, I felt like a normal girl living a normal life. I'd met a hero of an old man and I'd given him a reward by robbing the priest walking beside me.

"That was a good thing, Callie," Fabrizio finally said, nudging my shoulder.

I shrugged. "Technically, you just congratulated yourself, and Pride is one of the Seven Sins."

He blinked. Then he burst out laughing. "You got me, but I'm not so proud that I'm willing to stand on principle and throw this desecration of a coffee in the dumpster where it belongs. I think my suffering overshadows my pride, or at least they cancel each other out."

Fabrizio suggested we head to Roland's church and I reminded him that I didn't have very much free time. I shrugged, though, not particularly caring where we ended up. I would Shadow Walk to Castle Dracula once I'd finished speaking with Fabrizio and checking in on Roland's evacuation of my vampires—evampuation—from all corners of the world to Castle Dracula.

The streets weren't crowded, but they weren't empty either. I kept my eyes vigilant, wary of any surprise attacks from either Nephilim or demons. The Sins were also out in the wild, and I now knew they could possess people to do their dirty work. I still didn't understand why the demons seemed so adamant about finding Wrath and Pride. It had seemed like each of the Sins wanted their own little pockets of the city to themselves. Pride had made it sound like they did not work together, yet suddenly everyone was concerned about the safety of their siblings.

Judging by Wrath and Gabriel's response to me merging Michael and Lucifer into one body, I was betting that the rest of their siblings were going to be just as upset with me. I'd married the Brady Bunch of Heaven and Hell, and now all the Archangel Marcias and the Archdemon Peters were getting uppity, growing nostalgic for their once unified family.

Eae had looked Lucky right in the eyes and hadn't recognized him. So... was the Anghellian actually a human? What about the two specters he could call up—the apparitions of Lucifer and Michael who knew how to kick ass and head bash even someone as strong as their brothers, Gabriel and Wrath? Simultaneously. Lucky had made them look like punks and he hadn't even known what he was doing.

And his display of power at the fountain had really put things into perspective about how much mental anguish the Anghellian was enduring. How much could he take without snapping? Where was the noble Michael within the Anghellian? Because all I'd seen was a whole lot of Pride. Literally, thanks to his nudity this morning.

Had I made a nuclear bomb? Maybe the arch-class crew from both sides didn't have the details, but they had definitely sensed some powerful magic coming from Xuanwu's home while I'd been in Purgatory. Maybe that was what they truly wanted to check up on—the power, and how they might get their hands on some just like it.

And why hadn't Wrath or Gabriel rallied their forces to come against me or Lucky? They all seemed to be of an equal mind when it came to saving their brothers. They could have each sent their combined forces against me rather than hiding.

Unless...they were scared of the two Divines I had rescued. That was the only logical explanation. I really hoped Solomon and Last Breath had some answers or could at least point me in the right direction regarding the Divines.

"You expecting trouble?" Fabrizio asked in a low tone, pretending to sip his coffee.

I snapped out of my thoughts and looked over at him. "No. Of course not. That's crazy," I said, jerking my head to glance behind me. "Why? Did you see someone following me? Was it that guy pushing the stroller? That's suspicious. Or maybe that old lady folding laundry and smiling at you."

Fabrizio furrowed his eyebrows. "You're proving my point. You're paranoid. What's going on?"

I let out a shaky breath. "Don't take this the wrong way, Fabrizio, but I don't know if I can tell you. Things are very...complicated right now." Because they were. I had abducted Fabrizio's resident angel. I'd also bitten a Nephilim and uncovered a conspiracy of secret Nephilim vampires who might destroy the bedrock of the Shepherds. What would Fabrizio say if he learned that his hallowed Nephilim were just a secret flavor of vampire the angels had been coveting and hiding? I could absolutely guarantee that there was no positive way to spin that, and Fabrizio was the First Shepherd of the Vatican.

Which reminded me. "Hey. Tell me about the new management team at the Vatican."

He clammed up so quickly that I thought someone might have pinched his ass. "They want to meet you, personally. I will let you judge for yourself," he said, guardedly. It was painfully obvious that he was *not* going to talk about it.

I did not like that one bit. "They requested a *meeting?*" I said, enunciating the last word. "Or did they use another fun antonym, like interrogation, or inquisition? And did they actually say *request*, or was it a *demand?*"

Fabrizio grimaced. "I might have oversold it as a casual request. It was not optional and they gave me twenty-four hours."

I came to a halt. "Excuse me?" Fabrizio turned and gave me a slow nod. "Who was the invite for, specifically?" I asked. "What title or name did they use?"

Fabrizio grimaced and hung his head. "Every title I've heard attributed to you. It...doesn't look good. I can vouch for the fact that it is not a trap to capture you, as they permitted you to bring one ally and promised your safety." He sipped at his drink. "To be completely honest, it felt more like a parlay extended to an enemy force."

I let out a breath, actually relieved that they hadn't singled out any one particular aspect. If they'd called me out as the Horseman of Despair, I would have wanted to show up with my three brothers, Hope, Justice, and Absolution—Nate, Gunnar, and Alucard. If they'd called me out on any other specific title, it might directly relate to my situation with Heaven and Hell. The fact that they'd used all of them likely meant they wanted to broker a peace. "Okay. I can't right now, but maybe later tonight. If it will be brief. Or tomorrow morning."

He almost dropped his coffee. "Really? Just like that?" he demanded, sounding upset. "I thought you were going to bite my head off and call me a shitty friend!" he seethed. "Do you have any idea how stressed out I've been over this?"

I smirked, sipping my coffee. "Well, I do now."

"And then for you to put me off so you could bang your ninja! How do you think that made me feel? Roland was horrified! But to hear that you also had a relationship with him?!" he bellowed. "Your own Shepherd!"

I stared at him, stunned. "Bang my ninja?" I asked in a breathy tone. "What the hell are you talking about?"

His mouth clicked closed and his eyes widened. "You told Roland you had to get off the phone because you and Ryuu were going to get lucky. Then when I asked about using protection, you told me you always use protection. That you were going to need a bath and a blow dryer because you were going to sin all over this man," he croaked. "Damn near made me have a heart attack! Talking about how he could do things no other man could do! Poke my ears out already!"

I was speechless, recounting my conversations on the phone, realizing that I had said all those things. But it only sounded bad if they didn't realize Lucky was actually a person. "Well. That...was not remotely what I was doing. Good Lord, Fabrizio. Are you okay?"

I could see the vein throbbing in his temple, and I realized I could sense his racing pulse. "You weren't..." he trailed off, unable to even make himself say it.

"Absolutely not. I was hunting a man named Lucky with Ryuu. Roland should have known that. And he definitely shouldn't have gossiped to you about it." I put a hand on my hip, growing mildly annoyed. "And so what if I was banging Ryuu to kingdom come. What business is it of yours?"

Fabrizio guzzled his coffee in an effort to escape my glare. "I...well, it was all Roland's fault. I was just supporting him. He was concerned, and then I got concerned about him being concerned about you, and then—"

I held up a hand. "That's enough. How about you keep your nose out of my private life and I'll pretend this conversation never happened."

He nodded eagerly. "Thank Jesus."

I took a calming breath and continued my walk, muttering to myself. As I replayed my side of the conversation to Roland and Fabrizio in my head, I realized it all had sounded incredibly scandalous. What made it worse was that I wanted nothing more than to do a fraction of some of those things to Ryuu. Which meant I needed to make a pit stop in St. Louis the second I heard Nate had returned. I made a promise to myself and let out a breath. I would do at least one thing for my own benefit this week. "Fabrizio?"

He jolted, almost spilling his coffee. "Yes?"

"For the record, I'm going to bang the hell out of that ninja one day. If either of you so much as twitch an eye and screw it up for me, even indirectly, I will kill you."

He shifted his attention straight ahead, fighting a smile. "Amen to that." I nodded satisfactorily, not bothering to hide my expectant grin. Ryuu would be mine. "I want to know what's really going on with Heaven and Hell," Fabrizio said, snapping me out of my daydream.

I took a sip of my coffee. "Yeah. That's not a conversation I'm ready to have."

"Eae has been uncharacteristically cagey, and it's making my neck itch. Have you seen him recently?"

I shook my head, careful not to look guilty in any way. "The last time I saw him we were at war," I said, choosing my words very carefully. "Remember the fight outside Roland's church?"

Fabrizio grimaced and spat on the ground. "Vividly." He lifted his collar to show me the crucifix I had retrieved from the Doors—the one that had belonged to his old friend, Shepherd Anthony. "Thank you."

I nodded, smiling. "Wasn't a big deal," I said. Internally, I was grateful that he had not picked up on my deceit. I had stated two separate claims, making them appear like they were connected. That I was at war with Eae—true—during the battle outside Roland's church—also true. When taken together, they sounded connected.

What I had meant was that the last time I saw Eae—this morning—I was at war with him. And, in other news, remember that time we fought outside Roland's church? Good times, right?

I felt slimy for it, but I couldn't come clean on the topic yet. The Nephilim were hunting me, and Fabrizio kind of worked with them. Maybe even for them. And I might end up taking them all from the angels. There was a high chance Fabrizio might find himself across a field of battle one day, facing my Nephilim. If he chose the Vatican over the White Rose. Faith over friendship. He'd seen where that had taken Roland, so I had high hopes for him.

"Let's find an alley and magic our way to Roland's," he said, guiding me by the elbow to a nearby alley.

"How do you know Roland is even at his church?" I asked, frowning. "He could be anywhere. Unless he's not doing what I told him to do."

Fabrizio chuckled and pointed up at the sky. "Dark clouds mean Roland is home. Lets him walk around in the day."

My eyes widened in disbelief as I glanced up at the dark clouds hovering over the city. "That's...amazing. Where the hell did he come up with that?"

Fabrizio chuckled. "Frozen. That snowman guy."

I burst out laughing. "Olaf's cloud gave Roland the idea to shield the sun in Kansas City?" I laughed. "I don't know whether to be proud or ashamed for him."

"I've given him hell for it," he agreed with a belly chuckle, "but you're welcome to kick a man while he's down."

"I don't mind walking," I said, taking a deep breath of humid air. "I need to stay in shape, and walking is good for the heart. Something you should start thinking about, Meatball," I said, eyeing his permanent gut. "You're sporting a dad bod." Fabrizio was big man strong—not the chiseled Viking type, but those hairy bear types who were just big all around.

He grunted. "I prefer father figure." He pointedly glanced down at my hips. "But maybe we should keep walking. It does look like you're smuggling two sacks of loose nickels in those pants." Before I could even squawk at him, he was hooting and laughing, running away from me towards the alley at full speed. "That was for calling me fat!" he crowed, rounding the corner of an alley ahead of me.

I found myself laughing as I ran after him. My boots began to tingle and I skidded to a halt in time to see Fabrizio fly back out of the alley as if struck by a semi-truck. He slammed into a utility pole with a meaty grunt and a low chiming sound as the whole thing wobbled. He crumpled to the pavement, shaking his head blearily, obviously more surprised than he was injured.

"Look out, Fabrizio. Demon," I told him, slurping at my drink.

23

He blinked up at me, somehow managing to glare. "Thanks. What would I do without you?"

I nodded self-importantly and sauntered up to the alley, peering into the dark shadows cast by the tall buildings and the charcoal sky. "What flavor of asshole am I looking at?" I asked. "You all look the same to me."

"That was rude," Fabrizio grumbled, rising to his feet and shaking his head from left to right to loosen up his muscles. It sounded like a string of fireworks each time.

The darkness called back. "Where is he?" it rasped. Fabrizio shot me a curious look but I pretended not to notice.

"I don't talk to strangers. Old habits," I said, slurping more of my coffee. "Give me your name."

"Your flesh will taste delightful when I roast it over the pits of Hell," the demon snarled, still huddling in the darkness somewhere.

"I have it on good authority that my flesh is quite fatty and tough." I scanned the shadows, my eyes adjusting to the darkness. I could see the far end of the alley, so it wasn't a particularly large demon or it would have blocked my view. "Come on out, pal."

"Where is Pride?" he snarled in a low, deep, baritone.

Fabrizio stepped up beside me. He gave me a flat, meaningful glare for not sharing that little nugget of information. The First Shepherd felt privy to silly things like one of his friends apparently knowing one of the Seven Deadly Sins. I shrugged. "You weren't being very forthcoming yourself." I let out an annoyed breath. "If that upset you, this next part is going to blow your mind," I told him. I cleared my throat and faced the alley. "I already told Legion I don't know where any of the Sins are. I even spoke to Lust earlier, so you guys really need to work on your communication skills."

The demon snarled and I heard a splash. My eyes locked onto the sound and I prepared for a fight. I saw a scurrying creature skitter across the ground and Fabrizio unleashed a ball of fire. The flames engulfed it in less than a second. The creature screamed as it smoldered. I winced. "That was a rat."

"Demon guy?" Fabrizio called, his voice echoing in the alley. No one replied and we shared a long look at each other.

I eyed the smoking remains and grunted. "That little thing knocked you into the lamp post?" I asked, frowning.

Fabrizio shook his head, storming into the alley to inspect the remains. "It was much bigger," he said, defensively.

I stepped up beside him and stared down. "That's not a rat. That's a raccoon." Fabrizio put his hands on his hips, shaking his head with a frown. "You got your ass kicked by a trash panda demon," I said, grinning.

"Well, I killed it," he argued, "so, I win."

The smoking carcass suddenly began to twitch and spasm, rising up on its hind legs. We both leapt back with a hiss of surprise. "Um...what the hell is it doing?" I asked. The still burning raccoon stretched and groaned, tearing through its smoking charred skin to reveal a larger, stronger demon within. I gagged as the alley was suddenly pregnant with the smell of burning eggs, thick enough to chew on. I dumped my coffee out on the fiery demon and it hissed and sizzled in agony.

And, like my coffee had been fertilizer, it doubled in size *again*—this time tearing out of its brand-new flesh. It looked like raw meat giving birth to raw meat, and the cloying stench of sulfur was beginning to make my eyes water.

"That is *disgusting*," Fabrizio muttered, and then he drop-kicked it into the depths of the alley. It landed in an oily puddle and almost instantly exploded to ten times its previous size, turning into a spider-like creature with long, spiny, segmented legs. "It seems," Fabrizio said, "that liquid makes it grow larger."

"Mogwais," I murmured, shaking my head. "Don't feed them after midnight and don't get them wet. Now we have a gremlin to deal with." I assessed the demon. "A spider gremlin. Wasn't that in one of the movies, too?"

Fabrizio shrugged. "Pretend I said something clever because I have no idea what you're talking about."

I sighed, shaking my head in disappointment. I threw a ball of fire at the spider demon, cringing as it let out an ear-piercing scream that sounded like metal scraping metal. The fire washed over its back and the demon stumbled into a pile of foul-smelling, leaking trash bags pressed against the brick wall. It drove its head into the pile and began gobbling it down like a buffet challenge. Fabrizio cursed under his breath as we watched the meal instantly add bulk to the creature. It once again erupted out of its own chitinous exoskeleton to reveal a huge, thorned, sickly yellow spider that stood taller than our heads. It reared up on its hairy, chitinous back legs, clicking its mandibles and front feet as if challenging us to a boxing match. "It's all mine!" the demon screamed, slamming back down to all eights to gobble up more trash bags in a feeding frenzy.

"This is so fucked up," I murmured. I spotted several more puddles and cringed. "We can't let it get any bigger," I said. "I'll handle the water; you keep it busy."

Without waiting for his agreement, I began hurling blasts of magic at the ground, freezing the puddles on contact and sucking the heat out of the air and casting it up into the gloomy sky above. The alley turned into a skating rink and the spider began slipping and sliding as it tried to maintain its footing. Fabrizio began hurling blasts of liquid fire at its head. The fire splashed over the spider-like body, causing the demon's skin to burn and bubble up as it emitted horrendous screams that would definitely draw attention soon. Because he was the First Shepherd and a veritable powerhouse with his magic, Fabrizio simultaneously threw blades of air at its legs. Each strike of air impacted with the force and sound of a car accident, the legs crunching and the demon squealing like Fabrizio was hungry for dinner and cracking open crab legs to get to the meat within. Unfortunately, each shattered appendage only caused a thicker, more lethal version of the sickly yellow appendage to emerge from within, increasing the number of spikes and defensive scales covering the thicker new muscle mass. Each blow only made it stronger and more powerful.

It reminded me of the infamous Greek Hydra.

"It's the reverse matryoshka spider of doom," I shouted. "Those little Russian dolls that keep revealing a smaller, cuter version within," I explained. Fabrizio grunted, alternating back to fire. The flames blasted over the bright yellow spider's fuzzy body and face like liquid napalm, crackling and sizzling and burning. The demon now sported massive mandibles large enough to bite me in half at the waist, and they oozed a green slime that was likely venomous. Thankfully, the fire seemed to be a way to hurt it without letting it grow larger. The smell of burned spider fuzz added to the sulfurous stench and the occasional whiff of urine from the alley's overnight homeless population, creating a perfume that made me want to actually vomit.

The yellow spider demon lunged at me, clacking its wicked mandibles together as the rest of its body burned. I flung up a wall of fire right in front of its eyes and then rolled underneath, calling up my silver claws. I felt my mouth suddenly salivate and that same heady sensation of an alcoholic buzz rolled over me as my claws sliced deep into the spider's abdomen. The spider demon's legs buckled and its body convulsed as it let out a scream that set off nearby car alarms. I kept my fist high as I crouch-shuffled, ripping a deeper gash as the creature continued to writhe and scream, pounding its feet into the slippery, icy ground. Warm gunk and guts began pouring over my hand and down my back, plastering my hair to my skull, and smelling like hot, raw sewage. I risked a look back to see a hazy heat emanating from my silver claws, leaving a long, gaping wound that glowed and steamed at the edges. I spotted a dumpster to my right and I decided to take a gamble.

I yanked my hand out from his stomach and called up claws from my other fist. Then I spun and sliced at the creature's legs, severing two of the four that were closest to the dumpster. The demon began to tilt and fall, the last two legs on that side skittering madly on the ice. As it began to tip, I called up my angelic gauntlets and wings, giving the spider an uppercut to the chest that sent it flipping into the dumpster.

"Close the lid!" I shouted at Fabrizio. He slammed it closed with a gust of air and immediately began looping ropes of magic around and around the dumpster. I did the same, crisscrossing my ropes over his to form a web that would be harder to tear through. "Now heat up the metal," I screamed, "but don't blast a hole through it. We're having some Kansas City barbecue!" I knelt down and pressed my angelic gauntlets against the front of the dumpster, calling up as much heat as I could in an effort to transfer it into the dumpster and turn it into an oven. I watched as the metal began to glow in a widening circle radiating outward from my fiery gauntlets.

Fabrizio cackled as he followed suit and pressed his now glowing hands against the side of the dumpster. The demon squealed and screamed from within his make-shift oven as the metal began to smoke and burn, causing the paint to peel away as the steel went from a deep red to a bright orange. I felt the goop and spider guts covering my face harden and tighten, drying onto my skin like a beauty mask. I called up a shield to protect myself from the immense heat.

The spider demon pounded at the walls and tore through the melting plastic dumpster lid, only to come into contact with our ropes of power. It punched and pounded at the inside walls of the dumpster but immediately squealed upon contact, burned by the glowing red metal that was now its prison cell.

Thick clouds of noxious black smoke rose up from the burning dumpster, adding to the already unbearable smells filling the alley. Thankfully, the heat wasn't burning my hands, but that was probably because of my angelic gauntlets.

I glanced at Fabrizio in sudden alarm, and I was just in time to see his eyes flutter and then roll into the back of his head before he toppled onto his side. His hands were smoking and burned to the bone in several places. I let out a horrified gasp at his ruined hands. He'd shielded himself from the indirect heat, but he'd had no way to protect himself from the direct contact of his hands on the dumpster. He had to have known the risks. Yet...he'd still done it.

Unfortunately, as Fabrizio passed out, so did his half of the magic ropes keeping the demon trapped.

24

The weakened metal dumpster rapidly cooled without Fabrizio's assistance. In my distraction, the spider frantically grabbed my ropes and tore them apart, kicking out at the walls to explode out of the dumpster with a hissing shriek. I only just managed to call up my elemental wings, sheltering Fabrizio and myself from the ricocheting, red-hot shrapnel.

Unable to see from behind my shield, I heard the demon roar and I felt it kick my wings with one of its legs, sending me flying. I struck the brick wall with a shattering sound, my wings taking the brunt of the force, causing flecks of what looked like frozen glass to fall to the ground with me in a tinkling downpour. I rose up on all fours and checked over my shoulder to see that my wings were not destroyed despite the horribly loud shattering sound. The vaporous cloud of ice chips, feathers, and raw power had simply reorganized, absorbing the blow and shedding unnecessary crystals.

I looked up to see the yellow spider snatch Fabrizio by one leg and hoist him high in the air with a rattling hiss. The demon rose up on its back legs, swinging Fabrizio back and forth like a pendulum. The long gash I'd torn into its abdomen was a bubbling, bright orange, smoking eyesore, but it wasn't fatal. Damn. "I will devour him and make him a part of me. Hit me and you will be hurting him. We are one. Tell me where to find Lord Pride and Lord Wrath or I will eat this sheep slowly, starting at the limbs so he feels every rip and tear."

"Before you eat him, do you mind telling me who you work for? Is it Legion or did one of the Sins send you? Because I've given it some serious thought, and I think we could be friends, sulfur widow."

The giant spider crashed down to all five remaining legs, still holding the unconscious First Shepherd in one claw and giving me a chance to see the rest of the damage we had inflicted. The demon was a smoking, smoldering ruin from its time in the dumpster. Two of its eyes had burst open from the heat and now oozed bright orange goop down its face. I knew that if it consumed Fabrizio, it would emerge healed, larger, and even stronger than before. Fabrizio was no joke in the magic muscle department. If bags of trash had made the demon this much bigger than a trash panda, what would the power of the First Shepherd do to it?

That heady buzz of adrenaline suddenly surged through my veins like liquid ice and I heard my wings quivering with raw power as my gauntlets crackled against the filthy ground. I felt my fangs snap out and my vision tunnel in on the demon, everything else in my peripheral seeming to darken and fade away. I sunk my silver claws into the concrete and pointed my ass in the air like I was on the starting blocks for a track meet, waiting for the gunshot.

Except I didn't wait for a gunshot. I tore forward, ripping through the concrete with my claws in an attempt to go faster. I took two steps before subconsciously flapping my wings in a powerful sweep that launched me a dozen feet up into the air. My rapid and unexpected change in elevation caught the demon so off guard that it dropped Fabrizio to the ground. Meatball went splat into the gooey ickiness of liquified, orange spider eyeballs that had pooled below.

The spider lunged forward, snapping its giant mandibles at my face. Instead of shielding myself, I grabbed each pincher with my angelic gauntlets. An uncomfortable vibration rocked up my arms at the direct contact of Heavenly gauntlets and Hellish snaggle-teeth. The strange force didn't repel my grip like the wrong ends of two magnets touching, but it was extremely uncomfortable.

I realized I was laughing, baring my fangs as I stared at my reflection in its six remaining eyes. What I saw should have given me pause—a white-haired demon with glowing white eyes, covered in dried orange gore, and wearing oversized gauntlets made of crackling blue light. My eyes shone like fire and orange slime coated my face in surprisingly artistic swirls.

But that demonic angel was laughing, and her teeth were gleaming silver vampire fangs.

I heaved with my angelic gauntlets, throwing my arms wide with a vicious roar that ripped at my vocal chords. My gauntlets blazed as I ripped the spider demon's head in half as easily as if I were opening a set of double doors onto a sunny veranda for some cold iced tea on a hot summer day. Orange gore splattered all over me like an explosion of paint.

The demon's terrified eyes went dull as the force of my pull sent me crashing right into the now-open skull of the demon—feet-first, thankfully—straight into its bright orange brain. Of course, my wings chose that moment to wink out of existence as my power high suddenly fled my body in a rush. The demon collapsed, and I rode the inside of the skull down to the ground, tumbling around on spin cycle with the load of wet laundry that had once been demon brain.

I vomited, twice, in my desperate attempt to crawl and claw my way out of the disgusting skull. I collapsed on my side next to Fabrizio and found him staring at me in dazed pain and disbelief. As if he'd woken up from a nightmare.

Despite the pain and exhaustion, I saw one other thing in the First Shepherd's eyes.

Fear...of *me*.

I groaned, averting my eyes to ignore that look before I thought too hard about it. My fangs had thankfully snapped back into place at some point during my skully-go-round, so maybe Fabrizio hadn't noticed. I grabbed his wrists to help him up and almost immediately vomited again as I felt a chunk of tendon or flesh crumble to dust and he let out a sharp hiss. He wheezed, panting desperately at the fresh pain I'd given him. "I'm so sorry," I rasped, carefully setting them back down. I stared down at what had once been his strong, callused hands. There was more bone than flesh, and what little was left was carbonized muscle and dried or snapped tendons. Both of his hands were utterly destroyed. "Oh my god," I whispered, fighting back my tears. Why hadn't I hulked out sooner? "Stay strong, Fabrizio. I know someone who might be able to help."

He grunted weakly. "H-high...f-five," he rasped, giving me an agonized, crooked smile.

129

My eyes flooded with tears, spilling down my filthy cheeks. "Air five," I whispered back, cupping his face with both hands and slowly leaning down to kiss him on the forehead. "Will Shadow Walking hurt you?" I asked, gently patting his cheeks with my thumbs as I saw his eyes begin to flutter closed again.

"S-safe," he mumbled. I heard sirens in the distance and I was baffled to see that no curious citizen had come over to check on the chaos in the alley. Then again, maybe they had. I could envision a curious teen whipping out their phone in hopes they could catch something on video that would make them go viral. Instead, the budding internet star had seen a crazy flying woman fighting a giant talking spider, causing them to promptly shit their pants and then run away to get right with Jesus.

Someone had called the police.

"Okay. Just hold on a little bit longer," I said, not daring to use my filthy clothes or hands to wipe away my tears. Fabrizio let out a tired wheeze and passed out, murmuring incoherently under his breath. "I might have killed one angel today, and he wasn't half as noble as you, Meatball. You're not fucking allowed to die. Hold on." I gathered up my dwindling strength to Shadow Walk to Xuanwu's estate. Aala's rebirth pond might be able to save his hands or at least alleviate some of his pain.

"S-save...me...vampire," Fabrizio croaked.

He had seen my fangs. Damn it all.

25

Upon delivering Fabrizio to Aala, I had been promptly ushered into a private bath of steaming water full of floating lotus petals and given a selection of seven different scented oils to choose from.

No one outright said *you stanky, girl*, but I could read between the lines. I'd soaked for half an hour and then scrubbed the hell out of my hair and skin until I felt raw. The water had been filthy and orange from the demon gore, causing the lotus petals to wilt and wither. Which was when a second nameless, voiceless, robed woman entered the room, draped me in a huge, fluffy towel, and then guided me to a second private room with a new bath of petals and scented oils.

Apparently, they intended to incinerate all evidence from my previous bath and banish the tub to the Neverwas or somewhere else that was equally inhospitable. I cleaned off much quicker since the woman remained kneeling at the side of the tub, giving me the option of either physically fighting her while naked or allowing her to wash my hair and back. It was a close call, but I erred on the side of caution since I had no way of knowing how many years she'd spent learning martial arts with Xuanwu and Ryuu. Could have been centuries. I closed my eyes and tried not to focus on her gentle cleaning over my more sensitive bits, but my mind continued wandering to darker problems on the horizon. She then pulled me to my feet, used a pitcher to rinse me off, and then finally permitted me to step out of the tub and into a long soft robe.

There were hardly any chunks of orange spider brain floating in the second tub after I stepped out. I chalked it up as a win and followed her to a third room, stepping through the sliding rice-paper doors. There, I found the set of clothes Aphrodite had made for me and I let out a sigh of relief. Had Ryuu picked them up for me before heading out to deal with his ninjas and trail Legion?

I had scooped up the gleaming white fabric and lifted it to my nose, grinning like an idiot as I scented Ryuu's familiar musk mixed with spice and sandalwood. For obvious reasons, those were the two oils I had chosen in my baths. I had then slipped into my new clothes, my boots, grabbed my katana and the two Nephilim cuffs along with various other items from the pockets of my filthy clothes—which were nowhere to be found, likely also having been incinerated.

I made my way back to the training fields to speak with Xuanwu before I headed out. I saw the massive black tortoise sitting in the grass, watching Qinglong, Zoe, and Bai playing what looked like a game of tag twenty yards away.

I smiled and then sat in the grass beside Xuanwu, staring out at the field of purple grass.

"Much better," Xuanwu murmured after taking a deep breath through his nostrils, not looking over at me. He caught me up on his morning's events and the three patients I'd dumped on him.

Aala was currently tending to Fabrizio's hands, floating in the pool with him, even though he was still unconscious. She had been very busy this morning, and had set up a row of sickbeds for all the patients I had given her. Eae slept on one, a bandage around his throat and abdomen, and his wings bound with silk ribbons that were strong enough to restrain him. Golden runes burned on the ground around his bed in a perfect circle, trapping him in the event he woke up without supervision.

A safe distance away, also surrounded by glowing runes—although blue and a different collection of symbols from the angel's—Adrian, the Nephilim, slept on his own cot. He had been sedated, having woken up once in a panic, swinging his claws in a wild frenzy as he demanded to know where I was. Not knowing if his reaction had been threatening or supportive, Aala had tranquilized him with some crazy ass potion that had been derived from a combination of frog semen, two heron tongues, and yak urine. At least, that was what she had told me. The bowl of flower petals on the bedside table gave me cause to doubt her explanation, but I hadn't called her out on it.

The third bed would be for Fabrizio, the First Shepherd of the Vatican. Currently, he was still in the pond with a very naked Aala, so I was now certain that nudity had something to do with the healing aspect and not that I had been given a unique experience. Likewise, Eae and Adrian were also naked, covered only by a white sheet at the waist. Fabrizio hadn't woken up, so Aala was aiding his back-float, doing magical curiosities to him in an effort to hopefully heal his hands.

Next, I told him about my morning with Ryuu. The ninja had likely already told him but men didn't know how to tell proper stories. They focused on all the wrong parts and skipped over the most important aspects. I doubted this was true for Ryuu, but it was better to be safe than sorry. Xuanwu already knew the major behind the scenes issues—and information about my parents that I didn't even know yet—so I had no fear of speaking freely. He was also wise as hell and often saw situations in incredibly unique ways. I trusted him with my life. More than almost anyone I knew, as a matter of fact, even though he hadn't told me all he knew about my parents or why Heaven and Hell feared all four of his Divine family so much. We weren't incredibly close, but he had formed a Trinity with my godfather, Samael, and everything he had ever done had been to benefit me, whether I had understood that at the time or not.

He nodded along as I spoke, not interrupting me once. When I was finished, I stared out at the field. Zoe and Bai now wrestled in the grass with Qinglong, amidst flames and zipping metal projectiles the size of needles, biting, tackling and hissing or yowling at each other. Qinglong merely smiled, playing referee and putting out fires here and there. Xuanwu smiled, clutching his sword cane in his fist like he always did. Legend said that he could never release it, and that it was one of the most powerful swords in the world. His claws flexed and contracted as he watched them.

I glanced down at the Nephilim cuff I'd placed in the grass between us while telling him what I knew about the jewelry, which wasn't a whole lot. I even told him about my fangs and new hyper senses, since it was relevant for explaining why Adrian had abruptly switched teams to protect me against his boss, Eae.

Xuanwu had not reacted in the slightest to the information that I might be some kind of metal vampire. Instead, he picked up the cuff, inspected it for a few moments, grimaced, and then set it down with a shrug. "Do you love yourself, Callie Penrose?" he asked after a few moments of silence, when it became apparent that I was finished speaking.

I frowned, glancing over at him. "Sure," I said, studying him. "You heard the part about me growing fangs and biting his buddy, right?"

He smirked, nodding. "Love yourself for your virtues and your vices. Honestly acknowledge your strengths and your weaknesses. Walk with pride and dance with humility. Speak with grace and dine with empathy. Do these things and you will never be a monster. Frightening your foes does not make you evil, it makes you into a symbol. The White Rose," he said, nodding pensively. "With the foundations I just laid out for you, the symbol of the White Rose will strike terror and despair in the hearts of the wicked and inspire loyalty and hope in the hearts of the innocent." He turned to look at me with a kind, eager smile. "The White Rose does not cast a shadow of gloom and endless night; the White Rose calls the valiant to war to fight for brighter days."

26

I stared at him, nodding. "I will do my best," I said, honestly. "And you will tell me when I step off the path, which I guarantee is going to happen. There is a whole lot of hate in this heart, Xuanwu. A whole lot of rage, and I've seen what happens to me when I let too much of it out. Keep me accountable."

He turned to me and grinned, nodding his approval. "Of course, White Rose. I will tell you when you fuck up the beautiful cosmic balance I just described to you," he said, choking on laughter at his abrupt change in sincerity to the philosophical lesson a moment ago. "Never take yourself too seriously. Laughter heals the soul."

I grunted, shaking my head. "Okay." My eyes settled on the cuff. "Anything you know about this could be a big help, Xuanwu," I pressed.

He glanced over at me with a sad smile. "I think we have helped quite enough this morning," he said, not unkindly but sternly, his eyes flicking towards the two sleeping men. I sighed, nodding as I scooped up the cuff and slipped it into my pocket with the other. Aphrodite's clothes fit me like a glove, and pockets were essentially bottomless.

"I'm sorry about Jin," I said, recalling the name of the ninja who had been murdered.

Xuanwu was silent, breathing steadily through his nose as he watched his siblings play. "I am not."

That drew me up short. I glanced over at the black tortoise, studying his obsidian eyes and his long, wicked beak. His shell was covered in gnarly spikes and rigid hoarfrost. He seemed slow and mellow, but Xuanwu was a goddamned berserker on the battlefield—like a Dr. Jekyll and Mr. Hyde situation. It was wise not to poke the tortoise too much.

"Why?" I asked, frowning.

Xuanwu smiled. "Because it has awakened Ryuu from his peaceful meditation to pursue his true calling. A phoenix of death and fear now haunts the streets of Kansas City to avenge Jin, and all will soon know Ryuu's name. They have not struck a blow against the ninjas; they have unleashed a terribly vicious calamity, a force of nature so profound that even I shudder in anticipation at what he might do to the murderers and their associates." He glanced over at me, the frost and ice constantly shifting across his skin cracked and fractured. "Do we know who was responsible? Heaven or Hell?"

I tried to keep my face calm in spite of his foreboding description of Ryuu. I had to admit that it sent a thrill of anticipation through me, too. Not because of the violence, but because an injustice had awakened that violence. Ryuu's wrath was not an instigation but a retaliation. "Heaven's minions taunted us about the murders, but they did not outright claim responsibility. It is vitally important that I interrogate those two when I return. Not just about the attack on Jin and my vampire, but about much bigger issues coming down the pipeline."

Xuanwu was silent.

"Which means you are not allowed to kill them," I clarified. "Even if they claim credit. Once I'm finished with them, you can do whatever you want with them, but not until I get my answers."

Xuanwu nodded, turning back to watch his siblings playing in the grass. "I will agree to that. If neither side takes official credit, Ryuu will indiscriminately assassinate the forces of Heaven and Hell, one-by-one. They should be very, very afraid right now." He took a sip from a cup in front of him. "Tea, Miss Penrose?" he asked in a cordial, upbeat tone, as if he hadn't just discussed Ryuu murdering countless angels, demons, and Nephilim.

I shook my head, wondering just how crazy all my new friends really were beneath the surface. "No. Fabrizio and I were interrupted on our way to see Roland about my vampires, but I want to take these to Solomon, first. He might have read something about them. The temple is pregnant with books, so if anyone has information on the Sins, Archangels, Olympians, or Divines, it will be there." I patted the cuff in my pocket, meaningfully.

Xuanwu tracked my motion and then glanced over at the sleeping Nephilim and angel. "A collar," he mused in a tone of disapproval, "to keep them from knowing their true natures are actually to hunt and kill angels. That is incredibly cruel. Making a lion work for a sheep, by making the lion think he's a sheep."

I nodded. "Sounds crazy when you say it out loud. The Nephilim were sired from angels procreating with humans a long, long time ago. Why would their offspring instinctively want to kill angels? I thought the trope of kids killing their parents was predominantly part of the Greek and Norse pantheons," I mused, rhetorically.

He cast me a very dry look that made my shoulders wilt. "If only there were some other group a wise old man told you about...a group basically founded on the principle of overthrowing one's ancestors and willing to destroy the world to do it. If only..." he trailed off, deadpan.

I grunted. "Yeah. I walked into that one. The Masters," I mused, staring off into the middle distance. I wasn't sure what they had to do with the Nephilim, but their modus operandi was eerily similar. I really needed to sit down with Nate Temple and Quinn MacKenna so we could hash this stuff out. Which only brought on concerns about the Olympian drama. I let out a tired sigh and climbed to my feet. "I'll think on the Nephilim, but please keep Adrian and Eae safe for now. I'm pretty sure me drinking that Nephilim's blood broke off Adrian's cuff, and he immediately sprang into action to protect me. Maybe that means I am destined to become their version of Count Dracula as well. I might not even have to spill any blood to do it."

Xuanwu grunted, shaking his head in disappointment. "What did the Nephilim you left for dead look like?"

I frowned. "Handsome. Brown hair and pale blue eyes. Why?"

"He wasn't there when Ryuu's men went to retrieve the body. Either someone from Heaven came to collect his body, meaning they already know what you did since you took his bracelet, too," he said, slowly turning to look at me. "Or your Nephilim wasn't actually dead when you left him. There was absolutely no blood at the crime scene, either. Almost as if someone had sucked it right up from out of the ground."

I cursed. "Damn it. But the angels would have wanted to clean up Eae's blood to hide the evidence. Not let anyone discover that they're vulnerable against the Nephilim," I said, thinking of Quentin at large on the streets of my city. What if he remembered his old orders and chose to hunt down Ryuu's ninjas? He had those wicked new claws, now...

Xuanwu nodded. "Perhaps. But if the Nephilim did survive and drank Eae's blood to heal his wounds...the last thing he would remember would be you stabbing him in the gut and ravaging his neck. I imagine he has strong feelings about that memory. Or Heaven has strong opinions about you stealing what they consider their property. So when you say you might not have to spill any blood..." he chuckled darkly. "I almost feel like you haven't been paying any attention." He stared at me for a few more seconds and then resumed his study of his siblings in the field. "Thought you should know."

I rose to my feet and adjusted my katana, unable to decide which option would be worse: a territorial host of angels knowing I had kidnapped their soldier and almost killed another, and that I had learned the Nephilim's naughty secret; or a bloodthirsty Nephilim stalking the streets to get revenge on the woman who had tried to kill him?

"Does Ryuu know about all of this?"

Xuanwu shook his head, not looking over at me. "I haven't seen him since he left with Lucky and Xylo to trail your demon friend, Legion, five minutes after he dropped off Aala's new patients. That was hours ago."

I pursed my lips. "Heaven and Hell both have assassins out there prowling the streets to hunt down my allies in order to bully me into handing over Gabriel and Wrath, who seem to have vanished. Or Pride and Michael, who I also can't turn in because they don't freaking exist anymore. Telling them about Lucky will only make things worse. Much worse." Xuanwu nodded in agreement. I glanced over at Adrian. "But I can start by getting answers on this," I said, patting my pocket with the Nephilim cuffs. "If I can turn the Nephilim to my side, I can then use them to neutralize the demon assassins, buying us some much-needed time to deal with Legion and the rest of the Sins."

He thumped his sword cane against the ground. "Sounds like a plan. We will look after our guests until you return."

I nodded. "Thank you, Xuanwu." Then I Shadow Walked to Solomon's Temple to talk to a lion about some Holy handcuffs.

27

A s usual when I visited Solomon's Temple, I arrived on the vast open balcony that overlooked his lands. The first thing I noticed was the sudden vibrancy in the air—the smell of fresh growth from the huge swaths of gardens as far as the eye could see. The second thing I noticed was the dark bubble in the near distance where Castle Dracula was located. There, it was perpetually night, even featuring its own moon. Colossal walls surrounded the huge estate for miles in every direction, preventing all but an aerial army from breaking into the private world of monsters, vampires, and nightmares. But even an aerial force would be hard-pressed to attempt an assault, because I had hundreds of gargoyles sweeping the skies on vigilant patrols.

For such a nightmarish place, Castle Dracula was uniquely sophisticated. We had a Keep, a Clocktower, a Coliseum, an Observatory, a Library, an Armory, a Village, paved city streets, hotels, and brothels, and stunning, labyrinthine gardens. I knew that plenty of monsters had expatriated to Castle Dracula over the centuries, filling the place with creatures that I had never even heard of. It was strangely exciting, in a way, because not all of those residents wanted to be bothered and were very much uncivilized. A wrong turn in the forest might lead to a literal life or death situation. I wasn't the ruler they loved unconditionally, but there was no longer a question that I was their ruler.

So, they bent the knee or they hid in caves. That suited me. For now. Until I instituted the military draft for the Omega War. That would likely cause some peaceful protesting.

I made my way towards the main doors to Solomon's Temple, smiling at the giant columns, marble floors, hanging ferns and flowers, and occasional statues featuring too many civilizations to count. A half-naked, buff Asian man jumped out from behind a column, his eyes flickering with blue light until he recognized it was me. "Callie!" Richard shouted, and then he was squeezing me against his chest in a death hug. I smiled, hugging him back, briefly, before extracting myself.

Richard could shift into a deadly white lion known as Last Breath. He was one of the supernatural world's most frightening legends. Their boogeyman. He killed his targets in impossible situations in impossible ways and hardly anyone ever saw anything other than his glowing blue eyes, a white blur, and fog.

When not murdering large groups of people or high value targets, he worked for King Solomon as a librarian. He'd been here with Solomon for as close to forever as one could get without becoming forgetful. He and Solomon knew more about human, monster, angelic, and demonic creatures and their histories than anyone else I could think of.

They had also loved my mother dearly, even though she had never told them she was pregnant with me. Twenty-some-odd years later, they put the pieces together and found me, setting me on a grueling obstacle course through the Doors to prove I was worthy to claim my inheritance.

Solomon's Temple, and all its secrets. But I didn't have time for that any time soon. Especially not right now.

"Hey, Richard," I said with a warm smile. "How have you been?" I asked, suddenly feeling a little awkward. At some point, I felt I needed to talk to him about me choosing Phix to be my ride as a Horseman. I had said a few things to or near Richard that might have led him to believe the job would be his. That could have all been in my head, but I knew I would feel better if I came clean. Just...

Not right now, or I was liable to have a stress-induced panic attack. It was easier to ignore this topic since he wasn't currently in his lion form.

He shrugged, took me by the hand, and led me to a pair of lawn chairs overlooking a splendorous hanging garden made of trellises that climbed

TRINITY

thirty-feet-high and almost reached the foot of our balcony. We sat down and he crossed his ankles before folding his hands behind his head. "I've been good. Bored, but good. Spend a lot of time reading and staring at the eyesore of our once elegant neighborhood," he said with a roguish grin.

I rolled my eyes. "Have they been breaking the homeowners association's regulations? Letting their grass grow too long? Parking their cars outside the walls and playing their loud music at all hours of the night—" I grinned. "Oh, wait. It's always night."

He chuckled good naturedly. "There hasn't been a single issue. In fact, I'd love a tour. You mentioned they have a Coliseum and that you wanted to open it back up for gladiatorial events, right?" he asked in an almost feverish tone.

I nodded. "They used to use it to kill thousands of abducted prisoners from the Earthly realm," I said in a grim tone. "But the Minotaur and King Midas in St. Louis have a successful Fight Club tied to a pocket dimension where the combatants can't actually die. Nate Temple even fought Mordred there with the help of the Biblical Four Horsemen. From what I hear, they didn't hold back in the slightest."

Richard sat up straighter. "You think you could bring that here?" he asked, stunned. He licked his lips hungrily, likely imagining the opportunity where he could also cut loose and murder monsters without permanent repercussions.

I shrugged. "With the right magic, I don't see why I couldn't link that realm to Castle Dracula for specific events. I still need to hammer out the details with Asterion and Midas." And by that, I meant the pursuit of all evil.

Scrilla, cheddah, benjies, hundos.

Money. King Midas was the world's most successful investor. Ever. Period. Mostly because he was savvy, but also because he cheated when necessary. If he bet on the wrong horse, he would touch the horse with his pinky finger and turn it into solid gold. The Midas Touch legend was very, very real.

"And Dorian Gray has a huge following for grandiose events. Remember when he filmed me fighting that demon, streaming it to the entire supernatural world?"

Richard nodded, even though we hadn't known each other then. "That

141

was when we first started hearing about a girl in Kansas City. We never expected her to be Constance's daughter," he said, warmly. "Best surprise ever." He reached over and squeezed my hand with a genuine smile. "Dorian can bring the audience and showmanship as the host of the event, Asterion can provide the magical aspect to eliminate the possibility of death, and you can provide the most spectacular venue in the entire world," he said, pointing at Castle Dracula. "A damned Coliseum at Castle Dracula! Tickets would sell just so Freaks could tell their friends they visited such a famous place! It will be like the Super Bowl on steroids. That would be...truly magical," he whispered, looking like a kid on Christmas morning as he stared out at Castle Dracula.

I nodded thoughtfully. It really was a good idea. A unifying idea. I even envisioned inviting various supernatural factions to such an event as an olive branch between us. A gesture of goodwill. There were more benefits than risks. But there were a lot of other things I needed to do at Castle Dracula before focusing on entertainment.

Primarily, defense. Because Archangels and Archdemons could enter Castle Dracula with impunity.

I needed to find a way to put an end to that. Now.

Aphrodite had warned me that Darling and Dear were shacking up at Castle Dracula, and that I needed to get them to help me get the forges of the Infernal Armory roaring to make weapons of war with the mysterious Eternal Metal—the same metal that made my claws, my time-distorting vision, Sanguina's eyes, the Seal of Solomon...possibly even my new vampire fangs and the Nephilim claws. I didn't want to think about my fangs, especially when I didn't notice any strange hankerings for blood or any significant mood swings. The only times it had impacted me were when I'd been in mortal danger, facing an angel or a demon.

But why had it never happened before this morning? I shook off the thought.

It was baffling to think that all of these events or connections between Eternal Metal were coincidences. Were we really all tied together and no one had known it?

Well, my mother had obviously known something. She had set my life up to knock down these seemingly unrelated dominos, and now I was finding all the connections between us. The Eternal Metal also helped heal Xylo's bones. I felt the weight of responsibility in my pocket and let out a sigh. I pulled out the two Nephilim cuffs and handed them to Richard, telling him about recent events. Like Xuanwu, I knew beyond a shadow of a doubt that I could trust him. I shared an unbreakable blood bond with him.

There were no secrets between us and no questions about loyalty.

Richard and Solomon were the only family I had left.

28

Richard inspected the cuffs, pensively, holding them up to the light and twisting them in his hands to study every angle of the golden jewelry. "I can look into it, but I can tell you up front that I've never heard about the Nephilim being anything other than what we all thought they were—offspring of angels and warriors for Heaven."

"Maybe Solomon knows something?" I asked. "Where is he, anyway?"

Richard smirked, "Sleeping in like a bum." He set the cuffs down on a side table next to a journal that was half full of scribbled notes. I must have interrupted him with my visit. "Do you need my help?" he asked in a concerned tone, and I realized that he'd been staring at me. "You look stressed out. Exhausted."

I shook my head, firmly. "The biggest help would be you finding out everything you can on those cuffs. Anything on the Nephilim actually being brain-washed slaves forced to work for the very people their instincts tell them to hunt and eat. Angels."

Richard pursed his lips, troubled. "It almost sounds too crazy to believe. So, Eae and Adrian are safely locked up with Xuanwu, but what about this other Nephilim? Quentin the boob man," he said with a mild grin. "I haven't heard that name for a saint before," he mused, scratching at his chin.

I frowned. "What?"

"The Nephilim often adopt the names of patron saints, much like the

Pope in the Vatican. It isn't necessarily required, but strongly encouraged," he said with a shrug. "Old tradition."

I nodded angrily, clenching a fist at his casual reminder of my oversight with Quentin. "I'm not entirely sure. I thought he was dead, but circumstantial evidence seems to imply that the angels either took him back and know about my discovery of the cuffs, or he's wandering the streets of Kansas City all by himself."

He grunted. "A Nephilim with a newfound need to kill and drink angel blood when you say angels and Nephilim are stalking the streets to murder your allies. That sounds like a terrible combination. Or...perhaps a fortuitous accident. Maybe he will be so upset at his years of imprisonment that he will kill all your hunters for you?"

I shrugged. "Not with my luck. Which is why I need everything you can find. I'll be back soon. I'm going to go get Ryuu and see if we can track down any of the Sins."

"While avoiding demon and Nephilim assassins, you expect to just kidnap one of the Sins?" he asked, dryly.

I shrugged. "Do you have a better idea? Plus, if you can help me find a way to bring the Nephilim to my cause, I could castrate Heaven's efforts to assassinate me. The angels will think twice about attacking if I have an army of their thirsty Nephilim standing by my side."

"The angels might think twice, but not the Archangels," he said in a foreboding tone.

I grunted. "Which is why I need you to find me answers. On the Sins and if any of them are tied to actual Archdemons—like how Pride was actually Lucifer. I also need to know about Archangel hierarchy, Eternal Metal, Anghellians, demon prophecy, and the Four Legendary Creatures. They might be referred to as the Divines or Daemons. Oh, and anything about a Trinity."

He had started jotting down notes on his pad the moment I had started branching out well beyond my initial topic. "Anything else?" he asked, reading over his notes and tapping his pen against his lip.

I furrowed my brow, thinking. "There is a fifth Divine," I said, recalling Xuanwu's carved front door. "I saw a depiction of them all with their respective traits, qualities, and elements. In the center was a yellow dragon, but I can't recall what it represented or if it was even real. No one ever talks about that one, only the Four Divines. Even Xuanwu and Qinglong don't ever talk about the yellow dragon."

Richard nodded, scribbling a few last-minute details. "I'll get to work. Looks like I'm going to have to wake up the old man. Some of these topics are definitely going to be in different libraries in the temple," he mused, scratching at his jaw. He glanced out at Castle Dracula in the distance and smiled faintly. "Nephilim vampires...maybe they could live here in the temple. It would be fitting to have them live next to their...extended family."

I nodded at the strangely logical idea. "As long as they aren't crazy psychopaths, of course. Then again, it's probably a worse idea to move a bunch of Nephilim into Castle Dracula. Too many old habits and old enemies."

Richard nodded. "Solomon's Temple would be more appropriate, and there is plenty of room," he added. "We have ties to Heaven, so they won't feel so out of place. If it's good enough for the man who was famous for trapping demons, the Nephilim should feel right at home. I won't lie, the company would be nice, too," he admitted. "Especially if you open up Fight Nights at the Coliseum!" he said with a boyish grin, staring out at Castle Dracula.

I rolled my eyes, unable to bite back my own smile. "Well, don't make the beds yet. We need to learn more about them before we invite them to a sleepover." I pointed at his notepad. "So get to researching, librarian lady."

"Shhhhh!" he hissed in a dramatic stage whisper with one finger over his lips. "This is a library!"

I laughed, shaking my head as I climbed to my feet. "Work as fast as you can. Time is not our friend. I'll be back as quickly as I can, but I have no idea when that will be."

He nodded and pulled me in for another, longer hug. "I miss you, Callie. We miss you," he said, gripping me by the shoulder as he took a step back. "You should visit us more. We already feel like we missed out on the entire first part of your life. Your family history is here, whispering in the halls, and written in millions of books. Your mother's laboratory is a treasure trove of secrets. Don't get so busy fighting out there that you forget to tend to your own roots. Your own history. Your mother's secrets. Your only living ancestor and his pet cat," he said, point his thumb at his own chest with a grin.

I nodded, blinking rapidly to prevent shedding tears from the raw passion in his voice. "Thanks for the guilt trip," I whispered. "But you're right."

He grunted, shoving my shoulder playfully. "Not a guilt trip. A request. At least stop by for dinner once a week. Hell, invite your rowdy ass gang of friends here. I'll lay out a feast so massive that your friends won't even be able to put a dent in it. We have a dining room designed for dozens of guests and it's never used. Let's fill up every damned chair with all the lives you've changed. Those monsters you showed a new path—one where they could be honorable despite their bloody pasts, directing their violence towards their old masters. Demon godparents, vampire preachers, Dorian Gray..." he trailed off, gesturing wildly with his free hand. His eyes twinkled with excitement. "Just imagine how wonderful that would be, Callie. I can almost see it."

"Okay! Okay!" I growled, shoving him back with a laugh. "We'll do it soon. Once I know everyone is relatively safe. Maybe in a few days? Might even work for a rehearsal dinner for Samael and Lilith's wedding," I mused.

He nodded excitedly. "I'll have to go pick from the gardens and get some meat. I know some incredible recipes that no living mortal even remembers. Meals from *centuries* ago," he laughed, grinning like an idiot. "It will be the greatest meal ever. Laughter and joy and love will echo in these halls once again. Food will bring us together."

I smiled, infected with his enthusiasm. We really did deserve a celebration. To set our weapons down for a minute and take a breather. "Deal. But only *after* you get me answers," I said, pointing at his notepad.

He laughed, shaking his head. "Of course. I'll go get Solomon now," he said, spinning on a heel and jogging towards the entrance of the temple. "Solomon! Get your wrinkly ass up! We've got work to do and a feast to plan!"

I sighed, shaking my head at his unbridled joy.

Then I pulled out my phone and called Ryuu. The phone continued to ring and I started tapping my foot nervously. Why wasn't he answering? Maybe they had followed Legion and actually found one of the Sins. What if they were hiding and couldn't make a noise for fear of being detected? I hung up quickly, not wanting to cause their capture. Instead, I closed my eyes and focused on my connection to Xylo, searching for his location. I hadn't tried it from this great of a distance before. I wasn't even sure it would work.

Silence answered me. I frowned, nervously. What if...they had been caught?

I shook my head clear of the thought, focusing harder on our Blood Bond. I felt sweat pop out on my forehead and my lips and fingers begin to tingle. I extended my silver claws and pricked the tip of my finger, hoping fresh blood might strengthen the connection. I touched the drop of blood to my forehead, focusing on the bone beneath my flesh and imagining it physically connected to Xylo. I felt Sanguina in the Keep at Castle Dracula, but I muted her presence, focusing harder on Xylo as I imagined that the fresh blood on my finger was a third eye. I called up a mental map of Kansas City, searching for an echo of my magical phone call.

I saw a faint blip near a familiar spot and I frowned. I let out a breath, opening my eyes. I spotted a pile of folded towels on a nearby wicker table. They were placed there because continuing down that area of the balcony would eventually take you to a set of stairs that opened up on the numerous pools of Solomon's Temple. I snatched up one of the towels and wiped the sweat and blood off my forehead as I retracted my claws.

Then I Shadow Walked to Abundant Angel Catholic Church, wondering what the hell Xylo was doing there with Lucky and Ryuu. Had Legion led them there?

29

I appeared in the alley behind the church, my hand on the hilt of my katana, wary of an ambush. The gloomy alley was silent. I frowned, spinning in a slow circle. I could see nothing concerning. Maybe they were inside. The sky was still dark, cloudy, and overcast, so there was a good chance Roland was still in Kansas City. I intended to have a long talk with him about gossiping with his pal, Fabrizio, about my personal love life, and a stern reminder that vampires would die if he didn't get his ass in gear and start rounding up the Sanguine Council. The Nephilim had supposedly killed two, but I hadn't heard of any demon attacks on my allies yet—just on me and Fabrizio.

I kept my eyes moving, scanning my surroundings for any sign of danger, even using my boots to try and identify any demonic presence like I'd encountered earlier with Fabrizio. Nothing. With a weary sigh, I made my way to the parking lot around the corner, thinking I might be able to sneak inside without encountering bulldog Greta. In my current mood, I was open to the idea of murder. Maybe I would even taunt her about a fictional conversation I'd just had with her grandson, Yahn.

Pettiness, thy name is Callie Penrose.

As I smiled at my cruelty, I swept my eyes over the parking lot, not picking up any damage or signs of attack. No sulfur in the air and no bloodstains. I frowned, growing uneasy as I turned to approach the church's back door.

I froze as my eyes settled on the black katana embedded in the wood. My heart skipped a beat and my knuckles creaked as I squeezed the hilt of my sword.

Ryuu's Angel Killer. I watched a drop of blood fall to the steps and I felt my fangs pop out as raw fury swept over me like a wildfire. The sword pinned a small piece of paper to the door. I bolted up the steps, grabbed the paper and yanked the Angel Killer out of the wood, feeling like my heart was about to explode it was beating so fast.

I shuddered, sucking in short breaths as I tried to unfold the paper. My hands were shaking so violently that I almost dropped the note, especially when I saw a drop of blood on it. Acting without thinking, I lifted the paper to my nose and inhaled. I immediately grew dizzy at the vintage bouquet of centuries of existence contained in that single drop of blood and I knew, with absolute certainty, that it belonged to Ryuu. I could taste him in the air. The hundreds of years of war, the thousands of victims to this blade, and the very essence of the man himself all resided in that single drop of blood. It was almost like I had gained a greater understanding of the man, his principles, his philosophies, his passions, his vices and his virtues, in that single sniff. It was dizzying and I almost felt drunk at the influx of awareness.

My life forever changed in that moment—both in my perception of myself, and the realization of how I truly felt for the shinobi Halo Breaker. It was almost as if I had watched childhood videos of little Ryuu—but dating back more than one thousand years. I knew him better than I had minutes ago. Smelling his blood, and the hundreds of answers I gained from it, had altered the course of my future.

"You're a vampire, Callie," I whispered, the paper trembling in my hands.

There was no more lying to myself, pretending nothing about me had changed, or pretending I was different than my predecessors and my followers. I was Count Dracula—the greatest vampire in the world.

My fangs, my erratic and unpredictable ability to measure heartbeats, and now my insane sense of smell. I might be very different from those in the Sanguine Council and the fledgling Nephilim vampires, but I was also the same.

Some parts of me were now more similar to a vampire than a human. I still had no desire to drink blood—from any type of being—but I was eerily aware of the numerous dimensions of blood, something I had never before considered. The scent of Ryuu's blood had taken me back in time, sending me images of him in hundreds of different battles in hundreds of different locations against all different types of men, monsters, and even angels.

Blood was life. Blood was death. Blood was vengeance. Blood was *all*. With the scent of Ryuu's blood filling my nostrils, I knew that there was absolutely nothing I wouldn't do to get him back. Nothing was off limits.

With that determination firmly embedded in my mind, I read the words on the page, feeling my blood grow cold and my soul shrugging off any sense of morality.

Tell a single soul and he dies. Meet me at noon on Chateau Falco's front lawn if you want to see him alive again. —Peter.

I lowered the paper, staring into the middle distance as I clenched my jaw and gripped the hilt of Ryuu's katana, imagining that I could sense his calm lethality flowing into me. I licked the tips of my fangs with my tongue, drawing and tasting my own blood. It hit me like a jolt of electricity or an energy drink. Peter was the name of one of the saints, so did that mean the Nephilim had taken Ryuu? That seemed highly unlikely, given Ryuu's skills— almost like saying a gang of toddlers had jumped a professional boxer. And if it was the Nephilim, why had they left his legendary sword? The weapon most capable of killing an Archangel would be a prize beyond comparison. And why meet at Chateau Falco? Was that a warning that the Nephilim and angels were going after Nate's people? I almost pitied them for such a foolish tactic.

No. This couldn't be Heaven. The fact that the note referenced Chateau Falco made me pause. Hadn't Nate mentioned a man named Peter from St. Louis? An enemy of his. "You've got to be kidding me," I snarled. "Another person to worry about in addition to the shitnado already tearing through Kansas City?" I muttered under my breath. I swept my gaze over the stairs and parking lot, spinning in a slow circle to look for any additional clues or evidence. Where were Lucky and Xylo—

I gasped, noticing Xylo curled up on the ground, tucked against the wall behind two trash cans, and not wearing any disguise whatsoever. An aged ivory and silver infused skeleton, wearing his crimson cowl and a pair of...

Air Jordans? What the hell? When had Cain taken him to get those?

The embers and sparks connecting his bones still flickered, but very weakly as if they were fading.

"Xylo!" I whispered, terrified as I leapt over the stair railing.

🦁 30 🦁

I assumed he was relatively unharmed. But anyone could have stumbled across him and they would have freaked the fuck out to see an obviously long-dead skeleton outside a church. He was supposed to be disguised from detection when out in public—wearing a long coat and hat, at least. I leapt off the stairs and knelt over him, scanning him for injuries. Xylo couldn't be killed as far as I knew, but I'd also thought he couldn't sleep. He didn't need food or any of the other essentials mortals required, so why was he unconscious—as if he'd gotten his ass kicked? I didn't see any wounds.

"Xylo," I hissed, shaking his shoulder.

I felt our connection flare to the forefront of my thoughts the moment I touched him. He woke up with a dry gasp and a flare of embers and sparks that made me recoil, lifting my hand up to shield my face. "Callie!" he hissed, jerking his smokey, hollow-eyed gaze in every direction as if fearing an ambush. "Where's my cowboy hat? My trench coat is gone, too!" he snarled, rapping his finger bones against his head. "I'm naked!"

I place a hand on his sternum. "Easy, Xylo. Speak softly and we should be safe. No one else is here. What happened?"

He sat up, nodding uneasily. "Where is the teddy bear?"

I stared at him. "Teddy bear?"

He nodded, seeming to relax a hair upon noticing we weren't under assault. "That's the last thing I remember," he said. "Did Ryuu catch him?"

"Catch *who*, Xylo? You're the only one here," I said, forcing myself not to throttle him. "And this," I whispered, showing him the note and Ryuu's deadly katana.

Xylo froze, staring at it. "Oh, no. I have failed you," he moaned, clasping his finger bones over his mandible.

I glanced over my shoulder, verifying we were still alone. "Tell me what happened, Xylo. Where is Lucky?"

Xylo nodded, lowering his hand. "Lucky left about ten minutes into our search, telling us he was hungry. He disappeared before Ryuu even had a chance to say no—"

I sputtered incredulously. "Hungry?" I hissed. "He's the most wanted man in town, even if no one can recognize him!" I growled.

Xylo nodded. "Ryuu and I continued on, trailing Legion to Dorian Gray's house. There was a party inside, so we couldn't sneak in. He didn't stay there long, and we followed him here to this place," he said, glancing up at the church. "The parking lot was empty and I heard a boot scuff the gravel over there," he said, pointing to a spot a few feet away. "I turned around and saw a stuffed teddy bear flying at my face. I caught it on instinct. Then, nothing. I fell asleep," he murmured, obviously ashamed.

I frowned in disbelief. "A stuffed animal? You didn't see who threw it?" I demanded in a low growl. Who the hell made enchanted teddy bears that could knock you out on contact? That was fucked up beyond all belief.

Xylo shook his head, miserably. "I didn't see."

I gritted my teeth, debating what to do. I had an hour before I needed to be at Chateau Falco to supposedly get Ryuu back alive, but they had tracked Legion here. "Did Legion go inside?" I whispered, eyeing the church to make sure we couldn't be seen from a window.

Xylo shook his head. "We didn't see him go inside. Ryuu was checking the parking lot to see if Legion had simply walked through it. That's when I got hit by the stuffed animal. I didn't sense anyone at all, so whoever attacked was exceedingly powerful."

Had Legion noticed their pursuit and led them into a trap? Xylo wasn't necessarily conspicuous, not with a trench coat and a cowboy hat. Especially if they'd been following him long enough to go to Dorian Gray's house and then back across town to the church.

I frowned up at the building, thinking. It was highly unlikely that a Sin had taken up residence here. They'd take one look at Greta and abandon their cause. Also, Fabrizio lived here, and he knew all about the Sins. I knew they could go about their day undetected, shifting, which meant that they could look like anyone. But I'd also seen Fabrizio's ward, and that thing would have booted even an Archdemon on his ass or at least tear away his disguise. It hadn't even let me inside.

I frowned at a sudden thought. Had the defensive rune kicked my ass because I was a vampire? It hadn't affected Greta, even though it had sent me tumbling down the stairs. And Fabrizio had given me a strange look upon realizing I'd triggered it. Yet he hadn't mentioned it after the fact, which was strange.

Which meant that, without Fabrizio, there was no chance I could get inside now, even if I saw Legion doing the dab at me through the window. Which left me only one choice.

I turned to Xylo. "I need you to go to Castle Dracula and help Roland. He's transporting the vampires from the Sanguine Council there, and he will need your logistical help in finding them all places to sleep and food to eat."

Xylo gave me a crestfallen look, eyeing Ryuu's sword. "I failed you," he said, obviously seeing my order as a punishment.

I shook my head. "If they managed to overpower Ryuu, I don't think there was anything you could have done to stop it. I can't have you walking around town without a disguise, and I need someone I trust to keep an eye on Castle Dracula," I said, meaningfully. He knew all about the likelihood of Archangels and Archdemons infiltrating the place.

He nodded. I didn't dare drag things out, so I made a Gateway right in front of him. "Go. I'll be back soon, and I'll want an update on the vampires. Keep your eyeholes open," I said with a cold smile. "Some of our guests might very well be Sins in disguise."

He tugged his hood up and the smoke in his eyes grew black as night. "The Bone Heir King will rise to the challenge, standing firm against the forces of Hell," he vowed.

I didn't have the heart to prick his bubble with a discussion about phrasing, so I gave him a solemn nod. "Thank you, Xylo. Observe, but don't engage. We can't let them know we know. I'll find you after I save Ryuu."

He nodded and then leapt through the Gateway to Castle Dracula. I closed it behind him and rose to my feet, gripping Ryuu's katana in one hand

and the note in the other. I stared down at the paper, my vision turning crimson at the edges as rage consumed me. "You will wish you had never been born, Peter," I promised, licking my silver fangs. "I will eat your heart for daring to take mine," I growled, imagining Ryuu in shackles and beaten to a pulp in some cold, wet, danky cell. Ryuu was not the type of man to obey his jailers or cooperate with their interrogations, which meant his torture would come sooner rather than later. I realized I was panting wildly, so I closed my eyes and took a calming breath. I slipped the Angel Killer over my shoulder, feeling the power of Aphrodite's suit grip it like a magnet.

I closed my eyes, focusing on nothing but a slowly rotating chrome feather in a dark void, forcing myself to think clearly over my fury. Peter. I was certain Nate had mentioned the name before, but I had heard it more recently than that. I focused on my breathing, using counts of five to inhale, hold, and then exhale as I let my mind wander, simmering over the situation. Less than a minute later, I opened my eyes with a grunt.

When Gunnar had woken me up this morning with his phone call, he'd mentioned something about Grimm Tech being broken into during the night. By two men, Peter and Alaric. I'd been groggy from sleep and then thrown off balance by the fact that Hermes had spoken with Gunnar and Alucard about Nate's mysteriously dubious, likely fraudulent, travel itinerary on Olympian Airlines.

And then Aphrodite had dropped by the park to warn me about events swirling around Nate. Were our two worlds colliding as a result of this man, Peter? Was he a pawn for Zeus' schemes? Was this what Aphrodite had been trying to tell me? The pre-war to end the Omega War? If so, there was no room for half measures. Whatever reason Peter had for taking Ryuu, the only acceptable response was blood, fire, and brimstone. The Horseman of Despair would ride through the streets of St. Louis, leaving death and destruction in her wake until she found her shinobi warrior, the Halo Breaker.

If Olympus had to fall as a result...

So. Be. It.

I pulled out my phone and made a call. "Gunnar," I growled by way of greeting. "We need to have a chat."

"I was just about to call you," he said, sounding suspicious and wary.

"Funny, I was just about to head to St. Louis. You mentioned a break-in at Grimm Tech this morning," I said. "A man named Peter, right?"

The other end of the line was silent for a few moments, as if Gunnar was considering his words very carefully. "Yes. What about it?" Gunnar asked.

"One of my ninjas disappeared, and I found a suicide note from a man named Peter," I said, ignoring the message's warning not to tell anyone.

"Suicide note?" Gunnar asked, sounding confused.

I nodded. "By writing the note, Peter was committing suicide. He signed his own death warrant. It was a cry for help and I always help those in need."

The alpha werewolf of St. Louis growled his agreement. "Give me details. What happened—"

"None of that *matters*, Gunnar," I interrupted in a firm tone. "I am not in the mood for talking. I am in the mood for retribution. Tell Alucard to get his ass in gear because I'm coming to St. Louis. The Horsemen are going to play today."

"I thought you were busy with a war?" Gunnar asked in a growl that sounded more eager than taunting.

"For this, I'll make an exception," I said in a cold tone. "My war here can wait a few hours. I've already killed a demon and mortally wounded an angel and two Nephilim this morning, so they'll be distracted for a little while. Long enough for me to visit my second favorite city before I destroy it."

Gunnar coughed on the other end. "Wait. What—"

"See you soon, Horseman of Justice." I hung up.

This motherfucking Peter guy had chosen the worst possible time to mess with me.

Ryuu was off limits. *Period.*

I ripped open a Gateway to St. Louis and stepped onto the lawns of Chateau Falco, Nate Temple's ancestral mansion, situated in a walled enclosure that was large enough to probably justify its own zip code. It had been in his family for so many years that the actual number was no longer relevant. It was revered by any who had the fortune to set foot on the grass. A rite of passage for those who valued all things pretentious and vintage, and given even greater respect for the fact that it was decidedly impregnable after so many centuries.

It. Was. Still. Here.

And would, apparently, always be here. It was not accurate to say that Chateau Falco was located in St. Louis.

It was more accurate to say that Chateau Falco and the Temple clan had leased out a significant chunk of their unused land holdings to St. Louis as an act of charity.

The mansion was three stories of gothic architecture mixed with an English lord's summer palace, encompassing close to twenty-thousand square feet of extravagant interior that included a solarium, libraries, dining halls, banquet rooms, gyms, studies, and secret inter-dimensional libratories ——a combination of an alchemist's laboratory and a wizard's magical library. The grounds consisted of flowing hills, lush, meticulous greenery and flower gardens, a pond with a cute little bridge, a labyrinth, a forest, an impossibly tall, otherworldly glowing white tree, and—

It was excessive, over the top—impossibly beautiful and indelibly decadent—and it would make any Christie's magazine decide not to feature any new homes out of shame. Whatever dreamy European estate you could imagine...Chateau Falco was better.

And that was the point. Kind of like the Temple clan itself. Generations heralding back to before America was even founded had lived here. Before that, the Temples had likely ruled Europe in a similar, or even more, ostentatious manner. I knew for a fact that the Temple family tree had featured many more branches back then, so they probably owned multiple estates just like this one.

Now, Nate and Chateau Falco were the last of the Temples.

Chateau Falco counted as a Temple because the mansion housed a Beast named Falco, very similar to how Castle Dracula was powered by Sanguina.

I took a deep breath of the heady, floral air and sought out the prettiest flower garden I could find. Birds chirped in the trees, accompanied by the warbling chatter of squirrels, chipmunks, or some other endearing rodent that God had disguised with an extra dose of cute fluffiness back in his old, rambunctious Genesis days. You know, right after he'd figured out how to flick on the universe's first light switch, and then produce and direct his very own reality TV show, titled Naked and Afraid, starring two oblivious humans named Adam and Eve after they'd been thrown into a jungle.

I smiled down at the kaleidoscope of flowers, admiring their innocence as I gathered my thoughts.

Ryuu. Peter. Ryuu. Peter.

I torched the flower garden with fire so hot that they had to have seen the twenty-foot tall inferno from the mansion. Within seconds, only scorched dirt and rock remained of the pristine landscaping. Birds squawked in terror, and all squirrel chatter ceased. I looked up, ready and waiting for an alarm to go off or a dozen werewolves to attack me.

Instead, I was immediately blindsided by a tackle that was so abrupt and violent that it knocked the wind out of me and yanked me completely off my feet. In fact, I had apparently been banished from the Earthly realm through an invisible Gateway because the splendor of Chateau Falco winked out of existence, replaced by a world of blinding blue light. I didn't even have time to shout before I was forced to slam my eyelids shut to protect my corneas from imploding.

God must have heard my cynical thoughts.

I struck the ground and...

I bounced. Confused, I squinted my eyes open right before I hit another patch of spongy ground, only to feel even more confused. It was a cloud. I gasped in alarm as I finally came to a gentle stop, but I struggled to catch my breath due to the air being thinner at this elevation. What the hell was I doing up in the damned sky? Had Phix kidnapped me?

I lifted my head to see a stranger seated on a throne made of clouds. "Don't shoot the messenger...god," the handsome man said, flashing me a playful wink and a debonaire grin of perfectly straight, white teeth. His eyes were the color of melting gold and he wore a stark white toga.

I scowled, rising to my feet and clenching my fists. I recognized that voice, but the toga would have been enough to name him true. His ankles sported shining tattoos of golden wings. I stared as the tips of the wings peeled away from his flesh like gold leaf foil, coming to life in a rhythmic flapping motion that sounded like a dagger's whisper in a dark hallway in the middle of the night. "Hermes," I muttered with as much disrespect as I could manage.

He nodded, pompously. "You didn't come to my meeting with the other two Horsemen about Nate Temple."

"I was binge-watching Buffy while eating a pint of Häagen-Dazs with my fingers. I like to pretend one of my hands belongs to Spike and the other to Angel, both of them taking turns feeding me," I said in a flat tone.

He pursed his lips, unimpressed. "What were you doing at Chateau Falco?"

I folded my arms. "What were *you* doing at Chateau Falco?"

His shoulders hitched up defensively and I realized I had struck a very sore spot. "Guarding the place, obviously. Now, here is what you're going to do—"

"Where is Nate?" I asked, interrupting him. Whatever was bothering him, Aphrodite's warning was playing on repeat in my mind. Hermes was involved. Somehow.

He narrowed his eyes dangerously. "He is off on a side quest, as far as I know. Any other stupid questions, or are you ready to listen?"

I thought about it for a few seconds, glancing left and right at the clouds.

"What kind of cloud is this?" I asked, absently. I'd never paid much attention in whatever class had categorized such things.

He frowned, glancing down at the clouds with a frustrated look. "How the fuck should I know what kind of goddamned clouds these are? Do I look like the god of goddamned clouds?" he demanded, flustered and agitated.

I nodded, pensively. *Time to press the attack*, I thought to myself. "Exactly. I mean, what kind of idiot would abduct me and bring me into a realm he didn't control? A realm where one of his fellow Olympians might hold greater sway and be able to overhear."

His golden eyes flashed, actually seeming to glint. But there was a very real sense of fear buried under all that anger, despite him doing his best to hide it. He hadn't considered the risk I'd brought up—which was incredibly stupid of him, all things considered. Aphrodite had made a similar mistake. Were the gods really so alarmingly aloof? Had they been elite for so long that they had lost their survival instincts?

"I'm not here to discuss secrets," Hermes growled, aggressively. "I'm here to tell you—"

"Oh, but I have plenty of secrets, HERMES!" I shouted, cupping my hands around my mouth to let his name carry far and wide through the skies. "SECRETS THAT OTHER OLYMPIANS MIGHT WANT TO KNOW!" There wasn't an echo, obviously, but my voice rang out like a bell, making Hermes twitchy.

"You're bluffing," he said, sounding as if he was trying to convince himself. "I am the god of commerce, so I know how to spot a woman who is overselling her wares," he said, with hollow confidence.

"You sure about that, Hermes?" I asked, softly.

He hesitated for a moment, and then nodded stiffly to try and make up for it. "We have never crossed paths, but your story is well-known to my fellow Olympians. I don't know why any of your secrets would be of any special significance to me, specifically," he said, licking his lips warily.

I grinned. "Exactly what I thought. Now I know everything I need to know about you, bud."

He blinked, narrowing his eyes. He opened his mouth and then hesitated, replaying our conversation in his head to make sure he hadn't missed something. Then he surprised me by closing his eyes and taking a long, measured breath.

I didn't trust it one bit, readying myself for round two. But when he opened his eyes, the way he looked at me almost made me feel like...he was an entirely different person than a moment ago. A flash of light at his side revealed a tall, ridiculously ornate golden scepter. Two huge, serpent-like dragons spiraled around the staff from base to tip, and their dragon wings flared out at the peak in four different directions at seemingly perfect ninety-degree angles. The wings looked sharp and sturdy despite their decorative beauty, so the weapon looked more like a four-directional scythe. The danger was hidden beneath the ergonomic beauty. I narrowed my eyes, realizing the dragons looked eerily similar to Qinglong. The Caduceus didn't have serpents around it; the legendary staff glorified the carcasses of Asian dragons.

His face had drastically changed into a blank, appraising mask, and I realized that he was studying me in such a clinical manner that it instantly made me feel...icky. It wasn't so much that he looked like a psychopath or anything, but that he had so efficiently categorized every single element of me and my life in those few seconds that I felt like I'd caught a stranger watching my childhood dance recital tapes. Ones that even I hadn't ever seen. It was an all knowing...well, godly look. His face was entirely blank, processing what he'd seen in me, but his eyes were calculating and feral, wild and primal.

Not violent, just hyper-natural. The lion didn't hate the antelope. But he would eviscerate it all the same.

I suppressed a shudder that threatened to make my knees buckle. *Keep the resting bitch face in place, girl*, I told myself with more confidence than I felt. *It's all you've got. Olympian Psycho just saw your business card and you used a better font and texture than his.*

"What could you have *possibly* learned about me from our conversation so far?" he finally asked in a cold, derisive tone.

I chuckled. "Your reaction was one of fear, thinly veiled by hubris and pomposity. Those things don't work on me, by the way," I suggested in a stage whisper. "I'm not trying to blackmail or extort you. I'm telling you that I have valuable information, but you are so paranoid that you instantly assumed—and partially believed—that I might have some dirt on you. If you were confident and in control of whatever shit show you're running with my friends by telling them you're working with Nate, you would have plopped your ass down at the negotiating table and started haggling with me about how much my secrets might be worth. You, the god of commerce, just missed out on a deal because you are paranoid and afraid." He had frozen completely still and was staring at me with a shocked look on his face. "This is the part of the negotiation where you deny my assertion and make a lowball counteroffer. Something disrespectful to make me angry and desperate—"

"I know how a fucking negotiation works!" he sputtered, outraged as he thumped the ornate staff into the cloud at his feet. Then he closed his eyes and took another calming breath. "I am not confident that you have any valuable information, but I am impressed with your ability to infuriate a man for no other reason than to feel a little more important about yourself."

I winced, shaking my head. "That...was not a good negotiation tactic. You know, I really thought you'd be better at this."

He gritted his teeth and curled his lip up in a snarl. "We. Are. Not. Negotiating!" He hissed. "I am here to tell—"

"I KNOW THE OMEGABET AND I AM A MEMBER OF THE MASTERS—"

He lunged for me with the Caduceus, snarling, his face a rictus of panicked rage.

32

But I'd been waiting for it, purposely antagonizing him into this exact scenario. I side-stepped, called up my Silver claws to bat aside his golden scepter, and then I stomp-kicked him in the ankle wing —*hard*. I hammer-fisted the back of his neck—not wanting to actually stab him with my claws—as he tripped and stumbled past me. The unanticipated, powerful blow sent him slamming face-first into the cloud.

And then he sunk *through* the clouds, disappearing below.

I drew my katana, leaving Ryuu's over my shoulder. I began to laugh, huskily, spinning in a slow circle. "Marco!" I hooted, relying on the reflex instincts Ryuu had bludgeoned into me in the event Hermes tried to blind-side me again. "Come on! You're supposed to say Polo!" I explained.

Hermes slowly rose up through the clouds, studying me from a safe distance with a thoughtful frown. His hovering skills were clunky and inconsistent because the ankle wing I'd kicked hung limp like a wet dishrag. "Polo," he said in a dull, lifeless tone.

I smiled. "There it is." I kept my sword between us. "Now, are we ready to have a reasonable talk or are you going to continue trying to godranize me?"

"Godranize?" he asked, furrowing his brow as he slowly settled his feet back onto the cloud.

I nodded. "It's like patronizing, but...godlier."

He studied me, curiously, and I could have sworn he was fighting back a grin. "Ah. I call it godsplaining." He flashed me a roguish smile. "It's like mansplaining but, you know." He winked, holding a hand out as if to emphasize his awesomeness.

I smiled back, nodding. "That one is better," I admitted. Then I regarded the Caduceus in his other fist. "Lose the stick and I'll put my sword and claws away."

His eyes tightened ever so slightly. "The Caduceus is not a stick. It is a powerful magic wand."

"Then *expelliarmus*, Hermione." He stared at me, obliquely, not catching the reference but knowing it had been rude. After a few moments, the staff winked out of existence and he spread his hands to show he was unarmed. "Truce?" I asked him.

He nodded, but he swept his mercurial gaze over the clouds as if making sure we were still private. "Truce. My ward should prevent any eavesdropping, but only for a short while. A very short while. Straining it with certain...topics and phrases," he said, meaningfully, referring to my Masters and Omegabet shouts, "is not advisable. For either of us. Had I anticipated this lengthier conversation; I would have put it in place before you opened your mouth."

I nodded, sheathing my sword on my back and retracting my claws. "Then maybe you should have started negotiating sooner."

He grunted, shaking his head. "Perhaps," he admitted. Then he let out a deep breath and a throne of clouds rose up behind him. "You are much more perceptive, and infuriating, than I imagined you would be," he said, smiling to show me that he meant it as a compliment. Between one second and the next, his white toga evaporated and he was wearing pale blue, almost white jeans, and a deep V-neck tee that showed off surprisingly well-sculpted pecs. He sat down, reaching down to massage his ankle where his injured tattoo wing was tucked back against his skin.

"Make me one of those thrones, FedEx guy," I said, frowning at the lack of additional seating. He belted out a surprised laugh and then waved his hand. A cushy cloud rose up behind me and I noticed that the seat was perfectly sculpted for my specific tushy. I shot him a suspicious glare and he grinned wolfishly, leaning forward. "Someone else is very perceptive as well," I scolded.

He shrugged, unashamedly. "Ya got me."

I sat down and crossed my legs, and the two of us started an elementary school staring contest. "Do angels hang out up here?" I asked, glancing out at the blue skies.

He thought about it for a few seconds. "I would imagine so. Why?"

I swept my gaze in a three-sixty, verifying we were alone. "They're actively trying to kill me, so we both have need to make this conversation brief." I settled my eyes back on him to see a troubled look flicker across his face. "How's your ankle?"

He grunted, checking the skies uneasily. "It's fine," he grumbled. "So, what was the point of your little show? Did you think that since my sweet sister made you some clothes that you could bully other Olympians with impunity?"

I shook my head, caressing the fabric of my thigh with a smile. "They're really fucking nice, right?" I asked him. "I was a ten before, but these things make me a twelve, easily."

He rubbed his chin, assessing me with a wry smile. "Maybe a seven. Eight, tops." I scowled and he leaned forward with a triumphant smirk. "Taste the hubris," he whispered, drawing out the *S* like the Skittles slogan.

My scowl cracked and I burst out laughing. "Okay. I'm finished. You?" He nodded, leaning back in his throne with some of his recaptured dignity. "The Nate working for the Olympians story doesn't pass the smell test," I said with a shrug. "Your media team—which is you, messenger god—tried to sell a fact-checker's wet dream."

He frowned, clutching at his chest in mock pain. "Hypothetically," he began, his face telling me that he wasn't being hypothetical at all but rather covering his ass for the benefit of his eavesdropping ward's endurance for sensitive topics. "Perhaps it was *precisely* the message I wanted spread. One might say I was disappointed to see that the audience members were too stupid to catch onto it." His gaze bore directly into mine and I felt my fangs instinctively pop out at the severity of the unspoken menace in those Olympian eyes. "Until now."

I focused on keeping my fangs out of sight as I nodded, thoughtfully. "You wanted everyone to call bullshit, but no one did. What's my prize?"

"Respect."

I pursed my lips in displeasure, considering his words. After a few moments, I felt my fangs retract. Why send a message you wanted others to debunk? He wanted something but had been unable to openly state it. "What's your angle?"

"Hmmm. I was just being a dutiful son, doing as commanded. One must never disobey a parent, after all."

I studied him, analyzing his choice of words. If I was to believe the Olympian—which Aphrodite had encouraged me not to do—then the story was summed up in simple terms. Hermes had been told to give Nate's allies a bullshit story about his whereabouts. Hermes had crafted the story in such a way as to be easily debunked, but the Horsemen debunking committee was run by optimists like Gunnar and Alucard. Until the cynic from Kansas City arrived at Chateau Falco, in which case Hermes had immediately and secretly kidnapped her to try bullying her into another command.

And if he'd been waiting for someone to see through his bullshit story, waiting to abduct them to a secluded area, then he likely had some important information to relay to that person.

The question that I wanted to know was whether the command Hermes had tried giving me a few minutes ago was another load of crap or not. If Hermes meant Nate harm, he wouldn't have wasted the energy for these schemes. Which Olympian parent was calling the shots here? Zeus or Hera? And why were Aphrodite and Hermes playing games rather than collaborating. She had told me that Nate's execution was scheduled for tonight, and that it would disrupt the Omega War. Was the messenger god trying to expedite that—heh—or delay it?

It hit me like a lightning bolt—which was a terrible metaphor after considering Zeus as the big bad.

Hermes was being watched, and much more closely than Aphrodite. Chateau Falco was likely also under surveillance.

I focused back on Hermes, thinking furiously. "Well, I am awfully busy with fighting angels and demons and Nephilim. I only came to Chateau Falco to express my displeasure and report a package that was stolen from my doorstep. Maybe you should give me that command you started to say a few minutes ago. That way I can get around to utterly disregarding it and back to focusing on more important things," I said, shaking my head *no* to contradict my words. "Like my missing package."

He grinned and then winked. "Right. I'm sorry to hear about your shipping dilemma. If there is anything I can do to resolve it, I will. Most of these delivery men mean well, but there is always a bad apple who ruins it for the others. Now, as to my problem, I am merely executing the orders I was given. I would encourage you to respect Nate's professional wishes—as his colleague, of course. I imagine he is merely doing what he believes best, and your unconditional support would be the most helpful thing you could provide him until he is finished. Tonight. After that, none of this will matter."

I swallowed, trying to pick apart his words and read the multiple layers of subliminal messaging. There were so many freaking ways to interpret it, which was the entire point. Was he telling me to stand true to Nate's typical stance—destroy absolutely everything in his way? To do as a fellow colleague —a Horseman—would do? Or was Hermes telling me to stand back and that Nate had it all under control, but to be ready to swoop in as backup? Either way, he'd basically admitted that Nate was scheming, doing what he believed best. But...what did that mean, exactly?

And that Hermes was executing orders before Nate finished his job tonight, which sounded suspiciously like Aphrodite's warning that Nate would be executed tonight. Hermes was trying to warn me or let me know he was working with Aphrodite. But...could I trust him? What if he was lying to make it look like he was on Aphrodite's side?

"Cool," I said, knowing that Hermes was unable to say one word more, judging by the intense, desperate look in his eyes. "Well, I still need to file that missing package report, so how about we head back?"

He nodded, rising to his feet. I did the same. "It was a pleasure meeting you, Callie Penrose. It would be a shame if we ever stood across the field of war from each other. Friends make the strongest foes."

I studied the severely calm look on his face. "And foes make the strongest friends."

He dipped his chin. "Anything else before we leave?"

I thought about it for a few moments and then nodded. "I want ten percent of Asterion and King Midas' entire Fight Club operation after you rubber-stamp my contract for the Kansas City branch partnership," I said, thinking about the Coliseum at Castle Dracula. "As a boon for being more perceptive than my siblings," I explained, referring to his crap story about Nate working for the Olympians and me being the wisest Horseman.

Hermes burst out laughing, slapping his knees. "Wow. Done," he said, shaking his head and chuckling. "That is actually quite impressive. And have you already discussed these terms with Midas and the Minotaur for Kansas City?" he asked, wiping at his eyes and grinning.

I smiled back, sweetly. "Nope. But you just did when you agreed to rubber-stamp it."

His laughter abruptly cut off and his eyes widened. He stared at me for about five seconds, not moving a muscle. Then he began to slow clap. I curtsied, dramatically. "How did you know I held sway over the Fight Club?" he asked, curiously.

"The Minotaur has mentioned it a few times, and Nate told me about your coin."

His eyes zeroed in on me like a raptor and I could have sworn he stopped breathing for a moment. I frowned, wondering what I had said. "My coin," he repeated flatly. "Yes. I see, now. I give coins as a token of my favor. To remember to always have hope, even when things seem most dark. I've given him a few over the years," he said, carefully. Then his serious demeanor faded and he appraised me with an admiring nod. "You truly are a devil, Callie Penrose."

"That's what they keep saying," I admitted. But inside, I was thinking about coins, wondering what the hell was so important about them. He'd said to always have hope, and Nate was the Horseman of Hope. Had he given Nate another magic coin without his parents knowing? "How about that ride?"

"You bet."

And that's when Hermes punched me in the face. "Expelliarm this!"

33

I flew backwards as my fangs burst free and I tasted blood in my mouth and nose. I flew through a hazy distortion in the air and the scene abruptly changed, casting me into a dim, gloomy interior of an old house. I landed on my ass on a hard surface, and then slid backwards until I slammed into an even harder wall, judging by the cracking sound my head made upon contact.

My vision spun wildly, and I groaned, slapping my palms down to support my weight. I blinked blearily, trying to understand where I was. I saw the same hazy distortion in the air, almost like the heat waves that rose up from broiling highway roads in the height of summer. "Had to make it look authentic, Horseman," Hermes said, his voice drifting to me through the haze despite the fact that I couldn't see him. "And I really wanted to do that," he added with a dark chuckle.

I vowed to myself that I would punch Hermes in the face one day.

The haze evaporated and I took stock of my surroundings, muttering under my breath in dark curses regarding the messenger god. I faced an old glass cabinet full of antique figurines and dusty books. I was in a wide hallway with marble pillars and a polished marble floor. Extravagant paintings hung from the walls, about a few hundred years out of date. Family portraits and landscapes and battles. Each painting was illuminated by a dim yellow light hanging above the frame. Was I in a museum?

The wall vibrated behind me strongly enough to make my teeth rattle. "Not a museum!" I squeaked, lurching to my feet and instinctively grabbing my ass. I almost fumbled Ryuu's katana to the ground in my attempt to draw it. I held it out before me, jerking from left to right, fearing Hermes had suckered me into a one-way ticket to Mount Olympus or something. I was all alone. I used my free hand to wipe the blood from my nose and lip before spitting a bloody glob onto the rich wooden floor. As hard as Hermes had hit me, there was very little blood to be found and it didn't hurt as bad as it should have. Horseman or vampire perk? I shook off the thought, not particularly caring. I froze as my eyes settled on a particular painting of a handsome man in a suit. His tie was undone, his blondish brown hair was unruly, and he had a mischievous smirk that promised trouble and dared a challenge.

It was Nate. "You really *did* have dirty blonde hair," I mused out loud, smiling to myself. He'd always claimed it as his hair color, but I'd never seen proof. He stood in front of Plato's Cave—Nate's arcane bookstore—but it looked different and more run down. Since Nate was dangling a pair of keys from a finger, I assumed it was the day he'd purchased the place before he'd made any renovations.

A tall, muscular, bearded man stood at his side, draping a massive arm around Nate's shoulder in a way that screamed, *I'm an alibi.* I grinned, lowering my sword. "Gunnar," I whispered. "You both look so damned *young.*"

I sheathed Ryuu's katana on Aphrodite's magnetic-like suit and sighed, realizing where I was. Chateau Falco. Hermes had sent me inside but with a security guard reprimand of a busted lip so that his own watchers wouldn't think anything particularly suspicious about it. I wondered how long our truce would last and what his cryptic comments had actually meant.

Because every single thing he'd said could mean two completely different things. The fact that he'd focused so hard to say anything at all to me, while making sure he didn't incriminate himself, was actually proof, in my eyes, that he was trying to encourage me. Which meant he was actually trying to help me. If he were against Nate and me, he wouldn't have bothered saying anything. He had used entirely too many significant words that echoed Aphrodite's concern for it to be anything but a warning.

Yet despite my concern for Nate, I knew I couldn't act on it. Olympians of some flavor were watching Chateau Falco, Hermes, and likely everyone here—primarily Gunnar and Alucard. I couldn't do or say anything to disrupt that facade or I would attract the wrong kind of attention and possibly endanger Nate. I needed to act like my encounter with Hermes was nothing more than him threatening me to stay in my lane.

But my mind was my own, and it continued to theorize and analyze the spider's web of possibilities triggered by Aphrodite and Hermes' frantic interferences.

Even though I didn't know what quest Nate was on, I knew the man himself. In any given situation, he was always angling for a Plan B because he had more trust issues than anyone I had ever met—deservedly so. I couldn't judge him. His parents had even managed to manipulate my parents and my life, so Nate had every justification for his territorial orphan attitude. Whatever Nate was *really* up to, I could guarantee that he was only following the letter of the orders Mount Olympus had given him, not the spirit of the order. And he had specifically chosen not to reach out to his Horsemen for assistance.

That either meant he thought contacting us would pull us into danger—because he was an overprotective, hypocritical idiot like that—or he knew he was being watched. Aphrodite cared for Nate, and she also cared for me, encouraging the both of us not to trust any Olympians. I knew, deep in my heart, that Aphrodite was trustworthy. She wouldn't have bothered helping me understand my own complicated feelings for Nate Temple—pushing me to confront him and end our supposed relationship—if she were certain his fate was sealed. She would have just told me to be patient, wait a little while, and then I would be free to begin a relationship with Ryuu.

I couldn't do anything about Nate's self-sacrificing hubris, but if Nate knew he was being watched, he would try to catch our attention indirectly, knowing he couldn't trust his handlers or do anything drastic. Nate's middle name was drastic, or possibly catastrophic.

So, Nate would be scheming.

He would be doing something to catch my attention if he found a sneaky path that would allow him to get away with it. How could he catch my attention while making it look like something entirely unrelated—

My breath caught and my eyes widened.

Ryuu...

Had...Nate actually been the one to kidnap Ryuu? Aphrodite had said he was on the same page as me, and that his heart had found—or was in the process of finding—someone else. Did that mean he knew how I felt about Ryuu? Because there was no way this Peter assclown could have known about Ryuu's significance. And this mystery Peter told me to meet him here at Chateau Falco, which was Nate's home—yet it was under surveillance, so why meet here?

Questions were often as good as answers. They served to get rid of distractions, narrowing the field of possible answers. One thing I knew for certain was that if Nate really was behind abducting Ryuu, I was going to kick him in the balls. Even if his intentions had been pure.

"As long as it's before tonight," I murmured aloud, rolling my shoulders, nervously. The walls of Chateau Falco rumbled ominously, fretfully, protectively at the idea of her Master in danger. I place my hand on the wall with a sad smile. "I'll be there for him, Falco. Always." The wall grew warm beneath my fingers. "But I'm still kicking him in the balls if he had anything to do with Ryuu," I promised.

If a sentient mansion could laugh, it probably would have felt like a mild earthquake—like the one that suddenly shook the floor beneath my boots.

I thought about Hermes' other comments and my smile faded. Whatever Nate was going through, he was all alone...

And that was one of the most terrifying things imaginable.

"Nate can never feel like he is all alone," I whispered. "I don't think they truly considered what they've done by ostracizing him and putting him in a corner. If Nate feels alone and abandoned, the entire Olympian Pantheon couldn't quell his wrathful storm," I whispered, feeling strangely excited and horrified at the prospect. There was a reason he was called the Catalyst.

Falco actually growled, sending a grating, unearthly sound through the halls of this distant, forgotten wing.

"I will figure it out, Falco," I promised, "before tonight." Because Aphrodite and Hermes had made it abundantly clear that his execution was going down and that he needed his colleagues—his Horsemen—to remain true to Nate's creed.

Fucking shit up for everyone not wearing a Team Temple jersey.

And I had to do that—and inform Horseman Tweedledum and Tweedledee that they were gullible fools to buy Hermes' lie—without alerting the Olympian watchers at Chateau Falco. I had to feign ignorance while rallying the troops to go to war the moment Nate threw up the Horsemen signal.

At least Kansas City was peaceful and calm right now, not on the precipice of war or anything terrible, I thought to myself, dryly.

To figure out Nate's issue, I needed clear answers about the Ryuu situation. This Peter guy had jumped Xylo and taken Ryuu with the aid of some enchanted stuffed animal, and he had demanded I meet him here at Chateau Falco in less than two hours. I would check in with Gunnar and Alucard to see what they knew about Nate's made-up Olympian initiative, either kill Peter to save Ryuu or find out what game he was playing, and then hop back to Kansas City to take care of my own business. Then I needed to hop back to St. Louis tonight to prevent Nate's execution, even though I currently had no idea when or where or how that would go down.

I wasn't sure which of us was winning in the *who can start a bigger shit show* contest, but it had to be close.

It was probably safer to say we were both losing.

I patted the wall comfortingly and then assessed my surroundings, trying to get a bead on which direction to walk towards to find the main area of the mansion. I sighed, chose the hall closest to the painting of Gunnar and Nate, and then started walking, wondering how long it would take me to find someone helpful since the place was so big and I hadn't ever been in this part of the mansion. In fact, everything seemed dusty and forgotten, as if not even Nate had ever visited this area.

Curious.

If we all survived, I'd have to ask him about it.

34

After about ten minutes, I entered a wide, expansive foyer with a grand staircase leading up to a higher level. A crystal chandelier the size of a car hung suspended over the base of the steps, and more artwork and paintings hung from the walls. There were two seating areas and separate fireplaces on either side of the sweeping steps, but everything here was covered in dust as well. The floor was a rich, dark cherry wood rather than the marble from the hallways. Strangely, I didn't see a large set of front doors opposite the stairs. It looked like an entryway to the mansion, but it obviously wasn't. And it was definitely unused. I knew for a fact that no one had been here in decades, at least. Not even cleaners or nosy explorers.

I could still feel Falco's gentle purr beneath my feet, but I saw absolutely no signs of human life, and no doors or windows to look through and figure out where the hell I was in relation to the rest of the mansion. I frowned at another thought.

The lights were on. Dim Tiffany lamps and Edison light bulbs hung from dated sconces and other tasseled stand lamps. But...there were no footprints in the dust.

"Falco? Did you turn these lights on for me?" Her purring grew louder, and I let out a sigh of relief. "Good. For a second, I thought there might be someone creeping around—" I felt a dark presence roll into the room like a thick fog, and Falco's purring abruptly ceased like a pricked bubble, making me feel like my ears had popped.

A dark blur in my peripheral vision made me flinch and spin, lifting a hand to my katana over my shoulder. In the distant shadows, I sensed eyes watching me, although I couldn't discern anything specific. Then I saw another blur zip past the top of the grand staircase, too fast for me to make out. I slowly began backing up, drawing my katana and keeping my eyes peeled.

"Falco?" I asked, nervously. "Mind introducing me to your friends? I'd hate for there to be a...misunderstanding."

Falco remained utterly silent as if she'd been placed on mute.

I muttered under my breath. "Goddamned ancient mansions," I growled. Another distant lamp winked out and I heard the tinkling sound of shattered glass, followed by a dry, raspy cackle, reminding me of a zombie hyena. The hair on the back of my neck rose and I narrowed my eyes. "Fuck off, whoever you are. I'm not an enemy."

"Nephilim..." a strange voice croaked from the top of the staircase. I glanced up, noticed a black, humanoid silhouette that was decidedly too tall and eerily animalistic, and then the creature swatted away the lamp on the table beside him, casting the landing into darkness.

"Dark witch," another voice hissed from a hallway behind me, punctuated by another breaking lamp.

"Fuck this place," I growled, jogging backwards, and swiveling my head back and forth for more of these...whateverthefucks. They obviously sensed my bloodline, having called out both my father and mother, but why was Falco silent? Were these invaders? "And goddamned the Roaring Twenties," I added, scowling at one of the broken lamps.

As if they took offense of my opinion, more lamps began smashing and breaking in a rapid succession and that menacing cackle turned into a sadistic chorus as darkness swamped the forgotten, dusty wing of Chateau Falco. I was beginning to see why this section had been forgotten and abandoned. It was haunted by a gang of elitist Templegeists. I turned and ran, realizing I couldn't fight what I couldn't see, especially not when I was outnumbered.

I didn't have time for this shit.

I ran down the hall as fast as possible, thankful for the lamps every ten feet or so that cast the way ahead in a dim glow. I imagined they were lighthouses, chasing after them even as I heard them exploding and breaking in my wake as the cackling pursuers tore after me.

I skidded to a halt in front of a set of wooden, twenty-foot-tall, double doors that were gouged and scarred; I guessed from the claws of the creatures trying to break free. I was locked in here with them? I tried to call up my magic to open a Gateway or Shadow Walk, but my magic failed me, blocked just the same as my connection with Falco had been cut off.

I hit one of the doors with my shoulder, grabbing at the doorknob. I let out a gasp of disbelief as it flashed with purple light and then turned with a rusty squealing sound. I shoulder-charged the door again—once, twice, three times—as the shrieking beasts closed in on me. The door finally let out a shockingly loud crack, raining dust down over me and then creaked open enough for me to slip through to the other side. I shoved the door closed behind me even as I heard my pursuers slam into it, rattling more dust free from overhead. I heard them scratching and screaming and laughing as they struggled to open the door, but none of them tried to use the doorknob.

I backed away, staring at the door with my sword held steady, ready for them to break it down. A minute went by while they continued to rail and screech, scraping at the wood with frustrated snarls and maddening laughter.

"What the fuck?" I whispered, shaking my head and staring at the apparently magical doorknob. What had that purple light been? How was it preventing them from using it and why had it worked for me?

I lowered my sword as I heard them growing quieter, slowly giving up on scratching through the door. Minutes later, it was entirely quiet. I let out a sigh of relief, shaking my head. I took two more steps backwards just in case they were trying to lull me into a sense of false confidence. On the third step, I felt Falco's presence return as the floor beneath me hummed soothingly. I placed my hands on my knees and bent over, breathing deeply and shaking my head.

"What the hell was that, Falco?" I whispered. She didn't answer me, but she felt concerned. I checked my surroundings to see that I was back in the more modern area of the mansion.

I glanced back with a frown at the mysterious doors.

Only to find that they were no longer there. Just a smooth wall. "Screw this place, Falco," I muttered, turning away and resuming my journey through the mansion. I pulled out my phone and called Gunnar. "I'm here," I told him.

SHAYNE SILVERS

"Oh," he said, sounding surprised. "Meet me in the office in ten minutes."

"Will do," I said, shoving the phone back into my pocket and sheathing my katana.

It took me a few more minutes of walking to begin recognizing where I was. Nate's mansion was just shy of twenty-thousand square feet, and I knew of at least two pocket dimensions that were not included in that number. There were unused dining rooms, more random cabinets of curiosities than in most museums, and cozy little lounges, reading nooks, and libraries branching out from the wide, elegant hallways that inconsistently criss-crossed the mansion. The place was easier to navigate by memory than by map or any logical system of architectural design. Each generation of Temples had added onto the home, choosing their own layouts and room types, so it was actually surprising that I hadn't been lost longer than a few minutes. Especially since I'd started in an area with a magical door that I had never seen before.

I hadn't seen or heard a single soul yet. I paused to study a glass cabinet that contained a crystal menagerie of exotic animals the size of large coins that looked so realistic they took my breath away. Lions, monkeys, peacocks, unicorns, and—

A metallic clanking sound behind me caused me to instinctively and blindly let loose a blast of air to neutralize the threat, since I was still on edge after my flight from the monsters behind the locked door of the historical wing.

I didn't hit anyone, but my magic knocked over something big with a loud crash that sounded like ancient pottery. It was safe to guess that whatever I had destroyed had likely been both priceless and prehistoric. Literally irreplaceable.

It was followed by the sound of shattering glass, making me wince. Nate would not be pleased with me.

Like I was opening up an unknown medical bill, I turned to assess the damage. I winced to see a new collection of china and crystal glasses spilling out from a broken, glass display case near the entrance of an unused dining room. To me, it represented a steady waterfall of burning money. But I didn't see a body or even any sign that there had ever been one. I tried focusing on my new vampire senses for any kind of heartbeat, but I was too worked up to focus. I felt like a piano wire strung too tight. But as I focused, I made

178

out the sound of running feet through the sound of breaking dinnerware. I narrowed my eyes, warily, not sure how to process the development. If some stranger had just hurled a blast of power at me, I would have probably run away as well. What if it just been a houseworker trying to do his or her job for the Temple estate?

Or...

It could have been an enemy. Forgiveness was the better part of failure, so I hauled ass after them instead.

35

I'd barely taken two steps before rapid, incessant barking drew me up short and I stumbled, terrified that I might have been attacking friendlies. I let out a relieved smile, realizing it was likely Gunnar's puppies—long story short, he and Ashley had sired wolves rather than human babies. Weird was the new normal when Odin's wife was running the delivery room.

The wolf pups were hyper intelligent, and definitely not typical puppies. It was almost like they were reverse werewolves. All I knew was that it had something to do with Freya, Odin's wife, giving them some form of protection during the delivery. She swore they would become human in the near future, but keeping them in wolf form for now would keep them safe. Safer.

Except the longer I focused on their barking, it didn't sound happy and playful. In fact, it sounded frantic and afraid. I was running again before even realizing it, racing towards the sounds and hurling more blasts of fire ahead of me. What if Peter had not only taken Ryuu, but was trying to take Gunnar's pups? The letter had said not to tell anyone about it. I hadn't even told Hermes, knowing that I could only trust him as far as I could throw him.

"Calvin and Makayla," I whispered, horrified. They were being taken. I knew it in my bones. I bolstered up my speed and started throwing more fire while shouting at the kidnapper to stop running if he didn't want to get hurt. I was ignored.

I almost felt bad for the poor bastard trying to hurt the pups, but there was also the chance that the pups were simply rough-housing and one had bitten the other a little too hard. Calvin and Makayla were werewolves, after all.

"And werewolves like to play ruff," I said with a humorless chuckle, trying to convince myself. I skidded to a halt, realizing that since I could use my magic again, I could make a Gateway to cover more distance faster. I just had to be careful not to appear in the wrong place and accidentally slice someone—like the pups—in half. I pulled deep on my power, remembering a sitting room that seemed close to the source of the barking. I released my magic and a jolt of energy exploded up through my fingers. I yelped in pain, staring down at my failed Gateway. I cursed out loud as I heard furious grown werewolves howling and roaring in the distance, approaching the frantic puppies from the opposite direction so that we might pin them between us. If the werewolves thought it was cause for concern, I felt vindicated in my blast first, ask questions later policy. "Why isn't my Gateway working?" I cursed as I began running again. A Gateway had brought me here to Chateau Falco's lawns, and then Hermes' Gateway had dropped me off in that old, haunted wing of the mansion.

So why wasn't mine working now? Some kind of ward that let me hurl deadly magic but not travel?

Falco continued to grumble her displeasure, making the walls and floor shake, but I couldn't tell if she was warning me not to use Gateways or if she was telling me to hurry up and save the pups. What the hell was going on here? Voices, shouts, roars, and now *vampire* screams grew closer as I ran, and then I heard a loud crash just around the corner from me. I reached an intersection of halls and cursed to find that a wall had collapsed, blocking the hallway with rubble, a thick marble column, an armoire, and a table. I set to work, using my magic to fling the rubble behind me and tunnel my way through the blockage. Loud howls and roars drew closer on the other side of the rubble but were still some distance away.

Similarly, the sound of screaming vampires, roaring dragons, and blasts of flame emanated from what sounded like the first floor. In fact, I saw a dragon swoop past the window outside, telling me that the fight wasn't just inside Chateau Falco. Who the fuck was attacking us?

I now heard echoing howls from the pups as they called out for what had to be their father's sudden roar of vengeful fury. I heard someone curse, trying to hush the puppies, but they were too far away for me to do anything, even without the rubble cutting me off from them. If I could hear the kidnapper, I was so damned close!

The mansion began to rumble more violently, and the barking grew more incessant. On a whim, I tried reaching out through my vampire bond, calling on Alucard. *What the hell is going on, Alucard?*

Callie? he thought back, sounding stunned. *You're already inside? How did you get past the wards? And since when could you use telepathy?*

I growled. *Priorities! Who is attacking us?*

No idea. We just got past the wards when I saw the dragons shift and sprint inside as if all hell was breaking loose.

I growled, still flinging rubble behind me, but the barking was now drifting farther away. *The pups are in danger*, I said, glancing out a nearby window. *I think they are on the second floor, near the guest rooms. Hurry.*

I heard an explosive roar and shattering wood in the far distance—on the other side of me and the pups. Gunnar? I continued tearing at the blockade with my magic, flinging furniture and stone behind me while simultaneously trying to simply blast through it, but it felt like every stone weighed twice as much as it should. As if Falco was trying to make my job harder. "What the hell, Falco? Help me save them!"

"There he is!" I heard Gunnar shout in a much deeper voice than normal. He was in full alpha werewolf mode. "He has Calvin! I will fucking eat your *heart*, PETER!"

I snarled, my vision turning red at the call to arms. Peter. The motherfucker who had taken Ryuu. "Come on, Falco!" I screamed. "Let me *through*!"

I felt the ground and walls vibrate beneath and around me, responding to my plea. But I felt that wave of power drift past me like I was on a boat watching a shark swim beneath me. Moments later, it sounded like goddamned bombs were exploding on the far side of my impenetrable blockade. Wood splintered, glass shattered, stone cracked and crashed, and it felt like Falco was breaking out of the eggshell of her mansion, a screaming, violent leviathan of rage that sounded like a high-pitched wailing cry.

In response, I heard Gunnar howling and snarling, sounding as if he were being bludgeoned or trying to withstand a tornado, shielded only by the relentless fury of a protective father. It made my heart skip a beat to hear the raw agony and rage in his bestial roars. Even on my side of the blockade, smoke began to fill the air, both from dust and debris and a very real fire that might trap and smother us all.

I heard Gunnar shout, and suddenly the air in the halls was filled with the burning stench of ozone as if lightning were gathering all around me, filling every surface with static demons just waiting for a little carnage. I heard a metallic pinging sound that instantly made my ears pop, and a dazzling explosion sent a blue shockwave that knocked me on my ass and flipped me over and over until I slammed into a wall with a gasp, struggling to catch my breath as my heartbeat skipped out of sync in an erratic drum solo.

I dazedly began hurling wizard's fire at the blockade, screaming Gunnar's name and telling him it was me and that I was here to help, even though I couldn't clearly hear my own voice. I climbed to my feet and raced towards the barrier in the hall, blasting away for all I was worth. I couldn't hear the puppies barking anymore, but I could hear vampires and dragons drawing closer, pulled towards the epicenter of the mysterious electric blast.

I felt Chateau Falco groan, almost like a weary sigh, and then whatever force had been impeding my efforts collapsed and the pile of debris exploded outward, creating an opening I could fit through. So she *had* been blocking me!

I stumbled through and ran towards the sound of voices. I rounded a corner to find Gunnar in full bipedal werewolf form, clenching a beefy, one-handed hammer in his fist and kneeling on the ground as he read a tiny slip of paper. Thor's hammer, Mjolnir. Gunnar had claimed it for himself when he and Nate had killed the god of thunder in recent weeks—or so I'd been told. Mjolnir crackled and burped little arcs of electricity to the ground around him, latching onto the marble like twitching spider legs. I saw Ashley standing in the center of a ring of shattered marble tiles, looking numb and hollow, her eyes vacant.

"My babies," she croaked.

Alucard skidded to a halt on the other side of her and met my eyes. He wore flip flops, swim trunks, and an unbuttoned dress shirt with black Ray-Ban sunglasses. The Daywalker Master Vampire of St. Louis was also the Horseman of Absolution and a dear friend, despite being my subordinate—one of the few vampires I knew I could trust outside of Roland in Kansas City. He clenched his jaw and gave me a brisk, resolute nod. Peter had just earned his execution, and no one here was going to let it be a slow one.

Gunnar rose to his feet and slowly turned to stare at us, a giant white werewolf with an eyepatch seemingly branded into his eye socket. His single blue eye crackled with lightning, similar to Mjolnir at his side. "I hereby condemn Peter to death," he growled, licking his massive ivory fangs. He met my eyes, and then Alucard's. The one-eyed wolf panted, his massive shoulders bunched forward and quivering with pent-up energy. "It is time to ride, Horsemen."

"Lock down Chateau Falco," I growled. "I think we all need to have a chat in private," I said, thinking of Falco's obvious efforts to hamper my aid in rescuing the puppies. Putting that together with Hermes' strange warnings and advice, it was blatantly clear that something very strange was happening behind the scenes here in St. Louis.

Gunnar nodded his agreement. "Secure Chateau Falco. No one in or out!" he bellowed. Ashley snarled, deciding to be the woman in charge of the security initiative and snapped her teeth at anyone not moving fast enough for her liking. Every single werewolf, vampire, or shifter dragon in the halls evaporated like ghosts to follow her lead. Gunnar grinned proudly and then turned to me and Alucard. "Let's go to Nate's office and compare...notes," he said, grimacing down at the crumpled note in his paw. "Literally."

So much for keeping our notes secret.

36

The three of us sat in Nate's office, not bothering to hide our anger. We'd compared notes and found them all exactly identical. Peter had been busy this morning, even before the abductions. I learned that he was an old friend of Nate and Gunnar's, and that he'd sold his soul to work for the shifter dragons when they first came to St. Louis.

A beauty of a golden dragon named Alaric Slate. The man wanted to perform some eclipse ritual that would make him the strongest dragon in the world—the Obsidian Son—but his son, Raego, had beaten him to the punch with the help of Nate Temple and...Hermes, believe it or not.

Curiouser and curiouser.

Alaric had been killed and Peter's throat had been slit almost at the exact moment he'd been frozen into an obsidian statue, and that had pretty much been the end of that. Peter's statue had been placed on Raego's lawn as an ornament and reminder of what happened to those who chose the wrong side against Raego, the Obsidian Son and ruler of all dragons in the world. That, apparently, did not apply to Qinglong. Maybe because he was not a shifter but an actual dragon?

It wasn't relevant, so I didn't bring it up.

Everything had been fine, for years, until the middle of the night when Peter had somehow broken out of his statue—still fucking alive—with the help of Alaric Slate—also still fucking alive—and they'd broken into Grimm

Tech. There, they had been seen on security cameras, acting very...strangely before abducting Yahn during his surprise birthday party when he'd come in for work that morning. The three had disappeared, and no note had been left behind.

The moment Alucard learned of this, he took the fight to the dragon estate, threatening to destroy everyone and everything inside if he didn't get an explanation on how and why the dragons had allowed the chaos to happen. In short, he'd acted like a damned emotional father for his adopted daughters' boyfriend, the chameleon dragon.

I also did not bring up the fact that Greta had been distraught about Yahn not calling her on his birthday.

Again, it seemed irrelevant, and Greta was the absolute worst. I didn't want anyone here helping her to feel better.

Soon after, Ryuu had been abducted, and now Gunnar's pups, both with similar notes about meeting Peter at noon on the lawns of Chateau Falco— which was rapidly approaching.

Gunnar had changed into jeans and a white tee and was clenching Mjolnir like a stress ball. Alucard's face was set into a menacing frown even as he reclined on the Chesterfield sofa.

I chose not to bring up my meeting with Hermes since I couldn't be confident of exactly how my fellow Horsemen were being observed by the Olympians. I cleared my throat since the room had been silent for a few moments. "What the fuck is living in the Roaring Twenties wing of this haunted mansion?"

Gunnar arched an eyebrow, his white eyepatch shifting so that the silver coin in the center glinted in the sunlight from the windows. "Roaring Twenties wing?" he asked, frowning.

"An old section that was full of dust, old school lamps and asshole shades of some kind. Also, I'm almost certain Falco was impeding my efforts to rescue the pups."

Gunnar and Alucard nodded, both of them looking troubled as they murmured their agreement.

I let out a frustrated sigh. "Why can't we sense Nate?" I demanded. "And why the hell hasn't anyone killed Peter?"

Alucard grunted, looking more alert at the already asked and answered question. "I tried to kill the man responsible for the statue's security and I was informed that I was being *irrational*," he said with a sneer and finger quotes in the air.

Gunnar dropped Mjolnir onto the table with a solid thunk, making us both flinch and look at him. "You threatened to lay waste to the entire dragon nation," Gunnar growled.

"And?"

I shot Alucard an empathetic look, but then said, "That does seem a little extreme. Raego is the one who killed him, so we can be sure he had nothing to do with freeing him and healing him."

"If it wasn't for the dragon's mishandling of the statue, Peter and Alaric never would have succeeded in robbing Grimm Tech and kidnapping Yahn!" he roared, jumping to his feet.

I grimaced. "Worst surprise birthday ever," I muttered, folding my arms. Before I'd even finished speaking, I felt Alucard's rage spike up a dozen notches through our vampire bond.

Alucard's fangs popped out and he clenched his fists. "You're not helping, Callie," he warned. I barely prevented my own fangs from popping out at his insubordination.

Gunnar cleared his throat. "You two ready to stop fighting each other? My children were just abducted. Actual children, not hardened warriors with a few fights under their belts."

That sobered me up. I took a calming breath. "All right. This Peter asshole knew how to get to us. The question is, what does he want?" I asked, hoping for a lead into the Olympian connection.

The meeting devolved from there, and I realized that we were an unco-ordinated hot mess without Nate's guidance.

After a dozen crazy suggestions of how we might murder Peter during our meeting, Gunnar's phone rang and we cut off, abruptly. He answered it, turning his back on us and speaking in a low tone. I walked over to Alucard, putting my finger over my lips. He furrowed his brows but nodded, sitting up straighter. I crouched down beside him, keeping an eye on Gunnar.

"Things are crazy in Kansas City, Alucard. Worse than I've ever seen. Far worse than when Roland went postal."

He pursed his lips, and I could tell he was already formulating an excuse to tell me he couldn't help. I placed a hand on his wrist and squeezed, smiling warmly. I felt the tension drain from his forearm and he sighed, flashing me a guilty smile. I peeled my lips back and let my fangs pop out with a mild effort of will.

Alucard hissed and leapt completely off of the couch, putting it between us. "The fuck!?" he hissed.

Gunnar glanced over his shoulder with a one-eyed scowl, placing a finger over his lips to tell us to shut up. We both nodded, doing our best to look innocent. Alucard turned to me with a concerned look.

I shrugged. "I tripped and landed on a Nephilim with my teeth. It just sort of came over me."

"A Nephilim?" he sputtered. "Heaven is going to be pissed. What is Eae going to do—"

"Once I bit the Nephilim, his buddy's bracelet fell off and he attacked Eae, almost killing him. He had a fancy new set of silver claws like mine, and they absorbed Eae's blood." Alucard's eyes were practically bulging out of his skull. I nodded, understanding his shock. "I think the Nephilim are a different breed of vampire who feed on angels. They wear these bracelets that bind them to the angels, and they have no freaking idea. The second the bracelet broke—after I whipped out these silver beauties," I said, tapping my new fangs, "the Nephilim instantly came to my call. Craziest shit ever," I said, shaking my head.

Alucard stared at me, woodenly. "The hell do you want me to do about it? I've never heard of such a thing. Brainwashed Nephilim vampires?" he whispered in disbelief, as if I might not have heard it said out loud before. I nodded. "What about you? Do those things crave angel blood?"

I thought about it for a few moments and then shook my head. "I have zero cravings, but it definitely gave me an insane boost of energy when I drank Nephilim blood."

He shook his head, muttering under his breath. "Damn, Callie. What about the Shepherds? Heaven? Even the Sanguine Council is going to be concerned about Nephilim suddenly joining our ranks."

I nodded. "Tell me about it. Which is why I'll need your help once we take care of things here. Roland is already rounding up the Sanguine Council and bringing them back to Castle Dracula. I'll need you to help him keep the new family together while we figure this all out."

Alucard frowned. "Wait. Why is he bringing the Sanguine Council to your castle? Do the Shepherds already know what you did?"

I shook my head. "No, but Heaven does. As do the Seven Deadly Sins."

"Wait. *What?*" he gasped, sinking his claws into the expensive couch. "The Seven Sins?"

I nodded. "Archangels are pestering me, too. Let's just say that no one is particularly happy with me right now. In fact, they're all downright terrified. War is coming to Kansas City, Alucard."

He froze, studying me. "All that is happening back home...and you still came here for us?" he whispered.

I nodded. "To be fair, they took one of mine, too." I pulled my silver butterfly from my pocket. The totem I used to hide my Horseman Mask. "And we are family."

He nodded his agreement, but it was a slow, thoughtful movement. "Thank you, Callie."

Gunnar hung up his phone and turned to us. I shot Alucard a meaningful look, informing him to shut his mouth, and the two of us turned to look over at the Horseman of Justice. "It's time," he growled, hefting Mjolnir in his palm. "We will play it by ear, but none of us will do anything to put the hostages in danger. Alaric Slate is still out there, so I imagine Peter has a backup plan to ensure his continued existence over the next few minutes."

We nodded, grimly. "Let's go."

37

The three of us advanced from different directions, zeroing in on the colossal, white, glowing tree that dominated the grounds of Chateau Falco. The tree climbed a few hundred feet high, and I spotted a treehouse in the upper branches. Nate's Beast, Ruin, lived there rather than with his mother, Falco. I wondered what he was up to. Possibly in hiding due to Olympian spies?

I gripped a katana in each fist, but I had folded my arms across my chest, so the bared blades created an X across my torso and extended past my shoulders at an angle. Ryuu's black blade felt warmer in my hand, and I once again picked up on his intoxicating scent. I took a grip on my emotions with a measured breath before my fangs popped out at the thought of Ryuu as a prisoner. My face was utterly blank as I scanned the mansion's grounds in search of Peter.

The three of us feigned mild surprise and suspicion at seeing each other, because our notes had told us to keep this a secret. Part of me had wanted to tell Gunnar and Alucard of my suspicion that Nate was behind this, but I knew their faith would shatter if I ended up being wrong. They had enough on their minds without me adding false hope.

Alucard walked like a young billionaire software developer heading to a board meeting where he fully intended to fire everyone who deigned to wear a suit as swiftly as possible so he could get back to his disc golf tournament.

With each step, his flip flops slapped and smacked, and his unbuttoned linen dress shirt technically followed his company's dress code policy, even though his swim trunks did not. He still wore his large Ray-Ban sunglasses and moved with an almost unnoticeable feral grace. I felt a strange kinship between us, now. I could recognize his scent—cigar smoke and scotch.

Gunnar carried Mjolnir loosely at his side, and his biceps threatened to tear through his sleeves if he flexed too hard. He looked like he should have had an American flag tattooed on his bicep and a bald eagle gliding over his shoulders at all times. The coin on his white leather eyepatch glistened in the sunlight, looking both regal and sinister. I was confident that the coin was what he'd chosen as a totem for his Horseman's Mask. I felt a strange pull every time I looked at it, basically confirming my suspicion. But I still couldn't sense Nate. None of us could.

A man materialized out of thin air in my peripheral vision, standing before the towering white tree. I spun to face him, holding out my two blades in anticipation of an attack, but he did no such thing. He was tugging an eyepatch down from his head, dropping it to hang down his chest, although he didn't appear to be missing either of his eyes. Was that what had made him invisible? That was ironic, an eyepatch for a missing eye that made one invisible to others. He wore Nate's satchel—the one I had given him. I had no idea who he was, which obviously made him Suicide Pete. Try as I might, I still couldn't sense Nate or his Mask of Hope. This wasn't him.

Gunnar obviously recognized the man, but I could see Alucard did not. We all stared at him with barely restrained fury, only held in check by the fact that he had our loved ones as his hostages.

"Long time no see," Peter said with a slimy smile. He patted his satchel. "I'm looking for Nate. He missed a meeting I requested, leaving this behind in his stead. You're going to help me open it if you want to see your loved ones again. I die, they die. Oh, and Alaric is watching," he said with a sneer, "so don't try anything funny. Let's go," he said, motioning for us to approach.

Then he turned his back on us—something you just didn't do with murderous monsters. We glanced at each other, set our jaws, and approached him. He brandished his hand dramatically, revealing a bracelet of some kind. A Gateway roared to life, but I could have sworn I heard the faint sound of breaking glass before it came to being. A Tiny Ball? Gunnar had mentioned something about a bracelet giving him access to wizard's magic, so why had he used a Tiny Ball? I couldn't sense any magic on him. He jumped through without waiting for us to join him.

I cast Gunnar and Alucard a wary look. Peter wanted us to jump in after him without telling us the destination. It could be a prison or a trap of some kind. But it was our only option to get back our loved ones. Gunnar and Alucard jumped through first, fanning out to either side in a defensive line. The prick was playing power games, giving us subtle reminders of who was in charge. Pouring salt on our wounds. I was the goddamned Horseman of Despair. It was time to remind him of that fun fact. I stepped through the Gateway and into the unknown, my face as calm and still as a frozen pond.

I sheathed my swords behind my back, leaving the hilts showing over each shoulder as I silently thanked Aphrodite for such a badass suit. No need to worry about sheaths when the blade stuck to my clothes like a magnet. Peter stood a safe distance away, facing us openly. I stared directly into Peter's eyes, unblinking, still unable to sense Nate in our new location. Then I calmly turned around and discreetly called up my angelic gauntlets— but to a lesser degree so they were almost translucent. I then grabbed the edges of the fiery Gateway, insulated from the flowing ribbon of sparks. It writhed in my grip, fighting me, but I swiftly twisted my wrists in a sharp gesture, and it shattered. The Gateway collapsed in on itself with a choking *thump* that sent a shockwave of air outwards. I released my gauntlets and calmly turned back around with an absent nod of satisfaction as if I'd done nothing more than taken out the trash.

Peter stared at me in disbelief. He hadn't known it was possible to break a Gateway. To be fair, I hadn't either.

Hence, why I'd called up my gauntlets. I gave him a truly wicked smile and a slow nod. I'd shaken his confidence.

He stood stiffly, as if wary of something dangerous, flanked by two stone gargoyles. I scanned our new meeting place, checking for strengths, weaknesses, threats, and opportunities. It looked like a bank, but a very strange one. No marketing material posted on the walls and no ATM. The space directly behind Peter was wide open for more than twenty feet—no chairs, desks, coffee stations, or couches. Gunnar and Alucard both grunted, looking as if they recognized the place.

If this was a bank, where were all the customers? The suspected teller line was empty, and it was noon—a time when most people went to cash checks or make a deposit. I had also never seen a bank with two big ass statues perched on pedestals near the entrance to the large, open lobby. Having spent some time at Chateau Falco and now Castle Dracula, I was one-billion-percent sure that they were not just statues. They didn't move or breathe but they looked eerily realistic.

I studied the puny man with a frown. One of him against three Horse-men? What the hell was going on here? He was obviously petrified, and if Alaric had been watching back at Chateau Falco, why had we come here where he had no backup?

Peter cleared his throat. "Consider this Switzerland. If any magic other than that Gateway goes off, these statues come to life and beat down *everyone*."

We remained silent. We could still beat him with our fists. Alucard looked more than willing. The man took a slow, deliberate step backwards and—

The three of us collectively gasped and stepped forward in disbelief as Peter changed in the blink of an eye, revealing another person entirely. Alucard even ripped off his glasses and crushed them in his fist. I sucked in a sharp breath and clutched at my chest, my knees growing weak and unsteady as the blood drained from my face to see Nate Temple where Peter had been only seconds before.

But...I still couldn't sense him? Was this some kind of maddening illusion?

I heard a solid thud as Gunnar dropped his hammer, shattering a section of the tile floor. The crackling blue arcs of electricity from the legendary hammer fizzled out as if grounded by rubber.

"Nate?" I whispered, struggling to process the fact that my wild hypoth-esis about Nate being behind Ryuu's abduction was actually spot on.

"What the *hell* is this?" Gunnar demanded.

"Where. Is. Peter?" Alucard demanded in a strained rasp. "If you killed him, I will never forgive you," he snarled, apparently not believing it was really Nate. Or maybe he did, and he was threatening his friend for stealing his chance at revenge. Long story short, we were all on edge, confused, angry, and suspicious.

"Yahn was never in danger," Nate said in a surprisingly compassionate and guilty tone. "I didn't mean to abduct him, believe it or not. He gave me a birthday tackle through a Gateway."

Alucard stared back at him, unable to speak. That...made no sense. Peter had abducted Yahn. Gunnar had seen it on the security feeds at Grimm Tech. I noticed two thick bracelets on Nate's wrist, making me frown. If they had put him under permanent illusion that I couldn't even sense...how had taking a single step backwards into the open lobby revealed the truth? And without even a flicker of magic that I could sense?

"Your pups are safe, too, Gunnar. Better than safe, actually," Nate said, smiling at his best friend. I still couldn't sense Nate via our Horseman bond, so I wasn't entirely sold on the revelation either. If the Peter illusion had been so compelling, then it made sense this was yet another trick. I hadn't sensed any magic when he changed his appearance, but he had deliberately stepped backwards as if passing through a ward. I eyed the statues again, wondering if they were some kind of illusion breaker or if it had been the floor itself. "They were running around like lunatics when I shared a drink with Yahn less than an hour ago," Nate said with a casual shrug. Then he pointed at Gunnar's hammer. "You almost killed me with that earlier." Gunnar stiffened, his mouth opening and closing wordlessly. Nate was the person I'd been chasing through Chateau Falco? No wonder she had tried to stop me from killing him! She had known the truth!

Which was enough to almost sell me on what my eyes were seeing.

"What about Ryuu?" I whispered, struggling to control my rapid pulse and the unpleasant feeling in my stomach.

Nate met my eyes and I almost took an involuntary step back at the depth of pain and commiseration in his eyes. It really *was* him. He nodded with a reassuring smile. "He's fine. He was sleeping when I left to come here. I'm not even sure if he knows he was taken yet," he said with a guilty smirk. "I'm sorry, Callie."

My eyes welled up with tears and I fell to my knees, drowning beneath the waves of rage that had threatened to consume me. I was relieved, but I was furious. With my new abilities as a quasi-vampire, controlling my passions was beyond difficult. What if I'd actually succeeded in murdering Nate back at the mansion? It was a sobering thought on the lesson Roland had always taught me—never let passion rule reason or allow feelings to overlook facts. "How...*could* you?"

My question cut him like a razor. He hung his head, taking our shared anger like a man facing a firing squad. The Horseman of Hope had knowingly hurt his fellow Horsemen...but he was taking ownership of it. I could see that he empathized with our pain but that he still stood firmly behind his decision. Humility was not a suit comfortably worn by Nate Temple—not in public, anyway. In private, sure, but hardly ever in front of others. Despite my relief at seeing him safe and relatively unharmed...

He'd better have a damned good reason for hurting his newest siblings, his closest allies, and his fiercest friends.

His Horsemen.

He was now on trial, and I feared the judgment we might demand. We were not impartial. What had been so important to him that he'd been willing to risk so much? And why all the secrecy? What were the Olympians up to that he feared his Four Horsemen might not be able to handle? Why not just take the fucking fight to them? Now!

There had to be a ridiculously good reason. Nate was always the one to suggest *exactly that* course of action.

He took a deep breath and lifted his head to meet my accusing glare. "To keep them all safe, believe it or not. And to give you plausible deniability. Zeus was planning to do exactly what I did to you. Because he's been running around town wearing my face, trapping me in the guise of Peter, and Carl in the guise of Alaric. He's the one who took Alice," Nate whispered, gritting his teeth.

And that's when it all clicked firmly into place. Alice. Of course it was all about a child. Nate would do *anything* for a child, but for Alice he would break the *world*. The girl's mother had died, willingly, to grant Nate and Alice the chance to defeat Mordred in Fae. Since that time, Alice had been firmly glued to his side. She was a startlingly powerful being in her own right, but she was now an orphan, and Nate considered himself the patron saint of orphaned children. Judging by the painful look on Gunnar and Alucard's faces, they at least empathized with his motivation. Whether his chosen solution was acceptable or not, the jury was still out.

His comment echoed in my mind. Zeus had kidnapped Alice. No wonder Hermes had been so sketchy. If he were caught snitching, Zeus would have killed Alice, sending Nate into a spiral of murder and chaos that no one would have been able to stop. It was his one major weakness—his people, especially his children or those who couldn't look after themselves.

But it was also his greatest strength. How fucking big his heart was when it came to protecting the less fortunate from bullies—whether they be gods, titans, monsters, or entire pantheons.

"She wasn't as lucky as your loved ones," Nate continued. "She got taken by a *real* monster. In your case, a monster *saved* your loved ones," he said, emphasizing the word and pointing a thumb at his chest. "If I'd approached you in any way other than this cloak and dagger scenario, Zeus had assassins watching you. All of you."

The implication was obvious. Innocents would have died. Our loved ones would have died. We would have died.

Tense silence answered him, and I glanced at Alucard and Gunnar, curiously. Had they received visits from Aphrodite or Hermes? Someone else? Despite Nate's explanation, our response was not as promising as he might have hoped. Especially Alucard. He looked ready to murder someone. Anyone.

The circle of trust had been broken. Whether it could be mended or not would be seen in the next few minutes. Our pain was real. Learning that it had been intentionally orchestrated didn't make it go away. In a way, Nate had humiliated us by beating us, succeeding in kidnapping the people we loved most. Rubbing our faces in it didn't make it better. He knew our weaknesses—shared with him in confidence—and he had exploited them. Our loved ones had seen us fail to protect them, and that was something that could not be unseen. No matter the intention of the kidnapper, they had been kidnapped, and our respective people had seen us lose. In one morning, Nate had hamstrung three Horsemen with very little effort.

Nate abruptly tensed with a surprised look on his face as his eyes shifted to something over my shoulder. "He speaks the truth," a woman's voice said from directly behind me. The three of us spun, crouching instinctively at the potential threat. A truly stunning blonde woman in gold, dented and scuffed armor faced us without even a whisper of fear in her bright—

I blinked. Her eyes were two different colors. One green and one blue, both sparkling like gems.

Then a man stepped up beside her and Alucard gasped like he'd been shot in the heart.

Was this whole place not warded? Because I hadn't sensed either of them appear, and they definitely hadn't been here when we arrived.

38

Yahn, the chameleon dragon and Greta's grandson, smiled reassuringly. Instinctively, I almost blurted out Happy Birthday—anything to fill the oppressive silence. He had filled out—a lot—since the last time I'd seen him in a neon leotard, dancing to some sort of techno garbage. He was very handsome, and he oozed confidence—both traits that the pudgy dancer had not had when I first met him.

"We were never in danger," Yahn said. "Well, Gunnar almost killed Nate, I heard," he added, calmly. "Other than that, not even a scratch." He glanced at Nate with a guilty shrug, pointing a thumb at the blonde warrior. "She asked about the risk to innocent bystanders and I realized that I hadn't even considered the customers or employees," he said. His eyes flicked past Nate's shoulder towards the teller line. "They're now in a private meeting to give us some privacy. Once I was confident these three had seen through the illusion, I had the manager disable the alarms, so you can use magic again. The anti-illusion field always stays on, which is probably a good thing right now," he said, shifting his attention from Nate back to us.

Why had I not sensed anyone here? I really needed to practice this vampire skill. Then again, neither Gunnar nor Alucard had sensed other people hidden in the back room. Maybe the place was warded. If it was a bank, that made a lot of sense.

Nate shook his head, looking mildly annoyed to be outclassed, but I also caught a faint smile directed past my shoulder at...the blonde woman. It was a deeply personal smile—not openly, but I noticed it because he'd once smiled at me in much the same way. Nate...was in love with this woman. My pulse suddenly escalated, realizing that Aphrodite had told me the truth. Whether he realized it yet or not, he'd moved on from thoughts of me. So. This hot ass bitch and a half was Kára. I judged her, as was appropriate, and permitted myself to hate her a little bit.

Nate's smile morphed into one of resigned gratitude. "Thanks."

Kára and Yahn shrugged it off, keeping their eyes on us.

"Mind stepping over here?" Nate asked her, sounding strangely excited, as if he'd had a sudden epiphany. I frowned, curiously, my eyes shifting to the illusion-breaking line. Nate wanted to see what she looked like beyond the line, which was strange. What was the woman hiding?

"Not a chance," she said with a knowing grin, already thinking three steps ahead of Nate. I narrowed my eyes at the statues. What kind of illusion did he think the Valkyrie was under?

Nate shot Gunnar a crestfallen look and a hapless shrug, begging for sympathy. Gunnar gave him nothing. At all. In fact, he broke eye contact with his once best friend and he may as well have kicked Nate in the chest, judging by the reaction on his face. I didn't blame Gunnar.

Nate turned to Yahn. "At least tell me you didn't leave Carl in charge."

Yahn smirked. "I left the pups in charge, of course." Gunnar tensed, shooting Yahn a sharp, anxious look. The younger dragon stood firm, not wilting under the alpha werewolf's glare.

Realizing I was still kneeling, I rose to my feet and directed my glare at Kára. Then I turned to share my ire with Nate. "Someone needs to explain. Now. Is Peter truly free or was that another stunt you pulled to terrify us? And why can't I sense you?" I demanded, eyeing Nate up and down. I now realized why he'd made up the excuse about *finding* Nate's satchel. Because he knew one of us would have paused upon seeing it if he hadn't dismissed our suspicion. Even then he'd been trying to protect us. He'd brought us here so he could reveal the truth in private, knowing there was no other way to convince us. As mad as I was, I couldn't imagine being in his shoes.

Gunnar and Alucard were suddenly shouting over each other, demanding answers to all kinds of questions, their voices echoing and competing for dominance in the large open space.

Nate held up a hand, silencing them. When they'd quieted down, he turned to Yahn. "Can you head back and keep an eye on everyone?" For some reason, he didn't ask Kára to do the same, which made her grin victoriously.

Yahn nodded, ignoring the arguing shouts from Gunnar about how he better bring the pups here right the fuck now. Alucard silently watched Yahn toss a Tiny Ball on the ground and hop through the resulting Gateway. Despite being so concerned, he hadn't said a single word to Yahn. Perhaps his own rage had surprised him. Scared him, even.

They turned back to Nate with grim scowls. Nate took a deep breath and then began to tell the most bizarre story I had ever heard, and that's saying something. He told us about the cuffs on his arms—Titan Thorns—and how they could only be removed by...true love. Cliche almighty! They were the reason he couldn't use magic and we couldn't sense him. He talked about Kára—more than absolutely necessary, in my honest opinion—and we were soon sitting down on the floor like children listening to the tallest of tall tales from a compelling raconteur. Nate had been busy battling one pantheon after another, freeing Fenrir for Loki, visiting Asgard to pick a fight and kill Thor with Gunnar. The werewolf's chest puffed up with pride at that one and he smiled, smugly, gripping the legendary hammer tightly.

Nate told us of how he'd been abducted by Zeus and locked in a prison with Prometheus and Carl for the past week, suffering daily inventive forms of torture from both Ares and Apollo. He told us about the sleep-inducing stuffed animal Carl and Yahn had used to abduct Ryuu, along with the eyepatch from Grimm Tech that rendered one invisible—just like the one hanging around Nate's neck. He even mentioned quasi-real dreams with Quinn MacKenna, an Underground Railroad in the foundations of Chateau Falco that he'd just discovered, and I began to see an alarmingly elaborate tapestry unfolding, weaving seemingly erratic, random events into one great big quilt of intrigue and conspiracy. And...it was beautiful.

And terrifying.

Zeus wanted our new band of Horsemen to answer his beck and call. To be *his* Horsemen. And Nate was doing absolutely everything he could to make sure that didn't happen. Like kidnapping our loved ones so that we didn't have to face what he currently faced with Alice. I could see the concern was eating him alive inside.

Through it all, I kept thinking back on Hermes and Aphrodite, having a newfound appreciation and respect for their exceedingly careful comments.

They were under just as much—if not more—scrutiny than even Nate. All were prisoners under the vicious tyranny of Zeus, and the Father of the Olympians had established dozens of safeguards to prevent them from messing up his plans to take over our new band of Horsemen.

As we listened in rapt attention, I realized another startling discovery. Nate was doing something magical even though his Titan Thorns prevented him from using his awesome powers.

He was...being brutally, painfully *honest*. Hitting us with raw truths that he normally kept under lock and key and behind several vault doors. He was inviting us into his inner sanctum as a means of indirectly apologizing for his actions. I wasn't sure if it would be enough to mend our wounds, but it was definitely helping, judging by the reactions on Gunnar and Alucard's faces. It made a difference to me. A big one. Nate had saved Ryuu from Zeus.

For *me*. Even as he had his heart set on the stupidly beautiful Valkyrie in our midst. Kára watched the four of us like a sleepy cat, her eyes vigilant but her posture utterly relaxed, almost sluggish.

Finally, Nate trailed off and Gunnar shook his head woodenly. "It's all tying back to the beginning," he growled, waving a hand at Nate, indicating the earlier Peter illusion. "When the dragons came to town with Alaric Slate."

Nate nodded. "We've all been played by the Olympians. By Zeus. Especially you guys. He's a sick, twisted, clever man. I have to give him that. But here is the important bit—and the reason for my secrecy." The three of us leaned forward subconsciously. "You cannot let on that you know any of this. I didn't kidnap everyone just to get your attention. I need Zeus to see you furious, emotionally wrecked, and focused like a laser on Peter. He needs to know you are broken and malleable. His hubris is his greatest weakness. I need you to do this for Alice. And me. And your loved ones—who are now safe from his reach, thanks to me."

I narrowed my eyes at his decision to pat himself on the back, even though he was right. Social grace was not in his repertoire—except when he was manipulating someone to get something he wanted. But his warning echoed that of Aphrodite and Hermes.

"I *knew* this would hurt you," he went on, "but I valued knowing that your loved ones would not become the next Alice *over* the pain of knowing that I had to hurt you to make them safe. I'll carry that guilt to my grave," he rasped. "But I would do it again in a heartbeat. That's part of the job, Horsemen."

The bank grew silent. Painfully silent. After a few moments, I turned to lock eyes with Gunnar and then Alucard, reading their body language and silently asking what they thought of his spiel. We came to the same conclusion and finally gave Nate begrudging nods of acceptance. He smiled, faintly, gratefully.

Nate, the Horseman of Hope, had been backed into a corner and had made the hard call—the one no one ever wanted to have to make. He was the leader of the Horsemen, and he'd just proven it by risking our fury to keep our loved ones safe in the long run. He had betrayed us in order to protect us. The stakes were that high, and I found myself respecting him more than I thought possible. The incorrigible billionaire playboy wizard was still inside those eyes, but there was so much more to him now.

In a way, Nate's act was much like Ryuu's training lessons. He beat the living hell out of me on the daily, all to prove to me that I could take it—and that I could take so much more. He gave my confidence calluses. Again and again and again. Nate had hit us where it hurt, and we had rallied as a team to confront the threat. We had answered the call.

We. Were. Horsemen.

He had reminded us what truly mattered, and that we could handle anything if we were unified. We had definitely not been unified in Nate's office, but now that he was here...

There was a magic to his words. A fire kindled to life in our chests. I could feel it growing between the four of us. We did not fight for duty, we fought because we had heart and compassion for those less powerful. He had given us a taste of just how bad things could get in the days to come. We had faced our worst fears, and we hadn't fractured. We were still here. Kára was staring at Nate with fiery, passionate approval in her dazzling, dual-colored eyes.

"We have spilled first blood, so now we have nothing left to fear," Nate said. "We have tasted the worst already, and we have overcome it. Together. Now, there is nothing we cannot do, my brothers and sister," he said, staring each of us in the eyes. As one, we climbed to our feet, resolved for the battle to come. "Go along with whatever Zeus asks of you. I don't know, exactly, how his plan will play out, but you need to be convincing if Hermes shows up with an ask."

I think I masked my instinctive flinch, but Kára glanced over at me for the briefest of moments.

"How do you know he will?" Alucard asked, speaking for the first time in a while. I kept my face studiously blank. Hermes was playing double agent, and he'd obviously chosen to single me out, pulling me aside before the others. Did that make him trustworthy? If he hadn't met up with the others, did that mean I was supposed to keep my trap shut? I decided to wait before speaking. I could always tell them later. We'd heard enough truth bombs for the time being.

Nate grimaced. "Oh, he definitely will. I've come to know him very well." He turned to me with a resolute gleam in his eyes. "Whoever shows up, get a good read on them. You know how to play people well. Convince them by manipulating their personality type. If you need to show a little aversion to authority or capitalize on your worry for your abducted loved ones, do it. The rest of you, follow her lead."

I turned to Gunnar and Alucard, smiling for another reason entirely. I'd already played Hermes like a fiddle, but some of his comments made me hesitant to share here. Nate had asked me, specifically, to manipulate Hermes, so I made the executive decision to keep my circle of trust small. After all, Nate could be wrong about who he had lent his trust to. "I can do that," I agreed with a firm nod.

"Peter is working for him—whether willingly or not, I don't know. You can tell us apart by my Sensates," Nate said, showing off a truly horrific mess of tape covering his bracelets and then pointing at his necklace to reveal a simple black stone. "He doesn't have them. Again, Callie will read the social cues and act accordingly. We will cross paths again tonight."

Already done, I thought to myself. *Unless Hermes is playing me and Nate, simultaneously*. Tonight, we would battle Olympians. Not just Zeus, but Ares and Apollo as well. If things went poorly and Zeus found a way to rein in Aphrodite and Hermes, it might end up being five Olympians versus Four Horsemen.

"What if he asks something of us that disrupts your plans?" Gunnar asked.

Nate gave us a roguish grin, proving that he was the same old trouble-maker. "I don't *have* plans. I have dice and a board that I think can be utilized for any situation. I'll let you know when to break character." He took a deep breath. "Horsemen, prepare for war. Tonight, we downsize the

Greek Pantheon. Tonight, we let every other pantheon in the world know we're here to stay. Tonight, the world will meet the new Horsemen—the Dread Four."

I grinned, wickedly. I *liked* that name. A *lot*. Gunnar and Alucard licked their lips, mirroring my smile.

"We won't have long," Gunnar said, his smile fading as he put on his *let's get down to business* face. "He said he will have Peter with him tonight and that we can extract our vengeance then." I cocked my head, frowning. Gunnar had spoken with Zeus? Had that been the strangely secretive phone call he'd taken in Nate's office when I'd been...strangely secretive with Alucard. I let out a sigh, admitting that trust was still a problem with the other three Horsemen.

Nate clenched his jaw. "Oh, really?"

Gunnar nodded. "You're sure my pups are safe?"

Nate's concern faded and he smiled. "They are the safest people in the world right now. I took them *swimming*."

Gunnar gasped, falling to his knees and making me flinch in alarm. "You mad bastard," he rasped. "You did it." I glanced at Alucard with a curious look, wondering what the hell they were talking about.

"That's what I do, man," Nate said. "Now get hold of yourself. The Dread Four do not get sappy."

❧ 39 ☙

Kára capitalized on the lull in conversation to storm over to Gunnar,
brandishing her trident at him while pointing at his hammer with a
scowl. He stared at her with a bewildered look. Alucard made his
way closer, highly entertained by Gunnar's plight. I watched them, silently,
trying to process everything I'd heard as I mentally weighed my responsibilities here as one of the Dread Four with my duties as Count Dracula in
Kansas City. At least I now knew that Ryuu was safe—as long as we were
successful in defeating the Olympians tonight. My talk with Hermes
weighed heavily on my thoughts, and I kept changing my mind on whether
or not to mention it to Nate. What if telling him gave Nate a false sense of
confidence in his plan? Wouldn't it be better for everyone if he proceeded
like we had no allies?

I was smiling as I watched Kára berating the alpha werewolf of St. Louis
like he was a puppy who had just peed on the floor when Nate touched my
arm. I glanced over at him, proud that I hadn't flinched to see Peter's face.
"Can we talk?"

I nodded, following him towards one of the sentinel statues. It was
disorienting to know I was talking to Nate but to see and hear a different
man, entirely. Thankfully, he stepped beyond the barrier to reveal the man I
knew. He smiled, knowingly, reading my reaction. "How did you know to
take *him*?" I asked, thinking of Ryuu. "How did you know—"

"What he meant to you?" Nate replied, softly.

I stiffened, shaking my head stubbornly. This was not how I had intended the Ryuu conversation to go. I had intended to start off with a kick to the balls, but I couldn't bring myself to do it. "No. I don't know. It's—"

"Complicated."

I grew still, sensing that he knew much more than he should. Like he'd been watching me or something. Or maybe Aphrodite had been entirely too loose-lipped—heh—with Nate about her conversations with me.

Alucard had been pulled into Kára's vortex and he earned a sharp slap to the side of the head for trying to touch her trident. Gunnar was scratching his temple with a puzzled look on his face as Kára continued to fume at the poor men. Nate watched me, thoughtfully, and I could tell he was just as wary of me as I was of him. We both had secrets we intended to keep, and too much mutual respect to give any sort of leg up in our verbal sparring match.

"Yes. Very complicated," I finally admitted. How much did he know? Had Aphrodite told him about me and Ryuu, much like she'd informed me about Nate loving another woman—who was obviously the secretive, highly intelligent, casually violent Kára currently bullying Gunnar and Alucard. If they cared for each other, why did the two of them seem to be eyeing each other across an empty dance floor, waiting to see who would make the first move? There was a tension between them, and it was explosive, but in an exciting way. I wondered how honest they had been with each other about their feelings. Pot, kettle, black. Just like my encounters with Ryuu.

Was I the source of the tension between Nate and Kára, just like he was the source of tension between me and Ryuu?

I needed to stop playing defense and stop worrying about Nate's love life. That would only make me look like I was deflecting. I needed to cut the cord of romance between us without breaking his heart or hurting his feelings. To let him off easy. It was highly possible that he hadn't yet consciously determined how he felt about Kára, despite Aphrodite's valiant efforts to shove them into bed together.

"He's a stand-up guy, from what I've seen," Nate said, gently, breaking the silence.

I nodded, realizing I was losing the upper hand in our conversation. If I wholeheartedly agreed with him, focusing on Ryuu, it would make me look fickle and temperamental. I needed to end this on my own terms. Ryuu was not a part of the conversation. Maybe Nate was trying to lead me towards Ryuu in hopes that it would restore some of his own dignity—giving him an excuse as to why we were no longer an item. A scapegoat for his self-esteem. That was the worst way to handle this.

Especially if he still had feelings for me and didn't know how to let go. What if he was trying to give me an excuse to end it so that *I* didn't feel guilty? To make himself into a martyr for my happiness. The whole *I'm the wrong kind of guy for you, Callie; you deserve to be happy* shtick.

So...I needed to sever the romance between us without involving any third parties and without stomping on his heart. If I agreed too vehemently with his encouragement to end it between us, I would come across as relieved that I had dodged a bullet. He would feel utterly rejected and unlovable at a point in his life when he needed to be focused. That might even cause him to rebound onto Kára, ruining any chance they might have at a real relationship.

I needed to go on offense. He'd said *complicated* in reference to my feelings for Ryuu. But we hadn't yet spoken about his own *complicated* situation, or who his non-mystery woman might be. In fact, we hadn't even addressed the topic that he *had* a mystery woman—something I only knew thanks to Aphrodite's meddling.

I squared my shoulders and faced him, averting my eyes so I could read his body language. "Who is she?"

Nate smiled, immediately glancing over at Kára. *Bingo.*

She was now holding her palm out and Gunnar was begrudgingly counting out cash into her hand. For some reason, Alucard had been roped into the apparent protection racket and was reaching back for his own wallet with a shell-shocked look on his face. She was extorting them. I found myself smirking in approval and wondering when we would be close enough for me to learn her tactics. I also found myself wondering why Nate believed she was under an illusion.

"My bartender," Nate muttered dryly, aiming for some levity.

I met his eyes with a slow, mischievous smile. "I wasn't asking about Kára. I was asking about your *complication*." Nate flinched and his cheeks flushed, only now realizing the trap he'd stumbled into. "Maybe they are one and the same," I mused, setting the hook now that he'd taken the bait. "You don't know who Kára *really* is, after all," I said, meaningfully, as my eyes settled on the illusion breaking floor he stood on. "Or else you wouldn't have asked her to walk over here and stand beside you."

Nate narrowed his eyes at my obvious victory. The Ryuu situation had just been neutralized and I could now focus on breaking it off between us without involving either of our *complications*. I absently wondered if the illusion barrier would work on revealing an Archangel or Archdemon's true identity. If so, I could find out where these statues were made and have some shipped to Castle Dracula to ferret out my own spies and traitors.

Nate let out a defeated breath. "To be honest, Callie, I don't know," he said, glancing at Kára again, attempting to deny his obvious feelings for her. "That's part of the fun, I guess."

As much as I wanted to discover who she really was, I couldn't afford to go down the path of talking about anything other than us. I had one goal— clear out any and all obstacles currently preventing me from going on a nighttime adventure with Ryuu, a bottle of wine, and a big fluffy bed.

"No," I said, firmly, flashing him a knowing smile. "You *know*."

Nate's shoulders sagged, defeatedly and he smirked. "If I do, I'm too dense to tell myself the truth," he said. I gave him a flat look that was about as subtle as folding my arms and tapping my foot. "I'm serious, Callie. I love a lot of people in different ways. You, for example. We could have been great together. Sure, we have our differences. Who doesn't? We could've worked them out, though, and had a great time in the process."

This. This was *exactly* what I'd been aiming for. I had to agree but not be cruel. I smiled, sadly. "I agree."

"So, why didn't we?"

I gathered my thoughts, staring off into the middle distance. "I...don't know. It never felt like the right time."

"Later," he said with a firm nod. "I'm thinking it was too easy. Or maybe our timing was just off. Or maybe we were both wrong. The point is, I love you, Callie. But there is a very strong doubt deep within me. I don't know why or what it means, but it's there. A gut feeling."

"You sound like Aphrodite," I said, smirking.

Nate stiffened, looking suddenly alarmed. "You've spoken with Aphrodite?"

I nodded. "She kept encouraging me—in unacceptable ways—to question my heart."

He licked his lips, nervously. "Did you, by any chance, have your doubts *before* Aphrodite came to you?"

"Yes. Otherwise I would have stabbed her in the heart for trying to manipulate me."

Nate let out a long breath, relieved by my answer. "Yeah," he said, too quickly. "Me, too," he assured me, lamely.

I cocked my head, surprised at how poorly he was lying. He was usually much better. Not when it came to matters of the heart, it seemed. "You...*liar!*" I crowed, swatting him in the shoulder. Then I doubled over with laughter, realizing why he was so embarrassed. "You totally fell for her *come hither*, didn't you?" I hooted, imagining Aphrodite seducing him into oblivion.

Nate's ears turned bright red and he folded his arms stubbornly. "It's not funny. I was vulnerable and we didn't do—"

I laughed even harder, surprised that I wasn't hurt or offended by his discomfort or the thought of him being seduced by another woman, even if it was the goddess of sex.

"No. Listen, Callie. I was her prisoner—"

I roared with giggles at that, fighting to breathe. "In her kinky sex dungeon! You idiot!"

Nate narrowed his eyes. "Okay, fine. I might have led her on. For strategic reasons."

I shook my head, struggling to catch my breath.

"No one takes me seriously, and I'm getting sick and tired of it," he complained, scowling.

I finally managed to get a hold of my laughter, forcing it down deep. I straightened and wrapped him up in a hug. I kissed his forehead and then rested my cheek against his chest. He hugged me back, looking relieved and awkward, all at the same time. "How about this. If we find out that Aphrodite fucked me like she fucked you..." I trailed off, waiting a few moments to see if he would admit to any specific event with Aphrodite that I could later use to blackmail him with. He didn't, so I continued. "We will save each other for a rainy day."

Nate sighed, resting his cheek on the top of my head. "And we come full circle," he breathed, his body relaxing.

I pulled away, frowning at his tone. "What?"

"*Later*," he explained. "It's always *later* with us. I think that's kind of the point."

I nodded, surprised that he had come to the same conclusion as I had. "Yeah. I guess you're right." After a few minutes of thoughtful silence, I nudged him with my hip. "Tell me about that bartender, loverboy."

He squirmed, uncomfortable, and I grinned wider.

40

He shook his head, purposely not looking over at Kára. "That really was a slip of the tongue."

"Exactly," I said with a shit-eating grin.

Nate rolled his eyes. "If she was the one, these cuffs would have fallen off," he said, showing me his Titan Thorns. And I could practically taste the pain and frustration in his voice. He wanted it to be Kára, but the cuffs were giving him doubts. I frowned vexedly, inspecting them. He'd taped them up, hastily and messily, to attach the black Sensates to the leather. The cuff was covered in runes and symbols, causing me to take a sharp breath of recognition. The Omegabet. I didn't know any of the symbols, but they tickled at me like the missing words of a catchy song chorus. I now fully understood why they were so effective in blocking his magic and disguising him. "Kára really likes me," he continued, choosing his words very carefully, "and I won't deny that I really like her, too. But she has a lot of secrets." I arched an eyebrow at him, and he chuckled guiltily. "I'm not making excuses or being hypocritical, I'm just pointing out facts. I'm sick and tired of being blindsided by those I let close to me. I want raw, unfiltered honesty."

"Is that your love language?" I asked. "Aphrodite asked me about mine."

Nate shook his head. "Physical touch."

I blinked at him a few times, and then I started laughing again. "You are such a *guy!*" I said, smacking his shoulder.

He shrugged, smirking shamelessly. "I am a proud member of the Man Club, and I've memorized our Code. United, we are unstoppable. I stand ready to serve."

I scoffed, glancing back at Kára—who was now pacing back and forth before Gunnar and Alucard like she was giving them a military dress inspection. The two men stood at attention, nodding stiffly. She and I would get along fine. Nate scowled at the pair, offended by their lack of spines.

"What was your love language?" he asked, focusing back on me.

"It was a tie," I admitted. "Acts of service and quality time." In my peripheral vision, I saw a Gateway open near Gunnar and Alucard. Kára stepped through into what looked like a bar before it winked out behind her. The two men let out a silent sigh of relief, refusing to make eye contact with each other. I barely stopped myself from bursting out with laughter.

Nate was staring off into the middle distance, lost in thought, so he didn't even notice her departure. After a few moments, he nodded, pensively. "Ryuu seems like he'd be good at those."

My smile was much toothier than I'd intended. "He is, even though I didn't notice it at first."

"How long have you known him anyway?"

"Not long enough to justify my feelings," I said, shrugging. "Maybe I'm wrong. Maybe we're both wrong. Who knows?"

Nate grunted. "Well, if we're both wrong, neither one of us has to tell anyone about it. And this way, you can't say I told you so."

I scoffed. "You're so childish, and Ryuu is so much more mature. I guess I'm glad I'm leaving you," I teased.

"Good luck with that. You can't leave me. The floor is lava," Nate said, pompously, pointing at the ground like a child.

I rolled my eyes. "It's always winning with you."

"I have it on good authority that winning arguments is the key to a happy relationship."

"Oh? Aphrodite tell you that?" I asked, dryly.

"Hera," he said, shaking his head with grim fascination. "I've never seen a woman hate her husband so much. It was endearing. She also said love is for losers."

I grimaced at mention of yet another Olympian in the mix. Apparently, Nate had been schmoozing it up with all of them. "Sounds like a real piece of work."

Nate nodded. "She's a lush. Reminds me of Miss Hannigan in Annie." A mental image of the drunk, red-headed orphanage director from the popular musical came to mind and I actually cringed. "Hey, on a serious note. Do you know why Carl was wearing a cowboy hat when he brought Ryuu back?" Nate asked with a perplexed frown.

I choked on a laugh, imagining Carl wearing Xylo's cowboy hat and a trench coat—and how horrified the Bone Heir King would be about the news. "It belongs to Xylo. He likes hats. Says they help him fit in." I shook my head, frowning. "I was wondering why Xylo was so agitated earlier. Why did Carl take *that?*"

"Some answers can be worse than the questions, Callie. I think twice before asking Carl *anything* these days. Apologize to Xylo for me. I'll get it back." He paused, reconsidering his vow. "You know what? How about I just write you a check for damages. Carl can be possessive."

I smiled. "Just forget about it." Sensing a lull in our conversation, and feeling a strong desire to get back to Kansas City to check on everyone and make preparations for my return to St. Louis tonight, I pointed towards Gunnar and Alucard. Nate frowned, momentarily confused. "She left through a Gateway about five minutes ago," I told him. "Looked like the inside of a bar. Need a ride?" I asked, gesturing at his Titan Thorns, assuming he couldn't make his own exit. Which meant...Kára had left him here on purpose, wanting him to finish his private, very important romance-killing conversation with me. She'd given him space to do as he saw fit.

Nate nodded, frowning with concern at her unannounced departure—because he was a big idiot and didn't realize that Kára had been doing it for everyone's benefit. *Especially hers*, I thought to myself with an appreciative grin.

"Please," Nate said. "Mind dropping me off at Buddy Hatchet? Unless you don't know where that is."

"Oh, I scoped it out," I admitted in a forced, blasé tone. Nate studied me suspiciously, making my cheeks heat up so I punched him in the shoulder for what felt like the tenth time today. "Heard you were a local there and I had one too many glasses of wine one night," I muttered.

Nate nodded, looking oddly serious rather than amused by my admission. "Nothing happened, Callie," he assured me. "I didn't—" He cut off abruptly and his face went pale. "I kissed her this morning—"

I leaned forward and pressed a finger to his lips, smiling dismissively. "It's okay, Nate. The fact that you even told me says a lot. And the fact that it was only this morning means even more. You had already made up your mind by then. And...I had too, technically. We just hadn't compared notes yet," I told him.

Inside, I was doing the happy lingerie dance. *Callie's got a free pass!* I chanted, over and over again in my mind.

Nate's shoulders relaxed and he let out a sigh of relief. Nate must have seen some of my suppressed joy because his look shifted to one of suspicion. "So...how long has it been since your last confession, Miss Penrose?" he asked, smirking.

Damn him.

"How about that Gateway?" I blurted, calling up a portal less than a foot away from him, causing him to stumble back a step with a muttered curse. "There. It leads to a nearby alley since I never actually had the stones to go inside," I admitted. "Well, I didn't trust my self-restraint, to be accurate."

Nate stared at it, silently.

"Did you have something else on your mind?" I asked, frowning uneasily. Why hadn't he leapt through as quickly as possible? Was he having doubts, or did he have something else important to say to me?

Nate nodded. "Someone needs to end the bank meeting," he said, sounding as if he'd meant to say something else.

I studied him, thoughtfully, waiting to see if he would come clean.

He didn't. Instead, he hopped through, taking my silence as an agreement. "Goodbye, Callie. I'll give Ryuu a very inappropriate hug for you and tell him how much you cried—"

"You wouldn't," I hissed, clenching my fists. He grinned wolfishly and I stared up at the ceiling with an annoyed sigh. "You're impossible," I snarled, wondering how he could switch back and forth between serious and mischievous without any apparent effort.

"I prefer incorrigible," Nate said, smiling wider.

I closed the Gateway on his smug smirk.

After a few moments, I felt a purely inappropriate grin split my face. I'd done it! Ryuu was mine. ALL MINE! I would have to make our first official date special. A nice dinner and a new dress. Privacy. We would definitely need—

"So..." Gunnar said from directly behind me, startling the hell out of me. "Does that mean we can leave now?"

I took a calming breath, fighting to get my pulse back under control. Only then did I slowly turn to give him a withering glare. "I don't know," I said, sweetly. "Did Kára give you permission to leave?"

Their sudden scowls made me deliriously happy, so I ripped open a Gateway back to Chateau Falco. They hopped through, talking over each other about what they needed to do to get ready for the ultimate meeting with Zeus later tonight. They took half a dozen steps before realizing I hadn't followed. Alucard turned, frowning at me. "You coming?"

I shook my head. "I have angel, demon, and Nephilim assassins after me right now. Hanging out near you guys will only put targets on your backs. And I need to get back to check on my people if you want me focused for tonight's debacle. Text me when it's time to fight the Olympians, I guess."

Gunnar slowly turned to stare at me with one widening eye. "Text you. When it's time to fight the Olympians," he repeated, deadpan.

"Do you know how insane that sounds?" Alucard asked in a high-pitched voice. "How insane *any* of this is? Have any of us stopped, taken a breath, and reconsidered our life decisions or are we just going to accept this crazy ass shit as normal?" he asked, flustered.

I shrugged. "I mean, you could call me instead," I suggested. "If you don't like texting..."

They blinked in unison. Then they blinked again.

"Right. Good talk. I'll see you guys later," I said. Then I closed the Gateway, leaving me alone inside the bank. I spun in a slow circle, admiring the beautiful architecture and antique decor with the gilded sconces and deep red, polished wood. Nate had said it was called the Vaults—a bank for Freaks to stash their gold. I smiled, nodding to myself. Then I took a selfie next to the illusion breaking floor and security statue, checked to make sure my smile was acceptable, and then I made a Gateway for myself.

I forgot to inform the tellers they were free to go. Sue me. That sounded like a Nate problem.

41

I stepped out onto lush warm grass, looking up at another mansion entirely. Dorian Gray's estate looked like a Bond villain's retreat compared to Nate's mansion. I kicked a red Solo cup into a pile of more plastic cups and counted over a dozen empty glass bottles of liquor and beer, grimacing distastefully. Loud music was thumping from within the building and I saw a pair of topless coeds splashing each other in a fountain and giggling maddeningly.

I sighed, wearily, realizing my last-minute decision to quickly and stealthily scope out Legion's other place of interest was not going to be as cut and dried as I had hoped. I guess it made me old to assume a party might die down by early afternoon. From the looks of it, this party had never stopped.

Some might think this looked suspicious—to have Legion visiting such a place and to find evidence of a never-ending party. Those people simply didn't know Dorian Gray very well. Or at all. On the contrary, everything I'd seen so far was par for the course—I'd just hoped to be surprised with a bare modicum of sensibility.

The fact that Legion had come here wasn't all that surprising, either. Dorian Gray was friends with everyone, so if anyone might know where to find the rest of the Seven Sins for Legion, it would be Dorian Gray. I didn't sense any nefarious blood sacrifices, but I did see two guys licking a tree and murmuring excitedly back and forth about the fact that every enlightened person knew trees communicated through sap—it was akin to a person's saliva.

More importantly, there was a guy peeing on the other side of said sacred tree, power-washing the trunk with freshly bio-filtered Bacardi, judging by the glass bottle he was barely managing to hold onto. He forgot to pull his pants up all the way before stumbling onward in his life's grand adventure.

This was also the reason I hadn't chosen to call for backup before stopping by. It only served to make me look pathetic when my bodyguards saw there was nothing more dangerous than someone potentially spilling their beer bong on me or asking me an offensively stupid question three times in a row before forgetting what they'd been doing before bumping into me.

I made my way across the lawn, not bothering to sidestep around the dozen or so drunken idiots scattered across the lawn like struck bowling pins. Some were sleeping, some were making out, and a few were even outright doing the dirty. I stepped on a girl's hair, three hands, and I even used one girl's lower back—who was on all fours for a reason I will let you imagine yourself—as a stepping stool. The guy working behind her didn't even notice my drive-by, taking her surprised squawk as encouragement for his efforts.

My boots didn't sense any demons as I climbed the steps and reached the front door. It was cracked partially open, and there were none of the flamboyant door greeters Dorian usually had for his more...dignified events. At the front, anyway. Dorian's life creed was much like a mullet—business in the front, party in the back.

But he'd skipped the facade this time. The scene so far looked more like someone's parents had left for a week and the pop-up party had gotten wildly out of hand. Police were inbound, but the remaining guests were the party crashers who had long since dropped the oft-repeated lie that they knew the host.

I kept my eyes peeled and my hands at my sides, ready for immediate violence in the event that any of these drunks was actually a Sin in disguise, waiting to catch me by surprise. I entered the foyer to find a sea of writhing, topless bodies bumping and grinding to house music with enough bass to make the walls vibrate and my skin tingle. The air was a cloud of smoke and laser lights swiveled back and forth in time with the beat, reminding me of Pink Floyd's *The Wall* laser light show.

A middle-aged woman, plumper than was typical for Dorian's employees, bounced towards me with a beautiful, soul-deep smile like I was her long-lost sister. Her pale gray eyes were inviting and genuinely jubilant, perfectly complementing her iron gray hair. Thankfully, she was not topless, so I didn't feel like a prude.

"WELCOME!" she shouted over the music, shoving a woven basket brimming with party favors into my arms. I accepted it on reflex and the woman was suddenly pointing an SLR camera with a foot-long lens at my face, taking at least thirty pictures of me in less than five seconds. This close, with that long of a lens, I surmised that she was actually documenting my brain activity through my flesh and bone. "MAKE YOURSELF AT HOME, DEAR!"

Then she was dancing away, welcoming someone behind me inside after their restful nap on the front lawn.

I studied the contents of my gift basket as I twisted and shoved my way through the crowd, heading for the main living area where I hoped to find Dorian or any other familiar face. It was full of random party favors, baggies of numerous drug samples, body paint, glitter, and even funky glasses and sound makers like this was a New Year's Eve party. I grunted, shaking my head as I searched for a place to get rid of the contraband. I slipped through a wide entryway into the living room where Dorian typically hosted his parties, and I saw a crowd of strangers focused on having a good time and ignoring everything beyond the walls of the host's home. They looked tired but unwilling to admit it, consuming more substances to keep the party going—to keep avoiding the responsibilities and duties of their real life outside.

I found a relatively safe and clear space to stand near the back of a couch and a long table. I glanced up at the second-floor railing, studying the epic, masterful art covering the walls. I didn't see Dorian's infamous self-portrait, but I recognized many others. After I'd broken the illusion he'd used to hide his one true weakness—break his portrait and cause serious harm to Dorian —he'd moved the painting elsewhere. I didn't see Dorian leaning over the railing, watching the party below—as was his typical custom. When he wasn't in a back room with a few frisky attendees, anyway.

A young woman was bent over the table next to me. Most of the table was covered in drug paraphernalia, plates of food and discarded drinks and cups. Strangely, the young blond woman was fiddling with a standing microscope that had at least six different adjustable lenses on swivels. I paused, curiously, watching as she plucked a large glass marble from a bowl, holding it up to the light with a distant smile on her rosy cheeks. Her fingers began to glow, and the glass slowly altered to a rich orange color as she transferred her heat to it with magic. Like a glassblower at an artisan craft fair. She began stretching it out and folding it in on itself like it was putty. Soon, I could actually feel the heat waves emanating from her work. Sweat beaded on her brow and I watched in sheer fascination, juggling my basket of drugs, glitter, stickers, and funky glasses, as the woman's fingers danced across the glass with masterful purpose.

I felt the tendrils of magic dancing to her command, but I'd never heard of anyone using magic like this before. After a few minutes of deft work, I gasped to see that the glass in her fingers now looked like a tiny gazelle the size of a matchbox car. She set it down and watched as the heat evaporated, leaving the clear, incredibly detailed and lifelike, glass gazelle in a prancing pose. She leaned closer and exhaled a measured breath directly onto the figurine.

The gazelle hopped, made a cute little honking sound, and then it trotted across the table, maneuvering around a plate of fresh fruit to dive head-first into a small mound of marijuana sitting on a silver platter beside a large bong. The gazelle began nibbling at it, honking excitedly. I cringed, unable to decide which was more disturbing—the fact that the gazelle had trotted past the plate of sliced strawberries in favor of the ganja or that the toymaker had brought the cute little creature to life with a drug addiction.

"Carla's amazing, isn't she?" a woman asked from directly beside me, making me flinch. I swore she hadn't been there a minute before. "My name is Ginny," the woman who'd given me that basket in the foyer said, and then she pointed her giant SLR camera at my face from three inches away and took a dozen pictures.

Thankfully, the flash wasn't on or I would have been blinded. "Um. Yeah, Ginny. We already met and you already made a dossier on me," I said, pointing at her camera. "And gave me a welcome basket of highly illegal contraband," I said, lifting it to show her.

"Oh, dear," she giggled. "So many people here that it's hard to keep track of you all. Don't want anyone to feel left out." She peered into my basket and pointed out a little baggie of blue and pink crystals. "Try those, first," she said, grinning from ear-to-ear. "It's even better with friends!" she added in a conspiratorial whisper, winking at me.

I gave her a brittle, hollow smile, pretending not to notice the three-way make out session two feet behind her. I was fairly certain one of them was a werewolf or a very furry human. "Right."

❧ 42 ☙

inny grinned at the ganjazelle, snapping an inordinate amount of pictures of the figurine. "Naughty little fuckers, eh? Carla is a toymaker—"

"*The* Toymaker," Carla corrected in a warning growl, crushing a new marble to dust between two fingers.

"Of course, Carla," Ginny said with a bubbly giggle. "My mistake."

I arched an eyebrow at the temperamental Toymaker, since she'd made it sound like a title. Crushing a glass marble to dust with two fingers? I hadn't sensed any magic. Carla nodded stiffly and scooped up a third marble, dismissing us. I noticed half a dozen other figurines on the table, all meandering about. A tiny glass elephant was using his trunk to drink from a puddle of alcohol dribbling out of a spilled glass and a monkey was squatting and throwing tiny glass beads at passing partiers—much to their dismay since they spun around, expecting a life-sized culprit rather than the feces flinging figurine.

I turned back to Ginny rather than thinking too long on the antisocial Toymaker. "So, you help Dorian run the place?" I asked. "Have you worked here long?"

She nodded, excitedly. "Oh, yes. I've been Mr. Gray's house manager for thirteen days!" she said, acting as if she were closer to reaching her pension than she was to finishing a new employee orientation. Less than two weeks?

My eyes widened a hair, but I forced myself to nod happily. "Wow. Well, you're doing a great job," I said, smiling at her overly cheerful demeanor. Ginny wasn't the typical *come-hither* type of employee Dorian normally hired. He usually chose employees based on their beauty, their exoticness, and their...extracurricular talents, planning ahead for those moments when he needed them to put in some *overtime*.

Ginny remained standing beside me, snapping dozens of pictures of nothing in particular around the room. When she turned back my way to snap a few more pictures of Carla's newest work in process, I cleared my throat before something else managed to distract her. "Do you know where I can find—"

"Carla made the Guardians for the Temple family in St. Louis," Ginny said, leaning forward to get an extreme close-up of the crap-hurling monkey. "The griffin sentinels at their family estate, Chateau Falco. Have you ever been?"

I almost dropped my gift basket in surprise, but I managed to play it off as adjusting my grip. I hesitated to answer, not knowing if I wanted to admit any familiarity with Nate Temple to strangers. Especially not when I'd just left Nate's home. "I've heard of them," I said, carefully. "I also heard about stone statues that guard the Vaults and can help break illusions. You know, the Freak Bank?"

The Toymaker paused and slowly looked up at me. "What did you say your name was?" she asked in a slow, clipped tone, eyeing me suspiciously. I hadn't known she was actually listening to me.

"Rose," I lied, smiling. "I'm looking for Dorian. He wanted to speak with me about something."

Carla eyed me up and down with an appraising smirk at my tight white jacket and pants. "I'll bet he did," she said with a chuckle before focusing back on her work—a tiny lion with a full, flowing mane. As I watched, she picked up a tiny paintbrush and made a few delicate strokes on the lion's mane. She pulled away with a satisfied nod, set the brush down, and then checked her work with the magnifying contraption, flicking the lenses back and forth with deft fingers. Then she made a hum of approval and leaned forward, almost kissing the lion. Again, she breathed on it like she was starting a fire from kindling. I gasped to hear it let out a tiny roar and then see it shake its head back and forth before sniffing at the air and focusing on the ganjazelle behind it.

The lion stalked after it and then pounced. I let out a sharp breath as the lion tore out the ganjazelle's throat with a faint crunching sound. Tiny drops of blood sprayed up from the wound, and then the lion began to eat. The ganjazelle managed a few dying honks before it grew still.

I turned to see a slow, devilish smile stretching across Carla the Toymaker's face.

No more arts and crafts for me.

I turned to Ginny, who was snapping pictures of the lion's feast with a bright grin on her plump cheeks. "I really need to speak to Dorian. He's expecting me."

Ginny straightened with a shrug. "He should be out back, playing corn hole with the boys."

Of course he was. Ginny did not hear the full hilarity of her own phrasing, but Carla smirked. I managed not to actually growl at my blatant waste of time. "Thank you, Ginny." I spotted a stack of business cards on the table, cringing at the tiny ganjazelle blood spatter on the corner. It was for Carla's services. I leaned forward to grab one, smiling at Carla. "Can I take one?" I asked her.

She waved a hand, vaguely, not making eye contact. "Go right ahead, *Rose*," she said, emphasizing my name with an amused smirk. "I do parties." Then she laughed—a very dark, wicked sound. I pocketed the card, convincing myself she wasn't as creepy as she seemed. Best case scenario, I could hire her to make centerpiece decorations for my godparents' wedding. Or I could try to get some information out of her about the statues at the Vaults.

I made my exit, winding back and forth through the sea of bodies, swatting a few overeager hands, and denying a dozen offers of drinks. As I moved, I began to get an overwhelming urge to get the hell out of the house and outside for some fresh, non-intoxicating air. In my haste, I bumped into a man, almost bowling him over as I lost my grip on the basket and spilled it all over the ground. Like piranhas to fresh meat, the crowd was suddenly clamoring over the party favors, but I was focused entirely on the man I had bumped into as he turned around to blink at me, blearily.

"Callie?" Dorian Gray croaked, sounding like he hadn't had a drink in weeks. His eyes were bloodshot, his eyes were dazed and droopy, and he had an uncharacteristic slouch. "Did you arrive with Claire and Kenai?" he asked, frowning. "Or was that yesterday?" he mumbled to himself, scratching at his head.

"Claire is here?" I demanded, grabbing him by the lapels and shaking him. I almost cringed to feel how unsteady he was. How hollow and worn out and frail.

Dorian nodded. "She was, but I haven't seen her in...well, a while, I guess. I feel like I haven't slept in days," he wheezed, snatching at a drink from a passing platter. He guzzled the champagne and then grabbed another flute to dump on his head. "Ah, much better."

I opened my mouth to press him further when my boots suddenly began tingling. I froze, realizing they were pointing towards the door. I was running for the door before I consciously chose to do so, ignoring Dorian's baffled shouts from behind me. I flung it open and snarled as I came face-to-face with one of Wrath or Legion's familiar red demons who had been climbing up the steps.

My fangs popped out and I hissed at him, causing him to trip and stumble back. I dove for him and sank my fangs into his neck as I sank my claws into his gut. His blood hit my body like an adrenaline shot and my skin began to tingle. I heard everyone behind me scream and begin to panic. I pulled away from the demon, shoving his lifeless body down to the ground as I savored the feel of his blood coursing through my body, igniting my veins with energy. I slowly turned to face the crowd through the open doorway. They all looked like they'd just woken up from a frighteningly realistic dream.

"Your party is over," I snarled.

I turned back to the circular driveway to see Phix, of all people, and a man fighting half-a-dozen of the same red demons. I counted several already bleeding out on the ground and more people running and screaming to escape the bloodbath.

"My party is just beginning," I growled.

And then I was running towards them.

43

I drew my katana rather than using my claws and stabbed the first
demon in the lower back, severing his spine before he even knew I was
there. He screamed as I kicked him down to the ground, searching for
another.

Phix pounced and tore through one demon, literally ripping him in half,
before hurling his upper and lower body at two other demons in a shower of
blood and gore. But I froze in disbelief to see that I recognized Phix's ally.

Quentin, the prick Nephilim I'd left for dead at the park—the one
Xuanwu told me had gone missing. Now that I was focusing on him, I realized I could sense him. The same sensation that I had mistaken for a
desperate need to get out of Dorian's house. It hadn't been the crowd itself,
but Quentin's nearby proximity calling to me.

He was using his newly acquired silver claws and he moved like a dancer,
spinning and slicing, ducking and dodging, making his fight look like a
choreographed kung-fu flick as a pair of demons repeatedly thrusted their
pointed tridents at him, always missing their mark. Quentin laughed as he
cut them down, slice by slice, only seeming to get stronger and more fluid as
his claws drank the demons' blood.

Sensing no immediate threats, my thoughts wandered to Dorian's
comment about Claire and Kenai visiting here. I'd forgotten all about her
with all the other insanity. I had a lot of serious questions for her, and she'd

been hanging out here at Dorian's party? Why had everyone seemed so distant and almost hypnotized, only snapping out of it when they saw me kill a demon and bare my fangs at them? What the fuck had Claire been doing here—the same place Legion had visited earlier this morning—

In my peripheral vision, I saw a trident swing towards my face, snapping me out of my thoughts. I ducked, rolled towards the attacking demon, and then exploded upwards with an uppercut that knocked him off his feet with a teeth-shattering crunch. He landed flat on his back with a grunt and I leapt on top of him, straddling his waist as I tossed my sword to the side. Without further ado, I began punching him in the face, repeatedly—left, right, left, right, left, right...

All I could think about was Claire. What the hell was she up to? I now had yet another reason to question her motives.

I paused after eight blows, frowning at the bleeding, whimpering demon. He was surprisingly tough, because I didn't see enough blood for my liking. I pulled my hair back in a ponytail and called up a ring of air, using it like a hair tie to keep it in place, distantly noting that I could no longer hear Quentin or Phix fighting.

Then I set back to work, beating the living shit out of the demon with my fists, alternating from one hand to the other like a metronome, smiling as I finally began to see enough damage to make me happy. The demon's body went slack and unconscious beneath me, so I stopped, letting out a breath as I inspected my knuckles. Undamaged but covered in the victory of demon blood.

I heard Quentin grunt from over my shoulder. "Well. I guess that answers my question about where to draw the line."

"I know, right?" Phix agreed in a pleased purr. "She's the best."

I glanced up at him from over my shoulder and he flinched, taking an involuntary step back. Phix was sitting on her rump a few paces away, grinning devilishly as her head swiveled from one of us to the other as if watching an invigorating professional tennis match.

I reached over to pick up my sword and then rose to my feet, keeping my eyes on Quentin the entire time. I studied him up and down with a thoughtful frown. Then I calmly stabbed the unconscious, battered demon through the heart with my katana, still not breaking eye contact with Quentin. I tugged my katana free and twisted my wrist in a sharp motion, shaking off the demon blood. I placed the sword back where it belonged over my shoulder, opposite Ryuu's dark blade, feeling Aphrodite's suit grip it firmly before I let go.

Not once had I looked away from Quentin, enjoying his awkward discomfort, not knowing whether he should smile or run, kneel or stand. I approached him with a slowly spreading smile, revealing my fangs. "Hello, Nephilim," I said in a soft voice. "It's so nice to see you again."

He impressed me by not backing up, even though he was noticeably freaked the hell out by my psychopathic and now sociopathic actions. "It's, um, nice to see you, too," he said, lowering his gaze.

"Dracula," Phix chimed in, sounding amused. "It's, um, nice to see you, too, *Dracula*. Say it with me, Quentin."

He did, repeating everything, even the um, which almost made me burst out laughing, but I managed to keep a straight face as I studied his claws.

"So. What's new?" I asked, dryly—obviously demanding an explanation for the odd couple's presence. "Death didn't suit you?" I asked, deadpan.

He shrugged, still not meeting my eyes, looking like I'd caught him stealing cookies from the cookie jar. "I don't know. I woke up in the park and felt a need to save my family."

Phix snorted, flaring out her wings and showing off her honkers, reminding me of her blatant disdain for the Nephilim. He'd tried to freaking kill her. "Tell Master Dracula the truth, Quentin dear," Phix warned.

He hung his head, looking ashamed. "Phix came back to the park and found me alive. She woke me up and took me into her...custody, I think she called it."

I glanced over at Phix. She lowered her wings and shrugged, shamelessly. "You morons never thought to remove the body, so I took the initiative." She turned to give Quentin a sharp look. "You do not get to speak to her like I do, Quentin. I am more important than you will ever be. Repeat after me —I, Quentin, will never be as important as you, Phix, to Master Dracula."

He did, scuffing the grass with one boot as he did. It seemed a little overkill in my opinion, but Phix deserved to humiliate him as much as she wanted.

"Let's stop the mantras and tell me what this is all about," I said, folding my arms.

Quentin nodded. "Phix told me that I had to pay for my crime if I wanted to earn your favor."

I frowned. "It's not a crime to be a Nephilim. You didn't imprison your-self with those cuffs—"

"The crime of gawking at my *breasts*—for a total of seven seconds—and then trying to kill me," Phix interrupted. "By my count, he owes me a debt of seven bodies—one for each second of leering." She glanced at the dead demons. "His debt is now five bodies, but I told him an angel counts for three," Phix admitted with a bored yawn. "I wanted to see what he was capable of. So far, I have been satisfied," she said, glancing at the two dead demons he'd handled with pizazz.

Quentin smirked, nodding to himself.

"You used him as...a guinea pig?" I asked Phix, not sure whether to be mad or proud.

She nodded. "Who better to use as a test subject than a disposable, presumed dead, asshole with wandering eyes who desperately needed to redeem himself? I am teaching him repentance. To earn his keep." She glanced over at Quentin, who had wilted at the wandering eyes comment. "Unless you prefer to execute him. You're his boss, not me."

I nodded, pensively, studying Quentin. "Look at me." He lifted his head and met my eyes. "What do you think, Quentin. A lot has changed for you since this morning. How does your situation make you feel?"

He pursed his lips and I saw a flicker of anger dance across his eyes. "I want vengeance," he growled in a low tone. "The angels gaslighted me, making me worship the ground they walked on. And this whole time..." he said, lifting his claws and staring at them with a look of proud awe, "I could have been my own man. The whole time, I had the power to make them kneel."

I kept my face blank. "And is that what you want? Power? To shame your old jailers?"

He frowned, shaking his head. "What? No!" he said, vehemently, only now realizing how it had sounded. "It's just...I have the chance to be my own man. Phix told me some of what you've done and...it is the exact opposite of what I've been taught about you. The angels painted you as this demonic monster, but Phix flew me around the city today, showing me places where you had helped people," he said, his words more of a shameful whisper at the end. "I realized that the tour of stops mapping my meaningful victories is pretty shallow. I just did what I was told, fought who I was told to fight, hated who I was told to hate. But since that cuff broke off, I felt something I'd never felt before," he mused in a dreamy tone.

I arched an eyebrow, still keeping my face blank. "Oh? A new monster to serve?"

He didn't immediately answer, choosing to consider his words this time. "Family," he said, softly. "I felt a sense of belonging that contradicted what I thought I knew, and it was so much more powerful. I'm still trying to wrap my head around it, to be honest. But...I'd like to prove myself to you, on my own merit. The fact that you don't hold a leash over my head makes me want to be better. To see what kind of man I am." He frowned, looking dissatisfied with his answer. "I want to find out who I am, and what this is. If you will have me."

I nodded, slowly. "You do understand that I can also make you do what I want."

He smirked. "But you *aren't*," he said, emphasizing the last word. "Just because you *can* doesn't mean you *will*."

I smiled back. "And how am I to know you won't go running back to the angels at the first opportunity of escape?"

He clenched his jaw and took an aggressive step forward. "Because they lied to me, Master Dracula. I will never go back to them. And for what it's worth, if you intend on lying to me, you may as well kill me now."

I nodded my approval. "That is all I ask of my people, Quentin. Honor, integrity, and loyalty. And the decisiveness to stand behind your convictions when it matters most." I pretended not to notice his smile and I turned to Phix. "For now, he is your responsibility since he still owes you a debt. Keep a close eye on him and don't toy with him too much. We need to show the Nephilim that we are not what they've been led to believe."

I felt Quentin's eyes on me but I remained focused on Phix. She pouted. "Maybe just a little misery now and then?"

I rolled my eyes. "Fine."

Quentin chuckled. "To be frank, I find it refreshing after spending a lifetime surrounded by hypocrites who acted holy only to keep us under their thumb. And I think we've all seen that...I'm a little rough around the edges," he admitted with a mischievous grin.

I laughed. "I can live with that." I glanced around the lawn, surprised that Dorian hadn't come out after the mass exodus at his party. Especially now that the threat was neutralized. But I had more important things to worry about than Dorian's feelings, and I was on a time crunch. He'd probably passed out after his however-long bender. "Let's go see Adrian and Eae," I said.

Quentin choked. "They're *alive?*"

I pursed my lips. "Correction. Let's go see if Adrian and Eae are *still* alive."

"This is going to be fun," Phix said as I opened a Gateway to Xuanwu's estate. "Be a good boy, Quentin. Don't attack anyone without my permission. Trust me, I'll let you know when you're allowed to play. It's my favorite pastime."

44

Our unannounced arrival at Xuanwu's estate caused quite a chaotic stir, but it was swiftly doused when they recognized who we were. I was pleased to see everyone on high alert. Xuanwu walked up to me and smiled warmly, his obsidian eyes flicking to Ryuu's sword over my back.

My own happiness faltered as I was reminded that I had semi-bad news to tell him. He pulled me in for a hug and I almost deflected it due to my guilt. Instead, I waited until he loomed over me to whisper in his ear. "Ryuu was taken, but he's safe. I already have a plan to get him back."

Xuanwu hugged me as if I'd said nothing of importance. Then he extracted himself and nodded. "I know. I have seen your future together. Parts of it," he mused. "Congratulations on leaving your baggage behind in St. Louis."

I stared at him, stunned, and unable to make my mouth work.

He turned to Quentin and thumped his sword cane into the dirt. "Have you calmed down or is your blood still up like the tall boy's was?" he asked, glancing down at Quentin's hands. Upon seeing no claws—I think that's what he'd been checking for—he nodded, matter-of-factly. "Good. Saves me the time of beating it out of you," he said, jovially. "My name is Xuanwu, the Black Tortoise, or one of the Four Daemons, as you probably know me. And that is likely the only *accurate* thing you know about my family." Quentin nodded, wild-eyed and skittish. "My siblings and I would like to...clear the air with you and Adrian. He's already inside," he said, wrapping his arm around the dumbstruck Quentin and guiding him towards the house as he continued in a soft, rumbling tone. "Tell me your name, Nephilim..."

I glanced over at Phix, prepared to complain about being left out of the meeting. Except she had abandoned me as well, and was already a dozen paces away, curled up and sleeping in front of one of the numerous Buddha statues. I scowled at her stupid Rainbownatti tattoo, muttering unpleasant things under my breath. Why hadn't Xuanwu invited me inside to hear about the Four Divines? Why tell the Nephilim and not their new boss, Master Dracula?

I sucked in a breath when I turned to see a man seated in a wooden Adirondack chair before the pond, facing away from me. "Fabrizio!" I hooted, already jogging towards him. He flinched and almost fell out of his chair, and I realized that he'd been sleeping. I skidded to a halt beside him, staring down at—

I cringed, eyeing the twenty pounds of gauze extending from each wrist. He met my eyes and gave me a forced smile. "Hey, Callie," he said, sounding extremely tired.

"Oh, Fabrizio," I whispered. "I thought I got you here fast enough," I said, fighting back tears.

He shrugged. "Doc Aala hasn't condemned me to death, Callie, and I'd do it again in a heartbeat," he said, gesturing for me to sit down in the chair beside him. I did, perching on the edge of my seat to face him rather than reclining and staring out at the pond.

"What did she say?" I asked in a hoarse voice.

Fabrizio stared down at his waffle-iron-sized mitts, sighing. "Not to peek," he finally said with a wry chuckle.

I cocked my head at the potential good news. "Wait. Does that mean..."

Fabrizio smiled, hopefully. "Possibly, but I'm not getting my hopes up," he said, letting out a breath. I felt a tendril of magic brush a strand of hair back from my forehead and I gasped. Fabrizio chuckled. "Who needs hands when I have magic?" he asked, shrugging.

I nodded, my lips trembling. "Y-yeah. Of course," I whispered in a hollow tone. He could say whatever he wanted, believe whatever he wished. The facts wouldn't change—he had lost his hands helping me fight the demon, following my orders to heat up the dumpster.

"Enough about me," he growled, meeting my eyes. "I think we've both seen our fair share of changes today," he said, meaningfully. And his eyes flicked to my mouth as brazenly as if he'd pulled my lips back to inspect my teeth. I tensed, my eyes widening in alarm. "I don't know what's really going on here, but just because my hands are busted doesn't mean I lost my sense of sight or hearing. Nephilim with claws like yours, an angel who can now say the Lord's name in vain, and your...*unique* way of handling that dumpster fire demon who cost me my hands. Spill, Girlie Penflower," he said, using his tired nickname for me as a peace offering. He leaned his head back against the chair, waiting.

I struggled to process the barrage of information he'd just dumped on me. Eae could say the Lord's name in vain? What the hell? "Eae and Adrian are okay?" I asked. Xuanwu had alluded to it, but it was nice to hear it confirmed.

Fabrizio grunted. "Much better than I fared in those waters. Then again, my damage was...extensive."

I grimaced, leaning back in the Adirondack chair and staring out at the pond as I gathered my thoughts. "Just give me a minute to clear my head. I feel like I haven't sat down in days," I told him, closing my eyes as I considered what to tell him and what to keep secret. There was no denying my fangs, but I wasn't sure what to actually tell him because even I didn't know all the answers. That was what Richard was looking into for me at Solomon's Temple. The soft hubbub of ninjas and monks going about their business and the gentle, soothing breeze kissing my cheeks lulled me into a dreamy awareness, and my frantic mind soon grew as calm as the pond before me.

I thought I heard Fabrizio chuckling, but it sounded so far away...

I SAT UP WITH A START, MY HEART RACING AS I JERKED MY HEAD LEFT AND right, scanning for dangers.

Phix smiled at me, compassionately, from less than a foot away. "You needed it, Callie. You slept like the dead, and Fabrizio said he'd only looked away for a minute before you were snoring and melting into the chair, bonelessly."

I took a calming breath, pulling out my phone to check the time. I let out a sigh of relief to see that it had only been a few hours. It would soon be night, but I hadn't missed anything in St. Louis.

"The others asked me to bring you to the training fields when you woke up," Phix said, appraising me with a critical eye and not looking convinced I was up to the task.

I nodded, straightening my clothes subconsciously. "Yes. Let's do that. Everyone is still alive, right? Xuanwu didn't eat the Nephilim or anything?"

Phix gave me a dubious look. "Maybe you need more sleep," she said, slowly.

"I know where the training fields are," I said, already striding past her. Phix chuckled at my defiance but then caught up to me and prowled gracefully by my side with a contented purring sound. I mentally ran over my to-do list, knowing I still needed to speak with Roland to make sure my vampires were safe. I also needed to meet up with Richard to see what he'd found on my long list of questions. I hadn't intended to nap at all, and now I felt rushed to prepare for my big, knock-out brawl with the Olympians at some undisclosed time tonight—and I couldn't tell anyone here about that or they might interfere, jeopardizing whatever Nate had up his sleeves. Phix would definitely make an issue of it.

We made our way to the training fields where I found Eae still secured to his sickbed and the two Nephilim speaking quietly with Fabrizio. They saw me approach and stiffened before casually drifting apart. Then they all smiled a little too wide for my liking. I narrowed my eyes to let them know I wasn't stupid, and then I noticed that Eae was also watching them with a healthy skepticism. I put my hands on my hips and glared at Fabrizio and the Nephilim. "Stop whatever it is you're doing," I said. They shot me mock looks of innocence, mumbling affirmatively.

Then I walked up to Eae to get a closer look. I jumped to discover that Aala was seated on the ground on the other side of the bed. She looked up at me with a warm smile. "Morning, sleepyhead. You here for a swim?"

I smiled back. "I guess I needed it more than I thought. No swimming for me. I've got...a thing," I said, gesturing lamely in the general direction of Kansas City. "Just wanted to check on Eae. You feeling okay? Have the Nephilim been bothering you?" I asked him.

Eae was still staring at the Nephilim but he finally glanced up at me. "By *bothering*, do you mean slicing my throat and stabbing me in the stomach with claws?" he asked, deadpan. "Because they already did that."

I grimaced. "Yeah, like that. But I guess I meant have they been bothering you *again*."

Surprisingly, Eae smirked, shaking his head. "No. But they do avoid me. I can't blame them."

I nodded. "After I broke their bracelets off, you made it sound like you knew all along. What the heck is going on in Heaven, Eae? First, you show up telling me that Eden calls and that I've been summoned for judgment. And for the record, the angels and their Nephilim have been awfully quiet—nonexistent, in fact—since our park fiasco." His face grew pensive. "But drop that for the moment. Next, you offer to play double agent, and *then* I learn that you knew the Nephilim were brainwashed prisoners—trained Dobermans who were strong enough to take down an angel one-on-one." Eae pursed his lips, looking both guilty and angry. "How long have you known about this fun little fact?"

Eae rested his head back against the pillow, staring up at the bright tree leaves that formed a canopy over his head. "Not long enough. I found out during a routine raid when two of my Nephilim were killed and the last one had his arm chopped off at the elbow after an altercation with two vampires. Between one second and the next, the Nephilim and vampires stopped fighting and stared at each other with strange, puzzled looks—no longer wanting to kill each other. Then the three of them turned their attention to me and I saw claws sprout out from the Nephilim's remaining hand before the three of them rushed me. I was forced to kill them all," he whispered, "and I kept the bracelet from his severed hand before incinerating his body. The paperwork I had to fill out on that job took me months, and I had no less than a dozen higher up angels harassing me by putting me through repeated depositions and inquiries on what happened to the missing third Nephilim." He looked up at me, his face troubled. "I never got an official explanation or found a smoking gun, but I could read between the lines. The angels were hiding something and it was all related to those cuffs."

"So, where does that leave you, Eae? I'm sure they're all out looking for you."

He was staring at the Nephilim, lost in thought. "I do not wish to be found," he said in a soft tone. He asked Adrian and Quentin to approach, even though he was vulnerable and tied down. They did, warily, as if expecting a trap.

"Some angels are good and some are bad," he told them. "Remember there is always someone higher up the food chain. The angels were treating the Nephilim as they were told to treat the Nephilim. Until recently, I wasn't aware that the cuffs were anything other than a mark of your station. A rank on a uniform." He took a deep breath. "Although I did not know what was happening, I am still complicit in your imprisonment. I ask your forgiveness."

I frowned. "Did you just admit that some angels are bad?" I asked, incredulously. "That's proof enough for me that you've changed. But I would really love to hear you say the Lord's name in vain," I said with a smile.

Because that would just break poor Greta's heart, and my petty game was strong.

45

Eae seemed hung up on my first comment, furrowing his eyebrows in deep thought. "I guess you're right," he mused, sounding just as surprised as I felt. "Some angels are *bad*," he repeated, seeming to be tasting the words.

Adrian and Quentin were studying him like they'd never seen him before. They hadn't responded to his request, but they didn't look hateful or anything either. "You two don't have an instinct to kill him and drink his blood anymore?" I asked. "Or did I just imagine you felt that way back in the park?"

Adrian shook his head. "I wanted to protect you. I'll admit that I wanted to hurt him before, and that I got caught up in the moment with a sudden hunger for violence when I thought you were in danger, but I don't feel anything like that now," he said, sounding concerned about his own lack of answers. "He feels different than before."

I eyed Eae's wings, wondering why they hadn't burned away for his blasphemy. "So...does this mean you *fell?*" I asked him, gently. He had only changed after Adrian stabbed him with his new claws—likely drinking some of the angel's blood in the process. So...how had Eae been changed by someone drinking his blood?

Because if I learned that he was now an angel vampire, I was quitting this job and moving to Montana.

Eae opened his mouth, and I was surprised that he didn't instinctively react with a horrified gasp at my question—talk about fallen angels was taboo. Instead of getting angry, his teeth clicked shut and his eyes widened, and I realized the thought had not occurred to him until I'd voiced it. "God-damn," he whispered, glancing up at the sky as if expecting a hurricane of smite from the Pearly Realm.

Nothing happened and I saw him let out a faint, crooked smile.

Lucky strolled up to us from the pond, naked and loudly slurping a Frap-puccino through a straw. "Hey! It's the boob guy!" he said, pointing at Quentin and glancing my way as if expecting me to hand him an award for tattling. He frowned at my lack of surprise or appreciation and turned back to Quentin. "Hey, boob guy. I hope you're cooler than this one," he said, pointing a thumb at Adrian. "Because he *is* a boob."

Adrian frowned, his feelings mildly wounded, but he masked it quickly. "Hey, Lucky. So nice to see you again," he said in a monotone.

Quentin was smirking, studying Lucky with a calculating gleam in his eyes. "You seem...different. Not human, but there is something familiar about you..."

Lucky lowered his drink and a slow scowl split his face. "I *am* different, boob guy. I am an Anghellian."

Eae choked, rocking his head instinctively as he sputtered in disbelief. "What in the world is an *Anghellian?*" he wheezed.

Lucky glanced over at him with an amused smile. "Part Archangel Michael. Part Archdemon Lucifer—or Pride, as the hip kids called me," he clarified with a wink. "Part banished grace from Purgatory. Shake them up and you get a full cup of awesomeness. Anghellian," he said, pointing a thumb at his chest. "Retro angel." Then he slurped his Frappuccino for dramatic effect.

Eae...

Well, he passed out.

Aala let out an annoyed sigh. "He keeps doing that," she muttered. Then she pulled out a stethoscope and began checking his vitals.

My eyes widened in alarm to hear Eae's reaction was a common occur-rence. "Have you found anything wrong with him? Are his wounds healing okay?" I demanded. Adrian looked completely healed. Fabrizio—who was watching in complete silence—was the only one who hadn't fully recu-perated.

She waved a hand. "Healthy as a horse. I think he's just overstressed. He's lived longer than anyone else I've personally met, and he's never had to deal with free will before," she said with an absent frown.

"Wait. Free will?" I pressed, feeling an icy shiver roll down my spine. Wasn't that what had caused Adam and Eve to commit Original Sin in the Garden of Eden?

Fabrizio frowned, leaning back against the trunk of the tree. "Free will is the one thing humans have that angels do not," he mused, frowning at the angel's feathers.

With those wings sticking out of his back, the gift of free will definitely hadn't made him human. In fact, I could still sense his power, even though he was asleep. Although recovering, he was still a veritable powerhouse. In fact, it might have been my imagination, but he actually felt *stronger* than before.

First, I'd made an Anghellian, and now I'd given an angel and two Nephilim an identity crisis.

Bang up job, Callie, I thought to myself.

"He'll probably be down for an hour," Aala said, interrupting us. "Shoo." We made as if to leave but she cleared her throat. "Not you, Fabrizio," she said in a gentler tone. "I have a few...questions, if you don't mind."

I arched an eyebrow as a broad smile split my cheeks upon hearing her drastic shift in tone. It had almost sounded flirtatious. I glanced back just in time to see Fabrizio's cheeks turn beet red, letting me know he'd taken it the same way. He turned away, stiffly, and approached Aala, pretending that none of us were present.

Lucky walked up beside me, eyeing Eae thoughtfully. "You're knocking down their house of cards, Callie," he said, his tone soft but full of pride.

I grunted. "But we don't have any real answers. What are they?" I asked, eyeing the Nephilim, who were being ushered ahead of us by Phix's barking commands. "Are they actually vampires? Adrian took down Eae like it was nothing. Now, I'm sure if Eae hadn't been surprised, the fight wouldn't have been so one-sided, but still. He was *able* to hurt the angel, and his claws consumed the blood just like a vampire's fangs. And I can *feel* them, Lucky. Right now, I can feel their emotions and eagerness to fight my enemies."

Lucky nodded, thoughtfully. "Yet they no longer seem to see Eae as an angel."

I nodded with a weary grunt. "For once, I'd like to not destroy something when I encounter it."

Lucky grabbed my shoulder, forcing me to a halt. "You're out of focus, child. You're too wrapped up in thinking that what you took from Eae made him a lesser person. What if you took something from him that was *harming* him? You gave him *free will*, for crying out loud. And because I'm all about encouraging pride, you should remember that the only other person to grant free will was *God*."

I rolled my shoulders uneasily, shrugging off his hand. "Technically, Adrian gave him free will when he whooped Eae's ass and absorbed his blood."

Lucky snorted. "And was it my imagination, or did Adrian jump out of nowhere to protect *you*—seconds after he had been willing to fight you to the death. The Nephilim are yours, Master Dracula. By extension, their victories are also yours. This is the way of kings and queens, and you are a Solomon," he added with a wink.

I nodded, glancing at the Nephilim. "But what does this mean? If Nephilim are vampires and have the power to harm angels, give them free will, and use their blood to grow stronger...what powers do my blood vampires have that we don't know about?"

Lucky was silent for a time, considering the question. "Hell. Maybe your blood vampires can absolve demons of their sins," he joked. Then he cocked his head at a new realization. "You seem to have formed another Trinity. You, the Nephilim, and the Sanguine Council. Interesting..." he mused. And then he strode ahead of me, reminding me that he was stark naked by causing me to stare at his perfectly muscled ass. He glanced over his shoulder at me and winked. "Made you look."

I averted my eyes and growled under my breath. "Trinity is not the word I would have chosen," I muttered. None of this explained why my fangs had chosen this moment to make an appearance. They hadn't popped out before I bumped into Eae and the Nephilim. Not even before Lust interrupted my picnic with Ryuu.

My phone rang and I jumped like a startled cat, causing Phix to glance back at me with a frown. I fumbled it out of my pocket and answered without looking.

"It's time, Callie," Gunnar growled in a clipped tone. "I just received word about when and where Nate needs us for a meeting with the Olympians."

I muttered a curse. "Of course you did," I growled, knowing I couldn't speak plainly over the phone. Who had given him the information? Fake Nate—Zeus? Or one of the other Olympians?

"Sharpen your swords and meet me here at Chateau Falco in an hour," Gunnar said, cryptically.

"Will do." I hung up the phone, feeling frustrated about my impromptu nap. It had stolen valuable time. An update from Roland would have to wait, as would answers from Richard about my book requests. I also didn't have time to check in on Claire about her supposed presence at Dorian Gray's party or drill Xuanwu about the Four Divines.

Because I hadn't seen any of the others since I'd arrived here with Quentin and Phix.

Speaking of Phix, I needed to get away from her without her asking—or demanding—to tag along. "Hey, Phix," I called out. "Keep an eye on your new students and give them a history lesson about me. I need to go talk to Xylo at Solomon's Temple," I lied, "but I'll be back later tonight. I need them to stay here where no one can find them," I explained, referring to the protective barrier around Xuanwu's estate.

She eyed me suspiciously and I held my breath. "Can I make them fight each other if I get annoyed?"

Quentin and Adrian slowed, turning to look at me with a wary frown. I nodded, hurriedly. "Only near the revival pond." I turned to the Nephilim. "Don't annoy her."

And I made a Gateway before anyone could argue with me.

46

Gunnar and Alucard faced me with determined scowls, wearing the same clothes they had on earlier. Chateau Falco loomed over their shoulders and I made a silent oath that we were bringing Nate home to her, no matter how many Olympians stood in our path. After all, it was the only way to get Ryuu, Yahn, and Gunnar's pups back. Gunnar had received a visit from Hermes and had been given a coin that would supposedly take us to the meeting. The messenger god had been strangely tight-lipped, according to Gunnar.

I did not bring up my own meeting with Hermes. It wouldn't provide any answers but it would ignite at least a dozen questions, and we were already swimming in a plethora of those.

Gunnar was gripping Mjolnir tightly, but Alucard held no visible weapon. He looked like he was ready for a road trip, only needing his sunglasses. They had agreed to follow my lead during the meeting, watching my back in case we were bait for the trap Zeus was obviously laying for Nate. The two men were playing chess, and we were the pieces, as were the other Olympians attending the meeting. I gave Gunnar a nod and he flipped the golden coin into the air. A wavering haze appeared before us—an invisible Gateway. I couldn't see or hear anything through it, so I had no idea what we were stepping into.

I took a deep breath, and then stepped through. Gunnar and Alucard followed, and we found ourselves standing on a vast expanse of flat rock near the peak of a colossal mountain, surrounded above and below by thick black clouds. Red lightning crackled in every direction, dancing from cloud to cloud, and thunder growled ominously like some great monster lurked just out of sight, waiting to devour us. It was the most ominous storm I could have imagined in my darkest nightmares. The very air felt pregnant with violence, intrigue, anticipation, and deep, deep hatred.

The actual peak climbed up from the plateau about fifty yards away—a sharp pyramid of stone that stretched maybe another hundred feet higher than our current elevation. I swiveled my head in a circle, assessing the shifting, roiling black clouds surrounding us. I saw no other mountains in the distance, making this feel like a lonely island in the sky. It was obviously not Mount Olympus, judging by the lack of buildings or structures, but we were in the right neighborhood.

Because a thirty-foot-wide set of stairs stretched up towards a raised pavilion ringed with elegant Greek columns that were topped with ornate marble entablatures to form a perfect circle overhead. I shared a long look with Gunnar and Alucard, spotting the upper half of an older man with long, iron-gray hair waiting for us.

"Let's go take our places," I murmured, striding up the stairs and keeping my eyes on the stranger. Even from a distance, I had a damned good idea who he was. Power radiated from him. Zeus, Father of the Olympians and, according to Nate, the biggest son of a bitch to have ever lived. *He would hurt his own children to get what he wants*, I reminded myself, steeling my spine for whatever came next.

As I crested the steps, my eyes latched onto something else, and my heart dropped into my stomach. Gunnar and Alucard flinched behind me. Peter knelt before Zeus—previously out of our view from the base of the stairs or I would have approached with more caution. His face was pale and he looked to be on the verge of passing out from pain. Probably because his hands had been chopped off at the forearms. The ends were now cauterized and black with burned skin and dried blood. I didn't see a Sensate hanging from his neck, and I managed to keep my face blank, even though I wanted to fall to my knees in relief. It wasn't Nate, and that was a win.

Gunnar and Alucard growled aggressively, thankfully also aware that it wasn't Nate or they might have charged to attack Zeus. But we still had to put on a show since Peter had kidnapped our friends.

I sniffed indelicately and then resumed my scan of our surroundings to make sure no one else was lying in wait as I led my group to the opposite end of the pavilion from Zeus.

I blinked to see that the Temple family crest dominated the center of the pavilion's polished marble floor; it was at least eight-feet in diameter and ringed in twin bands of gold and silver. The crest was stained with liberal splashes of golden ichor—the blood of the gods—reminding me of a murder scene. What the hell was Nate's family crest doing way the hell up here?

I looked up at Zeus, directly across the Temple crest from us, careful to keep my face blank and neutral since I was supposed to believe Nate had been working for him. As far as I was supposed to know, Zeus was our ally. He was a tan, older man in the prime of his life, and his eyes seemed to flicker with electricity. He had a long white beard and wavy, iron gray hair. His body was chiseled with muscle, exactly like every statue depicting him, but his face was devoid of wrinkles or liver spots. A few creases at the corners of his eyes were the only indication of age.

I flicked my gaze down at Peter, curling my lip in disdain. "Charming," I said. "He kidnapped our friends, so don't expect any tears from us. We only came for blood." Zeus nodded, almost imperceptibly, but I caught a flicker of doubt in his eyes. That wasn't good. We couldn't afford his suspicion before Nate even arrived. I glanced from left to right, indicating the lack of people. "Where is Nate? Hermes told us to meet him here."

The suspicious gleam in his eyes faded. "I'm sure he will be along shortly. Isn't that right, Aphrodite?" he asked, sounding amused. Alucard and Gunnar grunted as the goddess of sex materialized out of thin air a few paces away from Zeus. Judging by their reactions, I realized that they had never seen her before. Either that, or they weren't getting enough attention at home. Thankfully, they didn't actually begin drooling, although Alucard did lift his sunglasses for an unimpeded professional assessment.

She didn't meet my eyes, but I caught her glancing at my clothes, point-edly, instantly making me feel self-conscious. What had *that* meant? What had she done to my clothes? I gave her a polite nod, acting as if we'd never met before.

The marble columns lining the perimeter of the pavilion made me feel like we were trapped in a bird cage, even though there was no ceiling. Beyond the marble pedestals was open, turbulent sky, meaning we were actually trapped up here unless we wanted to fly. I felt no sense of vertigo, even as the wind slapped and pushed at me. Then again, I had fucking wings, so it almost sounded exciting to peer off the edge of the world and take a flying leap with both middle fingers held high.

Between one second and the next, Nate Temple stepped out of thin air onto the Temple crest. I stared, momentarily impressed that he'd managed a Gateway without any of us sensing his magic. Then I recalled the coin Hermes had given Gunnar, and my wounded pride faded to realize that I had given Nate too much credit.

He no longer wore his Titan Thorns or he would have looked like a two-handed Peter. I bit back a smile, realizing I could sense his magic in addition to our Horseman bond. If he'd broken the Titan Thorns, did that mean he'd found his true love? If so...where was Kára? Or had he given his heart to someone other than the Valkyrie? Maybe she was keeping an eye on Ryuu and the other hostages. That made me feel better.

Nate wore an impeccable suit with his satchel slung across his chest, and the top few buttons of his white dress shirt were undone, revealing two necklaces tucked against his flesh. One of them was the Sensate and the other was a familiar coin—his Horseman's Mask of Hope. He looked relatively unharmed, but his eyes were dark, menacing, and committed.

He was the glint of light on Death's scythe, and the instant tightening of Zeus' eyes told me he sensed it as well.

Nate turned to look at us and discreetly shook his head—so faint that I could have mistaken it for a trick of the eye. His eyes were screaming at us, reminding us to maintain our roles while Nate led us down the rabbit hole. I knew things were about to get exceptionally strange, especially violent, and that I would have a lot of questions after the fact since I was not up to date on all things St. Louis.

That was fine. I was, primarily, here for Ryuu, but a close second was fulfilling my role as a Horseman and supporting my friend, the man who had given me the job in the first place. Nate was our brother in arms.

The leader of the Dread Four. Tonight was our official debut, and it was expected to be a doozy.

Nate completely ignored Aphrodite and turned to Zeus, seemingly unfazed by the god's smile. Zeus' eyes were calculating, confirming my assumption that this was going to be a long, confusing night of schemers getting their scheme on. Zeus didn't look remotely surprised to see that Nate no longer wore his Titan Thorns, but he did look mildly annoyed that the first small win of the night had gone to his foe. He'd also anticipated a bigger reaction to Aphrodite's presence.

Nate gave him nothing. Instead, he focused on Peter with a wicked grin. "Deja vu," he said. "So weird. Reminds me of the time you betrayed me to work for Alaric Slate," he said, glancing back at Zeus with a pensive expression.

Zeus stared back at him with a small, insincere smile. "I am so glad that you made it, Temple. I just heard the most troubling news from your Horsemen. That this man," he said, pointing at Peter, "abducted several of your friends."

"He's pretty much the worst," Nate agreed. "I had to teach him to keep his hands to himself, which is ironic since that involved taking them away from him," he added, chuckling like a psychopath. So...*Nate* had severed Peter's hands. Apparently, he'd had an eventful afternoon and had wasted no time in punishing his old friend, Peter. No naps for Hope.

Zeus' face remained perfectly calm, but his eyes were a window into madness.

"I'm sure—as a gesture of goodwill—the Horsemen would appreciate you *handing*," Nate paused to aim a cruel smile at Peter for the bad pun, "him over to their custody." Peter narrowed his eyes at Nate in a hateful glare, but he didn't make a sound.

Aphrodite eyed Nate's suit with a pointed look, and I could see that it had bothered him. Had...she made a set of clothes for Nate as well? She'd given my clothes a similar look. Zeus shot Aphrodite a dark glare. "I too know something of betrayal, but I think we've come to an understanding," he growled.

She nodded stiffly at her father, refusing to look at anyone else. What familial dysfunction had we stumbled into? I wondered if any of this was going to make sense any time soon. I resigned myself to listening and acting stoic. Nate needed us here for a fight; the rest was just two cocks fighting over a chicken coop. Empty pageantry as they got a better read on their opponent before the final battle.

Zeus smiled. "I must applaud you on incapacitating this criminal," he said, indicating Peter. "It bodes well for our future partnership. Loyalty is vital."

"Cool. Why isn't he walking past me yet? The Horsemen are right there," Nate replied, pointing a thumb at us.

"Maybe he needs a hand," Alucard drawled, lifting his sunglasses as if to get a closer look. Then he chuckled.

47

Zeus pursed his lips. "I have a few questions for him and then he is all yours. It seems my sons are missing, and I believe he might know where they are. Hermes is looking for them as we speak. Once he returns, the criminal is all yours." Peter's eyes widened in shock, but he still didn't make a sound. Not even a muffled one. Judging by the pain in his eyes, he should have let out some kind of agonizing groan, or at least a deep breath, by now. Zeus must have gagged him—which actually served to validate our ruse, now that I thought about it. Peter couldn't deny Nate's allegations about kidnapping our friends. Unless...Zeus already knew that had been a lie.

"Oh, I'm sure they'll be here any minute..." Nate said with a shit-eating grin.

Aphrodite looked up sharply and Zeus' smile slipped for a second.

"I spoke with Hera, believe it or not. Boy, is she a talker," Nate continued, shaking his head and walking a few steps away from the crest, appearing to scan his surroundings in an absent, half-handed assessment of potential danger. But Nate hadn't looked surprised at our location, so I was betting he knew it well and needed no threat assessment. Nate never did anything without a purpose, so I watched him very closely while pretending to look annoyed and impatient. Nate set his hands on his hips and squinted up at the raging skies with a distant smile. "This is so beautiful. The red on black. I *swear* I've seen it before…"

Zeus' eyes may have well been daggers, still hung up on the fact that Nate had taken his wife out for a date. "Oh?" he asked. "Did my wife—"

"How about we just cut the shit, Zeus," Nate interrupted, turning to face him with absolutely zero respect in his posture or tone. I felt goosebumps on my arms, mentally preparing for the inevitable fight. "You're going to give me the girl back. Then we can discuss our *partnership*." Nate actually spit on the ground after saying the word *partnership*.

"Do you mean Alice?" Zeus asked, frowning. "You brought her here yourself. To keep her safe," he said in a faux puzzled tone. Nate narrowed his eyes, obviously having done no such thing. In the confusion, I motioned for Gunnar and Alucard not to react, one way or another. The slightest miscue could ruin whatever games Nate and Zeus were playing. Zeus turned to Aphrodite like a stage manager directing a play, finally revealing why Aphrodite was present.

She waved a hand, and Alice was suddenly standing between her and Zeus. I sucked in a sharp breath of relief to see the child entirely unharmed. She wore a cute little yellow dress with white tights and shiny black flats. Alice blinked, momentarily confused at her surroundings, and then she saw Nate. Her eyes lit up with joy like a kid seeing Santa.

"Nate! You're back!" she squealed. "Look!" she giggled, excitedly. "Freya helped me make a magic purse so I can be just like you!" she said. A bright blue shoulder purse suddenly appeared at her hip. She caressed it with all the love and affection a purse deserved. Freya had made her an invisible purse.

Nate was so shocked and relieved to see her healthy and unharmed that he didn't even complain about Alice referring to his satchel as a purse. Although she was currently safe, she was obviously a hostage, and she obviously believed that Nate really had delivered her to Zeus, which was strange. Alice could see through almost any illusion. She was, in fact, a Seer. A startlingly powerful one. How had Zeus managed to trick her?

"It's beautiful, Alice. I'm so glad you're safe," Nate finally said, and I could tell his mind was racing with half-cocked ideas on how to get her out of Zeus' reach where he could keep her safe. As much as it hurt, I kept my face blank, occasionally shooting hungry, murderous looks at Peter—as if that was the only reason I was wasting my time here. Gunnar and Alucard did the same, following my lead.

Zeus placed a hand on Alice's shoulder in a gentle but possessive manner. Alice smiled up at him. "Safe?" she asked, turning to Nate with a slight frown. "Safe from whom?"

Nate pointed an accusatory finger at Peter. "He was abducting people I care about—"

Without waiting for Nate to finish, Alice promptly clutched the hem of her dress and shuffled up to Peter to kick him in the kidney. My eyes widened in surprise and Gunnar actually coughed. Alucard chuckled, nodding his approval. Peter groaned in utter silence, proving he really was gagged with magic. He didn't move from his spot or fall down on his side, either, which meant he was also restrained. Alice turned her nose up at him. "Bully!"

Even Zeus looked surprised by her reaction. "Good job, Alice. He is a terrible, terrible man," he said, squeezing her shoulder and meeting Nate's glare with a mockingly kind, grandfatherly smile.

Alice took one look at Nate's scowl and she frowned, nervously. "Are you mad at me?" she asked in a soft, scared voice. Nate immediately shook his head, but I saw a strange look pass over Alice's face, as if she'd just seen something in Nate, using her Seer powers. Then she let out a sharp gasp. "Oh! Don't be scared. I've kept your Catalyst book safe. It's in my magic purse," she said, sounding on the verge of tears as she reached inside to pull out a tattered book.

I froze, not liking the sound of that one bit. The fucking Catalyst book? A text that probably described, in great detail, why Nate was so important for the upcoming Omega War. Pretty much the entire reason Nate's parents had fucked with everyone's lives? Well, shit.

Before anyone could stop him, Zeus calmly reached over her shoulder and plucked it from her grip with a hungry grin. "Finally," he breathed with a rapturous smile, staring down at the book and dropping all pretenses that he cared for Alice. This was what he had been waiting for—why he'd abducted Alice. To get leverage on Nate and, ultimately, the Dread Four.

"Hey!" Alice snapped, kicking the god in the ankle. "Give it back, you big bully! That's mine!"

Zeus cursed in surprise, but rage swiftly took over and his face morphed into a visage of violence. "Move even a finger from that spot, or utter another syllable, and I will end your miserable existence, you wretched creature," he snarled, his eyes suddenly crackling with electricity. Alice froze at his startlingly abrupt change in demeanor. "You can't count the number of times I almost threw you off the cliff to cease your endless babbling," he muttered. "This makes it all worth it," he said, smiling at the deadly book.

Alice hung her head, her shoulders shrinking. Then they began to tremble. She sniffled...

I cringed, discreetly checking up on Nate, fearing that he was about to kick off the Omega War right here, right now. The raw pain and molten fury in his eyes made my heart skip a beat and I felt Gunnar and Alucard shift their feet behind me. "No," I breathed, firmly, but only loud enough for them to hear.

Zeus gave Nate a triumphant grin, not seeming to notice Alice's reaction. "This will be of great help in the upcoming war. Knowing how the Catalyst ticks." A shadow of fear settled over me. If Zeus could control the Catalyst with that book, he really would single-handedly control the Dread Four. "The book you found in Fae," he mused. "The book that got her parents killed. The book about the Omegabet and the Catalyst."

Nate stared back at him and I saw his eyes narrow ever so slightly, as if he'd had an epiphany of some kind. I wasn't sure anyone else saw it because it was gone almost the moment I saw it. His attention shifted to Alice for a brief moment, and then he licked his lips, nervously.

"One step closer and I'll burn it to ashes," Zeus warned, staring straight at me for some reason. "You need it just as much as me, Temple. That much I know. Right, Alice?" She nodded stiffly, still sniffling.

Despite everything, Gunnar growled loud enough for everyone to hear. "I'm here for my kids. That scumbag will pay for what he's done," he snarled, glaring at Peter. Alucard echoed his agreement, forcing me to do the same or attract suspicion.

"Let's make a deal, old man," Nate said, reaching into his satchel and pulling out—

I gasped. And I wasn't the only one. Nate held Pandora's Box in his hand. What the *fuck* was he thinking?

Zeus frowned suspiciously, and then he licked his lips at the opportunity to seize even greater power and control. "She's inside?" he asked, warily. Nate nodded. "I will not be handing over my leverage, Temple," he said, dryly, lifting the Catalyst book. "With this, I can *make* you do what I want."

Nate shook his head. "Keep the book. Give me Alice."

Zeus grunted. "Why? A vile slip of a girl for Pandora and her Armory? That's foolish."

Nate shrugged. "Think about it, Zeus. All the scary stories you've heard about me...the stories that keep you awake at night. I did all of those things *without* the Armory," he said with a chilling smile. "I don't need the trinkets within to be the Catalyst."

Zeus reconsidered the exchange in silence. "One condition," he finally said, crouching down and beckoning Alice closer. She shied away from him, careful not to move her feet due to his earlier threat.

"Touch her and the Omega War starts *now*," Nate snarled, clenching a fist.

Zeus scoffed. "I need a quick favor, is all. I will not touch her. Consider it rent for her visit. I had to send Hermes to buy crayons just to get her to shut up for more than five minutes." Speaking of, I wondered where Hermes was right now.

"Alice?" Nate asked, offering her the choice to make her own decision on the matter before he agreed. She nodded nervously, putting on a brave face as she gave him a weak thumbs up.

Brave girl, I thought to myself, mentally preparing myself for the worst.

"Fine," Nate muttered.

"Come here, child," Zeus said, smiling like a snake. I saw Nate slip his hand into his satchel, preparing some form of attack, but he didn't look my way for back-up so it obviously wasn't a discreet signal for us to raise mayhem. Alice walked up to Zeus and the god bent down to whisper in her ear. I shot Alucard an inquisitive look but he shook his head. He hadn't been able to eavesdrop.

Alice slowly turned to look at Aphrodite, her eyes growing distant and dazed. Then she glanced at Nate for a moment before turning back to Zeus. "I can see that your daughter is loyal," she said.

I felt my blood run cold. Wait...if Aphrodite was loyal to Zeus, things were about to get very fucking complex.

Nate looked just as confused. One thing I knew about a Seer was that they could read a person so clearly that they could often accurately determine their intentions and innermost desires. Yet she hadn't seen through Zeus' false hospitality. What was really going on here? Had Alice just lied, or had Aphrodite been lying to both me and Nate?

Aphrodite smiled, looking relieved.

Two bodies suddenly slammed into the pavilion and slid across the marble floor, leaving a fresh slug-like trail of ichor emanating from the Temple Crest design. Everyone jumped in alarm, equally shocked by the sudden comets.

I risked a quick glance to see two horribly beaten, bloody men whimpering and groaning in agony, unable to stand. Mist rose up from their clothes like they were smuggling dry ice.

I couldn't even make out who they were through all the blood and dirt covering their faces, but the golden ichor told me one thing—they were gods, and probably Olympians. I remembered Zeus saying he was waiting on Ares and Apollo to arrive, and I took a wild guess.

They had just fucking arrived. And we were two bodies closer to war.

48

Zeus scowled at his sons with a disgusted look. "Incompetent pieces of shit," he growled.

"The box for the girl," Nate reminded him.

Zeus studied Nate with a calculating eye. Then he shrugged. "I can't say they didn't deserve a little payback," he admitted, unconcernedly. Talk about fatherly love. "And if the two of them couldn't get the best of you while you were shackled and tied to a table, they deserved what you gave them."

I frowned, glancing at Gunnar and Alucard to see if they'd known anything about Nate somehow beating the hell out of two Olympians all by himself. He had to have done it since we last saw him. Had he whooped the shit out of Hermes as well? Maybe Aphrodite's advice had been spot on— don't trust *any* Olympian. Even Aphrodite. Gunnar and Alucard shook their heads, just as surprised as me.

Nate smirked. "I left them alive as a show of goodwill."

"Or a stroke of cruelty," Zeus suggested, not sounding upset in the slightest about it. Nate shrugged and held out the box. After a few tense moments, Zeus finally nodded. "Bring it over."

"No. I'll give it to Aphrodite," Nate said, firmly. "You now know you can trust her, and I know she would never hurt a little girl. It's fair. I've learned to always trust the boobs of the operation."

Which was one of Nate's most glaring flaws. Gunnar and Alucard nodded, absently, unaware of their idiocy.

Zeus glanced at Aphrodite with a threatening glare and finally nodded. Nate sidestepped around the two whimpering Olympian brothers and approached Aphrodite.

"Is this a good idea, Nate?" Alucard asked.

Nate glanced our way. "I would do anything to protect a child, Alucard. *Anything.* Even if it hurt my friends and those I care about. Even if it hurt me." The double meaning was heavy, even though Zeus remained oblivious, focused solely on the box in Nate's hands.

Alucard stared back, looking as if he'd been slapped—no doubt thinking of Yahn. He finally nodded back. Gunnar and I both shot him a reassuring look before turning back to the action.

Aphrodite looked extremely uneasy, licking her lips and practically quaking in her sandals as Nate handed her the box. Nate calmly backed away, staring her in the eyes the entire time. Zeus gave Alice a dismissive shove, and she used it as a boost to sprint to freedom. Nate knelt down on the ground, holding his arms out, and Alice hit him like a flying octopus, wrapping her arms and legs around him and burying her head into his neck. Nate rose to his feet, his eyes a little wild around the edges as he held her tightly and backed away from the Olympians and towards us. "It's okay, Alice. Dad's got you," he whispered, trembling slightly.

My heart was racing. This was no fucking place for a child, especially not after Nate had so easily handed over the keys to the kingdom. Something terribly clever was about to happen.

Alice murmured something into his ear and then I heard her let out a soft, relieved giggle. Nate missed a step, and then played it off like nothing had happened, whispering back to her. The raging storm made it impossible to overhear their secret conversation.

Aphrodite stared down at the box in her hands with a dreamy smile that made me feel particularly squeamish. She didn't notice that Zeus was frowning at her impatiently, his fingers twitching at his side, desperate to get his hands on the box.

Nate set Alice down in front of me, and then turned back towards Zeus, advancing a step as if to shield us from the Olympians. I felt a rush of air race past my face as something smacked Nate's ass with a sharp slap, causing him to flinch. I looked down to see that Alice was suddenly gone. I sucked in a breath but Nate glanced back at us with a firm shake of his head and an amused grin. What the hell? Nate had an invisible, ass-slapping, altruistic kidnapper on call?

I sniffed at the air, briefly catching a familiar scent, but the constantly shifting wind from the surrounding storm dispersed all traces before I could define it.

"Hand it over, daughter," Zeus warned, drawing my attention. "Or have you forgotten who has Hephaestus?"

She slowly looked up at him, cocking her head with an amused frown. "And will that matter when I open this box and watch your flesh peeled from your bones?"

For the millionth time, I expected for us to throw down. Zeus pursed his lips and I swear his eyes flared brighter.

"You see, Father," Aphrodite continued, "I think I've reached that age in a young woman's life where she needs to spread her wings. You know what I mean. That special day when you wake up and just know that today is the day your father dies," she said, smiling sweetly. "Because you just love him too much to let him keep on living," she said deadpan.

Although she'd just proven to be a psychopath, I felt relieved to have her back on our side. Or at least not on *his* side.

"Be very, *very* careful, daughter. My patience has limits," Zeus warned.

"You are destroying our legacy," she seethed. "You are a monster. And I will not stand for it. I care more about my *own* family. My loving husband and his daughter, Pandora. *Our* daughter. Your warmongering is over." She stared down at the box wistfully. "I can feel her inside. The power," she breathed, her eyes dilating.

And...I suddenly felt like an idiot for doubting her. I'd completely forgotten about her desire to save Pandora from Zeus' reach as a boon to her husband, Hephaestus. To remove her father's ability to blackmail the black-smith god.

So, once again, this was about loving or hating one's children. Zeus claiming father of the year as he did absolutely nothing for the still bleeding and crying Ares and Apollo while he threatened his daughter, Aphrodite.

On the other hand, Aphrodite being willing to risk pissing off the head honcho—her dad—of all Olympians in order to protect her husband's child, totally obliterating the evil step-mother cliche. Nate, of course, being willing to throw down with absolutely anyone for Alice, and risk permanently losing his best friends' trust in order to save their loved ones from Zeus' clutches...

In a way, Aphrodite and Nate were doing the exact same thing—fighting for a child who wasn't even theirs at the expense of losing something they held most dear. It was the very definition of self-sacrifice.

Zeus spun to glare at Alice, searching for any kind of leverage at hand. I watched his face go still for at least two seconds to see her missing, and then it contorted into a mask of rage that threatened to bring the whole mountain crashing down on top of all of us—even himself.

In that moment, Zeus lost the war. All that was left was for the archers to pick off the stragglers.

For the cavalry—the Dread Four—to ride over all resistance. Gunnar and Alucard smiled hungrily, licking their lips.

Nate shocked the hell out of us by bursting out with laughter. Zeus' eyes were actually crackling with electricity as he spun towards Nate. "I didn't even plan this one," Nate cackled. "You did this to yourself, you sick bastard."

The ruby-red lightning and distant peals of thunder raced closer between one moment and the next, and the maelstrom of wind began whipping my hair back and forth. "What is the meaning of this, Temple?" Zeus demanded, patting the book in his hands with the same level of violence as if he was cocking a pistol. "I thought we had an understanding."

"I'm not very good at understanding," Nate shouted back, fighting to be heard over the growling storm threatening to swallow us whole. "Oh, and before I forget, Alice wanted me to tell you something before she left. Page three is her favorite," he shouted, pointing at the Catalyst book with a triumphant grin.

I shared a meaningful look with Gunnar but he shrugged, absently adjusting his eyepatch as he focused back on Zeus. The Father of the Olympians frantically flipped open the old book and a bookmark slipped out, floating to the ground even as it was pushed and pulled by the inconsistent wind.

I gasped in disbelief, recognizing the long, black feather with a red orb at the tip. It belonged to Nate's unicorn, Grimm. I turned to look at Nate only to find him grinning like a madman. Like he'd just received the signal he'd been waiting for all this time.

"Grimm," Nate hissed. "Come to me."

I stepped up beside Nate, as did Gunnar and Alucard, and we stared up at the skies, mirroring Nate's excited smile. Within seconds, the familiar black unicorn appeared in the skies, his shadow wings spread wide, silhouetted against the ruby glow flashing behind the ominous black clouds. It was breathtaking and instantly made me envious that I hadn't brought Phix, but I'd needed to keep her on Nephilim duty. If I'd told her to come, everyone and their mother would have wanted to know what I was doing in St. Louis tonight that might be more important than taking on the Seven Sins, rogue Nephilim, or the mysteriously absent Archangels.

"Hidey Ho, motherfuckers!" Grimm's voice boomed through the skies, louder than the rolling thunder. "Check this out. I can shoot freaking rainbows from my freaking *head*!"

I stared in horror as a nimbus of dark energy blossomed around his horn, accompanied by the breathless sound of a soul-shredding scream that only grew more desperate as the black sphere grew larger. Within that orb of destruction was a lone white light, shining as bright as a star.

"TASTE THE PAIN-BOW!" Grimm screamed.

And a colorless, achromatic rainbow erupted out of his horn, slamming down to the pavilion in a smeared beam of grays and blacks that reminded me of a smudged charcoal sketch. The smell of burning ozone filled the air as it struck the polished marble where Zeus had been standing moments before. Unfortunately, Zeus had jumped clear, so the concentrated blast missed him by no more than a foot.

A spider's web of crimson lightning exploded across the sky, illuminating Grimm from behind, and I saw Nate's hand instinctively reach for his Horseman's Mask as he murmured something under his breath with a hopeful look in his eyes.

One of the bolts of lightning abruptly lashed out like a striking snake, latching onto Grimm's horn and exploding into a supernova of red light that made me squint for fear of getting blinded. I heard Zeus' cruel laughter, and I opened my eyes to see him seated on the ground, pointing a finger up at where Grimm had been flying. The unicorn was nowhere to be seen.

Barely a second later, Grimm slammed down onto the pavilion, his fiery hooves crushing either Apollo or Ares' outstretched hand, eliciting a desperate scream. Grimm did not apologize for this. In fact, his tail flipped up and...

I stared in disbelief. Grimm took a steaming crap on Ares and Apollo's broken, bleeding bodies. Literally. He scraped his back hooves like a dog finishing his business and then shook his coat of long black feathers while emitting a motor boating sound. "That loosed my bowels a little, thunder-snatch," he said, staring directly into Zeus' eyes.

But something else caught my eye. Underneath his feathers, Grimm's flesh looked to be made of black-diamond armor, just like when Nate fully drew on his Horseman's Mask. I grunted, impressed, realizing why Nate had grabbed at his Mask. He'd used it to armor Grimm for Zeus' impending lightning strike. Talk about quick thinking.

Otherwise Grimm would have been nothing more than unicorn dust raining down from the sky.

Peter, the poor bastard, was now standing up with a panicked, terrified look in his eyes, pointing his stumps at his reddening face. He was definitely trying to scream or shout or beg for help, but he couldn't move and he couldn't open his lips. I'd completely forgotten about him. Handless Pete—kind of like Shoeless Joe—had accidentally pissed his pants at the near miss from Grimm's painbow blast. I dismissed him as I saw Aphrodite on all fours, clumsily crawling towards Pandora's Box, which she'd lost during Grimm's attack.

Zeus lunged for it, snatching it for himself with a triumphant shout. He held it close to his heart and shot Nate an evil grin, panting heavily. "We've both played our games, Temple, and you played better than I anticipated, but we both knew it would come down to this," the god said, benevolently accepting his victory as he tapped the box with a finger.

Nate laughed dismissively. "Unless it's empty," he said, turning his back on Zeus to face us. He made the universal *let's wrap it up and go* gesture to us with one finger high above his head. "I'm starving. Anyone want pizza?"

"I was holding out for a gyro," a woman's disembodied voice purred right in front of my face, scaring the living shit out of me and causing Alucard to stumble back into Gunnar's broad chest with a cry of alarm. "But I'll settle for you, Pharos," the voice continued, still invisible but right in front of me. Why did it sound familiar—

"Kára?" I hissed, finally recognizing it from our brief encounter earlier in the day. She smelled of citrus and flower petals, and I recognized it as the same scent I'd picked up when Alice had disappeared and someone had slapped Nate's ass. Which, now that I thought about it, made perfect sense.

So...who was watching over Ryuu and the others? Kára had obviously taken Alice to safety, so they were likely all together.

"What do you mean?" Zeus shouted, furious that we were ignoring him. Grimm was pawing at one of the bloody gods, chuckling darkly at each new whimper of pain he discovered, like a child playing a keyboard for the first time.

"Alice is safe," Kára said. "But I have something to do before we leave."

Gunnar and Alucard had recovered, puffing their chests out to prove that they were not afraid of the invisible Valkyrie, and they looked as if they had as many questions for Nate and Kára as I did. Nate grinned. "Don't look at me. The girl does what she wants. I'm just along for the ride."

"You wouldn't dare bring me an empty box!" Zeus shouted. Nate rolled his eyes and turned back around with an annoyed look on his face. "I can feel her power within," Zeus continued. Was Pandora hiding around here somewhere? How else would Zeus feel her power if the box was empty "It's undeniable," he continued, adamant about the fact that he could sense her. "Aphrodite, get your husband out here. I put him in Temple's old cell. He will verify that his daughter is inside the box or he will die sobbing at your feet."

Aphrodite flinched, hesitated for half-a-second, and then meekly caved to her father's command. She obviously loved her husband more than she hated her father, because she stumbled to her feet and all but ran down the stairs in a drunken, weaving pattern. There were prison cells here? And then it hit me. This must be where Nate had been in jail for a week, tortured daily by Ares and Apollo? That was why Nate hadn't been surprised by the surroundings. Holy shit—

A forceful grunt snapped my attention back to see Peter was now sporting three sizable holes in his gut, as if impaled by...Kára's trident? No fucking way! Peter choked, silently, his nostrils flaring as tears poured down his cheeks and he slapped at the holes in his stomach with his stumps.

Then he was flying across the ground at a dizzying speed, obviously propelled by the invisible Valkyrie, but it looked more like he'd learned how to levitate and didn't know how to control it. Like an adult trying to use one of those self-propelled skateboard contraptions sold at every mall in America.

He slammed face-first into a marble column with a disgusting, entirely fatal, *splat* and Kára finally shimmered into full view, tugging a Greek era helmet from her head that made me think of Leonidas' legendary Spartan helm.

Her golden armor, although dented and scratched in places, gleamed in the crimson glow of the storm as fingers of ruby lightning exploded in the distance. She smiled down at the limp body of Peter with a satisfied grin. I glanced over at Nate to find him all but drooling as he stared at the Valkyrie. The way he looked at her told me everything I needed to know about how he had finally broken free of his Titan Thorns. I had questions on the particulars, but there was no denying how he felt about Kára.

Love was an understatement. Despite him being suspicious of her being under an illusion, he still loved her, unconditionally. I smiled, admitting that this was not the place for love. Then again, maybe it was.

Grimm had taken time away from his Olympian keyboard lessons to let out a loud neighing sound. "She's so badass. Never argue with her. Ever," he warned. Gunnar and Alucard murmured their agreement, and then seemed embarrassed about it.

Kára let out a huff. "That was *empowering.*" She set her boot on Peter's lower back and yanked her trident free. Then she glanced from Zeus to us, brushing a few loose strands of hair back with a gauntleted hand. There was simply no damned fear in her eyes. At all. It was almost frightening. Alucard made an approving sound and Nate elbowed him in the gut in a reflexive motion, knocking the wind out of the vampire. Gunnar smirked, squeezing Mjolnir's handle as if desperately needing to use it before he imploded.

"ENOUGH!" Zeus roared, shifting his attention down to the box in his hands, obviously unwilling to wait for Aphrodite's return. I watched him hesitate as a whisper of fear drifted across his face. Pandora's Box was no freaking joke. I didn't blame him at all.

"All right. Pay attention, everyone," Nate said, snapping me out of my thoughts. We huddled around him, leaving room for Grimm and Kára, who was already jogging back to us. "You're about to see a man look into the abyss," he told us in a severe tone, his eyes flicking towards Zeus to gauge how long we had.

"What do you mean?" I demanded, frustrated. "Why would you give him the box?"

Nate rode right over my question, still staring at Zeus. "And the abyss is about to fight back," he growled, licking his lips. "I can practically taste the fear in the air already."

"I'm here," Kára said, skidding to a halt beside Nate. She blindly squeezed his hand, but her eyes were also locked on Zeus rather than our huddle. "Did you do it?" she asked Nate.

"Yup."

"He's going to shit," she replied, smirking.

"Wait. How do you know what I did?" he asked, frowning at her.

She shrugged. "Alice is a talker. Apparently, she's been learning quite a bit from Freya," she said with a proud smile.

What the hell were they talking about?

"Anyone else about done with the cryptic lovers?" Alucard grumbled, as if reading my mind. "Because I want to hit something. Now." Gunnar pounded Mjolnir into his palm and clenched his jaw, nodding.

"Good," Nate said as he blindly pointed at Ares and Apollo with all the concern he might show a vaguely unique tree on a three-day hike through a forest. "Because they're faking it. Empty bottles of Ambrosia in their hands. Heals them right back up. Any minute now."

I snarled, shifting my feet so that I faced the new threat.

Grimm chuckled. "Now I feel bad," he said, laughing even harder as his hoof pawed at the ground, leaving a trail of white fire. I bit back my own laugh, recalling him taking a crap on the two gods and then playing Chopsticks with them.

"What were you two talking about?" Gunnar pressed, frowning at Nate and Kára. "What did you do?"

"Just watch," Nate murmured, still staring at Zeus as he struggled with the lid, finally committing to opening it. "You should probably put on your Masks. There might be fallout..."

49

We all turned to Zeus as he fumbled with the box, even though my full attention was actually focused on Ares and Apollo, waiting for their surprise attack. A thick, milky-white mist suddenly flooded the pavilion as I felt Nate draw on his magic.

"When you see them get up," Nate said, discreetly pointing at Ares and Apollo, "I need you to howl as loud as you can, Gunnar. I want you to make your vocal chords hurt. Howl for Calvin and Makayla."

Gunnar grinned wickedly. "I take it they're scared of wolves?"

"They weren't a few hours ago, but they spent some time in your old vacation spot," Nate said, chuckling.

Gunnar laughed. "They'll think the mist is from Niflheim," he breathed, nodding eagerly. I grunted. That was where Nate had sent them? To freaking Niflheim, the realm of deadly mist? Why would a wolf howl frighten them? The only Norse wolf I knew of was Fenrir, Loki's son—the giant wolf destined to kill Odin in Ragnarök.

And then it hit me. Nate had just *saved* Fenrir from captivity before he was captured in turn by Zeus. He must have stashed Loki and Fenrir in Niflheim—and then sent the two Olympians there for a party with their cousins. No wonder they looked like they'd been gnawed on and beat to hell. They'd just survived a giant freaking wolf strong enough to kill Odin. I eyed Nate with grim respect. That was downright cold of him to call up mist so soon after their encounter. Talk about PTSD.

"If they don't scream it, I need one of you guys to do it," Nate urged. "Loud enough for Zeus to hear." We nodded our agreement. "And put your damned Masks on!" he snapped. Then he snaked his hand around Kára's waist, pulled her close, and kissed her with so much passion that it was almost primal.

She melted into the kiss as the mist swirled around them. I growled, maybe a little jealously but also happily, as I reached into my pocket and grabbed the silver butterfly charm that I used to disguise my Mask of Despair. I pulled it out and slapped the mask over my face, gasping at what felt like a thousand fingers massaging my cheeks as the Mask fused with my skin. With very little effort, I could enhance my vision to move faster than everyone around me, almost seeming to freeze time. Like entering the Matrix.

But after sitting on the sidelines for so long through the Olympian soap opera *All Zeus' Children* episode, I really wanted to get my hands dirty. I knew the precise moment Gunnar and Alucard put their Masks on because I sensed a chiming hum of power connecting the three of us together, strengthening us like a braided rope rather than three separate strings.

Nate and Kára had separated during our wardrobe change, and were now staring at us with feverish grins. "They're all growed up," Nate mused, proudly.

To them, I knew my mask looked like uncut white crystal with six silver teardrops spilling down my cheeks. From the waist down, my body became ephemeral, blending with the glittering white mist Nate had summoned so that it looked like the roiling fog was an extension of me. As I moved my arms, I left a trail of misty vapor in my wake. I knew I could shift fully into mist and zip through walls, but the first time I'd done it had burned up almost all of my energy. This time, however...

I wasn't sure I'd *ever* felt so energetic, as if Gunnar and Alucard were feeding power into me like extension cords.

I glanced over at Gunnar, grinning with anticipation. The Horseman of Justice was a towering white wolf, easily eight-feet-tall even though he was slightly hunched forward. His golden mask had reformed to fit his canine face, making me think of those old plague doctor masks with the long beaks.

His paws sported long black diamond claws, and his thick shaggy fur looked to weigh a few hundred pounds all by itself.

The Horseman of Absolution—Alucard—hovered above a scorched circle on the ground. His quartz-like skin gleamed with emerald light, and claws of pure flame hung from his fingers like whips. I could feel their heat even though we were five feet apart.

"Ahh, shit!" Grimm neighed, prancing about excitedly. "It's *happening!*"

"Make your legend, Riders." Nate said, dipping his chin in respect. He pointed behind us and we turned to see Ares and Apollo climbing to their feet, looking alarmed at the blanket of mist surrounding them.

Ares wore a deep red toga trimmed in gold and cinched with a wide, leather belt. His fiery red hair was tied back in a man-bun, his cheeks were grotesquely scarred, and he had a thick ginger beard. His head was the shape of a worn boulder that had tumbled down Mount Olympus a few times. There was nothing symmetric about it at all. He was big and strong, but he definitely wasn't ripped or running at a low body fat percentage. He was just a massive man—like the guys in those strong man competitions. He was just *big*.

Apollo, on the other hand, was tall and lithe with broad shoulders like a swimmer, but legs like a thirteen-year-old long distance runner. The stark contrast between his torso and his lower half made me cringe—built more similar to an ostrich than a humanoid male. His once white and gold toga was stained with blood and filth, and his long blonde hair was a bird's nest from his time in Niflheim. He had a gaunt, imperious look on his face as if he was always looking down upon anyone who might attempt to talk to him. He was the guy who lifted his pinky when he took a drink.

Gunnar let out a bone-chilling howl that actually caused the mist to stir and roll. The two Olympians jumped in fear, waving their arms at the fog in hopes of dispelling it.

"NIFLHEIM!" Apollo screamed, terrified to the bone. "Why is it so dark—"

Ares grabbed him by both shoulders and violently shook him before pointing at the three of us. "This ain't Niflheim," he growled, seeing through Nate's plan to mess with their heads. "Get your shit together." He drew a flaming sword, and I found myself grinning as he doubled in size, becoming almost as large as Gunnar. As he grew, close to thirty skeletons rose up from the mist like wraiths, their eyes glowing with red fire to match Ares' sword.

Apollo tried to look tough by angrily scowling at us, but he smelled scared. He began to glow, powering up—

Absolution zipped towards him to tackle him in midair, burning a clear path through the mist in his wake. He hit the god so hard that they both flew entirely off the pavilion and then *through* the black clouds and out of sight. Golden and green flashes of light intermixed with the red lightning, creating a dazzling light show.

"Wow," Nate murmured. And then he cursed as a swirling knot of green and gold light exploded out of the clouds and zipped right back towards us, barely missing our heads as the Horseman of Absolution and Apollo chose a change in scenery for their battle.

I heard Nate and Kára talking to each other, but I tuned them out, locking my gaze on Ares and his small army.

It began to rain, hard, the water pouring down on us in great heavy sheets. Gunnar stepped up beside me, huffing heavily as we assessed Ares and his small army. The water striking their skulls resembled fresh blood every time a blast of ruby lightning crackled across the sky.

Zeus was playing weatherman in an effort to slow us down and dispel the mist. I saw Nate and Kára racing through the fog, skirting the skeletons as they closed in on Zeus. Olympian politics and retrieving Pandora's Box were up to them; the war zone was up to me and Gunnar. Oh, and—

Alucard zipped past us again, and I instinctively slowed time to make sure I knew which way to lean so as not to get clotheslined. For my efforts, I clearly saw that Alucard was laughing as he literally rode Apollo like a surfboard, crouching at the knees to tug hard on a fistful of the god's hair while grinding his lead foot into Apollo's face. Alucard was laughing as he stomped his back foot into Apollo's groin in a steady rhythm. I grunted, resuming my perception of time to normal speed to deal with my own Olympian.

Ares, the god of war.

I stepped forward, crafting the mist around me into a long, wickedly sharp spear that glowed with inner light. "They are just skeletons," I said in a calm tone, but my voice exploded across the pavilion like thunder, making Ares flinch. "And bones *break*."

I pointed my spear at the closest skeletons and they exploded into clouds of dust.

Ares snarled, slamming his fiery sword down into the ground. This time, *hundreds* of skeletons rose up from the mist, and these all wore armor and wielded gleaming weapons. They didn't bother with Nate and Kára, but focused directly on me and Gunnar—Despair and Justice.

Justice tucked Mjolnir into a thick leather belt at his waist, reached down and grabbed one of the new skeletons, and then ripped it in half with a bestial roar. His massive tail wagged, beating at the mist and bowling over a handful of armored skeletons. Then he proceeded to beat the closest skeletons with the remains he held in either paw, swinging them like clubs. Since he was bigger than me and could cover more ground, I let him focus on the skeletons as I squared off with Ares and his massive, fiery sword. I knew mist didn't work well against fire so I hurled my spear at the god of war. He swatted it aside with a dismissive sneer, not realizing it had only been a distraction, allowing me time to reach behind my back and draw my silver katana.

Our size difference was comical, but he still looked cautious. I took a moment to imagine all the things he had done to Nate Temple on this mountain. The full week of torture Ares and Apollo had given him several times a day, every day. Any shred of decency or honor for the fight ahead evaporated in my mind.

This wasn't a battle. This was a humiliation for all to see.

"Most people say you are evil and violent, Ares," I said, holding my katana between us. "But I think you're myth-understood. You look like a big old whiny bitch to me."

50

He gritted his teeth and his sword hand quivered with rage. "The things I'm going to do to you, Horseman—"

I sped up my perception of time—making the pavilion stand still—and rushed the god of war. I stabbed him in the gut and then sliced his sword wrist before the pressure of manipulating time throbbed at my temples. I backed up a few steps and let it go.

Ares roared with pain, dropping his sword and clutching at his gut. The fiery sword impaled him straight through the foot and he squealed in agony. His eyes locked onto mine and I knew there would be no mercy from him.

"You were saying?" I asked, smirking.

He snarled and then made his way towards me, limping and furious. I took a moment to glance back at Zeus, and I was just in time to see him finally open Pandora's box—only to be blasted with a shower of embers and sparks that lit his beard up like a wildfire. He dropped the box, swatting at his flaming beard, and a fist of molten lava burst out of the box to punch him in the face with volcanic knuckles. What the fuck was going on over there, and why wasn't Nate doing anything useful?

I focused back on my own problems rather than worrying about Nate. Ares batted a wandering skeleton out of the way without breaking eye contact. Then he swung his sword down at me, fully intending to smash me like a bug. I pivoted and spun, flicking my sword out to slice through his knee before I rolled between his legs and called up my silver claws in my free hand to stab him straight in the groin—without looking because I was directly under his toga and I wasn't eager to see a two-thousand-year-old fire-crotch. He gasped and fell to his knees, unable to support his weight after my gash to his leg.

I jumped onto his back and stabbed him in the shoulder, burying my sword through his collar-bone. He reached back and grabbed me by the shoulder, but I grabbed onto his man-bun to use as a tether. He flexed in an attempt to throw me clear across the pavilion but I held tight to my fistful of his hair, so he paid the price of ripping an alarming chunk of his own scalp free for the benefit of tossing me a few feet away. Right before impact, I shifted to mist and disappeared from his sight as he screamed and cursed about his new bald patch.

Which was when Gunnar hit him like a truck, sinking his massive fangs into Ares' chest and sending him crashing into a pavilion. The two of them tumbled and rolled, fighting with claws and fists because Ares had lost his sword.

I heard shouts and screams coming from Zeus' direction, as well as blasts of lightning, flares of orange light, geysers of molten rock flying through the air, and unrecognizable voices screaming at each other. I spun to see Zeus hovering high overhead, clutching his stomach. Ichor and what looked like lava dripped down from his wounds, and his beard was almost burned entirely off. I glanced down at the ground to see Pandora had arrived and that she was wielding a scythe at least twice as long as she was tall. A large, fiery man stood beside her and his fists glowed like molten rock.

The black clouds began to swirl around Zeus, the crimson lightning screaming as it grew, piling on top of itself. Zeus' eyes glowed like stars and I knew he was about to blow up the entire goddamned mountain.

ABSOLUTION! Disrupt Zeus! I mentally screamed at Alucard. *He's getting ready to throw something big!*

Alucard's voice came to me, sounding amused. *Ready or not, here I come!*

Alucard and Apollo screamed across the sky, aiming directly for Zeus, forcing him to release his gathered power. After a few quick passes, Zeus finally gave up, spun around, and then took off through the clouds, fleeing the mountain and abandoning his children. I saw stunning, metallic wings flare out from Kára's back, reminding me of a magician fanning out a deck of cards—except her feathers looked like a fan of swords rather than paper.

She shoved that Greek helmet on her head and promptly disappeared. Nate climbed atop Grimm and took to the skies, pursuing Zeus like a hunter pursuing his prey.

Looked like we were all on our own.

Apollo slammed into the ground directly in front of me. I grabbed him by the hair, feeling the power of the Horseman mantle flow into my muscles as I took stock of our fight. Apollo groaned weakly, obviously disoriented from the aerial manhandling he'd suffered under Alucard's surfing skills.

I saw Gunnar hoist Ares over his head with both hands and let out a roar as if he intended to perform the WWE backbreaker on the god of war. Instead, Alucard swooped down from the sky and halted about a foot away from Ares' face, hovering in mid-air. He made a kissing sound and then blasted him in the face with a beam of fire that sent the god cartwheeling through the mist and into another column, cracking the marble. The entablature above wobbled precariously and Ares climbed to his feet, lifting his arms high to catch it right before it crushed him. Then he flung it at Alucard, knocking him down to the ground.

"JUSTICE!" I shouted, drawing the ridiculously large werewolf's attention. With the power of the Horseman's mantle powering my muscles, I lifted Apollo up as easily as a rag doll and began to swing him in a dizzying circle. "FETCH!" I screamed, releasing the god of the sun and sending him flying through the air.

My aim was off, so Gunnar tore across the pavilion, destroying the dozens of skeletons who were somehow still alive and currently in his way. Gunnar leapt into the air and caught Apollo in his teeth by the knees, chomping his jaws hard enough to shatter the sun god's tiny, tiny legs and create a tiny, tiny shriek of pain. Gunnar landed on all fours and began shaking his head back and forth, slamming Apollo repeatedly into the ground.

Ares ran up and punched Gunnar in the jaw hard enough to make him stumble and send Apollo flying into Alucard, right as he was climbing to his feet. They both went down and, once again, I saw blasts of gold and green light burning away at the mist and scorching pavilions. Gunnar and Ares squared off, circling each other like combatants in a UFC prize fight.

But I had my own problems as several dozen skeletons rose up from the mist, surrounding me. I called up my claws and began tearing through them, drawing on everything Ryuu had taught me about fighting.

The skeletons fell like wheat at harvest, and I felt myself moving faster than I ever had before, riding through the mist like a ghost to appear wherever I wanted without having to cross the space between. Skeletons died before they even knew I was behind them, but more and more rose up in an endless spiral of obvious necromancy on Ares' part. After what had to be a few minutes of my game of whack-a-skull, I froze and let out an amused laugh.

"Ashes to ashes, dust to dust," I snarled, and the skeletons all crumbled to powder. I flung my hand and called up a blast of air to send the skeletal dust out into the sky so it couldn't reform.

I glanced back to see Pandora and lava guy watching me, looking like they wanted to help. Pandora's scythe was gone, but her eyes were feral and hungry.

I shook my head at them. "No. This is our fight. Go find Hephaestus and Aphrodite, and don't let them leave!" The pair nodded and then jogged down the wide stairs towards the prison cells.

I turned to see Gunnar swing Mjolnir in an uppercut fashion and knock Ares into the air. I grinned, calling up my angel wings and gauntlets, and I leapt up high to intercept him. I caught Ares by the throat and flew higher and higher, into the black clouds. Ares punched and kicked at me but I was used to taking blows from Ryuu, and my Horseman's armor over my skin made his attacks more of an annoyance than anything.

"Let me go!" Ares choked. "You wretched bitch!"

I grinned at him. "Okay, Gingersnap." And I let him go.

He plummeted like a pallet of bricks, screaming and cursing as he fell over a hundred feet. I tucked my wings and pursued him all the way to the ground, laughing so that he knew I was close. Gunnar was waiting for him and took a full swing with Mjolnir, clobbering him right before he hit the ground, altering his trajectory into a marble column. He struck it with a crunching sound and did not get back up.

I landed beside Gunnar and released my wings and gauntlets. The massive golden wolf's mask studied my back and then grumbled unhappily, annoyed that he didn't have wings. I shrugged. "Should have picked a better mask, Fido."

He snorted, tucking Mjolnir back into his belt. Then he pointed off to our right. Apollo was crawling away, unable to use his legs. Alucard followed him, occasionally slashing the god's back with his fiery finger whips, urging him onward towards his still motionless brother. Glancing around, I let out a sigh and tugged off my Mask. I expected a full-body shut down of exhaustion, but instead I just felt like I'd had a good long run. I tucked my mask into my pocket and grinned. Gunnar took off his mask and let out a tired breath, shaking his head.

"That's...not so bad, actually," he growled in a parched voice. "I expected to feel a lot worse."

Alucard had herded Apollo next to his brother, and I saw Pandora and lava guy leading Aphrodite and a tall, burly man towards us. Alucard took off his mask and slipped it into his pocket. A perk of the Horseman form was that none of us needed a change of clothes after such extreme transformations—even Gunnar, who was used to such chores.

"We did it, guys," I said, patting them each on the back.

Alucard grinned proudly. "Now what?"

The three of us turned to look towards the sky where I had last seen Nate. "I can still sense him out there, but he's far away," Gunnar said, softly, sounding concerned.

"Then we wait," I said. "Make sure these idiots don't do anything stupid."

⚜ 51 ⚜

he last hour had been ridiculously uneventful. The three of us
Horsemen had kept a firm eye on Ares and Apollo, who now sat
in a corner, humiliated, not daring to attempt an escape. Apollo
couldn't have run anywhere if his life had depended on it, and Ares looked a
little concussed.

But we remained vigilant, standing guard over them. Pandora had intro-
duced the lava guy as Prometheus, the freaking Titan. He'd been entirely
antisocial after his failed attempts to defeat Zeus, and had opted to go sit on
the edge of the pavilion, hanging his legs from the ledge as he lit up a cigar. I
was still struggling to process the fact that he was here, hanging out with us.
One of Zeus' most infamous prisoners, sentenced to thousands of years of
torture for the crime of giving mankind fire. For such a benevolent guy, he
sure wasn't interested in befriending us Freaks.

Pandora and Hephaestus loomed over Aphrodite, who was kneeling on the
ground with her own set of Titan Thorns that Hephaestus himself had placed on
her wrists. He was a tall, stoic man, and his knuckles calluses had calluses. One of
those rugged, say little, do a lot, types who are often found in the Midwest.
Those grouchy bastards you couldn't help but love. But he doted on Pandora,
keeping her close and smiling at her every time she wasn't looking at him.

I thought about asking for his help with the forges at Castle Dracula, in using the Eternal Metal for weapons, about a dozen times. Hell, Aphrodite had all but begged me to get to work on it, and the blacksmith god was her husband. But the tension between them was palpable. He'd put her in Titan Thorns which meant there wasn't a whole lot of trust at the moment, so I chose to leave it alone.

All was relatively calm as we waited to hear from the last member of the Dread Four. The earlier rain had washed away a lot of the mist, but the pavilion was still thick with it, looking more like a haunted cemetery with the black and red clouds blanketing the skies both above and below us. I sensed Nate approaching through our Horseman bond and let out an internal sigh of relief that was echoed by Gunnar and Alucard on either side of me.

He'd gone after Zeus, after all, the most powerful Olympian ever—the god who had managed to defeat and imprison the infamous Titans. I very pointedly did not look at Prometheus. One man, even Nate, stood long odds against Zeus. He had killed Athena, but could anyone really kill Zeus? Was that even possible? I stared up at the stormy sky, realizing the crimson lightning seemed to be moving away from us, the thunder changing to more of a sleepy growl as it retreated.

Through that darkness, I saw Grimm emerge. He tucked in his shadow wings and plummeted to the pavilion, landing in the thickest section of mist that had stubbornly refused to dissipate. He practically disappeared in the thick fog, and I hadn't been able to verify the faces of his riders.

Ares and Apollo stared, hopefully, at the new arrival, licking their lips nervously. We all watched in utter silence as Zeus' head rose up out of the fog. My breath froze. Wait...

Did that mean Zeus had won? Had he imprisoned Nate like we'd imprisoned the three Olympians. "Zeus lives! Father lives!" Apollo shrieked, sensing his imminent salvation.

Salvation did not answer the sun god.

Grimm's voice drifted out from the fog with a malevolent chuckle. "Don't get *ahead* of yourself, sunshine. I ain't yer daddy," the unicorn said, exiting the mist at a steady walk to reveal that Zeus was definitely *not* here to save his sons.

Zeus' severed head was impaled on Grimm's freaking horn. That's why we'd seen it first. He'd been mounted like a hunting trophy.

Everyone gasped, either in horror or shock. I stared, shaking my head in disbelief. Zeus...the Father of the Olympians...was dead. *Really* dead.

Nate had killed one of the most infamous gods in ancient mythology, and then he'd propped the head onto his unicorn's horn, forever ruining the peaceful, magical, benevolent tropes about unicorns that children all around the world held as truth. Grimm crapped on gods, murdered rainbows, cursed like a drunken sailor, and—

I gasped. He really *did* have a Rainbownatti resistance tattoo on his rump! Phix hadn't been lying. Did Nate know about this insane conspiracy? Someone needed to nip that in the bud before it got out of hand.

Nate hopped down from Grimm's back and held out a hand to help Kára down. He held a gnarly pale staff in one hand that looked like an aged piece of driftwood, but the smoking crystal at the top and the glowing runes down its sides told me it was much, much more.

He swept his gaze over us, assessing the situation, but his attention locked onto the wallflower Titan with a thoughtful frown. He leaned over to Kára and whispered something in her ear. She nodded and then trotted over to us, her boots crunching the remaining pulverized skeletal remains like dried twigs. Of course, Nate made sure to watch her departure, smiling like a big idiot. Then he made his way over to Prometheus, squatting down on his heels beside the Titan.

Kára took one look at the fallen Olympians, laughed, and then swatted me on the ass with a giddy giggle, making my eyes bulge. "Tell me everything. I want to hear about every whimper," she said, her eyes twinkling with merriment.

I found myself smiling back as I told her about the fight. Gunnar and Alucard even momentarily forgot about their fear of the Valkyrie and added in their own favorite parts. We were laughing about the bizarre battle back and forth, much to the shame of Ares and Apollo, when I saw Nate approaching out of the corner of my eye.

Nate eyed us up and down as he spent a few moments patting our shoulders and arms as if looking for the wounds he assumed we were hiding. I'll admit that I wanted to do the same with him, verifying he wasn't hiding a severe injury or gaping cut. All in all, it showed how nervous he had been for us. How much he cared. "Everyone all right?"

Gunnar rolled his eye at his childhood friend, looking amused. "Stop mothering us, Nate. It was fun," he said. Alucard wore a smug grin, staring down Apollo and making the Olympian fidget nervously.

I smiled. "No problems, and it *was* fun," I agreed, catching Gunnar's infectious grin. "We made a great team, right Ares?" I asked, taunting the god of war. He clenched his jaw, angrily, but he didn't have the balls to meet my eyes. In fact, by the way he was sitting, he might have lost one or two in our fight.

Nate turned to address Pandora and her dad. "Lord Hephaestus, I presume?" he asked, politely, before making his way over. I hadn't realized he'd never met the blacksmith god before. I bided my time, listening for an opportunity to acquire his services at Castle Dracula or at least plant the seeds for a future discussion. The Omega War was coming, and it was in all our best interests for me to fire up the forges to start crafting weapons with Darling and Dear.

"You must be the Master Temple my daughter keeps raving about. Sorry, I've been a little out of touch with current events," Hephaestus said, rubbing at the pale band of flesh around each of his wrists—evidence that he'd worn cuffs for a very, *very* long time. The two of them spoke back and forth for a bit, but I found my thoughts drifting to Ryuu. The fight was over and I wanted to see him. Now.

Aphrodite's voice snapped me out of my thoughts. She hadn't spoken a word since leaving the cells with her new Titan Thorns. "You helped me right a wrong," she said calmly, speaking to Nate. "Thank you."

Hephaestus pointed at Aphrodite's wrists. "I slapped some new Titan Thorns on—and the key is not love, like the ones you wore. Pandora implied —very strongly—that I needed *your* permission to deal with *my* wife," he growled at Nate, territorially.

Pandora rolled her eyes. "Father," she said in an embarrassed tone. Hephaestus smirked faintly at the victory of embarrassing his daughter. Dad win.

Nate seemed distracted, studying Aphrodite in deep thought. "Can you give me a few minutes, Lord Hephaestus? There is a lot more to the situation than meets the eye, and I would hate to make a hasty, emotional decision. Tempers are high tonight."

Hephaestus straightened at Nate's formal tone. "As you wish...Master Temple," he added, looking surprised he'd added the last part. He watched Nate turn and approach the rest of his Dread Four.

He swiftly and succinctly told us about his own battle, giving us only the highlights. He'd executed Zeus in front of several big-league Olympians and Asgardians, including the elusive Hermes. In an effort to cool concerns, Nate had made an agreement that, essentially, the Dread Four were going to be the universal policemen of the various pantheons. We did not want to start picking off gods, but we had no problem doing it if they crossed a line. He'd created the staff he now held, using Odin's Devourer, to form a truce between Asgard and Olympus. A pact to remain united for the upcoming Omega War—which didn't have a specific start date, so we were agreeing to something fairly generous.

To that effect, he now needed us to swear not to go rogue and start picking off gods without legitimate cause. None of us had any problem with it, so we each sliced our hands and gripped the staff, repeating the oath after him.

Once finished, we turned to address Ares and Apollo, who had heard everything we'd said and now looked absolutely horrified. Stunned silent. To hear they'd been ostracized...had broken them. They'd never believed that such a punishment could happen to gods like them. Which was the whole point of the Dread Four. To teach the gods about Hubris. After three seconds of Nate staring at them, they began begging for their lives, suddenly finding themselves in the position of mortals standing in judgment before gods.

Gunnar calmly stared at them, his lone eye cold and pure.

He turned to Alucard and me, drawing a line across his throat. "I've already killed a god, so they are yours if you want to claim them. Nate and I can handle it, if you do not want to," he said in a neutral tone, not passing shame or judgment on either choice. I nodded my agreement, not even feeling a flicker of doubt in my mind. I knew what they had done to Nate for a solid week. I knew Nate wanted nothing more than to do it himself, with his bare hands. He was giving us a gift that he himself had earned. I felt honored.

Alucard stepped up to Apollo...

I stepped up to Ares...

And...we killed them. If it mattered, I used my katana and Alucard used fire, each of us obliterating their beating hearts. We turned to each other and nodded. I saw no shame or guilt in his eyes, and I knew he saw none in mine. Instead, it only served to bring us closer together.

As they died, their souls flew through the air and struck the crystal atop Nate's staff, illuminating it with red and white light before it grew dim again. Aphrodite let out a sharp breath, assuming it was her turn next.

52

Nate and Kára made their way over to Aphrodite, and I chose to
involve myself in the situation, not knowing how I felt about the
determined look in Nate's eyes. The sudden anxiety I saw in
Pandora's eyes only made me more concerned.

When the gal who just murdered an unarmed guy in cold blood is the
voice of reason, someone made a bad decision a few miles back.

Nate faced Hephaestus and dipped his chin. "Thank you."

The god nodded solemnly. "They deserved worse," he said in a low whisper. "Much worse."

Nate nodded, shifting his attention to Aphrodite with a calculating look
on his face. The threat was obvious. Did she deserve the same fate as her
brothers? Personally, I didn't think so, but I didn't know everything she'd
been involved in regarding St. Louis. She had definitely done more good
than Ares and Apollo, but had she been involved in other crimes that I knew
nothing about? She had obviously schemed with her brothers, but had she
only done so to keep them preoccupied? Or had there been a more nefarious
intent behind her little coup?

She'd helped Nate find his heart's true love in Kára, and she'd done the
same for me. But more importantly, she'd risked everything for the chance
to prevent her father from capturing Pandora. And not for personal gain.
She'd done it to grant her husband freedom from Zeus' tyrannical plans.

To end Zeus' threat of blackmail. And to reunite a father with his daughter.

Nate finally cleared his throat, and I found myself holding my breath. "You should know that she did all this for you—even more than for her hatred for her father. You," Nate said, looking at Pandora and Hephaestus, "were the catalysts who finally pushed her to act rather than remain silent. If Ares and Apollo hadn't been working for her, they would've been working for Zeus. Either way, we would have fought them. And ended them. They would have likely died fighting, but dead all the same." Pandora smiled sadly and Hephaestus looked torn, wrapping a protective arm around his daughter as he stared at his wife.

"The crimes they committed were not at my request," Aphrodite said, lifting her chin proudly. "I did the only thing I could to try and harness their cruelty to a better purpose. I merely distracted them with trying to steal Pandora's Box before Zeus could. So that I could reunite my husband and his daughter. I accept your judgment." She met Nate's eyes with confidence. Then she did the same with Kára and finally me. "I can die with pride. I have accomplished more in the past week than the last millennia. Remember the good times," she told us.

Nate smirked, boyishly, glancing at Kára with a warm, appreciative smile. "Well, she changed my life," he admitted. Kára smiled, nodding her agreement.

"Me, too," I piped in, recognizing a sudden opportunity. "I could...take her for a while. I know a safe place," I explained. If I could become Aphrodite's prison warden, a certain blacksmith god might find a need to swing by Solomon's Temple for some conjugal rejuvenation with my prisoner. That might be pushing it, judging by the somber look on his face, but Hephaestus would definitely be more inclined to visit if Aphrodite were under my roof. And that might give me an opportunity to discuss Eternal Metal and the forges at Castle Dracula. If anyone knew how to work with Eternal Metal it would be Hephaestus.

Aphrodite pursed her lips. "I would prefer a clean death."

I blinked, momentarily confused. Then it hit me. She'd misunderstood my suggestion—which was entirely logical since she'd just seen me murder her brother, Ares, without a lick of remorse. I shook my head and gave her a reassuring smile. "I was not implying torture. I think you might have more to teach me. Maybe some things I could teach you. About family. Perhaps love should not die this night," I said, choosing my words very carefully in hopes they might resonate with both her and Hephaestus.

My words hung heavy in the air, and everyone turned to look at Aphrodite's husband. I crossed my fingers. Literally.

He finally nodded. "That could work." He stared at his wife for a long while, looking torn. "I will need time to think on you, wife. I do not know if I trust you any longer. Perhaps, over time, I could try."

Pandora clutched her father's hand with a hopeful nod. "*We* could try," she corrected, smiling at her stepmother.

A single tear fell from Aphrodite's eye and she nodded, unable to voice her feelings. Then she stopped trying to hold up the world on her shoulders and, like a woman taking off her heels to walk home barefoot from a bar after last call, she gave up. She hung her head to her chest and softly wept, overcome with gratitude and hope for the future of a reunited family.

Kára smiled, reaching out to grasp Nate's hand.

Okay. I was about finished with watching them love all over each other. I cleared my throat. "I can make a Gateway to Solomon's Temple," I explained, facing Pandora and Hephaestus. The temple leased space to Nate's Armory—Pandora's home—so it would be extremely convenient. I tried not to oversell it and sound desperate—although my anxiety and impatience were rapidly increasing as my thoughts began drifting to the problems currently waiting for me back home.

Pandora grinned in understanding—knowing exactly how easy that would make the logistics for their future family get togethers—and nodded her agreement. I felt like I was Pandora's co-conspirator in hooking the two Olympians back up. "You can stay with me in the Armory," she told her dad. "We'll be close enough to visit mother whenever we wish," she said, eyeing Aphrodite. When Pandora voiced the word *mother*, Aphrodite's breath caught, and then she began to sob even harder—a happier, messier cry.

I grinned, watching a father fall victim to his daughter's smile, like a car wreck in slow motion. Finally, he nodded. "That would be...nice," he said, gently, smiling down at Aphrodite in time for her to meet his eyes.

I tried not to let out a huff of relief to keep it professional. Nate sighed, nodding.

"Sap," Kára teased Nate, but she rested her head on his shoulder, obviously finding his reaction endearing. He smiled, shamelessly, and glanced back towards Prometheus. His smile faltered and he grunted. "He left," Nate said with a troubled look.

Since he was male, Kára made the prudent decision to double-check his observational skills. She did not compliment him for his passing grade—one can't give a dog a treat every time they perform a trick, after all. "Why?" she asked.

Nate furrowed his brow, slowly shaking his head. "I'm not sure. I hope he's okay," he murmured, staring out at the turbulent sky with a pensive look. I stepped up beside Nate and Kára, and discreetly motioned for Gunnar and Alucard to get their asses over here—they'd been maintaining their distance from the scary Valkyrie as well as the possibly contagious romance in the air, preferring the two heartless Olympians for company. They shot anxious, wary looks at the Valkyrie, but finally bolstered up enough courage to approach, making sure that Nate was between them and the dreaded emasculator. The five of us stared out at the storm in silence, taking a minute to process all that had transpired this night. The blacks and reds were strangely mesmerizing, reminding me of my time in the Neverwas...

Freaking *yesterday*, I realized with a small twitch. I needed a damned vacation.

"A new one is coming," Nate said in a gravelly voice, studying the storm like he was seeing the future.

"We'll be waiting," Gunnar said, confidently. Then he glanced at Nate sidelong. Except there was nothing discreet about Gunnar's sidelong glances. He was massive and he only had one freaking eye, so if he picked the wrong angle for his target—like right now—he had to turn and directly face his target to succeed. Nate—since he wasn't entirely oblivious and had already passed Kára's visual observational skills test—noticed, and I saw the corner of his mouth curl up in amusement. "We've been talking..." Gunnar said, sounding awkward and uncomfortable as he jerked his chin at me and Alucard, making us accomplices in whatever he was about to say. Kára and Nate turned to look at him. I frowned, because we had *not* been talking, as a matter of fact. But I had to force myself not to burst out laughing at his discomfort, and Alucard let out a nervous breath, peering at Kára from over Gunnar's shoulder like the werewolf was cover for anticipated gunfire. "We want you two to come to family movie night," Gunnar finally blurted in a rush, his eye flicking from Nate to Kára and back like a ticking clock. I couldn't help but grin.

He was sweating, for crying out loud, and I'm pretty sure Alucard was holding his breath. What the hell had Kára said to them in the Vaults to make them this nervous?

Nate chuckled, shrugging. "Okay," he said, drawing the word out. "That wasn't so bad, was it?"

Gunnar eyed Kára like she was a spitting cobra. "She makes me nervous," he admitted.

Kára beamed as if he'd just paid her the greatest compliment. "Do we need to have another talk?" she asked in a soft, meaningful tone.

Gunnar and Alucard tensed, shaking their heads vehemently.

I studied her, humbly admitting that she had valuable things to teach me. "I think we need to have a talk. Whatever Valkyrie mind games you played on them works like a charm," I said. She smiled back and winked before nodding.

Gunnar's phone suddenly belted out the *level-up* mushroom sound from the original Super Mario Brothers game, and Nate burst out laughing. The werewolf fumbled with it, pounding the silence button. He stared down at his phone as if it was a bomb he needed to defuse. "Ashley's probably wondering where I am."

Alucard grunted. "Was there a curfew on saving the world?" he asked, dryly.

Gunnar shook his head uneasily, shifting from foot-to-foot. "I might have told her I was getting groceries..."

I threw my hands into the air and cursed up a storm. "I'm *done*. See you morons later. Where's Ryuu?" I demanded, rounding on Nate and waggling a threatening finger in his face. "I don't want him catching whatever idiocy Gunnar's sick with."

Nate grinned, toothily, and Kára hooted with laughter, doubling over to hammer her gauntleted fist into her armored knees. "You're a dead man, Gunnar," she wheezed.

His face grew sickly. "It was the first thing I thought of," he mumbled, defensively.

Nate shot a look skyward as if beseeching help from on high. Then, realizing gods were no longer the ones to grant wishes to men such as him, he lowered his head with a tired sigh. He motioned for us to huddle around him. "We did a good thing tonight," he said. "And we did it for our families. Our *family*," he amended. "I can guarantee they are more worried about you than you are about them," he said, meeting my eyes first.

Then he lifted his hand and ripped open a massive Gateway to his Armory. Our friends huddled on the other side, but the crowd of faces became a blur as my eyes locked onto one man with perfect clarity. Ryuu leapt through without waiting and flew towards me like an arrow shot from a bow. He cupped my face with both hands and pressed his forehead against mine. I wrapped my hands around his waist and squeezed reassuringly, unable to speak as I breathed in his familiar scent. My fangs extended and I shuddered. He let out a shaky breath, his shoulders seeming to melt now that he'd physically verified I was all right. "My White Rose," he whispered, wiping away a tear that spilled from my eye with his thumb.

I heard my friends rejoicing as they were reunited, but it may as well have been static as Ryuu's physical presence consumed me, igniting each of my senses like fire to gasoline. But one voice snapped me out of my reverie.

"Groceries?" Gunnar's wife demanded. I pulled away from Ryuu, laughing through my tears to see Gunnar awkwardly shifting from foot-to-foot as he attempted to withstand his wife's fury. Ashley Randulf was a handful, and that wasn't taking her werewolf form into account. Or her motherly ferocity.

"That's our cue to leave," I told my ninja in a soft whisper. I grabbed his hand and pulled him away, making a beeline for Aphrodite. Pandora and Hephaestus were staring at the Gateway, curiously, but they shifted their attention to us as we approached. Hephaestus eyed Ryuu with a respectful nod. "I'll take Aphrodite with me and make sure she's taken care of. But you can visit whenever you like," I said with an inviting smile. Then, thinking of Richard's idea to host a feast, I continued. "In fact, I was planning on hosting a big dinner event soon and I would love to have you join us." I gestured vaguely behind me at the chattering voices surrounding the Gateway. "I'll probably be expected to invite that ghastly horde, so it's sure to be...entertaining," I said with a laugh.

"That would be nice," Pandora said, "wouldn't it?"

Hephaestus smiled. "It would be our pleasure," he said, his eyes drifting towards Aphrodite. He cleared his throat. "I hope to find other reasons to visit," he said, cautiously. Yowza! Point for Team Callie!

Aphrodite shot him a smile that made my ears burn, and it wasn't because she was incredibly sexy. The smile she gave him was one of hope and love and...future possibilities. She gave him a shy nod. "I would like that very much," she said in a soft whisper. Then she climbed to her feet, absently brushing her toga straight and blushing.

Inside, I was reenacting a cheer squad. Hephaestus could at least point me in the right direction regarding the Eternal Metal and the forges at Castle Dracula. And I would get the chance to quiz Aphrodite on...all manner of womanly things.

Speaking of which...

I grabbed her hand and ripped open a Gateway to Solomon's Temple, making hasty goodbyes to Hephaestus and Pandora, encouraging them to visit any time, and to explore Nate's Armory. Pandora glanced at Ryuu and then shot me an amused grin before leading her father away towards the others.

I pulled Ryuu and Aphrodite after me through the Gateway, and then we turned for one last goodbye wave. Nate was staring directly at me with a happy smile. He gave me a faint nod and I let the Gateway wink shut.

53

We arrived on the balcony of Solomon's Temple and Aphrodite studied her surroundings with a curious smile.

Phix barreled out of the entryway leading into the temple and skidded to a halt before us, her claws tearing gouges in the marble floor. "Callie Penrose!" she snarled, fuming. "Where in the *hell* have you been? I've been worried sick—"

Aphrodite cleared her throat and took a step forward, cutting Phix off from her tirade. "I am honored to make your acquaintance, Great Sphinx. I am Aphrodite, and Callie Penrose has committed herself to be my jailer," she said, lifting her hands in front of her face and clicking her wrists together. "She informed me that you are her most loyal confidante, and that she only trusts you to escort me to my prison cell until she has time to meet with me."

Phix stared at the goddess with a perplexed yet agreeable demeanor. She shot me a bemused look and I nodded. "It was a secret I couldn't risk anyone discovering. A room should suffice, not a prison cell. Her manacles prevent her from using her abilities," I said, going along with Aphrodite's impromptu suggestion.

Phix's anger petered out and she gave Aphrodite a stiff nod. "Of course she said that. I am the Sphinx. Follow me."

And then she turned around, leading Aphrodite away. Ryuu grunted, shaking his head. "What just happened?"

I was staring at Aphrodite, so I clearly saw the moment when she glanced back at me with a truly salacious smile and wink that included both me and the ninja. I felt my pulse quickening as I realized what she'd just done. She'd played wingwoman for me.

I turned to face Ryuu, breathing heavily. Then I shoved him, hard, using both palms against his chest. "How dare you get kidnapped?" I demanded.

He stared back at me, his face unreadable.

I pushed him again, harder, forcing him to shuffle back a step. "Do you know how worried I've been about you?"

He stared straight into my eyes. "I think I can imagine."

I ripped open a Gateway behind him and shoved him through before he could realize what I'd done, and then I pursued him, drawing both swords from over my shoulders. His back struck a solid surface, not permitting him to escape. I let the Gateway wink shut behind me and stared at him with his back pressed against my bedroom door. My chest was heaving as he stared right back at me, mercilessly. He did not ask stupid questions, and he made no apologies. Those dark eyes glittered, a direct challenge to my fury.

"I talked to Nate," I growled.

Without waiting for his response, I stabbed both katanas into the door over each of his shoulders, less than an inch from slicing into his flesh and hard enough to bury the tips through to the other side of the thick wood.

He did not flinch. He did not even blink. Instead, he smirked. "Oh? And what is this?" he asked, his voice a low, rasping growl.

My heart raced wildly and I felt like my skin was on fire. "A warning," I breathed, and then I stepped forward, close enough to taste his breath, and I reached over his shoulder to trail my fingertips up the back of his neck and across his scalp before gripping him by the hair.

His eyes dilated and he stared back at me, defiantly. "Warnings are for children. I am a man."

I tried not to collapse into a whimpering puddle at the way he said *man*, but I did reflexively tug his hair hard enough to bump the back of his head against the door. The bastard smiled, not giving me an inch.

I bolstered my courage, my fear, my desire, and my trepidation, forming it into a knot in the back of my mind. Then I licked my lips and parted them enough to reveal my silver fangs. He needed to know what I'd become. He needed to see what he was buying.

I needed him to see that I might no longer be the woman he thought I was. That wasn't a cry for help—I knew I was still the same woman, but naked honesty was Ryuu's way, especially when voluntarily given.

He continued to stare into my eyes and I began to fear that he hadn't even noticed my fangs. Maybe it was like how men didn't notice the drastic change in appearance after a woman spent three hours in a salon to get her hair done. I slowly licked the tips to emphasize the point.

He snarled, wrapping one arm around my waist and squeezing our hips together.

Oh. He'd noticed *something* all right...

His other hand deftly opened the door and he pulled me into the dark interior of my Master's Suite, spinning us as we moved so that he could kick the door closed behind him. In the darkness, I felt his Shadow Skin cloak wrap around us, pulling us closer, squeezing our bodies together with questing, unseen fingers of dark magic.

He angled his head and pressed his lips against my neck, biting gently. My skin exploded with tingles and I felt like my eyes rolled into the back of my head as I let out a shuddering gasp and tugged at the fistful of hair I still gripped in one hand. "I saw your fangs at the park," he breathed. "Show me something I haven't seen before, White Rose."

I laughed, huskily, as his mouth explored my neck like an animal. Why had I not assumed he'd noticed? He was Ryuu. He noticed *everything* about me. He just didn't need to talk about it like most people because he wasn't so insecure that he needed external validations to corroborate his feelings.

Ryuu was not a man of words. Ryuu was a man of action.

My fingernails dug into his lower back and I moaned, breathlessly. "You're going to need to rehydrate after your harrowing ordeal," I whispered, licking my lips as we made our way, step-by-step, closer to Dracula's great big bed.

He growled. "I was well taken care of. Do not worry about me. Do your worst."

I laughed and then shoved him backwards onto the bed. I tore off Aphrodite's clothes as he struggled to take off his own. I stood before him, naked in the darkness, marveling at the sensation of the cool, gentle breeze kissing my feverish, sweat-damp flesh, giving me goosebumps. I drew upon my magic to ignite the dozens of candles spread around the corners of the room, casting us in a warm, cozy glow that still left much of the room in shadow. His hands froze as the wavering candlelight gave him his first clear view of me. His eyes glittered with raw hunger, and he seemed unable to breathe or use his hands as he took in every inch of my body from head-to-toe.

"You're taking too long," I growled. I pinned him down to the bed with bands of air and then used a blade of air to slice his clothes open down the center from throat to ankle.

I released my magic and he didn't hesitate to tear them the rest of the way off—literally. He hurled his boots and shredded clothes to the side, shamelessly, and my eyes raked over his body, drinking in the view of his broad chest, his chiseled stomach, his ridiculous obliques and...

Why let my eyes have all the fun?

I slowly climbed onto the bed and crawled towards him, not even bothering to retract my fangs. In fact, I was panting with my mouth open, unable to get enough air as I straddled his waist and stared into his eyes.

"Teach me something, godkiller," he growled in a challenging, hoarse tone, gripping my waist with both hands.

"Gladly, Halo Breaker. Gladly," I purred, digging my fingers into his chest and lowering my hips at a glacial pace...

Some hours later, I lay back on the bed, smiling to myself as I listened to Ryuu's steady breathing as he slept beside me. For the life of me, I had a jingle stuck in my head and it simply would not go away.

Go ninja, go ninja, GO!

Ryuu had definitely lived up to the song's lyrics, and I used it as a lullaby to send me off into the sweet embrace of much-needed sleep.

❧ 54 ❧

I woke up in the morning with a smile on my face, scratches on my back, and my body sore in places and ways that only made me grin wider. I kept my eyes closed as I stretched my arms above my head and my toes as far down as I could before rolling over to...

Ryuu's side of the bed, which brought a fierce hunger out of me.

I nuzzled my cheek into his pillow, inhaling his scent as I reached my hand under the covers to see what was up.

I frowned, feeling only cold sheets. I opened my eyes with a growl, sat up, and swept my gaze around the room. I yawned, seeing no sign of Ryuu. I focused back on the bed and saw a slip of paper with writing on it.

No training today. You looked so peaceful in sleep that I didn't want to wake you. Meeting with Xuanwu to review current events, but will be back soon. You're busy this evening, so don't make plans... —Go ninja, go ninja, GO!

I squawked, crumpling the paper as my face caught fire. How the hell did he know that? Had I been singing it in my sleep? I rolled out of bed, noticed the two sword points still wedged in my door, and grinned. Ryuu wouldn't leave the Angel Killer out like that unless he intended to be back very soon. Still, there was always the possibility of Archangels and Archdemons lurking the halls of Castle Dracula. I made my way over to the door, peeked my head out to check for witnesses, and then I slipped out into the hall, butt ass naked, to tug our katanas out of the wood.

I hurried back inside without incident and closed the door. I laid the two swords down on the bed and made my way to the shower to get freshened up. I spent an hour getting cleaned up, and then I slipped into my white suit, finding that it was perfectly, magically clean. I sheathed my sword at my waist, covered up Ryuu's sword with a blanket, and decided to go check in on Richard, deeming a morning of research was just what I needed after my eventful night fighting Olympians.

I grinned shamelessly, mentally replaying acts two and three of the eventful performance that had taken place in my bed.

I Shadow Walked to Solomon's Temple, surprised that I didn't feel hungry. Even stranger, I still had no craving for blood. Even being intimate with Ryuu—several times—with my fangs out hadn't activated any kind of thirst factor. It had definitely heightened the experience by electrifying all my senses. But none of the typical vampire stuff.

Another reason to get some answers from Richard before checking in with Roland or any of the more dangerous items on my to do list. Fabrizio had told me that the Vatican had given me twenty-four hours to meet with them, but I'd slept right past that deadline without a care in the world. I'd only just remembered.

And here we were. The world was still turning.

I appeared on the balcony overlooking the infamous gardens spread out before Solomon's Temple. I took a deep breath, inhaling the vibrant smell of raw, fresh greenery and flowers. In the distance, I saw the dark sphere of Castle Dracula that I had just departed. I dismissed the strange logistical observation and made my way towards the entrance, wondering if I should stop by and check on Aphrodite. And Phix, for that matter.

I owed Aphrodite a hefty, hefty *wham-bam, thank you, ma'am* for getting Phix out of my hair last night.

But I owed Phix an explanation. She was my partner and she needed to know everything. That sounded exhausting as an initial task of the day item, so I opted for finding Richard, first.

I heard two men talking around the corner and followed the sound of their voices to find Solomon and Richard chatting together over coffee and croissants.

The two finished speaking before turning to me, not looking remotely surprised by my arrival. They must have heard the familiar crack of power that announced Shadow Walking, and they knew I was one of the very few people able to come here without permission. The wards around Solomon's Temple were ridiculous. Not even the residents of Castle Dracula could visit Solomon's Temple without prior approval.

But with the Archangels and Archdemons able to sneak into Castle Dracula, I knew no area was foolproof. Even these two could be Archdemons or Archangels hoping to lure me into a trap. Now that they were all after me, and that Ryuu was no longer here to protect me from them, I wasn't actually confident in how wise it was to be running figurative errands. This was the best opportunity to take me—while Ryuu was elsewhere.

I smothered that cowardly thought under a warm blanket of denial and let out a long breath. "Morning," I said, smiling at the both of them. "What are you two whispering about?" I asked, wondering if they were even aware they had a sexy new roommate-slash-prisoner named Aphrodite.

They grinned, boyishly. "The dinner tomorrow night," Richard said, excitedly. "I kept the guest list small for our first run, but it's going to be a blast."

My eyes widened, even as I smiled at the joyful look in his eyes. "Oh. So soon?" I asked.

He nodded. "I already sent out the invites," he said, tapping a stack of cards on the table beside the tray of croissants. "Here are ten out of twelve RSVPs. Waiting on two stubborn men—Roland and Ryuu."

"Wow," I said. "That's...pretty quick. Why the rush? We just talked about this yesterday. And how did you already get invites sent and responses back?" I asked, incredulously.

"Magic," Richard said, solemnly, waggling his fingers. "That, and I refused to leave them alone until they gave me an answer. In writing," he said, tapping the stack of cards, "because that's what professionals do."

I laughed, shaking my head. "Right. Have either of you seen Claire lately?" I asked, eyeing their coffee cups longingly.

They shook their heads. "Few days ago," Solomon said, glancing at Richard.

He nodded his agreement before turning to me. "Spending time with family is vitally important and never an inconvenience. We should all spend a little more time appreciating what we have rather than focusing so much on tomorrow. At one point in your life, today was your ultimate goal. Living in the moment is taking the time to enjoy the gift earned from your past labors and efforts. There is a reason it's called the present —it's a gift."

I smiled, nodding. "It's easy to forget that sometimes," I agreed, letting out a breath. Solomon smiled at me, kindly. "Well, I look forward to it. Thank you. But I actually swung by to ask you about the research we discussed."

Richard nodded, rising to his feet. "Perfect. I put everything I found in two different libraries," he explained. "Some books are warded from leaving the room, so that's the best I could do," he explained.

Solomon rose to his feet, sipping his coffee with a concerned look in his eyes. "The Seven Sins," he said, shaking his head. "It's been a long time since I banished one of them. They're slippery, tricky creatures. The usual tactics won't work," he said, eyeing the Seal of Solomon on my finger.

I nodded, having assumed as much. I hadn't realized that he'd ever encountered them before, though. "Join us. Your experience would be a great help as I look through the books. Especially since I was under the impression I could take them back and study them at my leisure," I said, sighing. Now I had to schedule research time, locking myself up in a specific library, when I had assassins out in the city trying to kill my people.

Solomon shook his head with a compassionate frown. "You could take most of them with you, actually. I think there are only three bound by the library wards. Not even I can take those out—a safety precaution I put in place so that even extreme leverage against me won't permit me to hand over such dangerous information to my enemies."

I grimaced. "How cynical of you," I said. "But effective and warranted," I admitted. "Well, let's go for a walk, gents."

Solomon shook his head. "Absolutely not. I have reached the age where I do not go looking for adventure; adventure comes to me."

Richard chuckled, shaking his head. "Lazy bum."

Solomon dipped his chin as if it had been a compliment. Then he turned back to me. "Take a look over the restricted books and then bring the others down. I'll tell you what I know and answer any questions you have."

I nodded. "Have a pot of coffee ready. I'm starving."

He arched an eyebrow in confusion. "That doesn't make sense. Do you want me to make some food?"

I gave him a stern glare. "Coffee *is* a food." Then I turned to Richard. "Let's go study Archdemons, kitty."

We made our way towards the temple entrance and then Richard guided me towards one of the main hallways to the right of the grand staircase leading to the second floor. I admired the beautiful art hanging from the walls, promising myself that I really would take a break to spend some more time exploring this place. Richard was obviously lonely and the place truly was breathtaking.

Richard drew me out of my thoughts by clearing his throat. "The first-floor library has a book that may prove most useful on the Seven, and it's not restricted. It's called the *Sev'n Most Sinist'r*."

"You're kidding," I said, feeling a thrill of excitement. Then I hesitated, frowning. "Wait. The Sinister Six were plagiarized from an ancient book about demons?" I demanded. "Is there *no* originality these days?"

Richard frowned, obviously not understanding my question. They weren't big on comics, here at Solomon's Temple. "One problem. I'm going to need your help finding it. We must have mis-categorized it a few hundred years ago."

I frowned on multiple levels—at how casually he'd said a few hundred years ago, and the fact that they'd misplaced a very important book on Archdemons. It wasn't like they were inundated with things to do around here. "Sure. But if that book is the most informative, yet it's not restricted, which books were too dangerous to leave the library?" I asked, shaking my head. "That makes no sense."

Richard shot me a wary look. "The books on Divines and the Azrael Scrolls," he said, making the sign of the cross.

I felt a shiver creep up the back of my neck at his tone. "Azrael, as in the Angel of Death? Didn't he lead the angels that came down to Earth and..." I trailed off, not knowing how to say it politely. "The angels who first parented the Nephilim with mortal women?"

Richard nodded, soberly. "The Watchers."

I rubbed my arms, feeling a faint chill. "Isn't that already public knowl-edge? The Book of Enoch talks about that."

Richard met my eyes. "I was recently informed that the Book of Enoch...*glossed over* quite a bit," he said, sounding troubled. "The Azrael Scrolls are the unadulterated truth."

I sighed. "Well, it's better than nothing. Have you read these restricted books?"

He shook his head, firmly. "I didn't even know about them until you asked for them. Solomon told me that when he first read them, he had nightmares."

I blinked, glancing at him sidelong. "Nightmares," I said, deadpan.

Richard nodded. "For six-hundred-sixty-six nights straight." I sucked in a breath of disbelief. He shot me a meaningful look. "So, no. Solomon locked them up, never told me about them, and then spent the better part of last night strongly advising me never to look at them."

I shuddered, wondering how badly I needed these answers. "He didn't seem very concerned a few minutes ago."

Richard did not respond immediately, but I could see him clenching his jaw. "Your father was a Nephilim and your mother was a Solomon. If anyone could read such apparent horrors without falling victim to them, it would be the amalgamation of Solomon and Nephilim bloodlines."

I grunted, trying to mask my discomfort. "Well, I sure as hell hope so. I don't have time for nightmares. My daily life is a nightmare. Sleep is my only escape from insanity."

I decided to shift topics to something less foreboding. "What did you learn about the Divines?"

He took a right turn at an intersection of hallways but I halted, inhaling through my nose. I...could smell something strange. I wasn't quite sure what it was, but it was enticing. Almost like a wisp of fresh baked rolls or something equally familiar. One of those smells from your childhood that made you smile before you even recognized exactly what it was. The kind of smell that could wake you up out of a deep sleep, like sizzling bacon.

"Let's go this way," I said, absently. "I haven't been down this hall."

Richard paused, glancing back at me. Then he sighed and spun on a heel. "Of course, you pick the direction leading to the library with the Azrael Scrolls," he said, warily. We continued walking and I did my best to not mimic Toucan Sam while cackling *Follow your nose!* "Why did you ask me about the Divines?"

His words almost made me jump because my thoughts were so distracted by the mystery scent. It kept fading and shifting to the point where I felt like I had almost imagined it, only to return a few moments later like a feather tickling my nostrils. "They are obviously rooted in Asian mythology yet Angels and Demons fear them. You are also a mysterious creature with ties to the Christian faith, so I thought that maybe—"

"And I currently resemble an Asian man," he said in a dry tone.

My cheeks heated at my unintended correlation and I swatted him in the arm. "No! You were close to my mother, who was close to Samael and Lilith. I'm just trying to connect dots. My mother spent some time here but then fled, not wanting to put you in danger. She didn't tell you about me and left you in the dark. While doing so, she secretly chose to make a greater demon and greater demoness my godparents. Then those godparents chose to form a Trinity—whatever the fuck that is—with these Divines. Finally, my mother chose to secretly plant one of these Divines here to guard her lab, which almost ended up killing her ancestor, King Solomon. That's why I'm asking you, moron!"

He smirked. "I was just teasing you."

I narrowed my eyes, dangerously. "Maybe it's not healthy for you to do that..."

He chuckled, lifting his hands up in a surrendering gesture. "Solomon and I have spent a great deal of time discussing those very things. Why the secret unions, and why secret unions with dark forces rather than asking for our help? It was almost as if she feared us. We have scoured the libraries about Samael and Lilith and any other number of curiosities you unveiled, but we had not attempted researching the Divines since we thought only two of them remained. We shifted our efforts to vampires after you picked up that after-school activity," he said dryly.

I froze, skidding to a halt as we passed a darkened hallway without the usual stand lamps or burning braziers. It seemed unused, dark, and smelled musty, but that wasn't what had made me stop. I could practically taste the mysterious smell, and my mouth had begun to salivate. "Callie?" Richard asked in a careful tone. "This way."

I didn't look over at him. Instead, I entered the dark hallway. "What's down here?" I asked, sniffing openly.

Richard jogged up behind me. "We shouldn't be back here. This is Solomon's private hall. The rest of the temple is public but he asks for this one slip of privacy. Your mother did the same with the laboratory corridor. You could do the same, but I must insist that you respect his one single wish and ask his permission before going this way," he said, jostling my shoulder.

I instinctively spun and my fangs popped out as I hissed at his uninvited physical contact. He lunged back, shifting to his white lion form as fog began pooling around his feet and his eyes flared to a cerulean glow. He loomed over me as a broad-chested, bipedal white lion. The world's deadliest supernatural assassin—at least by reputation—going back hundreds of years. Until I'd met Ryuu, anyway. "I will go where I please," I growled, extending my silver claws at his escalation to the problem he'd created, no longer caring that he'd seen my fangs.

Last Breath curled his lips at me and let out a coughing snarl. Then he shook his head, looking startled at his own reaction. "S-sorry," he growled in a low, rattling purr. "For a moment, you didn't quite seem like yourself," he said, cocking his head as he studied my face, blatantly giving me the opportunity to explain the silver fangs that he could clearly see for himself.

I swallowed, forcing myself to dial it down a notch, even though I couldn't explain why his touch had triggered me. "I apologize, too. I've had a very rough couple of days and I have no idea how to explain this recent development," I said, touching the tip of my fang with my finger. I let out a nervous breath, waiting for him to say something.

"Is this the real reason why you're so curious about the Nephilim?"

I shrugged. "One of three reasons, to be precise." I glanced down the dark hallway, feeling as if it was pulling me closer. "I'm going down this hall whether you like it or not, Last Breath. I don't know why, but I *need* to do this. My instincts are screaming at me, and I've learned to follow them, even when it hurts someone's feelings."

Last Breath's shoulders loosened and he gave me a hesitant nod. "What do you sense?" he asked, sounding entirely on board now that he knew I sensed a danger of some kind. He was highly protective of Solomon, me, and this place. "Did you see something?" he asked, eyeing me up and down. "No offense, but if we're talking about senses, your skillset is not as fine-tuned as mine. Even with the killer instincts you picked up...yesterday," he teased, tapping his own fangs for emphasis.

I shook my head, firmly. "I can practically *taste* it," I said, feeling both disgusted and strangely euphoric. A very sickening feeling came over me, recalling the last few times I'd felt so...invigorated.

Blood.

Without further commentary, I turned away from Last Breath and called up a ball of light to hover over my palm. I tracked the scent, which grew stronger with each step. It didn't taste or smell like any blood I'd encountered before, but that was just semantics. It didn't smell the same as Eae's angel blood, the Nephilim blood, the demon blood from Dorian's party, or even the Olympian ichor from last night. Yet it was still similar. This tasted...crisp and fruity, reminding me of an apple.

"I don't hear anything," Last Breath said, speaking in a breathy whisper. His purring continued, but it was a comforting, rumbling noise that reminded me I wasn't alone. "I can't see or smell anything either. Are you following some kind of magical trail? Maybe Solomon was working on an experiment in his quarters and left a potion on the burner..."

His words faded from my mind as I focused all my attention on the crisp, fruity taste in the air. I closed my eyes, realizing I could focus much better on the scent without the figurative noise of my other senses bombarding me as they vied for my attention. I inhaled deeply, filling my lungs with the crisp, bitter-sweet scent, trying not to drool. It didn't make me hungry—which was a *huge* fucking relief—but it did make my jaw ache. Kind of like how you can smell a pickle and want it so badly that the first bite, for some weird reason, makes your jaw ache for a moment.

Unless I was weird and that happened to no one else, ever.

My jaw ached exactly like that pickle nibble, and I hadn't actually tasted anything yet.

My boots squeaked, and I froze, not realizing that I'd actually been walking. Last Breath cursed and I opened my eyes, staring down at the ground. A motionless pool of blood fanned out into the hall, originating from an old wooden door that looked like nothing more than a janitor's closet.

A shiver went down my spine. I'd just scented this all by myself. Even Last Breath hadn't noticed a pool of freaking blood. Not even after I'd warned him something was wrong. I really was changing.

I pointed down at the blood, sniffing the air and feeling my heart drop into my chest at an abrupt certainty in my mind. "That...is Solomon's blood," I whispered, my voice shaking.

Last Breath snarled, crouching down to sniff the blood. "Why can't I smell it?" he murmured, sounding terrified that his senses were at war with each other. He could see it right in front of him but not smell it. He then yanked open the door and let out a savage yowl as the light from my ball of magic illuminated a nightmare.

A pile of ancient books, manuscripts, and historical parchments were piled up on the floor, looking like it had all been swept up here in a hurry. King Solomon sat upon the millennia of recorded history and mythology and philosophy like it was a throne of wisdom or a shrine to his life. Yet all that wisdom had not been enough to protect the wisest man in the world. Solomon's throat had been ripped out, and feather quills had been gouged into his eyes.

My breathing slowed and I stared, feeling numb. Solomon's bare feet had been slashed to ribbons, the entire alphabet seemingly carved into the sole of his left foot and an equal number of angelic and demonic runes carved into the sole of his other foot. His fingernails had been torn off or pierced with iron nails, hammered into tall wicker baskets that propped his arms up like armrests for his death throne.

I stared into his eyes at the white feather quills buried into his pupils, unable to even blink as I stopped breathing entirely. Last Breath let out a mournful, choking yowl behind me, but it sounded distant and distorted and stretched out, as if I was hearing it under water.

Despite staring into my ancestor's tortured eyes, my peripheral vision was perfectly clear, almost as if I was staring at one of those optical illusion puzzles where a magic ship appears if you stare at the center and unfocus your eyes. Except the optical illusion was perfectly clear rather than vaguely noticeable.

I knelt down in the pool of blood, feeling a tear roll down my cheek.

Solomon's feet had been pressed against the door, and gravity finally combined with the pool of semi congealed blood to send his body slowly sliding out into the hallway, knocking over the two wicker baskets.

Massive black cobras as thick as pythons suddenly slithered out of the baskets and into the blood, lifting their heads until they were taller than me kneeling. They hissed, revealing gleaming black hoods with a red circle on either side that reminded me of Grimm's feathers. Their fangs were at least as long as my pinky, and they glistened with milky, yellow poison that made the air taste like burned hair. Despite the fact that I was still staring into Solomon's ruined eyes, my peripheral vision saw all.

I did not move.

I did not react.

I did not care.

The world was burning before my eyes, and all I wanted to do was get a little warmer before my heart turned to ice.

My last remaining relative was dead, his body mutilated and then made into a trap. For me.

My instincts screamed at me, telling me that direct eye contact with the cobras would be certain death, so I locked my eyes on my ancestor's tortured, ruined face, only assessing the cobras in my peripheral vision.

The cobras were obviously not any kind of natural creature but rather some genetic hell-spawn mutation. They were too big and their eyes glowed like burning rubies. They began swaying back and forth, hissing at me.

I slowly, ever so slowly, began to frown as I tried to see through Solomon's mutilation and imagine the kindly old man he had once been. I found myself wishing I'd spent a few more minutes sipping mint juleps or iced tea with him on the terraced balcony. Let him read me a story or tell me more about my mother as a young girl.

I realized that if I ever had a little girl, she would not get to sit on his lap or fall asleep in his arms.

I realized that our big dinner feast tomorrow to celebrate family and unity was going to have one empty chair at the head of the table. The host had not survived long enough to receive the toast he'd so adamantly earned.

Another tear rolled down my cheek and I felt my pulse slow further than it ever had before. I waited, calmly, feeling dead inside. I didn't call upon my wizard's magic or my Horseman's coin. My instincts screamed at me that doing so would guarantee my death. These cobras were designed to kill the most powerful of beings. Any attempt to use my powers would get me killed. Last Breath must have had the same instincts because he had not moved a muscle, made a sound, or attempted to help me in any way whatsoever. So, I waited.

After a few painstakingly long seconds, the cobras lunged for my face at the exact same instant, competing for the kill.

※ 56 ※

Without breaking eye contact with my notorious grandfather, my hands lashed out to blindly catch each cobra by the neck. My instincts shouted at me to call up my angelic gauntlets before I dared look into their ruby eyes.

Now!

I obeyed without question, calling up my gauntlets. I heard the crackling sound of rapidly forming ice that stretched out for an eternal heartbeat. Only then was it safe to look at their eyes directly. I finally blinked and turned away from the murdered king—my greatest great ancestor.

The cobras screamed and hissed, snapping their fangs at me as their bodies wrapped around my forearms in an attempt to squeeze me hard enough that I might release them. The frigid cold from my gauntlets coated their necks, and I watched as the hoarfrost slowly trailed down their bodies. I did not let the frost climb up over their heads.

That would be too dignified.

Thankfully, my wings hadn't reflexively ripped out of my back because they might have torn Last Breath in half. I stared into those hateful crimson eyes and relished the frantic shift from rage to terror to agony. I watched as their bodies grew sluggish and cold, frozen and burned, from my gauntlets. Finally, they went stiff and rigid, and their eyes flickered to a dull, sooty rubies rather than living fire. I calmly set them back inside one of the baskets and replaced the lid.

Last Breath grabbed my shoulder. "How the *hell* did you move so fast —Oof!"

As if snapping out of a daydream, I realized that I was now facing him with one palm outstretched. My instincts from training with Ryuu had taken control of my body, causing me to dip and roll my shoulder before spinning and striking the threat with my open palm in the upper thigh. Last Breath had flown into the wall, shattering the stone so hard that his body was halfway wedged into the wall. He groaned, pulled himself out, and grasped his thigh with a furry paw, glaring at me warily.

I did not apologize.

I turned back to Solomon, assessing the scene, and committing it to memory. A demon had done this. A strong one. And they had wanted to send a very personal message to the man who had spent millennia imprisoning other demons. They had desecrated his corpse, torturing him with knowledge. But what were all the books doing here?

I sucked in a breath to see a familiar title under his forearm. I gently moved his arm, ignoring the hiss from Last Breath behind me, to reveal a large black book with crimson, Old English font on the front—like those old, illuminated texts written by monks copying a bible for some forgotten king.

Sev'n M'ost Sinist'r.

The cover, binding, and the gold foil edged paper was dripping with thick, oily blood. I grabbed the book and clutched it to my chest before rising to my feet. I slowly turned to Last Breath and cocked my head suspiciously, staring at him with absolutely zero empathy.

"Did you do this?" I asked. My voice sounded raw and parched to my ears.

His eyes widened in horror. "NO! Of course not!"

I could sense his heartbeat raging inside his chest, but I knew it wasn't from fear. It was a deep, aching pain.

I stepped closer, my eyes hollow and my voice flat. I felt the bond between us, confirming my thoughts that he could not ever betray me, but I didn't know if there was a way for an arch-class angel or demon to fraudulently mimic my blood bond. They'd found a way around every other precaution—even the sanctity of Solomon's Temple. "Then who, *the fuck*, were you eating croissants with on the balcony?" I whispered. "He's been dead for *hours.*"

"Ohmygod..." he wheezed, only just now considering the fact that we'd seen Solomon less than half-an-hour ago. He'd been so emotionally affected by seeing his friend's mutilated body that he wasn't thinking clearly. Last Breath was a notorious hunter, tracker, and killer. If anyone could catch this demon, it would be him.

"You were played by one of the Seven. He even helped you research books about himself, all the while knowing what he'd done. How fucking nihilistic can he be?" I muttered under my breath. Last Breath looked like I'd ripped his heart out with my bare hand. I remembered how his senses had been useless and I cursed. "That's why he had breakfast with you. He must have done something to neutralize your senses. You said he was sleeping in yesterday when I visited you. When did you see him after that?"

Last Breath thought about it, looking like he wanted to vomit. "Last night," he rasped. "He made me dinner and then we visited the libraries for your books."

I nodded, grimly. "Snap out of it, Last Breath. Solomon needs your head in the game. I need your head in the game. The only thing we can do for him now is to avenge him. This asshole is obviously clever, so we need to play this smart. If we run out there guns a'blazing, he'll just disappear on us. He is sick and twisted, but he's not a fighter."

Last Breath took my words to heart and his eyes began to glow brighter. "If he was a fighter, he would have taken me out first, so that he could spend more time torturing Solomon."

I pointed a finger at him. "Precisely. He wants you to feel this pain. Wants the both of us to taste failure. He wanted to destroy what we love most—Solomon and his books," I said, pointing at the king and his throne of mockery and wisdom, "us with our misfit family."

"He...helped me make the dinner invitations," he snarled, curling his lips back in barely restrained rage.

I grimaced, running through the list of Sins in an attempt to guess which one we were dealing with. Greed? Wrath? Gluttony since he helped plan a dinner? I shook my head, not believing they were responsible. Wrath and Greed would likely be fighters. We were dealing with a spider who coveted what we had: books, dinners, family.

Envy. It had to be Envy. I briefly thought of Claire and her suspicious actions days ago, but banished the thought as paranoia.

"How do we get close to him? He will know the moment he sees us," he whispered. "He might even know, now. What if those cobras were his eyes?"

I pursed my lips. "Nothing we can do about that. All we can do is head down there, get a read on the situation, and resort to extreme violence if necessary."

"My senses are useless," Last Breath said in a neutral tone. Not pitying himself but stating a fact.

I shrugged. "You've hunted stronger monsters than yourself before. You fight with your brain. You misdirect and get upwind, lay bait and traps and lure him into the optimal killing field." I frowned at a new thought. "When is the last time you were in this form rather than your human form?"

He cocked his head, thinking. "Yesterday afternoon."

I glanced at Solomon's body with a sickly assessment. He hadn't seen Solomon again until that evening. "The timing seems close enough. He waited until you were in human form to do his work. Hell, he could have even used a demonic persuasion tactic to make you subconsciously not *want* to shift into your hunting form."

"Okay," he said, seeming to regain some confidence. "You obviously have sharper senses than me right now, because you found this all on your own, and then there're your gauntlets," he said, eyeing my hands. I hadn't realized that I had released them or that I was still clutching the bloody book. "I've never seen anyone move as fast as you did with the cobras, and I've never seen *anyone* faster than *me*. What *are* they?"

I shrugged, uncomfortable under his scrutiny, because I had no answers for him. "If we survive this, I'll tell you what I know. We've been gone long enough, and I don't want him getting suspicious. I need to wash this blood off, and I need to take this book," I said. "Solomon looked like he was hiding it for a reason. Either that or the Sin wanted this book hidden away where you couldn't sniff it out." I frowned. "Speaking of books, do you think some of them really are restricted, or do you think that's just what the Sin wanted us to believe? When did he tell you about these specific books being restricted?"

Last Breath grimaced, his ears tucking back. "Last night," he breathed.

I nodded woodenly. "The one in the library wasn't miscatalogued," I said, glancing down at the bloody book in my hand. "It's right here." I frowned, suddenly remembering that I'd dropped off Aphrodite and Phix at the temple last night. I told Last Breath about them, and then asked if he'd seen or heard anything from them.

He shook his head. "I had no idea they were here," he said, sounding alarmed.

Shit. "Now I really need to get my hands on this Sin—to either protect them from harm or to find out what he's done with them."

Richard nodded, determinedly. He glanced at Solomon, took a deep breath, and then approached his old friend. He leaned close, careful not to get his paws in the blood or disturb the potential evidence at the crime scene and murmured a prayer over his oldest friend. I didn't hear the words, but even watching the way his shoulders shook and his voice caught was enough to make my eyes burn. He couldn't even touch his friend for fear of marking himself with blood and possibly alerting the imposter Solomon once we confronted him.

He then calmly reached into the closet and pulled out a rather small satchel the size of a tiny messenger bag. The front was emblazoned with an Old English *S* branded into the trunk of an ancient tree. Last Breath snatched the bloody book from my hand and slipped it into the satchel. He swung it back and forth and I blinked to see that it behaved as if empty rather than swinging with the weight of the book within. He smiled sadly. "For a man who loved to read, he never liked lugging around the weight of a decade's worth of books on his travels." He held it out to me. "He would have wanted you to have it. No one can sense anything within."

I smiled at the bag, realizing it was very similar to the properties of the satchel Darling and Dear had made for Nate Temple at my request. "Did Darling and Dear make this?" I asked.

Last Breath neither confirmed nor denied. "Who?" he asked in a tone that meant he was purposely avoiding my question and had no intention of answering, ever.

"Put the cobras in there, too. If they really are the Sin's eyes, it might confuse him or throw him off track. And I want a damned souvenir for my troubles."

Last Breath eyed the wicker basket, grimacing. "They're dead, right? Because I really hate snakes."

I rolled my eyes. "If they're not dead, they're cryogenically frozen for at least a few hours. Take the satchel with you and go collect a few of the books you discussed with Solomon so we can corroborate our story. Do it as fast as you can."

"Where are you going?" he asked with a protective frown.

I smiled. "I'm going to go to my mother's lab and wash up. I'll come up with a story that will buy us some time. I won't hide the fact that we split up. I need to grab a few things."

He grinned and turned back to the closet. He came back with a similar bag. "This one is mine. Same properties," he said, handing me a black bag with a similar design. "I would like you to have it, Callie. For helping me avenge my friend," he whispered in a hoarse rasp overflowing with despair. He glanced at Solomon and my heart broke to see a tear roll down his furry cheek.

I blinked away my own tears. "We're going to get him, Last Breath. I *swear* it."

He nodded, shaking his mane as if to get his head in the game. His lip curled back to reveal long ivory fangs, and a coughing snarl bubbled up from his throat as he narrowed his glowing blue eyes. "Purrrfect," he growled.

I forced a laugh, even though it was terrible timing for a joke. "I'll flaunt the fact that we split up, telling him that my mother had a secret stash of books on the Divines, since that topic seems to concern him so much. I'll taunt him with the comment, providing him with some bait that is so enticing that he might not even notice you enter from behind, or won't care when you do. That's when you strike."

His eyes glittered hungrily. "I regret that this is our first hunt together, Callie Penrose Solomon. Queen Solomon, now," he added, glaring at his old friend.

I curled my lips, baring my silver fangs. "Then let's make our first hunt together legendary, Last Breath. Let us be the reason to raise our glasses in toast at our feast tomorrow night. Not just in memory of Solomon, but in celebration of avenging the wisest man in the world."

He shuddered and a tear rolled down his other cheek, leaving a trail through the wet fur as he nodded miserably.

I couldn't help it. I wrapped my arms around him and buried my face in his thick white mane. I felt his shoulders stiffen and then relax, melting over me like hot wax as he squeezed me, purring like a locomotive. "I'm sorry about Solomon," I whispered. "We will spend the whole feast listening to you tell stories about Solomon. The good and the bad. The embarrassing and heroic. We will honor him tomorrow, Last Breath. But we will avenge him *today!*" I hissed.

Last Breath growled passionately, a sound of both dreams and nightmares, smiles and cries. "I...will try to make everyone laugh tomorrow," he croaked. "I will...try very hard," he rasped, squeezing me tight enough to hurt.

I squeezed him back just as hard, weeping into his fur as I tried to soak up his pain and lessen his burden. "We can talk about the vine thing," I whispered. "How the big nosy idiot tried to snoop in a young woman's room and almost turned into a tree." Last Breath coughed, nodding stiffly. "Or how he always tanned in the nude," I added. "Crazy old bastard."

Last Breath chuckled miserably. "Thank you, Callie," he whispered, squeezing me tightly. Then he let out a faint laugh. "You are doing a great job of knocking the world back on its heels. I think...you would have even given your mother a run for her money, and before I met her, my fur was golden. Why else do you think Solomon and I have white hair? I aged a thousand years for every one of hers," he teased.

I laughed, wiping my snot and tears off in his mane. I stepped back and winced at the bloody smears I'd stained his fur with. "Damn it. I didn't mean to—"

He shook his fur and the blood evaporated, leaving his gleaming coat pristinely white. He smirked at the surprised look on my face. "I murdered battalions of men at a time, Callie. It was my job. I know how to clean up for a photo op, and a cat hates being dirty," he said.

"Then why didn't you..." I trailed off, glancing at Solomon.

Last Breath hung his head. "The scene needs to be preserved and recorded. He was left like this to deliver a message, and that message might be vitally important." He swallowed, audibly. "And...if I touch him, I will lose what little courage and resolve I have left," he rasped.

I nodded. "We will get him. I swear it."

Last Breath nodded, taking a deep breath Then he pointed a claw at my own white clothes—the set given to me by Aphrodite. "Seems we're a matching pair, but your face and hands are a mess."

I stared down at my white outfit and blinked. He was right. No blood on my knees or anything. My hands were coated in blood from the pool on the floor, but not my clothes. I wiped my thumb on my stomach, grunting to see no blood transfer. I'd forgotten about that little perk. "Well. Aphrodite knows her stuff."

Last Breath began backing away, his tail swishing with anticipation. "Let's go trick a trickster."

I nodded. "Which way to my mom's laboratory?" I asked, frowning. "Or the nearest washbasin."

He pointed back the way we'd come. "Two lefts and a right."

I was already jogging away the moment he'd pointed, the glowing sphere in my palm causing the shadows to flee my advance, so I heard his directions from over my shoulder.

Between my second and third stride, I heard a strange grunt, followed by a bubbling, gurgling sound behind me.

I skidded to a halt as my heart fell into my stomach. "Last Breath?" I asked, my voice sounding entirely too small in the echoing hallway as I slowly turned around.

57

My mind could not fully process what my eyes saw as I stared down the hall back the way I had come.

A naked blonde woman faced Last Breath, giving me a dim side profile of each of them since I had taken the light with me, leaving the hallway in shadows. Neither moved, neither spoke, but she looked familiar, even in the darkness. I heard a steady dripping sound, like pouring water. I frowned, feeling numb.

"Claire?" I called out, taking a step closer. She did not answer me, but she seemed to be smiling at Last Breath, who still hadn't moved. I began jogging closer, my pulse accelerating. Claire's hand was dripping for some reason.

Last Breath fell to his furry knees.

Then his great white lion head fell from his shoulders, landing on the ground with a sickening bounce, before stabilizing so that his dimming blue eyes stared up at the ceiling. Claire lifted a bare foot and kicked Last Breath's body in the chest, sending him sliding into Solomon's dead body. "Aww, now they're holding hands," Claire said in an overly sweet voice. Then she shook her hand off and slowly turned to face me. In the darkness, her eyes looked blindingly white and I saw her lick her dazzlingly bright teeth before she smiled at me.

My heart stopped beating and I froze, unable to think as I stared at Last Breath's head lying in a pool of blood. Last Breath...one of the most notorious killers ever, had just been murdered with hardly any effort whatsoever. I heard a shattering sound in the deepest recesses of my mind as I slowly met the woman's eyes. She had once been my best friend, but that was all gone now. "Claire," I growled.

She smiled, calling up a ball of sickly yellow flame in her palm, and I realized that she was entirely covered in blood. Last Breath's blood. Her fingers sported long black claws, easily long enough to decapitate my friend. She rubbed the blood into her skin like it was lotion, purring happily. Then she let out a jubilant laugh. "It is *so* nice to see you again, Callie."

I hurled magic at her, screaming loud enough to make my vision waver. She swatted it aside with a familiar laugh that made my skin crawl.

And then I was running for her, closing the distance impossibly fast. She flung her hand out at me and a black sphere of evil screamed at my face. I batted it aside with my angelic gauntlet and grinned as I saw her eyes widen in disbelief. She flung three more and I batted those aside, snarling as the tiles shattered under my feet with each step—I was moving entirely too fast for them to support the force of my strides.

I saw the moment she chose to flee, and I dove forward, grabbing her by the throat with my angelic gauntlet. Her eyes bulged and she choked as I squeezed. I spun and slammed the back of her head against the stone wall, shattering the rock to pieces. I screamed incoherently, wanting nothing more than to rip her in half.

She laughed, taking my beating like it was a pillow fight.

"Y-you...wouldn't kill your b-best friend," Claire choked in a taunting tone. I heard shouts from further down the hall, and they sounded familiar.

I squeezed harder, feeling cartilage crack. "Cut the shit, Envy," I snarled, naming her true.

She tried to respond but couldn't beneath my grip. I relaxed my fingers just enough for her to speak and she coughed, hoarsely. "I *am* Envy, child. What I want, you cannot have," she croaked, smiling through her pain. "And let me tell you, this body is so much better than that doddering old bastard, Solomon. One day in that meatsuit was worse than a year in Hell." Her claws trailed over her hips and she moaned. "But this one got to play with Kenai quite a bit, so I'm understandably biased. He fucks like an animal! I wonder what he'll do when he learns he was fucking one of the Seven Sins, not his sassy girlfriend, Claire." She laughed huskily, obviously relishing the thought of his pain and guilt.

"Where. Is. Claire?" I demanded. I shuddered at the thought that Envy had been Solomon from out on the balcony this morning, having breakfast with Last Breath. And Kenai was going to lose his fucking mind when he learned the person he'd been sleeping with had been Envy. I gritted my teeth, remembering that Claire and Kenai had last been seen at Dorian's party. "Was that you at Dorian Gray's house?"

Envy grinned—exactly like Claire grinned, and I had to force myself not to release her on instinct. "You interacted with many of us yesterday, you silly fool. Greed, Gluttony, and Lust." My blood ran cold to hear that I'd been close to more Sins without realizing it. Who? "Lust *really* hates you, by the way. This," she said, waving a hand at the two dead bodies, "is nothing personal, I hope you know. Strictly business."

"They were my *family!*" I roared, tugging her into the center of the hallway before my emotions got the best of me and I bludgeoned her head against the wall.

Envy tried slicing at me, but her claws did no damage, and I realized my angelic gauntlets now emitted a hazy light that acted as full body armor. "Well, they aren't anymore, are they—"

I reared back with my free hand and punched her in the face, rocking her head back. She laughed as I hit her again. And again. And again. I screamed at the top of my lungs until my voice was hoarse, and I never once let go of her neck.

I panted, staring into her eyes as she spit out a tooth with a broken grin. "Give me more, mommy," she cackled in Claire's voice. "I will never tell you where your friend is—or if I killed her like the rest of your pathetic family," she snarled, smirking at Solomon and Last Breath.

I squeezed her neck, knowing I didn't have the strength to kill her but desperately needing her to shut up.

Her eyes bulged and I saw blood vessels bursting in her sclera as she struggled to escape my grip. She had already shrugged off the majority of the pain from my overpowered blows, since Archdemons could do things like that. But that was why I held onto her firmly with my gauntlets—in hopes that it would lock her into place for a few moments to see if I really did have the ability to kill her outright, like Ryuu.

Blood began to drip from her nose and the corners of her eyes as she struggled against me, looking frantic. I loosened some of my pressure, trying to think of anything I could do to actually hurt her.

She took advantage of my leniency. "How are you holding me?" she snarled.

"The Halo Breaker taught me a few things, bitch," I lied. "This is just foreplay."

Envy's eyes darted over my shoulder to look back the way I had come, and then they widened in terror as I heard a snarl from the far end of the hallway. I spun, froze time, and released the Archdemon's throat.

Ryuu stood a dozen feet behind me, all his weight on one foot and his arm outstretched towards me like a pitcher on a baseball mound after releasing the ball. But Angel Killer, his black katana, hovered directly in front of my face, floating in mid-air. I leaned my face to the side, analyzing the intended trajectory, and saw that it had been intended for Envy's mouth and would have missed me by a hair had I not noticed Envy's fear and moved.

He'd been trying to kill her for me.

Fuck.

That.

I felt a monstrous leviathan of rage bloom deep within my breast and it whispered great and terrible things to me. The Omegabet tickled my ears like a lullaby. I listened with great interest. Then, I snarled, baring my fangs, and snatched the Angel Killer from the air by the hilt. I drew the blade down my forearms, whetting the dark metal with the blood of a Nephilim and a Solomon—one side of the legendary blade for each arm.

I leaned close to the demon and drew a symbol on her forehead with my blood—a symbol I hadn't known moments ago. It crackled to life with green fire, burning into the Archdemon's flesh as I patiently stared at the space above her head. As the fiery rune burned itself out, a dark, thorny ring flickered into view.

Envy's Halo.

I reached out and grabbed it, feeling my arm spasm as my muscles locked rigid. I gritted my teeth and screamed, tearing it away from her with a startlingly loud tearing sound. I stood there, panting.

Only then did I release my grip on the flow of time—the ability to speed up my perception of it, at any rate.

Envy screamed in agony, her eyes latching onto the halo in my hand with a look of unadulterated horror and fury. "MINE!" she shrieked in a hoarse croak.

I smirked and shook my head. "That's the problem with you, Envy. You think everything belongs to you, when in fact, *nothing* belongs to you. How can I get it through your *head?*"

She opened her mouth to say something, but my sword arm was already moving. She had time for her eyes to widen in understanding before the Angel Killer slammed into the side of her neck with truly shocking force, powered by my angelic gauntlets. The black katana tore through her neck and whipped out the other side, showering me in her blood.

Just like she had done to Last Breath.

Her head lobbed up into the air and I thrust my sword arm forward in a piercing strike, impaling the severed head at the base of the neck. The body continued to spurt blood out of the gaping wound before Envy's knees gave out and she collapsed to the side, a large pool of blood forming beneath her.

"Oh. *That's* how I get it through your head, bitch!" I snarled, panting heavily.

Ryuu skidded to a halt by my side, his grim face analyzing the chaos of the hallway, noting the evidence and cataloging it in the span of one second. He stared at the severed head as I lowered my arm to inspect it at eye level. We watched as Claire's face changed to a grotesque, scaled monstrosity, more reptilian than human. The body did much the same, shifting into a wretched, slimy, semi-humanoid structure covered in long, wiry hair and blistering sores.

Ryuu glanced down at my other hand, thoughtfully. Envy's Halo seemed to be powering down but I could still sense energy throbbing deep within.

"You never cease to amaze me," he rasped, gently gripping my waist in both hands, and resting his forehead against mine. "What do you need from me right now?"

He didn't chastise me for putting myself in danger or taking unnecessary risks. He didn't try to take control of the situation and tell me what he thought we should do. He didn't comment that I'd just become a Halo Breaker. He...

Asked what I *needed*.

My lower lip trembled, and I realized I was panting, imagining Claire in some cell where I would never find her, or perhaps tortured to death like Solomon. How long had Envy been using her body? Since I outed her at Castle Dracula days ago? What figurative fires had she started using Claire's guise?

"I...think I just want a hug," I whispered.

Even though I was covered in demon blood, Ryuu didn't shy away from kissing my forehead in a gentle, compassionate manner. His kiss said he didn't care about situational details like demon blood. All he saw was me, Callie Penrose, alone on the field of battle—the last warrior standing. And that was cause for celebration.

He pulled me close and gripped the back of my head, pulling it to his shoulder as he hugged me, firmly. "I can do that," he breathed, kissing the top of my head.

58

After a time, I pulled away, staring down at the halo in my hand. "I guess Legion was right," I said. "I really did see his Hello."

Ryuu furrowed his brow for a moment, confused, but then his features slipped into a grim smirk. "Cute," he said, shaking his head. "Gallows humor A Hell Halo. Hello."

I gave him a hollow smile, shrugging as I studied the thorned ring. "It's literally the only thing laughable about this," I whispered, my smile fading as I found I had shifted my attention to Last Breath's severed lion's head. The fur and mane were perfectly clean even though it sat in a pool of blood. His magic eraser lion's mane repelling the blood was a horrifically stark contrast.

There would be no embarrassing stories about Solomon at his great big dinner. The one thing that had made him more excited than I'd ever seen, had been taken from him. From all of us. And all the while, Envy had been helping him plan it, pretending to be Solomon, knowing what she'd done and what she intended to do to Last Breath before it could come to fruition. It was insanely, maddeningly wicked. If she couldn't have a family dinner herself, she would take ours.

"He did not die afraid," Ryuu said, kneeling down on one knee and bowing his head, honoring the fallen warrior.

I saw something vaguely familiar poking out of Ryuu's pocket and I frowned, pointing. "What is that?"

Ryuu glanced down to see what I was pointing at. He sighed, pulling out a small, thick card and I gasped. "It was my RSVP to a dinner. Richard said that I was a part of the family," he said, clenching his other fist hard enough to crack knuckles. "He came by this morning to invite me to a private dinner tonight with just the four of us, but only if I promised to fill out this RSVP for a...celebration dinner party tomorrow with a lot more people. He said something about it being professional to hand deliver this back to him," he said, petting Last Breath's mane with two of his trembling fingers. Then he turned to look up at me and his eyes were red-rimmed and furious. "I wanted to speak with you, first, but when I returned to your rooms and saw the hilt of my sword poking out from the covers, I knew you had left. I felt you come here, and I assumed you were speaking with Aphrodite, and that I could drop off my RSVP like Richard had asked. I found Roland, who was also searching for you and he had an RSVP of his own to deliver, so he made a Gateway here for us."

I frowned. "Roland is *here?*" I whispered, my knees trembling. Ryuu leapt to his feet and caught me before my legs gave out entirely. He smiled down at me, sadly. "I told him to stay back as soon as I saw the blood and realized you held Envy. I didn't want anyone else dying. He would have been a liability."

"I can hear you," Roland's voice growled, and I looked over to see him jogging towards us, his face pale, and his fangs out. Ryuu gently set me down, remaining close in the event my legs gave back out. Roland's crimson eyes glowed with protective fury. He brushed some of my hair back and clenched his jaw in relief to see that I was all right. His eyes flicked towards Solomon and Last Breath and he shuddered. "Oh, Callie," he whispered, cupping my cheek in his palm.

I didn't even try to hide my tears. "Where are Aphrodite and Phix?" I croaked.

Roland smiled. "She might have those cuffs on, but that crazy woman sure knows how to use a blade. She killed two demons before we even knew what was happening."

My eyes widened in alarm. "What?"

Roland nodded, motioning for us to follow him. "The temple is secure. When we arrived, we bumped into Solomon. He took one look at us, cursed, and then fled. The next thing we knew, half-a-dozen demons spilled out of a side room and attacked. Aphrodite and Phix leapt into the fray and I stayed back to help while Ryuu ran to find you. After that, I just followed the screaming," he said, dryly.

My eyes widened suddenly. "My sword!"

Ryuu grunted, lifting up Envy's head on the end of the Angel Killer. "*My* sword," he corrected with a faint smirk. His eyes drifted to my hands and I realized I still held the Hello. It no longer vibrated or hurt, but I could sense the dormant power within. "I don't want to think about that right now," I breathed. I slipped it into the satchel Last Breath had given me...

The last gift he would ever give me. I pointed back over my shoulder. "Can you grab the satchel Last Breath is holding. He was keeping it safe for me." Roland nodded, disappearing for a moment to do the grim work of retrieving it from my friend's lifeless body. He returned and handed it to me. I slung it over my shoulder and gritted my teeth. It was time to get to work. I turned to Roland. "Give me an update on the vampires. Did you get them all?"

He shot Ryuu a wary look before turning back to me. He finally gave a grim nod. "Actually, they are all waiting for me at Castle Dracula. Everyone is waiting to hear why hundreds of vampires moved in over the last twenty-four-hours."

I frowned. "What do you mean *everyone?*"

Ryuu cleared his throat. "The Divines. Eae. Your Nephilim. My ninjas. They have all come to see you."

I slowly turned to look at the two of them. "And was I supposed to tele-pathically get this calendar invite?" I asked.

Roland shrugged. "Well, Hermes showed up with Asterion and King Midas to sign paperwork of some kind. Alucard came back with them, bringing a hundred werewolves as if he thought we were under siege. Then everyone started coming for one reason or another. All I did was announce that I would speak to the new and old residents about the vampires moving in so there weren't any...bloody misunderstandings."

Ryuu cleared his throat. "Perhaps, given the mornings events, we should postpone—"

"Oh, *hell* no!" I snarled, glaring at him.

He smirked. "I was going to say postpone long enough for you to clean up."

I frowned, staring down at my hands and all the blood covering my skin —a blinding contrast to my white clothes. I could feel the blood drying to

317

my hair and face. I turned to Roland and bared my fangs. "Make a fucking Gateway, Roland. This is *exactly* how my people need to see me," I snarled. "This is *me*. The White Rose. Master Dracula. The Horseman of Despair."

Roland grinned wolfishly and ripped open a Gateway. I plucked Envy's severed head from the tip of Ryuu's sword and calmly stepped through to the ramparts of Castle Dracula and an eternal night sky. The Four Divines stood at the edge of the ramparts, staring downward. They turned to me and gasped at the sight of me covered in blood.

Hermes stood off to the side, pointing at the Coliseum in the distance as he spoke with Asterion, King Midas, Dorian Gray, and Alucard. They turned at my arrival, smiled, but their joy faltered and they suddenly looked less eager to negotiate the Coliseum deal with the blood-soaked White Rose.

Claire was nowhere to be seen, but Starlight, Kenai, and Armor stood opposite the St. Louis crew, their arms folded across their chests. They grinned upon seeing me, approving of my makeup, and I realized that it had been forever since I'd seen Armor. I smiled back at him, dipping my chin. Kenai looked concerned and I couldn't make myself meet his eyes.

Eae, Adrian, and Quentin stood with Fabrizio and Aala a few paces away from the bears, looking slightly uncomfortable but excited. Two days ago, this would have been hell itself to them. Fabrizio stepped forward, looking ridiculous with his gauzy oven mitts.

"The Vatican reached out to me," he said in a low tone, grimacing warily at the head in my hand. He licked his lips. "They were...disappointed you did not meet them this morning."

I grinned wickedly. "You have your phone on you?" I asked. He nodded, frowning in confusion. "Then you should record this next part and send it to them," I growled. "Get shots of everything." He stared at me, his jaw hanging open. "That was not a question, Fabrizio. Get out your fucking phone. *Now!*"

He actually jumped, pulling out his phone and holding it up. "Okay. Go."

I cleared my throat, turning to Ryuu. "How's my hair?" I asked him.

Ryuu smirked. "Just the way I like it," he growled. "You're practically glowing."

I nodded, realizing that Fabrizio actually was already recording, shifting the phone to catch our conversation. I laughed, harshly, and called up my silver fangs. Then I grinned at the camera, baring them for the camera. "Good morning, Father Ignatius and esteemed members of the Conclave.

This is the White Rose. I regret missing our meeting this morning, but I had a dentist appointment," I said, tapping the tips of my silver fangs and then grinning, wolfishly. "I wanted to take this time to give you a message," I said, warmly. Then I motioned for Fabrizio to follow me as I made my way to the balustrade overlooking the grounds at Castle Dracula.

Gargoyles screamed in the skies, suddenly spotting my arrival, and a roar louder than anything I'd ever heard before exploded from below the balustrade. I walked up to the edge and stared down at thousands of monsters, vampires, werewolves, frogmen, witches, and other creatures I had no names for. Fabrizio cursed, panning the phone up and down, left and right.

The horde screamed even louder, shaking their fists and staring up at me with bloodthirsty grins. I smiled back at them and slowly lifted Envy's head by the hair for all to see. I called upon my magic to carry my voice far and wide.

"Welcome! As your Master Dracula, I want to welcome you *all* to my Castle. A new age is upon us. An age where fresh lines are drawn, and long-time enemies will soon become the closest of friends. We are FAMILY!"

Their roars momentarily overwhelmed me, so I gave them a few seconds to die down.

Then I slowly swung Envy's head back and forth. "Behold! One of the Seven Deadly Sins dared to attack me this morning. I wanted to introduce her to you before I put her head on a pike at the Castle Keep. Envy's brothers and sisters will soon join her, and our triumphs will know no bounds."

The crowd screamed and snarled.

"There will be changes here in the days to come. The Coliseum will reopen. You will see many new faces. We now have Nephilim brothers to welcome into our fold," I said, motioning for them to step up to the balustrade. "We even have an angel," I added, smiling at Eae. "Show them your wings!" I said. Eae, surprisingly, smiled, baring his teeth as he flared out his wings to the roars of the crowd below. I raised my voice. "As you can see, pantheons and factions that used to be your enemies will soon flock to Castle Dracula, and you *will* welcome them as distant family reunited. Anything less than peace will result in public executions," I warned, staring down at the crowd. "So rejoice and make new friendships," I said, gripping the wall with my angelic gauntlets and calling upon them to glow with crackling blue light. The crowd hushed excitedly, leaning forward.

I flared out my wings, stretching them wide, and then I called up the Spear of Destiny. It exploded to life in my fist, blazing with golden light that shot up into the night sky and stabbed at the heavens. I slammed Envy's head onto the tip, and the beam of light broke, exploding out of her eyes and mouth instead of the clouds above.

"A WAR IS COMING, AND THERE WILL BE BLOOD!" I screamed, hefting the spear up high over my head. Then I bowed...because...why not?

The thousands of freaks at Castle Dracula exploded into a deafening roar, repeating my words in a thunderous, echoing chant.

I turned away and smiled at Fabrizio's camera. "I'll see you soon. When I have time."

I gave Fabrizio a nod and he ended the recording with trembling hands. "You sure?" he asked, lowering the phone.

"Send it," I told him, turning away.

I thought about Last Breath and Solomon. Their dream for a family—starting with tomorrow night's dinner—had inspired my speech. They had wanted to make us into one unified family, and their dream had died with them. So, I would honor it. I would make these monsters into a team. "I will destroy them all," I vowed, thinking of the rest of the Sins. And the Archangels if they wanted to make an issue of it. I turned to see Ryuu staring at me, his dark eyes smoldering. He licked his lips and nodded his approval.

I glanced up at Solomon's Temple in the distance, thinking of Solomon and Last Breath.

"I will miss you so goddamned much," I whispered to myself.

Then I retracted my wings and walked over to Hermes. He winced uneasily, knowing full well what I had done last night to his brother. "Great speech, Callie—"

I punched him directly in the throat, sending him flying into a wall. He lifted his head, blinking dazedly. "Now, we're even." I turned to the Minotaur, who looked like he was ready to agree to whatever I demanded. "Let's go make a deal," I snarled. "The Coliseum isn't going to fight itself."

As we made our way into the Keep, I had no end of requests to answer. Roland, Alucard, and Eae vowed to work with Xylo to find the vampires and Nephilim new homes or places to stay.

Ryuu pulled Fabrizio aside to go secure the crime scene back at Solomon's Temple and check on Phix and Aphrodite.

And a dozen other things as I led Hermes and his crew to the heart of the Keep to set up our first Fight Night. My monsters were bloodthirsty and needed an outlet—especially with all the new changes coming.

I smiled at a new thought. Samael and Lilith wanted a wedding...

What better way to bring everyone together than a demon wedding?

Because Last Breath had taught me that the present was a gift and needed to be cherished.

I would honor his dying wish...

And then I would give the world a gift...

The White Rose marching to war.

*CALLIE PENROSE WILL RETURN IN **HALO BREAKER**...*

DON'T FORGET! VIP's get early access to all sorts of Temple-Verse goodies, including signed copies, private giveaways, and advance notice of future projects. AND A FREE NOVELLA! Click the image or join here: www.shaynesilvers.com/l/219800

*Turn the page to read a sample of **OBSIDIAN SON** - The Nate Temple Series Book 1 - or **BUY ONLINE**. Nate Temple is a billionaire wizard from St. Louis. He rides a bloodthirsty unicorn and drinks with the Four Horsemen. He even cow-tipped the Minotaur. Once...*

(Note: Nate's books 1-6 happen prior to UNCHAINED, but they crossover from then on, the two series taking place in the same universe but also able to standalone if you prefer)

Full chronology of all books in the TempleVerse shown on the 'BOOKS BY SHAYNE SILVERS' page.

TRY: OBSIDIAN SON (NATE TEMPLE #1)

There was no room for emotion in a hate crime. I had to be cold. Heartless. This was just another victim. Nothing more. No face, no name.

Frosted blades of grass crunched under my feet, sounding to my ears like the symbolic glass that one would shatter under a napkin at a Jewish wedding. The noise would have threatened to give away my stealthy advance as I stalked through the moonlit field, but I was no novice and had planned accordingly. Being a wizard, I was able to muffle all sensory evidence with a fine cloud of magic—no sounds, and no smells. Nifty. But if I made the spell much stronger, the anomaly would be too obvious to my prey.

I knew the consequences for my dark deed tonight. If caught, jail time or possibly even a gruesome, painful death. But if I succeeded, the look of fear and surprise in my victim's eyes before his world collapsed around him, it was well worth the risk. I simply couldn't help myself; I had to take him down.

I knew the cops had been keeping tabs on my car, but I was confident that they hadn't followed me. I hadn't seen a tail on my way here but seeing as how they frowned on this kind of thing, I had taken a circuitous route just in case. I was safe. I hoped.

Then my phone chirped at me as I received a text.

I practically jumped out of my skin, hissing instinctively. "Motherf—" I cut off abruptly, remembering the whole stealth aspect of my mission. I was off to a stellar start. I had forgotten to silence the damned phone. *Stupid, stupid, stupid!*

My heart felt like it was on the verge of exploding inside my chest with such thunderous violence that I briefly envisioned a mystifying Rorschach blood-blot that would have made coroners and psychologists drool.

My body remained tense as I swept my gaze over the field, fearing that I had been made. Precious seconds ticked by without any change in my surroundings, and my breathing finally began to slow as my pulse returned to normal. Hopefully, my magic had muted the phone and my resulting outburst. I glanced down at the phone to scan the text and then typed back a quick and angry response before I switched the cursed device to vibrate.

Now, where were we?

I continued on, the lining of my coat constricting my breathing. Or maybe it was because I was leaning forward in anticipation. *Breathe*, I chided myself. *He doesn't know you're here.* All this risk for a book. It had better be worth it.

I'm taller than most, and not abnormally handsome, but I knew how to play the genetic cards I had been dealt. I had shaggy, dirty blonde hair—leaning more towards brown with each passing year—and my frame was thick with well-earned muscle, yet I was still lean. I had once been told that my eyes were like twin emeralds pitted against the golden-brown tufts of my hair—a face like a jewelry box. Of course, that was two bottles of wine into a date, so I could have been a little foggy on her quote. Still, I liked to imagine that was how everyone saw me.

But tonight, all that was masked by magic.

I grinned broadly as the outline of the hairy hulk finally came into view. He was blessedly alone—no nearby sentries to give me away. That was always a risk when performing this ancient rite-of-passage. I tried to keep the grin on my face from dissolving into a maniacal cackle.

My skin danced with energy, both natural and unnatural, as I manipulated the threads of magic floating all around me. My victim stood just ahead, oblivious to the world of hurt that I was about to unleash. Even with his millennia of experience, he didn't stand a chance. I had done this so many times that the routine of it was my only enemy. I lost count of how many times I had been told not to do it again; those who knew declared it *cruel, evil, and sadistic.* But what fun wasn't? Regardless, that wasn't enough to stop me from doing it again. And again. And again.

It was an addiction.

The pungent smell of manure filled the air, latching onto my nostril hairs. I took another step, trying to calm my racing pulse. A glint of gold reflected in the silver moonlight, but my victim remained motionless, hopefully unaware or all was lost. I wouldn't make it out alive if he knew I was here. Timing was everything.

I carefully took the last two steps, a lifetime between each, watching the legendary monster's ears, anxious and terrified that I would catch even so much as a twitch in my direction. Seeing nothing, a fierce grin split my unshaven cheeks. My spell had worked! I raised my palms an inch away from their target, firmly planted my feet, and squared my shoulders. I took one silent, calming breath, and then heaved forward with every ounce of physical strength I could muster. As well as a teensy-weensy boost of magic. Enough to goose him good.

"*MOOO!!!*" The sound tore through the cool October night like an unstoppable freight train. *Thud-splat!* The beast collapsed sideways onto the frosted grass; straight into a steaming patty of cow shit, cow dung, or, if you really wanted to church it up, a Meadow Muffin. But to me, shit is, and always will be, shit.

Cow tipping. It doesn't get any better than that in Missouri.

Especially when you're tipping the *Minotaur.* Capital M. I'd tipped plenty of ordinary cows before, but never the legendary variety.

Razor-blade hooves tore at the frozen earth as the beast struggled to stand, his grunts of rage vibrating the air. I raised my arms triumphantly. "Boo-yah! Temple 1, Minotaur 0!" I crowed. Then I very bravely prepared to protect myself. Some people just couldn't take a joke. *Cruel, evil,* and *sadistic* cow tipping may be, but by hell, it was a *rush.* The legendary beast turned his gaze on me after gaining his feet, eyes ablaze as his body...*shifted* from his bull disguise into his notorious, well-known bipedal form. He unfolded to his full height on two tree trunk-thick legs, his hooves having magically transformed into heavily booted feet. The thick, gold ring dangling from his snotty snout quivered as the Minotaur panted, and his dense, corded muscles contracted over his now human-like chest. As I stared up into those brown eyes, I actually felt sorry...for, well, myself.

"I have killed greater men than you for lesser offense," he growled.

His voice sounded like an angry James Earl Jones—like Mufasa talking to Scar.

"You have shit on your shoulder, Asterion." I ignited a roiling ball of fire in my palm in order to see his eyes more clearly. By no means was it a defensive gesture on my part. It was just dark. Under the weight of his glare, I somehow managed to keep my face composed, even though my fraudulent, self-denial had curled up into the fetal position and started whimpering. I hoped using a form of his ancient name would give me brownie points. Or maybe just not-worthy-of-killing points.

The beast grunted, eyes tightening, and I sensed the barest hesitation. "Nate Temple...your name would look splendid on my already long list of slain idiots." Asterion took a threatening step forward, and I thrust out my palm in warning, my roiling flame blue now.

"You lost fair and square, Asterion. Yield or perish." The beast's shoulders sagged slightly. Then he finally nodded to himself in resignation, appraising me with the scrutiny of a worthy adversary. "Your time comes, Temple, but I will grant you this. You've got a pair of stones on you to rival Hercules."

I reflexively glanced in the direction of the myth's own crown jewels before jerking my gaze away. Some things you simply couldn't un-see. "Well, I won't be needing a wheelbarrow any time soon, but overcompensating today keeps future lower-back pain away."

The Minotaur blinked once, and then he bellowed out a deep, contagious, snorting laughter. Realizing I wasn't about to become a murder statistic, I couldn't help but join in. It felt good. It had been a while since I had allowed myself to experience genuine laughter.

In the harsh moonlight, his bulk was even more intimidating as he towered head and shoulders above me. This was the beast that had fed upon human sacrifices for countless years while imprisoned in Daedalus' Labyrinth in Greece. And all that protein had not gone to waste, forming a heavily woven musculature over the beast's body that made even Mr. Olympia look puny.

From the neck up, he was now entirely bull, but the rest of his body more closely resembled a thickly furred man. But, as shown moments ago, he could adapt his form to his environment, never appearing fully human, but able to make his entire form appear as a bull when necessary. For instance, how he had looked just before I tipped him. Maybe he had been scouting the field for heifers before I had so efficiently killed the mood.

His bull face was also covered in thick, coarse hair—he even sported a long, wavy beard of sorts, and his eyes were the deepest brown I had ever seen. Cow-shit brown. His snout jutted out, emphasizing the golden ring dangling from his glistening nostrils, and both glinted in the luminous glow of the moon. The metal was at least an inch thick and etched with runes of a language long forgotten. Wide, aged ivory horns sprouted from each temple, long enough to skewer a wizard with little effort. He was nude except for a massive beaded necklace and a pair of worn leather boots that were big enough to stomp a size twenty-five imprint in my face if he felt so inclined.

I hoped our blossoming friendship wouldn't end that way. I really did.

Because friends didn't let friends wear boots naked...

Get your copy of OBSIDIAN SON online today!
http://www.shaynesilvers.com/l/38474

Turn the page to read a sample of **WHISKEY GINGER** *- Phantom Queen Diaries Book 1, or* **BUY ONLINE**. *Quinn MacKenna is a black magic arms dealer in Boston. She likes to fight monsters almost as much as she likes to drink.*

TRY: WHISKEY GINGER (PHANTOM QUEEN DIARIES BOOK 1)

The pasty guitarist hunched forward, thrust a rolled-up wad of paper deep into one nostril, and snorted a line of blood crystals—frozen hemoglobin that I'd smuggled over in a refrigerated canister—with the uncanny grace of a drug addict. He sat back, fangs gleaming, and pawed at his nose. "That's some bodacious shit. Hey, bros," he said, glancing at his fellow band members, "come hit this shit before it melts."

He fetched one of the backstage passes hanging nearby, pried the plastic badge from its lanyard, and used it to split up the crystals, murmuring something in an accent that reminded me of California. Not *the* California, but you know, Cali-foh-nia—the land of beaches, babes, and bros. I retrieved a toothpick from my pocket and punched it through its thin wrapper. "So," I asked no one in particular, "now that ye have the product, who's payin'?"

Another band member stepped out of the shadows to my left, and I don't mean that figuratively, either—the fucker literally stepped out of the shadows. I scowled at him, but hid my surprise, nonchalantly rolling the toothpick from one side of my mouth to the other.

The rest of the band gathered around the dressing room table, following the guitarist's lead by preparing their own snorting utensils—tattered magazine covers, mostly. Typically, you'd do this sort of thing with a dollar-bill, maybe even a Benjamin if you were flush. But fangers like this lot couldn't touch cash directly—in God We Trust and all that. Of course, I didn't really understand why sucking blood the old-fashioned way had suddenly gone out of style. More of a rush, maybe?

"It lasts longer," the vampire next to me explained, catching my mildly curious expression. "It's especially good for shows and stuff. Makes us look, like, less—"

"Creepy?" I offered, my Irish brogue lilting just enough to make it a question.

"Pale," he finished, frowning.

I shrugged. "Listen, I've got places to be," I said, holding out my hand.

"I'm sure you do," he replied, smiling. "Tell you what, why don't you, like, hang around for a bit? Once that wears off," he dipped his head toward the bloody powder smeared across the table's surface, "we may need a pick-me-up." He rested his hand on my arm and our gazes locked.

I blinked, realized what he was trying to pull, and rolled my eyes. His widened in surprise, then shock as I yanked out my toothpick and shoved it through his hand.

"Motherfuck—"

"I want what we agreed on," I declared. "Now. No tricks."

The rest of the band saw what happened and rose faster than I could blink. They circled me, their grins feral...they might have even seemed intimidating if it weren't for the fact that they each had a case of the sniffles —I had to work extra hard not to think about what it felt like to have someone else's blood dripping down my nasal cavity.

I held up a hand.

"Can I ask ye gentlemen a question before we get started?" I asked. "Do ye even *have* what I asked for?"

Two of the band members exchanged looks and shrugged. The guitarist, however, glanced back towards the dressing room, where a brown paper bag sat next to a case full of makeup. He caught me looking and bared his teeth, his fangs stretching until it looked like it would be uncomfortable for him to close his mouth without piercing his own lip.

"Follow-up question," I said, eyeing the vampire I'd stabbed as he gingerly withdrew the toothpick from his hand and flung it across the room with a snarl. "Do ye do each other's make-up? Since, ye know, ye can't use mirrors?"

I was genuinely curious.

The guitarist grunted. "Mike, we have to go on soon."

"Wait a minute. Mike?" I turned to the snarling vampire with a frown. "What happened to *The Vampire Prospero*?" I glanced at the numerous fliers in the dressing room, most of which depicted the band members wading through blood, with Mike in the lead, each one titled *The Vampire Prospero* in *Rocky Horror Picture Show* font. Come to think of it...Mike did look a little like Tim Curry in all that leather and lace.

I was about to comment on the resemblance when Mike spoke up, "Alright, change of plans, bros. We're gonna drain this bitch before the show. We'll look totally—"

"Creepy?" I offered, again.

"Kill her."

Get the full book ONLINE! http://www.shaynesilvers.com/l/206897

MAKE A DIFFERENCE

Reviews are the most powerful tools in my arsenal when it comes to getting attention for my books. Much as I'd like to, I don't have the financial muscle of a New York publisher.

But I do have something much more powerful and effective than that, and it's something that those publishers would kill to get their hands on.

A committed and loyal bunch of readers.

Honest reviews of my books help bring them to the attention of other readers.

If you've enjoyed this book, I would be very grateful if you could spend just five minutes leaving a review on my book's Amazon page.

Thank you very much in advance.

ACKNOWLEDGMENTS

Team Temple and the Den of Freaks on Facebook have become family to me. I couldn't do it without die-hard readers like them.

I would also like to thank you, the reader. I hope you enjoyed reading *TRINITY* as much as I enjoyed writing it. Be sure to check out the two crossover series in the Temple Verse: The **Nate Temple Series** and the **Phantom Queen Diaries**.

And last, but definitely not least, I thank my wife, Lexy. Without your support, none of this would have been possible.

ABOUT SHAYNE SILVERS

Shayne is a man of mystery and power, whose power is exceeded only by his mystery...

He currently writes the Amazon Bestselling **Nate Temple** Series, which features a foul-mouthed wizard from St. Louis. He rides a bloodthirsty unicorn, drinks with Achilles, and is pals with the Four Horsemen.

He also writes the Amazon Bestselling **Feathers and Fire** Series—a second series in the TempleVerse. The story follows a rookie spell-slinger named Callie Penrose who works for the Vatican in Kansas City. Her problem? Hell seems to know more about her past than she does.

He coauthors **The Phantom Queen Diaries**—a third series set in The TempleVerse—with Cameron O'Connell. The story follows Quinn MacKenna, a mouthy black magic arms dealer in Boston. All she wants? A round-trip ticket to the Fae realm...and maybe a drink on the house.

He also writes the **Shade of Devil Series**, which tells the story of Sorin Ambrogio—the world's FIRST vampire. He was put into a magical slumber by a Native American Medicine Man when the Americas were first discovered by Europeans. Sorin wakes up after five-hundred years to learn that his protégé, Dracula, stole his reputation and that no one has ever even heard of Sorin Ambrogio. The streets of New York City will run with blood as Sorin reclaims his legend.

Shayne holds two high-ranking black belts, and can be found writing in a coffee shop, cackling madly into his computer screen while pounding shots of espresso. He's hard at work on the newest books in the TempleVerse— You can find updates on new releases or chronological reading order on the next page, his website, or any of his social media accounts. **Follow him online for all sorts of groovy goodies, giveaways, and new release updates:**

BOOKS BY SHAYNE SILVERS

CHRONOLOGY: All stories in the TempleVerse are shown in chronological order on the following page

FEATHERS AND FIRE SERIES

(Also set in the TempleVerse)

by Shayne Silvers

UNCHAINED

RAGE

WHISPERS

ANGEL'S ROAR

MOTHERLUCKER (Novella #4.5 in the 'LAST CALL' anthology)

SINNER

BLACK SHEEP

GODLESS

ANGHELLIC

TRINITY

NATE TEMPLE SERIES

(Main series in the TempleVerse)

by Shayne Silvers

FAIRY TALE - FREE prequel novella #0 for my subscribers

OBSIDIAN SON

BLOOD DEBTS

GRIMM

SILVER TONGUE

BEAST MASTER

BEERLYMPIAN (Novella #5.5 in the 'LAST CALL' anthology)

TINY GODS

DADDY DUTY (Novella #6.5)

WILD SIDE

WAR HAMMER

NINE SOULS

HORSEMAN

LEGEND

KNIGHTMARE

ASCENSION

CARNAGE

PHANTOM QUEEN DIARIES

(Also set in the TempleVerse)

by Cameron O'Connell & Shayne Silvers

COLLINS (Prequel novella #0 in the 'LAST CALL' anthology)

WHISKEY GINGER

COSMOPOLITAN

MOTHERLUCKER (Novella #2.5 in the 'LAST CALL' anthology)

OLD FASHIONED

DARK AND STORMY

MOSCOW MULE

WITCHES BREW

SALTY DOG

SEA BREEZE

HURRICANE

BRIMSTONE KISS

MOONSHINE

CHRONOLOGICAL ORDER: TEMPLE VERSE

FAIRY TALE (TEMPLE PREQUEL)

OBSIDIAN SON (TEMPLE 1)

HURRICANE (PHANTOM...9)

BRIMSTONE KISS (PHANTOM...10)

ANGHELLIC (FEATHERS...8)

CARNAGE (TEMPLE 14)

MOONSHINE (PHANTOM...11)

TRINITY (FEATHERS...9)

SHADE OF DEVIL SERIES

(Not part of the Temple Verse)

by Shayne Silvers

DEVIL'S DREAM

DEVIL'S CRY

DEVIL'S BLOOD

DEVIL'S DUE *(coming 2020...)*

NOTHING TO SEE HERE.

Thanks for reaching the last page of the book, you over-achiever. Sniff the spine. You've earned it. Or sniff your Kindle.

Now this has gotten weird.

Alright. I'm leaving.

Made in United States
Orlando, FL
19 March 2024

44967291R00191